GOLDENS ARE HERE

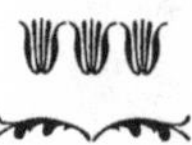

GOLDENS ARE HERE

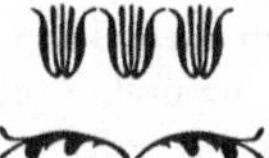

A Novel

Andrew Furman

GREEN WRITERS PRESS
Brattleboro, Vermont

Printed in the United States

10 9 8 7 6 5 4 3 2 1

Green Writers Press is a Vermont-based publisher whose mission is to spread a message of hope and renewal through the words and images we publish. Throughout we will adhere to our commitment to preserving and protecting the natural resources of the earth. To that end, a percentage of our proceeds will be donated to environmental activist groups. Green Writers Press gratefully acknowledges support from individual donors, friends, and readers to help support the environment and our publishing initiative.

Giving Voice to Writers Who Will Make the World a Better Place
Green Writers Press | Brattleboro, Vermont
www.greenwriterspress.com

ISBN: 978-0999076620

COVER IMAGE: ARCHIVAL PRINT

PRINTED ON PAPER WITH PULP THAT COMES FROM FSC-CERTIFIED FORESTS, MANAGED FORESTS THAT GUARANTEE RESPONSIBLE ENVIRONMENTAL, SOCIAL, AND ECONOMIC PRACTICES BY LIGHTNING SOURCE. ALL WOOD PRODUCT COMPONENTS USED IN BLACK & WHITE, STANDARD COLOR, OR SELECT COLOR PAPERBACK BOOKS, UTILIZING EITHER CREAM OR WHITE BOOKBLOCK PAPER, THAT ARE MANUFACTURED IN THE LAVERGNE, TENNESSEE PRODUCTION CENTER ARE SUSTAINABLE FORESTRY INITIATIVE® (SFI®) CERTIFIED SOURCING.

For Eva

Persuade a careless, indolent man to take an interest in his garden, and his reformation has begun.

—SUSAN FENIMORE COOPER

Is not the tree of the field man?

—DEUTERONOMY

Florida, 1961

BOOK ONE

LATE HARVEST

One

ISAAC GOLDEN shuffled the potatoes about the plate, his cutlery clinking profanities. He had identified the counterfeit liquid at a glance, resting undisturbed in the fancy Lucite pitcher. Coonskin-capped Eli somehow knew not to reach for it.

Did Melody think he was blind? Where in the fridge had his wife hidden those tiny tin cans of concentrate?

Color was okay, Isaac thought. They got that down pretty well. A precise dosage of pulp, too, formed filament archipelagos at the surface, lapped the Lucite circumference. Just something about its viscosity, the way the reconstituted orange liquid—he could hardly consider it juice—resisted the morning rays streaming in the bay window from over the Atlantic, its greater opacity, vaguely chalk.

He stabbed each of the three loose yolks, watched the eggs bleed about the Pfaltzgraff. For their *milchik* meals, Melody still insisted upon using her mother's service, the winterberry design at the rim clashing against their current environs. A vague reproach? Nostalgia only? Mere habit? Isaac exhaled audibly through his nostrils.

"Forgive me, I just thought we'd try some," Melody finally burst the silence, raising a paper napkin to her mouth as if to capture the escaped words.

"Yes, I see." He cleared his throat.

"Oh, don't be such a pill, Iz." His laconic sullenness was too much for her to bear, apparently. "Is it such a crime to sample a glass? It's really super."

She loved that word. Super. Everything with her these days was super. Or not.

"The things they can do," she continued, then sighed, her head swiveling back and forth on its axis to punctuate her point, leaving it to the family to speculate upon the several examples. Color television? Air-conditioning? Project Mercury? Plastic wrap? Isaac's wife was someone ever primed to be awestruck by this and that new thing, while he was slow, or unwilling, to concede the purported advance.

"Really, Iz, you'd have us all living in caves for crying out loud. Next you'll deprive the baby her evaporated milk."

Isaac glanced over at their youngest, Sarah—healthy as a horse, this one—mewling through her frothy mouth and making a general mess of her soggy cereal oat rounds on her tray. Goodness.

"Concentrate's all they serve now at Janisse's and everyone . . ."

Whenever Melody got going like this, it was no use resisting. She radiated an enthusiasm that had drawn him—opposites and all—but her vim was ill-suited, Isaac worried, for this hot drowsy state. It was a state slow to excitement. A state that took its time. That curious expression bandied about in town—*honest as the day is long*—hadn't made much sense to him at first. No one uttered such things in Philadelphia. About long days. About honesty for that matter. But the very days were longer and slower here, the sun vaulting itself high in the sky at daybreak and staying put, only reluctantly teetering toward the earth's bruised horizon by nightfall.

He rose from his chair, reached for the pitcher, and topped their cups. "*There*," he said. "We're trying it. Satisfied?"

"Mmm," Eli let slip, then cleared his throat.

"So what do you think, Iz?" Melody's eyebrows rose with her voice. Her hands clapped silently below her fine chin, before her lovely slender neck, just this side of Modigliani. A dark beauty, Isaac had married. "Super, right? You have to admit. And the dear cans take up so little space. And every pitcher tastes the same. Never sour. And you can *potchkee* it up any old way you please by adding more or less water. Amazing what they can do—"

"Sorry, dear heart, but it tastes like that Johnson's baby aspirin if you ask me. What's the difference if they're consistent about it?"

"Well now you're just being silly, Isaac Golden. Such a fuddy-duddy. There's simply no speaking with you."

Something about the way she said this—the lilt of her voice, the precise angle she set her raven do atop her delicate frame—betrayed her unswerving, if exasperated, affection for his fuddy-duddy-ness, his peccadilloes. Affection above all, which offered him license to continue:

"We're fresh-fruit people, Mel. Parson Browns, Hamlins, Valencias—"

"Midsweets!" Eli cried in his bewildering falsetto, only half-mocking him, Isaac hoped. "Gardners! Duncans! Marshes!"

Sarah pounded her fists and wailed falsetto too, flashing a wet pair of bottom teeth Isaac hadn't noticed before.

"Christ!" he shouted, covering his ears with his thick mitts.

"Eli," said Melody. Then, casting her gaze toward her husband: "We're Jews from West Philadelphia, Isaac. We're *no* kind of people. . . . Juice-wise, anyway."

"Well I didn't buy a hundred acres of choice grove land on the river to start selling pound-solids to the frozen people. That's for sure."

Before the words had fully escaped his lips, Isaac thought he saw Eli roll his eyes behind that bird nose of his. He wasn't certain, though, so he let it slide. "Remove that ridiculous hat at the table," he said instead. "It'll be eighty degrees in a couple hours."

"Okay, dear. Calm down." Melody rested a hand atop his. Isaac could feel its soft warmth, her cooler platinum wedding band against his knuckle, swollen from yesterday's labors. "You're going to give yourself palpitations."

The frozen people. A few scientists from the woolly interior of the state had caused all this trouble. They boiled, pasteurized, and evaporated fresh juice to crude-oil consistency in behemoth Short Time evaporators festooned with octopus arms spewing a steady sludge. That was the easy part. The tough part was making it taste half-decent upon reconstitution at the tap as various orange essences wafted off into the ether during evaporation. And so the scientists, shortly after the war, concocted the cutback—fresh juice, mostly, but also d-limonene, that piquant peel-oil potion, and other mysterious, unadvertised compounds. Esters? Carbonyls? Hesperidin? Lycopene? The frozen people, Isaac worried, would be the end of them. (And before he'd even had time to carve out a proper beginning!) He didn't quite know how he knew this. Only that he did. Perhaps it was its very obliterating popularity that worried him. Its leveling force. Concentrate. Isaac pondered the word. The nation used to aspire toward big things. Cars. Rocket ships. Skyscrapers.

Why labor toward this shrunkenness, whittling fine things down to smaller, ersatz components?

Other fruit stands all along the US 1 didn't even serve fresh chilled, anymore. They still advertised their Hamlins or Valencias in their vintage E. Bean orange crates to motorists from the north, yet thought nothing of administering medicinal doses of concentrate, distilled from some mish-mosh concoction of early-, mid-, and late-season cultivars. People, orange people, didn't even talk about oranges anymore, but acids, sugars, and degrees Brix! So yes. Maybe it always tasted the same, as Melody insisted. Yet what was so terrible about a little variety, the more acid Parson Brown and Hamlin nectar in October—the most complex nose and palate tang—the rounder, fatter flavor of Pineapples and Midsweets come December, the audacious Valencias in spring, the sugary juice bursting the Brix scale? And what about the manifold additional citrus varieties petering out toward extinction, or undiscovered? The craft edged closer and closer to monoculture. No one else in Isaac's co-op fathomed wasting acreage on improvement, experimentation. Walt, Edwin, Doyle. Even Clay. They left the crossing and hybridizing for others, scientists from the commission on secret state plots, university laboratories, and enclosed orangeries (for all Isaac knew), inland.

Boom!

The Goldens flinched at the table from the deep-bass discharge.

Boom!

The concentrate quivered.

"Son of a . . ." Isaac refrained from completing the curse. The children. "He's doing it again!"

"Isaac," Melody warned.

Boom!

"Sunday, for crying out loud!"

Sarah cried upon the third report, the flesh underneath her faint eyebrows rubicund with rage. Melody rose from her chair to pacify her.

"What's Mr. Boehringer doing, Dad?" Eli asked—his own tender scion—then issued a rich cough into his seashell palm.

"Eli?" Melody asked. "You okay?" Eli nodded his head, raised a small hand high toward his mother as if to ward off a blow.

Boom!

"That ignoramus!" Isaac's Pfaltzgraff hopped as he pounded his fist against the pine table.

"Isaac, don't confront him now," she warned, bobbing Sarah in her arms. "Not while your dander's up, not while he's carrying a rifle for heaven's sake."

"Shotgun, Mel," he corrected her as he rose, the legs of his chair squealing against the lemon linoleum. He threw his paper napkin on his plate, a puny gesture.

"Shotgun? What's the—"

He ignored his wife as he fled to the scene of the struggle, only taking enough time on the porch to throw work boots on his oversized, unsocked feet.

"He has a *gun*, Isaac!" he heard Melody shout after him.

"Daaad! Don't!"

"A *gun* Iz! Don't be a crazy person! You're acting like a crazy—"

Rifle. Shotgun. A distinction without a difference to his wife, Isaac considered as he tromped out back past Melody's vegetable garden and the wild tamarind (which had no business growing so far north); the triad of live oaks beyond that had been permitted to stretch their arms and grow their shaggy beards a respectable distance from both the house and planted acres. He followed his beeline along the dusty path between the scruffy patches of palmetto and lantana, the taller spice-smelling islands of wax myrtle and privet where the towhees and scrub jays and cardinals and mockingbirds loitered, and disappeared into the raised rows of his experimental, untagged, unharvestable crosses, hybrids, and chance seedlings toward the property line. These ten acres of his larger property. Eli's grove, he called this parcel he set aside for the perfection of fruit.

A gun was a no-good gun to his wife. *Pasht-nit,* in the vernacular of the tribe. Not for them. Why make fine distinctions? But such distinctions mattered now, mattered here. That Walt, say, prided himself on his 12-gauge Winchester, while Clay was a Browning man. A new livelihood in a new state with new people and new rules and new words! A new life, they had embarked upon. Because the climate would be better for Eli's lungs. And because their parents had already died early deaths, anyway. And because why not?

"Walter!" Isaac shouted, still several rows from their irrigation ditch border.

Boom!

"Walt! You hear?!" He glimpsed him, finally—*boom!*—picking off butterflies hovering over the Hamlin and Valencia orange trees with his Winchester. Some swallowtails, broader than sparrows, disintegrated upon impact, vanishing into the atmosphere, redolent now with pungent gunpowder, while others, clipped, dropped helter-skelter from the sky like wounded kites. Poor creatures. Isaac felt his hackles rise. He imagined crossing the irrigation ditch and throttling his neighbor, watching his face grow scarlet above his grip, his bloodshot eyes bulge. He shook his head to clear the terrifying image from his mental screen, exhaled volubly. It wasn't only, or even mostly, this shoot 'em up that inspired Isaac's rage. Walt wanted Isaac out, having never wanted him in, and barely concealed the sentiment. What's more, a vandal had been attacking random trees on Isaac's grove the past year with an axe or machete, four thus far, issuing near-lethal scars, piercing the cambium. While Isaac couldn't bring himself to name Walt as a suspect (not wanting to *pish* in his cereal, as his father would have put it), he couldn't quite dismiss him from suspicion, either.

"Tomfoolery," Sheriff Wright downplayed the gravity of the offense, while promising to increase his patrols. "Bored teenagers up to tomfoolery," he had speculated.

In any case, Walt had called him here this morning. To have it out. That's what all this shooting was for, Isaac knew. His neighbor might as well have used the rotary. Had Walt not meant to draw him near, he wouldn't have so carefully avoided Isaac's gaze until he reached the very edge of the ditch. Just yards from Walt now, in plain view, Isaac lifted his palms as if to say, *Well?* He was a big man, Isaac, nobody's *nebbish,* fair-haired with hands like frying pans, forearms rippled with muscle-cords beneath, hardly looked the city Jew at all. His heft meant something more here in Florida, across these dusty rows of grove trees—his new, outdoor life—more than it had meant in Philadelphia. Emboldened him.

Walt lowered his shotgun, bent it open at the middle and laid it at its crease across his elbow, pasted with red fur. His mustache—a furious, untended weed—blanketed his upper lip. Tobacco bulged beneath his lower lip like a malignancy. There were standards of decorum, Isaac knew, standards that held fast. Which was why he knew that he needn't fear confronting his neighbor over the irrigation ditch, bone dry now in advance of the rainy season. Which was why, too, he didn't truly figure that Walt was the culprit attacking his grove trees. Walt would disable his shotgun before engaging a fellow grower in conversation, no matter how angry. He would spit a bolus of tobacco-stained saliva to the side, never toward his neighbor, and then he would speak.

"I ain't doin' nothing wrong, Ike. These durn butterflies of yours'll destroy my whole row. Look at these poor Valencias already."

Isaac studied Walt's row across the ditch. Robust ten-year Valencias, the copious foliage from spring flush mildly degraded, gnawed at.

"Look fine to me, Walt. Now we've been through this. You want to shoot up the swallowtails, bully for you. But keep your Winchester pointed over your own trees. I can't have you firing into my grove, Eli tromping about half the time."

Bully for you. Shoot up the swallowtails. Tromping about. Where the hell had Isaac picked up these phrases? Since migrating southward to the underpopulated coastal center of the peninsula, since joining this co-op of salty citrus growers, Isaac's vernacular had been shifting in kind to the frequent surprise of his own ears. What had happened to the essential Isaac? *Was* there an essential Isaac?

"Hell, Ike"—Walt spat again—"just spray like the rest of us and we wouldn't have no problems. Didn't we all just give you the commission's new spray schedule at Janisse's a month ago?"

Isaac exhaled through his nostrils. "You know I won't spray, Walter. And you know why. Eli's lungs."

Walt's face fell as soon as the words escaped Isaac's lips, which made Isaac regret the utterance. Walt's humane qualities were much more bothersome, somehow, than his red-faced truculence.

"Aw, hell, Ike," Walt gathered himself. "Aw, hell. If you don't want to use no malathion or aramite on account of your boy, 'least use DDT. Keep those skeeters and no-see-ums from pestering y'all too. Them bugs can't be no good for that Elly of yours, either. Skeeter bites sure pester Jo Ellen. Something terrible they pester poor Jo."

There seemed a new and separate accusation here—Isaac's mosquitoes looping across the irrigation ditch to harm Walt's daughter—but he chose to ignore it.

"We're doing just fine by our ladybeetles and fungi," Isaac insisted. "Plus mineral oil, sesame and fish oils too. Just fine."

Isaac, despite the co-op's objections, had gone the biological route to combat the countless biting and sucking insect insurgents: red mite, rust mite, bud mite, thrips, whitefly, blackfly, aphid, pumpkin-bug, wax scale, soft scale, red scale, chaff scale, mealybug, leafhoppers. The two-spotted and blood-red ladybeetles kept the aphids and most of the scale in check. Purple scale was a bit more trouble lately, but there was a new parasitic wasp he hadn't tried that the commission was pretty optimistic about. The white, red, and gray fungi ably choked up the whitefly larvae works. Keeping matters "in check," however, wasn't Jake by co-op standards. Complete and utter annihilation was expected, his partners' attitude toward pests and weeds approximating the nation's sentiment toward human enemies across the waters, the communists.

"Fine by whose standard?" Walt continued. "Old Man Hawley worked these acres to a pound-solid yield near a third more than your piss-ant harvests. You gotta *work* the land, Ike. Can't just play with it."

Everyone argued from time to time, it seemed to Isaac, but some people just didn't know when to drop it.

"Yes, you've told me, Walt. I've had to turn over some acres." *Why was he explaining himself?* "And I've been working on some things here, not playing." Isaac could see Walt's eyes glaze, his mouth fall agape, a peaty well of tobacco juice rising just inside his drooping lip. Walt crossed his meaty right forearm underneath the left one, just above his paunch, to help support the Winchester. Isaac should have left well enough alone, too. Yet it seemed that he, like Walt, was one of those people who just couldn't drop things, which was probably why they got under each other's skin so. It wasn't mere Jew-hating on Walt's part, which might have been easier for Isaac to truck.

"We have to think long term, Walt. Not just about this year's harvest. What's a few acres here and there? Might come up with something that'll help us all in the end."

Walt issued a copious spurt of tobacco-juice to the clayey soil. "Hurts us *all* when one don't pull his fair share, what I know. Those Simply Citrus folks on the ridge been beatin' the tar out of us with their yields. We've got hardly no leverage no more with the bird dogs, those Suncoast fuckers. And your Dr. Frankenstein crap over there ain't helpin' none. That's what *I* know, partner." Walt spat again, a purely rhetorical gesture, it seemed to Isaac, the tiny squirt scarcely meriting the effort this time.

Isaac watched as Walt's pale eyes glanced over his shoulder, as if his thoughts had drifted elsewhere. But no. Walt had spotted their approach. Isaac turned and saw them too, the men with lacquered hair walking clumsily up his row in their irrelevant shoes, thick ties, and short-sleeve oxfords, laminate badges dangling on clips from their chest pockets.

"Sweet Jesus," Walt groaned. "Now what do those suits want?"

Two

SOON AS HE CROSSED Janisse's threshold—"Afternoon, sugar!" she greeted him from behind the behemoth register—Clay Griffin could tell that Walt was stewing in his juices about something, crouching over his elbows ready to pounce, Scottish skin back of his neck redder than usual with his heat. What was it with red-headed folk? Clay wondered. They did seem to run hotter.

The men of the Central Indian River co-op on or near the island consumed long lunches at the diner Sunday after church, nursing their Camels and Kents, their Winstons and Lucky Strikes, sitting out the searing heat, having eaten dusky breakfasts to tend their small groves at sunup for an hour or two before church. Beneath a dense plume of smoke, they could chew the fat at the Formica counter for hours on the Lord's day, precious respite from their hectoring wives. Lord's day aside, important business to discuss, they explained to the ladies. And Janisse was pretty smart about things, Clay thought, what she did and didn't let slip to the girls at Junior League. Discreet. She'd make a fine mistress to someone so inclined. If she weren't two hundred odd pounds, anyway.

"It just ain't right is all I'm saying. Letting a Jew buy up that choice land 'cross the river practically from the base." *That old chestnut,* Clay mused, groaning into his stool down the bar, past Edwin and Doyle. Isaac never went to church, of course, so never lunched with them either, Sundays. And so Walt could carry on. Clay thumped his cardboard case of Winstons against the Formica, partly to offer vague dissent, partly to pack the tobacco within their sheaths, mostly out of habit. "Spittin' distance!" Walt continued. He paused to gulp his iced coffee, which beaded against his furious mustache. It was a beverage that just didn't seem to suit Walt. "And with that new colored boy in a suit tromping about lately. Could be in cahoots all we know."

No one seemed to recognize the new Negro about town wearing that suit and tie. They worried about him. What was he up to? But they hadn't recognized him.

As Clay had recognized him.

"Now I don't cotton to vandalism. Killing trees no matter the grove. But these times. After what happened few years back."

"You mean those Red spies, Walt?" Edwin asked. Young tow-headed Edwin, nursing that sickly sweet RC Cola along with his cigarette. Impressionable Edwin. "That what you mean, Walt?"

"Hell yeah, Win, that's what I mean. Everyone knows the coloreds and the Jews lean that way. Those Jew spies just tip of the iceberg. Rosensteins, Rosenblooms—"

"Bergs," Clay sighed, lighting up. "Rosen*bergs*, you mean."

"What other proof you need there's a risk? I'm not saying put them in camps like we did with the Japs. Jews had a tough enough time in those camps over there with the Krauts. Got nothing against them, personally. We're all God-fearing Christians here. They want to grow oranges all of a sudden they can buy up as much sandy land on the ridge they want, far piece from here. Like everyone else been doing. But we can't just have them living any old place, next to sensitive military operations. And now with this new colored in a suit—"

"It's not exactly a military base," Clay interjected. "Space program's different. Science and all."

He wasn't sure why it was so, but from the moment Ike bought up Hawley's grove—three years back now? Four?—Clay found himself defending the man over this and that. It wasn't like he had any great affection for members of the Jewish persuasion, not having known a Jew besides the Krupnicks in town until Hawley keeled over during spring harvest without a proper will—"intestate," the papers said—and a sister swooped down from South Carolina and put the groves, the equipment, the house, the whole kit and caboodle up for public auction, and that giant loping stranger, overdressed in a suit, frying-pan hands holding his hat, who didn't look like a Jew at all, nothing like those Rosenbergs, hair practically blonde, and had the President's own true-blue American name even, Ike, and quietly outbid Walt, who sat there fuming, Walt's face looking like the inside of all those pink marsh grapefruit he wouldn't be harvesting off Hawley's land, after all. Didn't even know Ike was Jewish until they settled in and that raven-haired wife, comely woman Mrs. Golden, no denying that—now *she* looked like a Jew, but in a fine way—declined the girls' second invitation to the church picnic and had out with it, because how long could you keep something like that a secret?

"You really believe it's about space, Clay? Science?" Walt flashed his woolly red eyebrows, stretched his furious mustache with his grin. "Think they give a gator's tit about sending a man to the moon, that worthless rock, even if they could?"

"Those Mercury boys sure got pluck enough," said Edwin, slurped his RC, swallowed. "Grissom, Schirra, Shepard, the rest of 'em."

"Sure 'nough," said Doyle. He tapped the gray worm at the end of his Camel into the plastic ashtray, nodded his head slowly, as if lost in thought over something else, maybe over that new plastic-lined sheet of postage stamps laid out before him like a second placemat. Doyle Newell collected things. Small things. Stamps, mostly, but also Depression glass and antique model trains—things that couldn't run away from him. Clay always felt bad for Doyle when he saw him with his small collectibles. Doyle was almost his age. Deep creases marked each side of his mouth, like parentheses. His mousy hair had beaten a hasty retreat years ago, but Doyle hadn't given up on the remaining strands, pomading them to make them look darker, more significant, organizing them atop his crown in an unfortunate middle part. His chain-smoking had aged him some, but life had also marked him more heavily than Clay. Doyle's wife, Joan, hadn't cottoned to the long slow days on the grove and up and ran off with a bible salesman from Tampa. That's the part that seemed to fester the most with Doyle. A bible salesman. Of all things. And there was Doyle and Joan's baby girl too, all grown up and living who knew where now, whom Joan had taken along with her, of course.

"What you got against the moon?" Clay asked Walt.

"It's all show, that space hoo-haw. So we don't get the tar scared out of us. National defense what it's all about, H-bombs launched from space, missile shields and whatnot. Soviets, bet the farm, got weapons perched right over us now, just biding their time."

"Hell Walt," said Clay, "you just have your knickers in a twist 'cause Ike beat you out at auction. Fair's fair. It's been how many years? Bygones already."

"Right across from Dummitt's grove," Walt muttered. "Give an inch they take an ell. 'Fore you know it, they'll own the lot of us, the stool you're sittin' in, Clay. Just you wait. Right across from Dummitt's grove. I'm surprised Ike didn't up and move into Dummitt's big ole heart pine house on the island while he was at it."

"Can't see Jewish folk leaving New York for Florida," Doyle opined. "Not in numbers, anyway. Not for this." Doyle opened his leathery palm before him, as if it were Janisse's bar he was talking about. The tip of his cigarette bobbed from between his parched lips as he spoke, like a conductor's baton. "Miami, sure. But not here. They's city folk. Ike's just different. Exception to the rule."

Clay sipped his sweet tea, pleased with Doyle. But he could tell by the way Walt shook his head slow over his coffee that he wasn't satisfied, that he was searching his bitter inventory in that half-baked noodle of his for something else to add to the litany. Dragging Dummitt into this seemed unfair, though—even if Walt claimed a forebear who had worked the grove. Dummitt, the progenitor of them all. Captain Dummitt had started sour orange stock on the river back in the 1800s when he wasn't fighting Seminoles or siring bastard offspring with his Negress in his great wooden house, built from heart pine and salvaged shipwreck wood. Still standing on the island, that big old gabled house. Vacant now, except for the varmints. His high grove was one of the few in the state that survived the hard freeze of 1835. Survived the '95 freeze too, pretty much, the freeze that started the southward march of citrus, and the railroad, and the people. Joe Buck Wilson's outfit owned Dummitt's grove now, right next to Clay's own smaller island holding, plus all that ridge land near Orlando Joe Buck owned, which was the only reason that Simply Citrus didn't gobble up those acres, too. A big fish, Joe Buck. Last of the big fish. Too big to join their piddly co-op. Feds had their eyes on the island now. *That* was the true danger, seemed to Clay. Not the Jews. Not the new Negro in town, whom Clay recognized but wouldn't reveal. Not the Simply Citrus frozen people. Not the Suncoast swindlers. But the likely federal incursions on the island and on this side of the river too, worst case. That outer space business.

"Should see Ike's rows," Walt complained. "Cover crops my ass. A God durn bramble what it is. Snake-infested you can bet. Diamondbacks, pygmies, corals, cottonmouths, you name it."

"Cottonmouths live near cricks and such," Doyle declared, wiping the mayonnaise from the corner of his mouth.

"God durn bramble in there all the same."

"Pigweed?" Edwin inquired. Edwin was deathly worried over pigweed, for whatever reason.

"Hell yeah, pigweed, Win. And pepperweed. And cudweed. And goatweed. You name it. Wandering Jew too, I bet!" Walt joked, rapped Edwin's shoulder with the back of his unclenched fist. Edwin lifted a knuckle to his mouth to keep the RC in, then removed his Chevy baseball cap and slapped it against his thigh as he laughed. Janisse set down Clay's heavy ironstone plate onto the bar, the flaccid flesh roiling beneath her elbow, the corrugated fries spilling over onto the Formica. She remembered his blue cheese. He enjoyed the dressing—never ketchup—with his fries.

"Now what's so funny, boys?"

"You don't want to know," Clay said. He sampled a blue cheese pasted fry, felt his innards relax under its savory influence. Janisse retreated, twisted her mouth into an expression of mild, or perhaps mock, disapproval.

"It's no joke," Walt declared, his sobriety restored. "It's bringing bad attention our way, whatever Ike's up to in that big piece he set aside. Commission fuckers paid him a visit this morning. Or Ag Feds, tough to say. Tromped right out there to find him middle of his grove. Who knows what they want? Can't be nothin' good."

"Commission men? In his grove? On Sunday?" Clay asked.

"Think so. They were wearin' those tags. I didn't stick around for the inquisition."

"Sure they weren't frozen people after some acres?" Doyle asked.

The Simply Citrus frozen people, an upstart division of a larger interest headquartered in Atlanta, had already bought up and reclaimed ten thousand soggy acres west on the ridge, smack middle of the state. Their loamier land on the river would be the next place they'd look to gobble up, Clay figured. Only logical. It didn't take one of those government rocket scientists to figure that one out. They'd already opened up a refrigerated warehouse at nearby Port Canaveral, the main shipping portal for their inferior juice.

Walt shrugged. "Didn't look rich enough to me to be the frozen people. Commission boys, dollars to donuts. Maybe Feds."

Clay held a generous clutch of Winston smoke in his lungs, sought counsel from the burn, exhaled finally through hirsute nostrils. "Interesting," he uttered.

Three

SHE PLUCKED A TENDER BULB from the wooden sill above the sink. Melody loved these dear fruits, their baby-bottom peel in her palm, their hue often as not tipping from yellow toward egg-yolk orange. That's something Isaac taught her, that cool temperatures, not heat, prompted the color break from green to yellow and orange, that if their late-season Valencias, say, weren't harvested before the broiling rainy season arrived, they'd change back to green from brightest orange, which wasn't good. Ethylene wouldn't even work then to change them back at the packing house. Nevin's Fruit Co., edge of town.

Sarah down for her nap, Isaac out of her hair doing who knew what with Ted in the nursery rows or greenhouse, Eli girding himself for the outdoors, two hours still before she needed to tend the stand—their Lord's day occupying her Christian neighbors till at least ten—Melody scrambled about the cupboards, marshaling additional ingredients for her mother's honey cake. One cup honey, one cup sugar, two eggs, one cup sour cream, two cups flour, quarter cup shortening, one teaspoon baking powder (here might be the problem). No time to lose, given Sarah's caprice. Who knew how long she'd stay down this morning, the little devil?

The Meyer lemon yielded beneath her sharp knife, its juice bursting from its severed purses onto her cutting board. She squeezed half the bulb over her stainless mixing bowl. Baking a decent honey cake, carrot cake, chocolate roll, cochin, or rugelach didn't seem like too much to ask of this hot as Gehenna, big-bully state. She could forgive Florida for most of its trespasses, having bargained on them: its humidity, its mosquitos and no-see-ums and sand gnats and love-bugs and God knows what other swollen insects, smearing the Pontiac's windshield with their ooze and gunking up the grill, the state's follicular assaults, her raven hair a tangled mess half the time, the faraway *shul* in godforsaken Orlando, the genteel hostility of its townspeople (or wariness, rather, hostility too harsh an indictment; she wasn't quite sure what to make of the vandalism against their trees, but wanted to believe Sheriff Wright, that it was only kids up to tomfoolery), and the lamentable shortage of wary people to talk to, period. But no one had warned her that even her mandel bread—which hardly took a *balabusta* to concoct—would settle like a puddle of pale mud in the oven and cool to a granite consistency.

"Hold it right there, mister!" Melody had glimpsed Eli flash across the narrow field of view beyond the pocket door as he bolted for the front. She heard him groan at her command. "Let me take a look at you."

She abandoned the mixing bowl on the Formica counter, rinsed her hands in the sink, and sat in the lemon vinyl chair to get a decent look at her son, grasping the knobs of his shoulders. He avoided her gaze. The butterfly, inflamed, stretched more scarlet across his bird nose today. She wasn't altogether convinced that diet wasn't a factor, yet she hadn't been able to isolate any food culprits. "Looks like you forgot something," she declared, rising toward the junk drawer.

"I have my inhaler," he countered, then groaned upon glimpsing the metal tube in his mother's hand. "I have to wear that gunk *every* day?"

"It's to protect you, sweetie. From the sun."

"I'll be under the trees. In the shade. And I'm wearing my special hat." He gripped the broad bill of his khaki fisherman's cap to underscore his point.

"Still."

"What's the difference, anyway? It doesn't get any better. Lotion don't do no good."

"The lotion *doesn't* do *any* good," Melody said, smearing the white paste across the ridge of his nose, across the scarlet wings dappling his narrow cheeks. His flesh felt hot against her fingertips.

"Exactly," he declared, his mouth curling into the hint of a smile, vanishing the next instant. "Why's it have to be so ugly?" Melody felt her throat constrict, her eyes well, but managed to gather her wits, pasting her son's hot rash with greater intensity.

"It's a beautiful butterfly is what it is, Eli. There's not an ugly thing about you. Not one ugly thing. You're my beautiful boy. My beautiful baby boy." She pulled him in for a hug.

"M*o*-*o*m," he shrank from her, as if embarrassed by onlookers. When did this start, she wondered, this pulling away?

"All right, go out and play." She rose and shooed him, mostly so he wouldn't read her face. "But stay in your grove," she called after Eli from the threshold. He had already bounded off the porch, raised off the ground on cinderblocks from the foundation to ward off the snakes, gators, and other creatures that the alien groves themselves, and their attendant human and machine noise, hadn't thoroughly chased off already. "I need you back in one hour! You hear me, Eli?! One hour!"

Melody returned to the honey cake batter and smoothed it into its baking dish with the rubber spatula, a dollop swirl at the center that would probably bake out. She deposited the nascent cake without much hope into the preheated avocado oven and, wheeling Sarah behind her in the bassinet, retreated to the family room sofa for a blessed span of rest, however brief. Leaning back, she flipped vacantly through the broad glossy pages of *Life*. Cute ad for Lucky Whip. Several photos devoted to space. *Gagarin Meets Krushchev. Inside Yuri's Capsule. Celebration in Moscow.* What else? *Sidney Poitier's "Raisin in the Sun." Red Skelton Top US Clown.* She never much cared for his humor. *At the Eichmann Trial.* The monster. The animal. The wild beast, Melody fumed. His cool demeanor an obvious ploy. Everyone could see this, yes?

Melody tossed the issue back onto the coffee table. Had they made a mistake coming here? Isaac didn't seem to think so, if the undeterred intensity of his labors were any indication, which bolstered her. All she had known of Florida was from that movie with Gregory Peck that made her weep at the end. "You're not proposing to take us *there*, are you? To live in the hinterlands with wild animals and guns and people who don't wear shoes?" This was all that she remembered about the movie, that it made her weep and that there were wild animals, and guns, and that certain characters ambled about without proper footwear.

"Not even close, hon'," Isaac had assured her. "We'll be near the coast. Besides, it's ancient history, that movie. The state's nothing like that anymore, not since air-conditioning and the railroad. It's a real place now. You'll see. And you know what Dr. Lippman said. Be better for Eli. That or Texas. Or Arizona. Or California. Talk about hinterlands. Talk about sticks."

The warm climate *had* been better for Eli, she assured herself. Only a few bronchial infections and asthma attacks since they moved down a few years ago. No terrifying winter nights at the edge of a narrow hospital bed, their son gasping for breath within a translucent tent, disappearing, disappearing, his chicken chest heaving. Hardly any breathing treatments at all here. Even her child's shrill voice had descended an octave or two in the balmy atmosphere, though his growing older might explain this welcome development. Melody stood and looked down toward Sarah on her belly in the bassinet (never on her back, Melody made sure), studied her steady inhalations and exhalations, her torso's rhythmic rising and falling like a ship traversing near-smooth seas. So this was what it was like, she thought . . . to have a healthy baby.

A chromosomal anomaly was to blame for Eli's illness, rarer than most such genetic flukes, though somewhat less rare among members of their Ashkenazi tribe. Improbably, impossibly, cruelly rare. They had known to be on guard against Tay-Sachs, Canavan, Crohn's, cystic fibrosis. But not this illness. It had taken months to diagnose. Eli's initial symptoms were concerning but indeterminate. Low birth weight. Failure to thrive. High-pitched baby squeals. Acute lung infection at six weeks. The telangiectatic erythema, as it was called, Eli's butterfly rash, had been the final determinative clue. The diagnosis was clear, suddenly. The prognosis too. He would be small, Eli. Painfully so. Perhaps only five feet tall. His Golden features forever disguised behind his bird nose, protuberant ears, and butterfly rash. Chronic lung diseases, asthma, bronchiectasis, and various dermatological maladies would plague him. Worst of all, odds stood at twenty percent that he'd develop leukemia, lymphomas, or carcinomas before his twenty-fifth birthday.

Melody felt tired, suddenly. Dog tired. She lay back down on the sofa and glanced toward her ankles, only slightly swollen. She permitted herself this one vanity, admiring her lovely ankles, unbesmirched by veins varicose or spider. All the same, she wasn't so dense that she didn't realize others found her pretty, beautiful even, and not on account of her ankles.

The egg timer in the kitchen would wake her. She closed her eyes.

Onetwothreefourfivesixseveneightnineten . . . Eli tallied the rows as he ran his grove. He liked the way the trees made him feel, flashing across the sides. Fast. Lightning fast, . . . *Twentyonetwentytwotwentythreetwentyfour* . . . which he never felt out on the wide-open macadam at recess, where he never won a footrace, and usually lost by quite a stretch, small as he was, the little wind he could muster through his narrow throat. He broke his stride, then began walking. He couldn't run the whole piece to their crossing spot at the border, where the irrigation ditch narrowed to a leapable crease in the tilled earth.

"What took you so long?" Jo Ellen complained from across the ditch as he reached the border, a candy cigarette twitching from her mouth. The wire and cord grass was allowed to grow tall here in clumps of green and brown they had to walk around. The blade of her hand protected her pale eyes from the morning rays out there in the open. Her other hand rested on her uncurved hip, as if anticipating that womanly ledge that wasn't there yet. Everything about her looked red. Red hair in tails, unbraided. Red freckles. Red skin beneath, either flushed or downright scorched. A raspberry knee smeared with a rusty Mercurochrome stain. Even that painted red tip at the end of her candy cigarette. Her classmates at school teased her by calling her Red, she sometimes complained, but she was a grade ahead of Eli so he didn't really know her classmates and didn't hear them call her anything. They both pretty much ignored each other when their paths crossed at Woodrow Wilson, not because they were embarrassed of each other—Eli was pretty certain—but because their friendship was a secret they kept from their parents, and so they had naturally extended the deception at school. And because Jo Ellen was a girl and Eli was a boy.

"Mom made me put on this stupid lotion again," Eli explained, pointing toward his bird nose, his butterfly rash.

"I don't see nothin'," Jo said, her cigarette twitching again. She must have gotten sick of the cigarette twitching when she talked, because she snatched the whole thing into her mouth right then without her hands, like a frog, and munched on it. Else she was just hungry. "Look normal to me," she added after she finished chewing.

Eli touched his cheek and felt his finger glide across the thin paste. He inspected the pads and noticed the white zinc. Either the bright rays rendered the paste invisible from across the ditch or Jo was just fibbing to make him feel better. She did that sort of thing, he thought, told him lies from time to time to make him feel better. About his sticking-out monkey ears. About his bird nose. About his chicken chest. Was it because she was almost two years older? Did it make her feel even older than that, almost like a grown-up, to lie to him to make him feel better? Or was she just nice?

"Well, you gonna come over, Jo?"

It was always Jo who jumped the ditch to play in Eli's grove, never the other way around.

"I gotta wash up for church in a half hour. Mom'll whip me if I'm not ready."

"Just a little while then."

Would her mother truly whip her for being late? Did they actually own a whip, and where did they keep it? It seemed to Eli that Jo often exaggerated to make her life seem more dangerous and exciting, like something on television. Like last week, when she bragged about her bicycle crash on the highway—fast as a motor car she was going, she claimed—pointing to that raspberry on her knee to prove it, which was never much bigger than a postage stamp.

Jo picked up her gnarly live oak stick and jumped the ditch, and they disappeared beneath Eli's grove into the too-sweet air. Spent blossom snow drifts littered the beds, raised on account of the high water table. Without words, they slipped off their shoes, because there weren't any sandspurs yet on the cover crops between the rows. There was just enough room between the raised rows of Parson Brown and Hamlin crosses and hybrids for the two to walk side by side without scraping their heads against the foliage, just high enough now to shade them some from the sun. They walked right on top of the freshly planted peanut, wax bean, and cowpea cover crop. They weren't for harvest anyway, but would be turned under after the rainy season to add nitrogen to the nutrient-parched soil. Eli liked the way the soft green felt beneath his feet. He scrunched his toes upon each stride, the plants and clay top layer yielding under his command.

"Wish my daddy planted beans and such around our trees."

"Why doesn't he, then?"

"Says it ain't worth it. Says they take up too much water. Says it don't keep weeds down no-how. Says they bring bugs and snakes."

Says this. Says that. Says this. Says that. It bothered Eli, as if her father was so smart or something when he was really an ignoramus, so his father said at night from behind the closed pocket door. A *momzer* too, whatever that meant. But Eli knew enough not to say any of this. Jo was the only other kid around for miles. Most lived in town or nearer to it, anyway.

A marsh rabbit darted before them, then disappeared into the next row.

"Rabbit," Jo said.

"My dad says it's good for erosion too," Eli declared. "The peas."

Jo made a farting noise with her mouth. "You don't even know what 'rosion is, huckleberry." She leapt from her feet—not too high on account of the soft soil—and slapped at the spring flush foliage. She would have rathered a bolder gesture to demonstrate her superiority, Eli knew, pluck a heavy orange, maybe, and throw it like Wally Post clear over three, four rows, but the season was all wrong, the trees having just dropped blossoms, setting their green beads. Only the tall Valencias far side of the grove still held their last overlooked remnants of fruit.

"Do too. It's when the rain comes hard and washes the dirt away and Dad and Mr. Ted and them have to shovel it back."

This silenced Jo, who began poking the lupine grass with her stick for rattlers and coral snakes. They had just reached the small clearing. A tree at the center of this carefully spaced design of trees had withered from foot rot and had to be grubbed out. Eli begged his father to leave the space be, and his father let it be, maybe so he'd know where to find him.

"Why d'you call him that?"

"Call him what?"

"Your father's Ted. Why d'you call him Mr.?"

"Cause he's a grown-up."

"Sounds funny."

Your father's Ted sounded funnier to Eli, but he held his tongue.

"All clear," Jo finally declared. Yes, she liked acting like the grown-up, Eli could tell, which was probably why she ate those candy cigarettes, which were hard and tasted like chalk. The last of the Boehringer children, and much younger than her brothers and sisters—who were adults, just like their parents—she liked being the big shot. Which was okay. Mostly.

They lay down in opposite directions, the tops of their heads not quite touching, but close enough that Eli could sort of feel Jo's head anyway, its heat. Eli held back the broad brim of his fisherman's cap so he could see. It would be a while before either of them uttered a word. They listened to the silence instead. The tender new citrus leaves lapped against one another like shuffled playing cards in the intermittent east breeze, the breeze which Eli could hear but not feel within the canopy. A pair of invisible birds in the foliage picked up a tune. An insect wheezed nearby. Distant machinery growled from the Boehringer's grove.

"Swallowtail!" Jo finally cried.

"Darn." Eli barely glimpsed the sharp black and white wings before it flitted out of view.

"Eagle!" Eli yelled the next moment, lifting his arm to point. "Bald Eagle!"

"That waren't no eagle. It was an osprey, you huckleberry. That don't count."

"You sure?"

"Sure I'm sure. Head was too small. Pretty neat, anyway. Don't see too many of them either lately, have we?"

"Nu-uh. Think we'll ever see a wildcat?"

"Sure. I've seen plenty."

Eli wanted to believe her. "You sure they're really here?"

"What do you think eats all the rabbits, huckleberry?"

It seemed to Eli that nothing ate the marsh rabbits. Why else were there so many of them?

"Ah heck, Eli, I can just lay here forever and watch the sky. Let's live forever, Eli."

"Not me. You maybe."

"Ah, turpentine!"

Eli chuckled at Jo's funny word. Turpentine.

"You're not hardly sick at all. Just small. Voice and that sunburn hardly count. I missed more school than you so far. You'll live forever like me. I just know it. Now that they can go to outer space and all they're gonna figure it out by the time we're old. How to live forever."

"Not me."

"Turpentine! They already made that food pill for those Mercury aeronauts you know. They don't have to eat nothin' up there. Just swallow that pill. Now if they can do that already . . ."

Eli hadn't heard about this pill. It didn't seem possible. He was also pretty sure that the space explorers were called astronauts, not aeronauts. But he liked the sound of the leaves slapping against each other in the breeze now and again and the sharp tweets of hidden birds—red birds, he was pretty sure—and the rising buzz of some new bug now, and the fresh-spent blossoms all about smelled so darn good, and the bed of ground cover beneath him felt so soft that he didn't want to argue just now and ruin everything, so he wouldn't say anything to Jo about her food pill or her aeronauts.

Minutes passed.

"I'd just sure like to see that wildcat," he finally said, feeling his voice vibrate against his throat.

Eli's parents didn't know that he knew why they dragged him to Dr. Olivet's in town every few months for those prickings inside his elbow. But he had seen the carbon copies on his father's desk and read them. Greatly Elevated Risk Factor for Cancer, the phrase read. And then other words that he didn't know. Leukemia. Carcinoma. Lymphoma. But he knew cancer, and knew that it was bad, that it had killed Grandma Ellen and Grandma Noma and Grandpa Seymour. (Something called Stroke killed Grandpa Harry quick, as if Adonai himself had reached down and struck his grandpa to the ground with a giant baseball bat.) No, Eli wouldn't live forever. He had been small and sick-prone long as he could remember and didn't expect that life would be any different down the road. Certainly not better.

"We'll see a wildcat soon," Jo said. "Promise."

"Okay." A stronger gust made the leaves dance around the borders of Eli's vision.

"And 'long as you got that breather doohickey—"

"Inhaler. It's called an inhaler, Jo."

"Yeah. 'Long as you got that."

"Okay."

Four

MELODY SHED COPIOUS TEARS, bent over her collapsed cake. One pregnant drop tilted over her aquiline nose onto the ruined honey cake and beaded on the impermeable surface. Now why was she crying? Was it truly over this silly cake, over all her ruined cakes and cookies? She didn't think so, but she couldn't quite tap the source of these schoolgirl tears. "Now stop this nonsense this instant!" she commanded out loud, and obeyed, wiping the last of her tears on her apron.

Eli bounded on the porch, jolting her. Sarah inhaled in a wheeze, then began crying. And just like that, Melody felt better. The return of her human traffic. Just as well that Eli woke the baby. She'd have to wake her anyway, matter of minutes. He always did that, her son, jumped the two stairs to land with a two-footed thud on the heart pine porch. Probably scared of some bogeyman under the raised foundation, Melody figured, lying in wait to grasp his ankles. Children and their fears.

It was a short walk down the loose river rock driveway to their stand. Besides citrus, they sold local tomatoes, peppers, cucumbers and squash, green beans from Deland and Apopka, strawberries from Plant City, melons from Newberry, pecans from the panhandle, orchids from the Seminoles, fewer eggplants and asparagus spears and okra and leafy greens from Melody's garden. Plus honey from their grove bees. Postcards and seashells, too, from a distributor in Cocoa. Melody wanted it to be a full-fledged store, something like the Krupnick's Cash Store in town. Well-stocked shelves and shoppers elbow-to-elbow along the aisles. A fleet of employees. A brisk business out in the world and under her command. But for now, it was still just a stand. Eli shuffled the loose rusty rocks with his feet, toting the meager cash tray like a book inside his elbow, while Melody walked Sarah in the perambulator on the scruffy grass berm. She could feel the strengthening sun pasting the back of her neck. GOLDENS ARE HERE, the rectangular wooden marquee read in bright black letters, framed by yellow. Erma, Melody trusted, had already stood up the smaller roadside sandwich boards either direction on the US 1, which read GOLDENS AHEAD, intentionally cryptic to court curious motorists. Plus a couple YOU'RE ALMOST THERE messages.

When they had first pulled up to the property in the middle of a sublime fall, the air still perfumed by Valencia blossoms, Melody had clamored for Isaac to stop the Pontiac at the foot of the drive so she could get a decent look at the frontage. This, before she'd lay eyes on the weed-choked vegetable patch out back, the triad of live oaks with their shaggy beards, the wild tamarind (which had no business growing there), the lantana and palmetto and privet and wax myrtle islands where small birds dove for cover. All she had seen were photographs, which her friends said was crazy, nuts, *meshugeneh*, insane. While her friends were beginning to decamp from West Philly to the leafier Main Line just outside the city limits—not least of all because Negroes had started their incursions into their city neighborhood—the Goldens had ventured a more dramatic migration. A new life. She had put her trust in Isaac. The grand scale of the enterprise had somehow made it more enticing, not less. Had Iz cajoled her to move to Pikesville or Short Hills or Scarsdale, Melody would have fought him tooth and nail.

"I can't believe we're truly here," she had uttered, leaving the heavy car door open behind her.

"We're here, Mel."

"I have to go pee-pee," Eli complained.

"So go pee," Isaac answered. "Who's going to see you?"

Melody scanned the flat horizon west of the groves, empty save for island thatches of low-lying palm-looking shrubs, the higher, shaggier palms here and there along with some great terraced pines, their needles much longer than the pines she was used to, forming great pom-pom clusters.

"I just can't believe it, Iz. It's so lovely. What is that tree called, a cabbage palm?"

"Sabal, they call them. I think. We'll have plenty of time, Mel, to learn all the palms. Royals, queens, coconuts—"

"I just can't believe we're here." She shook her head slowly, taking in their new environs. An enormous white bird with black legs glided overhead—heron, she would have guessed, or egret, whatever the difference.

"Believe it, Melody. The Goldens are here."

"Goldens are here!" Eli squealed in his falsetto, having taken care of his business but neglecting his open fly. "*Pow-pow!*" He shot his silver gun, then dropped it back quick into its holster. "Goldens are here! Goldens are here!" He drew his gun and aimed at an invisible antagonist along the sleepy highway. "*Pow-pow!*"

The stand's name inspired a good bit of confusion from tourists, but a productive sort of confusion, the sort of confusion that prompted questions, which prompted conversation, which prompted, at worst, the obligatory purchase of a single net of Hamlins, or a fresh chilled quart, or a jar of their orange blossom honey, or a net of pecans, or a postcard. *Is that a variety? Golden oranges? No? Oh, it's your name? How about that.* Sometimes she'd elaborate, tell them that the "golden apples of Hesperides" in Greek myth were probably oranges, so, in a sense, they *did* have Goldens here. She'd share all sorts of entertaining nuggets, starved as she was for adult conversation. That citrus wasn't native to Florida, or the New World even; that hundreds of years before Jesus, the first citrus seeds migrated from the China Sea to the Malay Archipelago, to the east coast of Africa and the Mediterranean, where Jews cultivated and popularized the citron; that the word "orange" evolved from the Sanskrit; that Columbus, Pizarro, Ponce de León, and various Jesuit missionaries introduced citrus to the Americas, along with pestilence, pillaging, and mass slaughter (usually good for a laugh, this last bit); that British mariners consumed citrus to stave off scurvy, hence the word "limeys"; that the blossom end of an orange was sweeter than the stem end; that fruit harvested up high on the tree was sweeter than low fruit; that south-facing fruit was sweeter than north-facing fruit; that they hardly grew any Valencias in Valencia, Spain, anymore; that those dreadful California oranges were mostly peel and albumen, that bitter white part, hardly a drop of juice to be had; that oranges, unlike stone fruits, didn't ripen any further once you pulled them from the tree.

She'd slogged through the definitive tome on citrus by Tolkowsky, a Jew from pre-war Palestine, and a half dozen other books too. Sometimes, she'd see the eyes glaze before her, but often as not the tourists appreciated her local-color bonhomie and expertise. It felt good to know so much about something that most people didn't bother thinking about, however trivial that something was in the grand scheme of things. Oranges. Grapefruit. Lemons. Still, most of her old girlfriends in Philadelphia didn't know very much about anything strange.

Melody glimpsed Ted's wife at the orange pyramids, culling soft or moldy Valencias. She had likely already culled and compiled their eggplant, bean, and tomato configurations, wiped clean the honey jar labels and set out their orchids. Erma's hands, ashen and lined, her only feature giving her age away—sixty or so, given the advanced age of her older children, who lived in faraway Plant City and Live Oak tending separate harvests. Strawberries. Beans. Peppers. Tomatoes. Melons. There was another son, too, up north somewhere. Like several colored women (Negro, the favored term now, which sounded coarse to Melody's ears), Erma's countenance reached fifty at some point and then halted. A lovely woman, Erma.

"Go help Mrs. Lomax," she told Eli. "Hand me the cash tray."

Oranges lasted pretty long off the tree, thanks to that Johnson's wax schmear at Nevin's. All the same, they'd only be in fresh fruit a few more weeks or so before they'd have to wait for the early fall harvest of those pale and pimply Parson Browns.

And what will Melody do to occupy herself this long hot summer?

"Good morning, Erma."

"God bless," said Erma, who flashed a silver smile. Then: "Melody," as if it were a separate sentence she'd found buried in the aging fruit she was sifting through.

Melody stepped behind the wooden counter and slid the cash tray into the register. It felt good each morning to slide the drawer shut, to strike the No Sale button and hear the register's bright reply. Open for business! Such as it was.

It had taken months to tease a "Melody" out of Erma. Colored people down here (Negroes, Melody reminded herself) acted differently than they did in Philadelphia. An increased deference obtained, if deference was the right word. Which explained why Erma had called her "ma'am" those first several months, and why she still waited each morning for Melody to greet her before reciprocating in kind, even though Erma had surely seen them coming a mile away. The field-workers, all of whom were Negroes, never quite looked her in the eye. So many Negroes about on the grove and stand during the season. Maybe this was the main difference between there and here. The sheer number of Negroes she daily encountered here, grove ma'am that she was.

"We don't have to stand on ceremony," she had told Erma shortly after they met. Her mother's phrase, *stand on ceremony,* had somehow spilled from her mouth. "We can stop all this ma'aming business, don't you think?" To which Erma nodded, then continued her same careful dance around the new grove ma'am. This southern racial deference had unsettled Melody. But she found herself, over the first year or so, growing more comfortable with all these sheepish laborers at her beck and call, which frightened her. Its intoxicating appeal. She could see how white southerners, even well-heeled Jews (although what kind of Jews could they have been?) owned slaves way back when.

Thankfully, Erma at least had managed over the past few years to shed most of her obsequious armor.

To wit: "Now what's that old bird want?"

Erma's remark prompted Melody to glance up from the ledger over her reading glasses and spy Mary Beth's approach, wearing her Sunday finest, hat and all. MB, as her friends called her, never patronized them. Her allegiances rested elsewhere, which was fair enough. There was something trailing behind her on wheels, something she was bringing for her. Melody instinctively lifted Sarah from her perambulator and bobbed her in her arms, either to shield the baby or vice-versa.

"My land, it's fixing to be hot as blue blazes today." MB fanned her thin face; the perspiration beaded through her Sunday makeup. *My land. Blue blazes.* Melody admired the local vernacular, although she wasn't quite certain how local any of it was. One thing that surprised her about Florida was how few of the locals, even the growers, could claim Florida roots deeper than a generation or two. Only the Boehringers and Griffins, Clay's family, far as she could determine. The others had migrated from the North and Midwest as adults, or as children with their parents. Like MB, whose my lands and blue blazes originated, Melody suspected, from some Michigan backwater.

"Good morning, Mary Beth."

"Morning, sugar. We missed you at Junior League last week."

In lieu of an apology, Melody shrugged. Sarah had been in a fussy mood—teething, poor thing—so Melody missed last week's planning meeting at Janisse's for their fall fundraiser, the spaghetti dinner.

MB didn't greet Erma, nor did Erma raise her head to acknowledge MB. Surely the two knew each other. Curious, this racial performance. Melody watched as MB reached down behind her, plucked something from her rolling cart, and placed it on the counter between them. A pie.

"Oh my," Melody exclaimed, lifting a hand to her heart.

"Thought it was about time I brought you one of my pies."

Something about the pie moved her. Not MB's dubious gesture (something up her sleeve, to be certain) but the pie itself—its surface, Melody realized, lacquered with perfect pecan halves, nestled together carefully like bedfellows, their sensual creases and curves glistening beneath a caramelized coating of (what?)—brown sugar? molasses? corn syrup?—the pale brown thumb-dimpled crust, lapping up high from the aluminum rim, like waves off a seawall. There was love in this *treyf* pie. She'd grant her that.

"Figured those 'fridges needn't sit empty all summer." Melody glanced behind her at the fresh chilled quarts and gallons within the glass-encased shelves. "More and more folks vacationing down this way all through summer," MB continued. "Cocoa Beach. New Smyrna. Palm Bay. All that outer space business. Pies might make a nice addition to your honey and flowers and such, you decide to keep those shutters open."

"I don't know, Mary Beth. How would we work out the—"

"Oh, sugar, let's just try a bite and see. Call Eli over. How's that child of yours doing, bless his heart?" The scaffolding of MB's face fell under the weight of her concern.

"Oh fine. Very fine. Thank you for asking."

This was another reason Melody was willing to leave Philadelphia—to escape the fallen scaffolding of familiar faces.

"I suppose a piece of pie never hurt anyone, though it *is* a bit early."

"Shucks, Hyram eats pie with his coffee for breakfast most mornings. Even if they are fruit pies, mostly. Let me hold that precious baby of yours and cut yourself a slice."

Melody obeyed, sliced a small wedge with the broad haft of a budding knife (never a shortage of these knives about), transferred the morsel to a paper napkin, and gazed, nonplussed, at the dark interior.

"It's *chocolate* pecan," Mary Beth declared, reading Melody's worry lines. She brandished a plastic fork from thin air, handed it to Melody.

"Eli!" she called before spearing into the wedge. "Pie!" Now where had that rapscallion taken off to? He was supposed to be helping Erma. Probably pestering Ted, tending to the trees, crouched over a sour orange liner, maybe, in the nearby nursery row. A fair number would be culled. Too many, it seemed to Melody. Wasteful. The prouder of the lot would be budded with scions after being inspected and tagged by the commission men, most of these transplanted to the grove a year later, but some they'd sell to motorists at the stand.

Oh well. Eli would turn up. It worried her, sometimes, Eli tromping about on the grove all by himself, especially with some *nogoodnik* vandalizing their trees time to time with what must have been an axe or machete. The vandal, she assured herself, wouldn't dare set foot on their grove in broad daylight, would he? If Eli couldn't roam about on his lonesome down here in the sticks, what was the point?

Melody pierced the lacquered top between two pecans with the fork tines and scooped up a mouthful to her lips. The crust and nut shell gave way upon the slightest incisor assault while the still-warm chocolate interior dissolved on her tongue. But it wasn't the bittersweet chocolate or the nuts that left the greatest impression—the crust, rather, its flaky layers peeling from one another in discernible sheets between her tongue and hard palate, its meat-rich depth of flavor. This crust! She knew its secret. Pig fat. Her eyes closed of their own accord under the sensuous influence.

Could it truly be a sin, such a crust?

Melody contemplated her disastrous recent efforts, baking-wise, and she knew what she would try. The sudden knowledge startled her, prompting a bout of hiccups.

"You need a spot of water, Mrs. Golden?" Erma asked from a faraway fruit pyramid, the *Mrs. Golden* for Mary Beth's benefit.

Melody waved off the suggestion, then placed a palm on her chest to settle her thumping heart.

"A little slice of heaven, my chocolate pecan, don't you agree?" Mary Beth inquired.

Melody nodded.

Melody Golden, who begat here on this toe-tip of the continent batches upon batches of rock-hard mandel breads, collapsed cochins, tragic honey cakes, and ruined rugelachs, Melody Golden, daughter of Harry and Noma Herskowitz of Philadelphia by way of New York by way of Galicia, Melody Golden, wife of Isaac Golden, mother of Eli and Sarah Golden, member of the Levantine tribe, daughter of valor, would bake with lard.

Five

ISAAC CONTEMPLATED THE SEED, not wanting to contemplate the men with the laminate tags who had confronted him on the grove, earlier.

Caustic kernels. Meddlesome pits. Pesky pebbles. Mandibular obstructions. Tiny sparks between compromised molars. Dental nerves aflame. *Ouch.* Choking hazards. Menace to mouth-feel, very least. Mastication interruptus. Triggers of troubled tongues. Juice-dribbles across chin and cheek. Throat-back surprises. Gag-reflex starters.

Most people didn't have a good word to spare for seeds. Bane of fresh fruit citriculture by most lights. Housewives coast-to-coast fairly banished seedy varieties of oranges, lemons, and grapefruit to the genetic ash heap, preferring the "seedless" varieties (six seeds or fewer per fruit, so the commission stipulated), driving the market ever thusward all the way down the supply chain. So much for the sublime, yet seedy, Duncan grapefruit; the Marsh seedless (orig. Lakeland, FL, 1860), Thompson variant (orig. Oneco, FL, 1924), Redblush (orig. Donna, TX, 1931), and Ruby Red (orig. McAllen, TX, 1929)—their cloying, simple sweetness be damned—was all the small river growers could afford to plant anymore, given the bird dog's purchasing orders.

Jackknife sliced soft sour orange equators under Isaac's command. He pressed grimy half globes above the sieve on the workbench, welcomed their pleasant bitter olfactory greeting. Ah. Here's what Isaac saw on the slatted sieve floor: a surfeit of seeds, the testa coat. Chalazal and micropylar poles. Here's what he imagined: the darker tegmen coat beneath, creamy-white cotyledons within, plumule and radicle awaiting germination, taproot bursting the micropylar base. An utter mystery, most citrus seeds. Hybrids, crosses, and mutations over millennia—at human and insectival behest—yielded mixed-up miscegenate citrus embryos. You just never knew what was inside a single citrus seed, most times. Yet sour orange, unlike most cultivars, grew true to type from seed. One of the reasons it was such a good rootstock. A good seed.

Isaac believed in seeds. From the time he swallowed a watermelon seed and his father warned him, crunching caterpillar eyebrows together, that it would grow now from his *pupik*, and Isaac uttered, too young to be horrified, "Honest, Papa? From my belly button?" A later, elementary school experiment on the kitchen windowsill of their West Philadelphia tenement. Apple-seed sprung shoots from the Mason jar. Miraculous milky shoots. Nascent creased leaf. "Where can we plant now, Mama?" he had asked, scanning the impermeable surfaces about the kitchen, the brick wall beyond the clotted-paint windowpanes offering even less hope.

"Plant?" his mother asked over her ironing, confused—she held a spray bottle of water in her left hand to affect the sharpest creases for her husband, the salesman—then glimpsed her son's wet drooping lip. "The park," Ellen Golden uttered. "The park we go, Isaac." For some time after, Isaac absconded with found concave objects—egg cartons, vegetable tins, paint cans—suitable receptacles for any variety of seeds splashed with soil. He had set out to green the entire city, though few of his curbside seedlings survived the lifted legs of canines, the weeding of unappreciative residents, or first winters. Still later, at the Free Library on 52nd, when he was supposed to be studying his science, he found himself thumbing through the crusty pages of an ancient volume, *The Fruits & Fruit Trees of America; Or, The Culture, Propagation, and Management, in the Garden and Orchard, of Fruit-Trees Generally; With Descriptions of all the Finest Varieties of Fruit, Native and Foreign, Cultivated in this Country,* scanning the hundreds upon hundreds of apple seeds and shoots and trees of America. Acklam's Russet, Allemand, American Summer Pearmain, Autumn Rose, Bachelor's Blush, Barton's Incomparable, Blinkbonny, Buck Meadow, Catooga, Chattahoochie, Cheltenham, Cornish Aromatic . . . The names! He spent hours reading about the "Amelioration of Fruits," techniques and strategies hopelessly remote to a child of the city, which partly explained their appeal. Top-working, inarching, banking, marcottage, any number of grafting styles—splice-grafting, tongue-grafting, whip-grafting, cleft-grafting, saddle-grafting. He had committed Dr. Van Mons' Theory to memory: *Cultivation is required to privilege flesh and pulp of fruit over vegetation and seeds.* Life started with a simple seed. Then, through intervention, one could create wonders. A tree! It would be later that he learned how few apples, wild or cultivated, had survived a new America. How many ignored, withered seeds were now lost forever. And so while his mother cried for a brother, unknown to Isaac, lost somewhere in alien Russia, he mourned, strange child, the obliteration of separate, nonhuman beings, or maybe only their names: Curtis Sweet, Dana Greening, Danvers Winter Sweet, Derry Nonsuch, Detroit Red, Devonshire Buckland, Dickson's Emperor, Disharoon, Dobb's Kernel Golden Pippin, Doctor Helsham's Pippin, Downing's Paragon . . .

"Commission boys came out to see me this morning," Isaac uttered to Ted, working the other side of the sieve. Ted always waited for Isaac to initiate conversation. They'd spend the whole day in silence if Isaac didn't get them started, he figured, staring over at Ted's more practiced ashen hands, manipulating sour orange spheres and budding knife with terrifying élan (he always used his ivory-handled budding knife, never a simple jackknife), his palms flashing pale time to time as he pursued his digital exercises.

"Reckoned so. Had a few words with me at the liners."

Isaac nodded, made a listening noise. He didn't know how to feel about Ted's tardy disclosure. When was Ted planning on telling him that he spoke with the commission men? And what did Ted say to them? There was something impossibly discreet about his foreman. Isaac couldn't tell how much of Ted's manner betrayed deference or plain old sneakiness. Definitely some sneakiness there, Isaac thought. He wouldn't put up with it, were it not for the fact that he couldn't quite entertain notions of THE SNEAKY, SHIFTLESS NEGRO—as a real thing, that is—and were it not for the fact that he never would have survived his first season without Ted, who spotted, diagnosed, and treated trees in various states of decline as if the specimens spoke their ills to him. "You'll want to keep Ted on," Clay had told him just after the auction. "Only bit of advice I'll offer, 'less you ask first. Name's Clay Griffin."

"Well?" Isaac asked Ted now. "What did they want?"

"Just where you were at?"

"And you told them?" Perhaps it was his Jewish upbringing, his once-removed but palpable sense of persecution. People with a sense of persecution knew that you avoided people with uniforms or badges or clipboards or pens, people conducting studies, people who wanted A MOMENT OF YOUR TIME. That you avoided pretty much any stranger who came looking for you, not unlike people with a sense of humor knew how to tell a joke.

"Reckon I did." Ted lifted the biceps of his muslin shirt sleeve to mop his creased brow. Salt-and-pepper coils above yielded to sporadic scalp lagoons, unpatterned baldness that smacked of insidious influence, fungal or bacterial encroachment that Ted would never tolerate on the trees. The temperature beneath the greenhouse panes was stifling, the air so thick you could nearly see it. "Apologize if I made a mistake."

Surely Ted, a Negro in the South, knew from persecution. If two officious-looking white strangers came looking for Ted, he'd sure enough find a way to elude them. He just didn't extend the same discretion toward his white employer. Jewish. White. White. Jewish. Distinctions too fine to mean much to Ted, probably, faraway Holocaust notwithstanding.

"Didn't give you no trouble, did they? Figured you might have called on them about the mischief"—that's how Ted referred to the vandals attacking Isaac's grove—"or they were just up to their usual 'spections, maybe. But we're all tagged proper, stock and scions. And we don't got no tristeza, if that's what's on their mind."

"That's not what they wanted," Isaac said, twisting a half globe above the sieve. "And I haven't reported the vandalism to the commission. Just Sheriff Wright. Not sure it's a commission matter." His hand ached, perhaps because it was so large. There were just so many extraneous muscles and tendons and ligaments in his clumsy frying-pan hands to ache, whereas Ted's hands seemed all skin and bones, just the essential machinery. For whatever reason (puny, peeved protest?), Isaac found himself not revealing what the commission men wanted, specifically, and, for whatever reason (pushback against Isaac's puny, peeved protest?) Ted didn't inquire. Rather, Ted hummed an inscrutable melody at a barely perceptible frequency as he worked, as if to release the pressure of unsaid words.

"Got 'nough seeds now, I expect," Ted declared, finally. "Start in on the rows now." The foreman clutched a fistful of mucusy seeds and repaired to the nursery row, where Hawley had formerly cultivated orchids. Ted often did this, took the lead, which Isaac didn't mind so much as he noticed, which maybe meant that he *did* mind. There was never any doubt about Isaac keeping Ted on as foreman—Clay's encouragement, unnecessary—as little as he knew about actually running a citrus grove. All of Isaac's knowledge vis-à-vis citrus, vis-à-vis grove proprietor, vis-à-vis Negroes, for that matter, was book-gleaned, theoretical. Yet he found it vaguely irksome that Ted acted so nonchalant upon Isaac's overture, as if Ted were doing Isaac the favor, when another new grove owner might have turned him out on his ear, brought in younger, more malleable, blood. Irked him further when Ted renegotiated more generous terms for his remuneration than Hawley's ledger warranted. And irked him even further that ever since, Ted undertook his duties with what struck Isaac as vague proprietorship. But what was Isaac to do? There were warrens of behavior that Isaac, a Jew, a Jew from the North to be precise, couldn't traverse with Negroes—at arm's length in Philadelphia, but now suddenly at his elbows—aware as he was of Emmet Till and Rosa Parks, Little Rock's mean-spirited Orval Faubus, the Woolworth's counter in Greensboro, those Freedom Riders firebombed out of their bus in Alabama just days ago. The Freedom Riders wouldn't be wasting their time on Isaac's underpopulated, insignificant state—on their way to New Orleans, instead, according to Edwards on the news. (The whole state of Florida was shaded dark like the northeastern and western states on that map of the Freedom Riders' hopeful route behind Edwards on the television, as if Florida didn't rate as true south at all, as a true *place* at all.)

You just couldn't be aware of all that was going on in the country and reprimand the UPPITY NEGRO, play the southern white landowner. For that's what it would be. Playacting. Theater. So, instead, Isaac deferred to Ted, offered him the widest of berths to command the field-workers. This impossible business of negotiating other people!

Isaac gazed down the row at Ted. He worked the seedbed like a magician, knuckle down above the rich soil, summoning seeds from his secret palm with his hidden fingers, taut ashen flesh riding barely discernible across metacarpal, then a longest middle finger poke at the invisible mucusy seed below the soil, muscle memories of the same hand filling the empty-air column with a deft pinch between thumb, ring finger, and pinkie. No playacting about that. Just good honest work with his hands. Isaac, across the bed, lagged behind, performing his more clumsy choreography.

"Gonna go fish for speck tomorrow," Ted announced, apropos of nothing. Monday was Ted's day off. Early morning Sundays too, when Erma dragged him to the AME Church in town.

"Where?" Isaac inquired. "St. John's?"

"Mmm-hmm. Tournament coming up. Brand-new aluminum boat the grand prize."

"Nice," Isaac said. He could never quite warm to Ted's favorite hobby. Fishing. It seemed to Isaac a hobby suitable only for children, a pastime that one was supposed to outgrow, which probably wasn't a fair interpretation as Clay, Edwin, and the others all fished for snook and redfish in the lagoon, in addition to slaying manifold fauna, mostly legged and mammalian, though God help the occasional rafters of turkey and bobwhite coveys that still roamed their groves.

"Now that I made longer outriggers," Ted declared, "got the trolling spread pretty near perfect." The foreman wiped his brow again with his muslin sleeve, paused above his labors, mostly to let Isaac catch up from across the row so he wouldn't have to shout. "Could take Mr. Eli out again sometime for speck."

"He'd love that."

Which was true. Eli had taken to the outdoors here. Any chance he got, he grabbed up his fishing rod and headed to the river. Dusty mile or so clear past the grove, across the Florida East Coast tracks, through the dense patch of sabal palms and the mangrove thicket to the river. Quite a hike. There, he had discovered mangrove snapper, redfish, sheepshead, and snook—depleted though they were from the haul seine poachers—larger piscatorial prizes than Ted's freshwater speck and bass. (Melody, consulting her *Joy of Cooking,* had learned how to clean and fillet the creatures, cringing all the while.)

"Why was it again that you like fishing for crappy so much, speck, whatever you call them?" Isaac inquired now. "Rather than snapper and such, I mean. Snapper's still around plenty, it seems, even with the poachers."

"Never much cottoned to saltwater fish. Raised in Live Oak, you know. Up near Georgia. Suwannee River. Sort of what I'm used to, freshwater. Cleaner than salt."

Isaac nodded.

"Best start budding soon," Ted declared, striding past Isaac to gather the hose, having finished his row. Isaac could tell, somehow, perhaps by the way his foreman waited until this late moment to suggest budding, when he could leave the words in his wake, that it wasn't merely a casual suggestion.

"I suppose."

"Before summer heat sets in," Ted shouted from the spigot. "That or wait for fall."

"Might as well get a jumpstart. Makes sense."

Ted returned, the hose trailing behind. "So, we'll let Mr. Eli's grove be 'nother season? That the plan?"

There it was! Ted had little more patience for Eli's grove than Isaac's co-op peers. It wasn't the money so much. Only a small part of Ted's pay hinged upon those measly acres. It just didn't sit right with him, Isaac knew. Pilfering away usable land.

"I figure at least another season or so. Can't tell much after only two seasons of bearing, right?"

Ted shrugged.

Isaac had migrated southward to lay hands on something essential and true. And for Eli's health, too. Yes, Eli's health. But perhaps Eli's health was only the excuse. There were words to describe his horticultural endeavors. Courageous. Bold. Imaginative. Adventuresome. Visionary. Good words, all. But there were other words too. Foolhardy. Self-indulgent. Presumptuous, even.

Contrary Isaac. Was this why he had actually pulled up stakes? Why he squandered so many acres, flirting perilously close to foreclosure? What gave him the right—this greenie, this Yankee, this Jew no less—to meddle with the satisfactory citrus status quo in this sunshine state? There was the commission, the Departments of Agriculture, state and federal, a whole division at the university, too, whose entire charge was citrus sustainability and improvement. And so the longer-standing co-op growers—Clay, Doyle, Edwin, Walt—didn't trouble the waters. They left well enough alone, season after season budded the same-old scions to tried-and-true rootstocks (sour orange here along the river). They left it to those impeccably credentialed and salaried others to fool around with the genetics.

Times were tight. Maybe Walt, and now Ted, had a point. You protected every inch of your modest profit margin. You worked the land. You didn't play with it. Only Isaac plied closed corolla buds with tweezers, emasculated unsuspecting stamens, painted foreign pollen to pistil with his clean camel-hair paintbrush, paper-bagged his specimens on the tree to ward off interloping insects sloppily trailing indeterminate pollen. Did his partners even scout their rows for unanticipated bud sports? Why bother when it all came down to sugar and acid ratios for the dumbed-down American palate? No one else seemed bothered by this homogenizing, which bothered Isaac all the more, this refusal of the co-op to be properly perturbed.

Where was their ambition? Most of the varieties they now cultivated arose as chance seedlings or bud sports on this or that grove, nursed by this or that grower, who merely paid attention. The Parson Brown, say. No genius, Reverend Nathan L. Brown. Landowner of a small parcel up around Webster. Figured he'd supplement his meager parish income by raising citrus. Bought five seedlings on a lark in 1856 from some fellow claiming to have gotten those precious pebbles from an orange off a British ship in Savannah, the orange having grown from a tree in faraway China. Seedlings grew into pretty standard looking trees, bearing downright unattractive fruit, the rind approximating an unfortunate dermatological malady. Here's what Reverend Brown noticed, though. When he sliced open the still-green fruit on those five trees early October, the pulp vesicles inside had already matured to pale orange, the earliest cultivar one could harvest by several weeks!

A hundred-odd years later and they couldn't improve upon the Parson Brown? There had been so many apple names. . . . Catshead, Chandler, Drop D'Or, Danver's Winter Sweet, Domine, Early Red Margaret . . . So few citrus cultivars, by comparison. Why not them? Why not *him*, Isaac Golden? Why not here? Why not now!?

He walked the greenhouse row, inspecting his twenty-day shoots along with Ted. Single, double, and triple shoots. The citrus seed was a strange little bundle, to be sure. Multiple embryos oftentimes in the same seed. Even sour orange. Vegetative and sexual. Isaac culled the misshapen and feeble shoots and set them aside for later retrieval, a practiced pluck between the calloused pads of thumb and forefinger. Once they reached a quarter inch or so diameter at the base, he and Ted would move them to the outside nursery rows, where they'd be budded a season later. His cohorts didn't bother anymore this far down the chain of citrus being. Handling seeds for stock. Closest they got was handling their own budwood. Why mess with seeds or seedlings when the Seminoles sold cut-rate the sour orange stock they grew from seed down in the Glades? And so here, maybe, was the problem. Here's what explained the rise of the frozen people, maybe. Once you cut yourself off from the source . . .

"They asked me to drive over for a visit," Isaac declared, culling an unpromising zygotic seedling between the meaty pincers of his forefinger and thumb.

"Beg your pardon?"

"The commissioner. In Lakeland. He wants to see me."

"I'll be."

They worked in silence until the heat sapped their strength. Or Isaac's strength, rather. He held out as long as he could, hoped that Ted might suggest calling it quits first. A vain hope. Days failed long before Ted ever would. His foreman found meaning, it seemed to Isaac, in the intensity of labor itself. Ted's smallest gestures—the furrow he held above his brow, his energetic deployment of his pruning shears—betrayed his single-minded commitment to the work at hand, whatever it was. Isaac lifted his eyes toward the sun, a nebulous smudge beyond the smoky greenhouse glass, hardly bleeding yet toward the horizon.

"We've done enough for now," he declared. "Let's take a break. I want to run in to Clyde's before supper for those drip lines I ordered." Clyde's Ag-Mart and Feed and Janisse's were the only businesses open on Sundays, Janisse's because folks had to eat, Clyde's because ranch, farm, and grove crises, the town elders agreed, didn't take a day off. Ted nodded, the trace of a slight smile dawning across his mouth, whether on account of the drip lines or his boss's fatigue, Isaac wasn't certain.

They made their way the short piece through the mowed path of wiregrass alongside palmetto fans and fewer fragrant wax myrtle shrubs, past the triad of live oaks with their shaggy beards, the wild tamarind, which had no business growing there—its light-green feathers of new growth bursting out everywhere now in the dense canopy—and past Melody's garden to the loose river rock driveway around front and the stand to check in on the women. Ted advanced toward Erma, culling soft Valencias from a pyramid, while Isaac made his way past the red-mesh pecan nets toward Melody behind the register. But not without glancing back toward Ted and Erma and seeing Erma do something strange, lift the blade of an open hand toward Ted's wet cheek, cupping it there for a moment, as if to offer it ballast. And more. Ted lifting his hand to cover hers a moment. Gestures so intimate, so real, that Isaac lowered abashed eyes.

Six

EVENING. You enter the home of a family at dinnertime, six o'clock, six thirty, say, and you know that it's a certain kind of place at a certain kind of time featuring a certain kind of people. Family people, that is. A special place and time for these particular people. Not any more special, perhaps, than other places and other times for other people, but a special time for these sort of people, all performing the practiced rituals of their station.

Isaac was this sort of person, a family man. Enough the Jew, anyway, that it hadn't occurred to him to contemplate alternative possibilities. There was nothing so resilient and indomitable as the American family, circa 1961. One view, anyway. All hell could break loose, but the family would hold fast. Again, one view, probably Mel's view, God love her, but not Isaac's view. Families, he worried, were bird's nest fragile. One crucial twig—Eli's precarious health, the grove's equally precarious footing, any variety of unforeseen but imminent calamities—and the whole thing might come tumbling down. Isaac's view.

But then there was dinner. Isaac left his caked boots and soiled socks on the raised pine porch, having spent the past few hours laying out those drip lines with Ted that he picked up from Clyde's, heat of the day. He crossed the threshold and entered his home. The smell was the first thing he noticed. He took his time in the family room, resting his bare soles on the warm pine floor before advancing to the kitchen, where Melody had probably labored the better part of two hours, took his time to register the distinct odors permeating the atmosphere: faint cruciferous sulfur, tomatoes cooked to a red-wine finish, earth-smoke of ground meat, an undercurrent of allium (yellow onion and less garlic). Filled cabbage. His mother-in-law's recipe, her memory be for a blessing. Sunday night. Poor Eli, having set the table, had most likely retreated to his room, sulking already over his comic books. *Green lantern*? *Superman*?

Isaac, like Eli, didn't much like the meal. Sarah's digestive system, lucky for her, hadn't evolved sufficiently to brave gassy cabbage. Melody, for her part, didn't care much for filled cabbage, either. And so, essentially, no one would be altogether happy this evening. Happy, though? It was a single dinner. What did happy have to do with it? Happy was for two, three meals a week. Satisfied for three or four, maybe. But not every dinner should inspire pleasure. There should be one or two dinners a week that families just soldiered through, fortunate as they were to have nutritious food to fill their bellies.

Isaac stood for a moment at the threshold between the den and the kitchen, filling the pocket door frame with his heft. "Here, hold your daughter," plaid-aproned Melody greeted him. Something of a challenge there. *Hold your daughter*. Sarah was *his* daughter. He should take the time to hold her a decent stretch at least once a day, look at her more often than that. "You don't *look* at her enough," Melody sometimes warned him. He wondered whether Melody attributed his practiced incompetence to her faulty diaphragm. They were hardly in a position, financial or otherwise, for another mewling offspring. But Isaac didn't begrudge his wife their daughter. It wasn't that. Sarah was his daughter, *his* child. Yes, he understood. You couldn't be the paterfamilias by half measures. You were in, you were in. Out, out. Isaac accepted the terms of the contract. In his head, anyway. But it was awfully hard. Hard since Eli.

"How's the little buttercup today?" he cooed as soothingly as he could muster, seated now on his own father's leather recliner. Under the influence of his ample weight, the chair released the faint aroma of his father's long-extinguished White Owls and Cuesta Del Reys. Its enormous arms tattered with bronze studs, the appointment was hopelessly out of place in their Florida den. Yet he couldn't bring himself to remove it, his patrimony, and Melody, to her credit, never hectored him to do so. He grasped Sarah from beneath her underarms so she could face him, bobbed her up and down on his lap. She downright refused to test the strength of her legs against his thighs upon her descent, letting the creased and dimpled ham-hocks dangle, pleased for her father to do all the work.

"How about moving those plump *pulkes*?" Sarah stared him down through her familiar blue eyes, her fat cheeks reminding him of that movie director, Hitchcock. "Give Dad a smile, maybe?"

Nothing. A thread of viscous saliva advanced downward from the corner of her mouth, gaining momentum as it plashed and pooled on his thigh.

Here's what Melody couldn't quite appreciate. Try as he might, there were certain frequencies of human exchange beyond Isaac's capacities now. Ever since Eli. He had steeled himself. Sarah sure knew it. The way his baby girl looked at him unnerved Isaac. No blank stare, this look from his daughter. Intent, rather. Purposeful. It was a look that knew things, that made certain unspoken demands.

"I'm doing the best I can, *pisherle*," he declared.

Nothing. Just that same look, more than purposeful, he reconsidered. Accusatory. He couldn't quite bear this look.

"I should really clean up before supper!" he called out to Melody, Sarah's weight now testing his depleted biceps.

"This instant!?" she returned the volley across the open pocket door frame. "You truly need to clean up this instant!?"

"I'm filthy, is the thing, Mel!"

"You can't spend five consecutive minutes with your daughter!? That's what you're telling me!? Not five minutes!?"

Isaac felt the heat rise in his face, exhaled to release the pressure. It wasn't as if he were lollygagging all day.

"Eli!" he shouted, shifting strategies. "Come out here and help me with your sister, would you please!?" He heard Melody's groan from the kitchen, maybe just imagined it.

"Coming!" Eli whined. Isaac heard the complaint of his son's mattress, the rustling of papers.

"You could help out a lot more around here, mister," he greeted Eli once he arrived, handing off Sarah. "Sit. I'll get a bottle."

Eli was down in the mouth upon Isaac's return with Sarah's evaporated milk. No picnic, he figured, being Eli. Shrunken Eli. Solitary Eli. It hadn't been fair to prod his son about helping out with Sarah. His boy helped out plenty, took more interest in his baby sister than Isaac could reasonably expect. He felt rotten about his first evening words to his son.

"Everything okay at school, sport?"

Eli shrugged.

"Those bigger boys aren't picking on you, I hope."

"No, Daddy." Eli bobbed Sarah gently in the cradle of his thin arm as he plied the glass bottle upon her. He had learned, Isaac noticed, that jostling his sister slightly, putting her off-balance, prompted her sucking reflex. Eli stopped rocking her once she latched on, but still stroked her fleshy cheek with his small finger. "No one picks on me," he continued, his eyes on his sister's furrowed brow. "No one's ever picked on me."

What Isaac heard in this was that not one of his peers at school had paid him enough mind to pick on him. The sickly Jewboy. He wasn't sure if that's what Eli meant to communicate. Perhaps he was reading too much into things. What Isaac would give to transfer some of his ridiculous outsized strength to his son.

"Well, I better wash for supper, kiddo." Something moved him to trouble Eli's shock of straight hair, his son bucking at the assault. Isaac was pretty sure that he would have appreciated this human touch from his father, absent most of the time selling "provisions" to various mid-Atlantic purveyors—mysterious food and food-related items—remote the few nights a week he was home, seated on his leather brass-studded throne with his *Inquirer* opened full before him, cigar smoke plumes wafting toward the ceiling from behind the shrouded source. But, again, it couldn't be any picnic being Eli. Few school friends, if any, his father hollering at him to watch his sister, then—oddly—reaching with frying-pan hands to trouble his hair.

Isaac's wife and son made busy orbits about the table upon his return, Eli placing forks on the napkins he had folded into rectangles, never triangles, aproned Melody setting down the Lucite pitcher of water at the center, Sarah braced in her other arm. Even had they completed their preparations, they wouldn't have taken their seats before Isaac's arrival. It sure was something, being the husband and father, the paterfamilias, whatever the burdens. It sure was something.

"Let's sit," he suggested. They sat, the wooden chairs screeching against the lemon linoleum, which Old Man Hawley had inexplicably pasted over the finer pine floor in the kitchen.

"The *hamotzi*, Eli."

"*Baruchatahadonaielohenoumelech—*"

"Like you mean it," Isaac interjected. "The *kavanah*."

Eli started over and completed the prayer, slower.

"There," Isaac said. "Was that so hard?" As if it were a prize for compliance, Isaac passed the basket of Wonder Bread to his son, who began slathering a foamy piece with Mazola.

"Not so much margarine," Melody warned, bobbing Sarah in her lap.

"Do we have to eat stuffed cabbage *every* Sunday?" Eli complained.

"We don't have it *every* Sunday," said Isaac.

"Seems like it."

"Don't talk back to your father."

"I wasn't talking back."

"There you go again," said Isaac, without heat. "People are starving in Armenia. Be a good boy now and eat your supper."

"A few bites, anyway," Melody declared.

Isaac sighed. "A few bites, then."

The meal completed—aborted, rather, the wreckage of unappreciated cabbage, ground meat, and rice strewn across their plates—the dishes scrubbed clean by Melody (cleared by Isaac and Eli) while she broiled a palette of brown sugar crusted Duncan halves, the family decamped with their dessert trays for the family room and the RCA. The Victor was an enormous twenty-one-inch indulgence that they could scarcely afford, but that Isaac regardless bought, UHF and all, so that Melody wouldn't feel so alone. She had developed a near sisterly fondness for that Lucille Ball—so funny, Melody declared, it was hard to believe she wasn't Jewish. Too bad the show was canceled. Thank heavens for reruns.

"We'll still catch most of the news," Melody announced, clicking the "wireless wizard" remote with one hand, Sarah braced on her knee with her other arm.

"It's not working," Eli announced.

"Now don't start."

"It *never* works."

"The tube just needs to warm up." Isaac smacked the top of the heavy walnut console.

"You'll only break it doing that," Melody warned, the "wireless wizard" lowered, bobbing Sarah on her knees, who, like Eli, seemed perturbed by the delay.

A star formed at the center of the tube. "There," Eli said. The star streaked across both sides of the screen, then the screen itself grew incrementally brighter, revealing Edwards behind his news desk.

"Sure takes a long time to warm up—"

"*Shhh,*" Isaac said.

"Go brush your teeth, Eli," Melody instructed, raising Sarah over her shoulder from her knee, as if to shield her view from the screen. "You're done with your grapefruit."

There was some debacle, Isaac could tell. The deeper pitch to Edwards' voice, his more deliberate cadence, the scaffolding of his face rigid. A botched assault on Cuba's coast, apparently. Dead, dark bodies in army fatigues strewn across the sand, the thick-bearded communist dictator perched tall above, surveying the carnage, gloating. US Ambassador to United Nations, Adlai Stevenson, denies US involvement.

"Well that's just terrific. There's your president for you, Mel."

"*Shhh.*"

"A fine mess we're in now, I bet."

"*Shhh,* Iz."

Sure, Kennedy was a war hero and all, but still a bootlegger's son, a *shikker*'s son. Didn't that trouble anyone? Too slick by half for Isaac's taste. Too good looking when it came right down to it. Isaac had voted for Nixon. A perfectly respectable hardworking fellow, that Nixon, one who didn't have the world handed to him on a silver platter. So what if he sweated like a *chazer* through the debate, if unflattering lines and shadows marred his countenance, if he could have used a fresh shave? It seemed to Isaac that anyone with his head in the game these days, the stakes as high as they were—that *momzer* Krushchev—ought to perspire some. Nixon had struck Isaac as the more serious man. And Isaac didn't like the way Kennedy ran down Eisenhower.

"When are you going to realize that he's in over his head, Mel?"

"Just be quiet, you," Melody admonished. She rose, pivoted on her hips to rock Sarah. "He's just a big brute," Melody exclaimed. "A merciless brute, that Castro. Look at him! That horrible beard!"

What Isaac thought: Eisenhower would have pulled it off. He wouldn't have botched the logistics. But Kennedy? What does he do? Sends a skinny ragtag crew of amateurs to take over an island.

What Isaac said: "That he is, Mel. A brute. That he is."

"Everything okay?" Eli asked, perched in his Superman pajamas beneath the threshold, wary of entering the room. Perhaps he had discerned the troubled postures of his parents, the newscaster's disconcerting sobriety.

"Yes, Eli," Isaac assured him. "Everything's okay, son."

"You sure?"

"Yes, we're sure," said Mel. Then, more softly: "Everything's fine, Elijah-le."

"Everything's fine," Isaac said again, sharper, as if it were true.

Eli stood silent for a moment, gauging the weight of the repeated words.

"Help me put your sister to bed," Melody said, rising. Isaac lingered at the television, then followed after the party to Sarah's bedroom, paused at the threshold. Eli leaned over the lip of the crib to kiss his sister goodnight.

"I can't reach her now," he groaned, his bony bird sternum pressed against the wooden rail. "I can't reach her to kiss, Mom."

"Like a Torah do it," Melody said. "Through the slats. Kiss her like you kiss a Torah."

Eli leaned back from the rail, reached his fingers through the wooden slats to touch Sarah's cheek, then kissed the inside of his fingers.

"Night, Sarah," Eli said.

"There," Melody said, and Isaac withdrew.

*

"I'm ready for bed too," Eli declared when he returned to the family room with his mother. "Ready for my tuck, Dad." For whatever reason, Eli liked his father to tuck him in at night, his nighttime tuck, shrouded in darkness, the last outright expression of paternal affection he still craved, and expected, despite having shrunk from his father's touch earlier in the evening. He shouldn't have scolded Eli about Sarah, Isaac admonished himself afresh. What was that all about?

"Your father will be there in a minute." Melody gripped Eli's small shoulders, pivoted them toward the hall behind. "Now go brush your teeth."

"Okay."

Isaac stood, but didn't advance toward the bedroom hall quite yet. "Incredible," he uttered, talking over the broadcast. The reporters seemed to know exceedingly little beyond the bare bones—an amphibious assault was attempted, it was quashed with brutal efficiency, there were significant casualties, arguable US involvement—but the gravity of the event, apparently, dictated the incessant repetition of those few details.

"Might not be so smart living near that aeronautics facility now. Not the way things are going."

"Hush, Iz. Don't even think like that."

"A fine mess we're in now, Mel. A fine mess."

"Isaac."

"Okay. I won't say another word."

"Go, already. Go. Eli's waiting."

The walls of Eli's room were festooned with his rubbings. His teacher at school had taught them how to compress leaves—palmetto, magnolia, sweet gum, live oak, beauty berry—beneath the pages of diaphanous paper, then shade the canvas with graphite pencil to summon their likeness. He had busied himself ever since gathering and sketching any number of found objects from the grove and beyond, which now almost completely obscured his corduroy wallpaper. Isaac reflexively scanned the room for new installations each time he entered. A new sample from the town's sprawling camphor tree, it seemed, had been added to the mosaic of twenty or so other tree and shrub specimens, the skins of garter, rat, and milk snakes, the various rock and twig outlines. Eli had catalogued a fair number of scourges to their citrus too: lubber grasshoppers, stinkbugs, leaf-footed plant bugs, Fuller rose beetles, cicadas, blue-green beetles. Eli didn't exactly see them as scourges, Isaac supposed. He appreciated his son's impulse, the desire to gather the shards of his new world, to hold them close.

"You're going to warn me if you spot too many of those blue-green guys, right? You're my right-hand man, yes?"

"Uh-huh."

"Promise, kiddo? They'll wipe us clear out."

"Promise."

"No butterflies, eh?" Isaac asked, scanning the wall again. Isaac's morning encounter with Walt still festered.

"Butterflies don't work, Dad. Too soft."

"Makes sense." Isaac walked toward Eli's twin bed, sat at the edge atop the quilt, threadbare now. Isaac's mother had stitched it for Eli shortly after he outgrew his crib and outgrew the gender-neutral yellow-and-white baby blanket she had knitted for him while he was still a mystery in Melody's womb.

"See lots of critters out in your grove today, sport?"

"Rabbits, mostly. Think I'll ever see one of them wildcats?"

"One of *those* wildcats, Eli. Let's not forget your grammar. You've been living here too long. That or watching too much *Wagon Train*. Or *Gunsmoke*, maybe. You keeping up with your factors?"

"Yes Dad," Eli sighed.

He wasn't a particularly strong student, Eli. A child's brain, Isaac remembered from *cheder*, was like the freshest parchment, the rabbis claimed, which hungrily absorbed a scribe's ink. But Eli's brain wasn't so absorptive. Part of his illness, probably, that stubborn brain, so it was difficult to fault him. Still . . .

"Six times four?"

"Twenty-four, Dad."

"Good. Six times nine?"

Eli paused for a moment. Isaac could see the fingers of his right hand working beneath his grandmother's quilt. But that was okay.

"Fifty-four!"

"Good. Once you get them all down, long division will be a breeze."

"I know."

"Well, goodnight Eli." Isaac had stopped telling his son that he loved him every night, hoping (perhaps foolishly) to toughen him up some. Instead of the words, he kissed his boy on the forehead, above his unfortunate butterfly rash. He listened to the workings of Eli's embattled lungs, trying not to appear to Eli that he was listening to his embattled lungs. Smooth, unimpeded air. Good. He rose from the bed.

"Goodnight Dad." Eli rolled on his side, pulling a stretch of quilt with him.

"And yes," Isaac uttered at the threshold.

"Yes what?" Eli asked, rolling on bedsprings toward the sound of his voice, the thread of the conversation having slipped from his grip.

"I know you'll see a wildcat, son. I just know it."

"So I'm heading to Lakeland tomorrow," Isaac announced a short while later from their marital bed, stripped to his Bogart tee and pajama bottoms. Melody lingered in the bathroom before the vanity mirror. She already finished scrubbing her teeth with the Pepsodent. Isaac had heard her discreet foam spittings into the sink basin. He figured she was troubling her gums now with the rubber stimulator at the end of the handle.

"Oh?" she called, invisible still beyond the threshold.

"The commissioner. He wants to see me. And I might ask about that new parasitic wasp to take care of the scale. I was going to take the Pontiac if that's okay. You don't have Junior League, do you?"

Melody turned off the bathroom light, approached the bed. The moon bully cast blue spears through the slatted shutters. "Not tomorrow," she uttered. "Take the car." She set her bottom down on the edge of their mattress, brushed a shock of her raven hair with deliberate, mechanical strokes. The moonlight summoned the silhouette of her flesh beneath her long, gathered nightgown. Isaac followed the line from her raised elbow down her torso, traced the tantalizing slope from waist to hip.

"You don't really think they'll do anything crazy, do you, Iz?"

Isaac knew what she meant. The Soviets. The Cubans.

"No, not really, Mel. We'll be okay. I was just talking, before."

Melody nodded, plied her hair with more rapid strokes of the brush, as if the matter were settled. Her dark hair had been much longer before the children, clear down to the small of her back. A profligate hairstyle, in truth, which Isaac's conservative mother couldn't quite abide. She had appraised Melody's appearance as exotic so she didn't have to say cheap. A real Jewess Isaac had married (fair-haired, hulking, *goyische*-looking Isaac), as if to set his allegiances straight, once and for all. Over meals, when they first started courting, Melody would twist the thick shock of her hair in her left hand and hold the cord over her breast, away from her soup. The reflexive gesture had affected him powerfully. His wife's still-lovely form on the bed now didn't affect him quite so powerfully. But he remembered how it used to feel to see her twist the thick raven cord above the modest rise of her chest, and he felt the memory, at least, thick in his throat.

"The baby is asleep," she announced, setting the brush down on her nightstand.

"Oh," he answered, knowing what *the baby is asleep* meant—detecting now, too, the reinforced tea rose in the atmosphere overtaking the lingering influence of her morning Camay beneath, the menthol from the single cigarette his wife allotted herself after the children were asleep. (Just one cigarette in the evening, ever since the *Reader's Digest* report.) He registered these cues in his lungs, his belly. He reminded himself to breathe. And after such a long hot day. Such a long hot day for the both of them. Sunday. He consulted his mental calendar. It had been some time, he supposed. He lifted a calloused hand, reached beneath her raven curtain, traced the tender button trail at the base of Melody's neck. She raised her knees and leaned back, slid her small bare feet beneath the sheets, rested her head atop her pillow, then turned on her side to face her husband. There was something irresistibly fetching about the way a woman—or his wife, anyway—advanced to bed. While Isaac (and most men?) propped a clumsy knee on the mattress, then sort of belly-flopped head first onto his pillow, Melody descended more gracefully, bottom first, then leaned back like a diver slipping beneath the skin of the sea.

"Are you too tired, dear?" She stroked the sun-bleached blonde fur of his forearm.

"No, hon'," he lied. "I'm not tired."

This particular place, Isaac thought. This spot of time. A special time and place for a family man.

"I was thinking, Iz," Melody announced some moments later, "maybe we can keep the stand open this summer. Fewer hours of course. But it seems a shame to shutter it up again all season. Don't you think?" Her voice seemed to come from above. She'd just returned from the bathroom and her ablutions, no doubt, washed clean any lingering perspiration on her face with upward (never downward) strokes of a wet washcloth. She hadn't yet slid once again beneath the sheets.

Isaac groaned, stricken by the verbal assault, turned over on his back and cracked open a single eye. There she stood, loomed over him between sentences like a victorious combatant. "Huh? What?" It occurred to him that he had been asleep, or mostly asleep. He ever marveled at Melody's rapid recovery of her senses, post-coital, that she could launch into substantive, spirited conversation now of all times.

"Open the stand? All summer?" Isaac lifted the crook of his elbow to his brow to shield his eyes—both open now—from the bathroom light, blazing. Melody lowered her bottom onto the side of the bed again, stroked the blonde fur of his forearm, her familiar comfort.

"Well, we can see how it goes, Iz. Just take it one week at a time. But with all that outer space business going on now at the Cape, we're getting more government people stopping in every day. Tourists too. Janisse says they're going to expand on the island next, if they don't head up to Georgia or Texas or down to The Bahamas.

All that moon talk. And even without oranges there's marmalade and pecans to sell, and the postcards and honey, plus the orchids, and I could make Borden's milkshakes, start baking pies and such . . ."

"Baking? When it's a hundred degrees outside?" Isaac asked, or perhaps only thought as sleep's riptide gradually pulled him back under.

"Isaac? Iz?" he faintly heard.

"Yes, Mel. Yes. Yes. . . ."

Seven

THE GROVE. The town. The river. The island and the Haulover Canal across the liquid expanse. Oak hammocks, pine flatwoods, sulfurous mangrove shorelines, and palmetto scrub. Miles and miles of scrubland. A place of abundance, from a certain perspective. A singular landscape.

That very word, landscape, would have been inscrutable to Isaac's parents. What business did a Jew have contemplating the landscape, the frivolous outdoors? And what would they say about this frivolous place? Hardly a place at all. They had no people here. Closest *shul* was in Orlando. The Goldens made the drive nearly every Saturday morning for services, along with the Krupnicks, Meyer and Freida, who owned the Cash Store in town—or Jew Store, as the locals referred to it without apparent malice—and along with the few other members of their tribe scattered across various central Florida backwaters: Sanford and Deland and Leesburg and Eustis and Cocoa and Apopka and Kissimmee and Deltona and Clermont and St. Cloud. But Orlando was boring, Eli complained. After services were over, there was nothing to do there. Was this small swatch of Florida enough? Isaac worried, gripping the wheel. Enough to hold them? He had gambled their modest inheritance on the grove.

No turning back now. Isaac cast stabbing glances at the Standard Oil road map, folded open on the passenger's vinyl seat. He'd follow the red US 1 signs past the tiny hamlet of Mims to town, proper. From there, the 22 to Orlando, then (it appeared) the 92 south to Lakeland. Wide open two-lane highway, mostly. He twisted on the radio dial to hear Brenda Lee crooning, *I'm sorry, so sorry that I was such a fool, I didn't know love could be so cruel*, then turned the radio off to focus on the road. It never seemed wholly safe to him, listening to the radio while driving a motor car.

Isaac exhaled in a sigh, savored the rare solitude. Windows rolled down, the menthol spice of the roadside wax myrtle invaded his nostrils, just crossing the threshold from pleasant to cloying. Scruffy thatches of palmetto, privet, stopper, and a few low-lying lantana with their tight white flower fists also competed for sandy ground between the groves. Melody enjoyed the fragrance of the lantana shrubs all about their property, but they smelled cat-piss pungent to Isaac. Not too many high trees about the highway. Only sabal palms and clusters of sand pine and slash pine above the palmetto carpet and more solitary oaks. The lush longleaf pine had mostly been cleared for its timber. Intermittent tropical storms and hurricanes and fires shaved the land close, fairly decimating the most vertically inclined foliage, save for the elastic palms and pines. The live oaks seemed to know what they were doing too, swooping low, nearly touching the ground with their thick arms before raising them skyward beyond the elbows. A chunky bird flitted blue across his field of vision and dive-bombed into a patch of palmetto. Florida's version of the jay. Dusty-looking thing without any real crest to speak of, but accented by a nice shade of blue, anyway.

Soon, Isaac knew, the interstate, which had already opened up north in Jacksonville and down south in Miami, would converge upon them a mile or so to the west. More lanes, fewer lights and intersections, and blazing fast speeds. A good thing, Walt thought. And Doyle thought. And Edwin, agreeable Edwin, thought. (Clay was more circumspect.) Smooth multi-lane highways and thick rivers of traffic from the frosty north. But what use was such traffic to them when drivers would just whiz by west of town at fifty-five miles an hour to Palm Beach, Fort Lauderdale, and Miami? If motorists could bypass traffic on US 1, would anyone pass Goldens Are Here, anymore? Would anyone even exit the interstate for the town itself? That outer space business, as Melody called it, might be their only hope, as much as Clay feared the government's possible encroachment on their acres.

Isaac stopped at his burg's first traffic light. Two lights in all. Downright metropolis these parts. County seat, anyway. Still bigger than podunk Cocoa or New Smyrna. He drove slowly, taking in the loping pedestrians and storefronts. Nevin's Fruit Co., their packing house. O'Flanagan's Furniture & Electric. Nelson's Feed

Store. Pritchard and Sons Hardware. The O.K. Barber Shop. Not too many Negroes out and about center of town. And never at night, rare exception of the Magnolia Theater, where they seemed to materialize out of thin air, seating themselves way up on the balcony next to the hot clacking projector. They mostly stayed east on and around Hopkins, where they lived, away from the heart of town in obeisance to well understood racial rules, mostly unwritten. A Negro civil rights worker (or rabble rouser, as Walt had put it at Janisse's) had been dynamited to death along with his wife in their bed on Christmas night in Mims. This was a few years before Isaac's arrival.

Now there was a new Negro about wearing a suit, who had the co-op fellows worried. Mostly on account of the suit, it seemed to Isaac. Not a zoot suit, Doyle said, but a suit all the same. They weren't certain, exactly, what his business was in town. They weren't certain where he was staying, who his relations might be, if he had any. Isaac hadn't seen the fellow.

He cut up Julia Street past Janisse's, the Spanish Mission Palm Hotel & Apartments and the Magnolia Theatre, then down Palm Avenue. He always noticed the Brevard Title & Abstract Co.—perhaps on account of the curious business (what was an abstract?)—before the county courthouse across the street, its ostentatious Doric facade. Whoever built that courthouse really thought this town would be someplace. More than its piddly six thousand or so residents by now. Would all the outer space business, Isaac wondered, truly breathe life into this sleepy hamlet, or would this development, too, somehow wound them?

As Isaac left the center of town behind, homes overtook the storefronts and civic buildings. A collage of architectural styles advertised themselves, as if the builders couldn't quite decide what age they lived in, or wished to retrieve. Conical towers of helter-skelter Queen Anne houses, the more enforced symmetry of Colonial Revival properties, replete with gabled roofs and dormers, Spanish-looking stucco abodes, and the more modest wooden bungalows, which Isaac preferred, still fancier than his cracker-style grove-land house.

Then it was a sleepy drive for quite a while. After reaching familiar Orlando, Isaac followed the southwest dogleg to Lakeland, which took longer than he expected. The Pontiac's engine revved some to negotiate the gentle hills, which trended slowly upward. There truly was an elevated ridge here smack in the center of the state between Leesburg and Sebring. Actual topography. Scrubland featured intermittent rafts of drowsy cattle, which gave way to acres upon acres of graded land, speared with scrupulously hedged, too-green citrus trees, plotted in perfect rows. Glancing down the endless rows of queer square trees while in transit, barren sand alleys between, made his head spin and forced his eyes back toward the highway before him. The Simply Citrus holdings. His foundering co-op's prime competition. Isaac had never taken the time to explore these groves on the ridge south and west of Orlando. Who tended these seemingly boundless acres? Not a family, certainly. Where would a family live with the land overtaken on all sides by these homogenous tree-rows?

There was something undeniably awesome about the scale of the enterprise. All the same, soil was for crap here, he reminded himself. It surely took pounds and pounds of costly chemical fertilizer—nitrogen, phosphorus, potassium, magnesium, manganese, calcium, sulfur, iron, copper (to counter "red rust"), zinc, boron, molybdenum (to vanquish "yellow spot")—to nourish the Hamlins, Midsweets, Marshes, and Valencias along these parched acres, equal amounts of herbicide and insecticide to assemble these manifold shock troop columns in their immaculate uniforms along this antiseptic terrain. Various orange and grapefruit scions planted on rough lemon stock, which matured faster than their sour orange stock along the river, but produced inferior fruit. Weren't for the concentrate craze, the fruit here would never pass muster. Not without surreptitious beet-sugar infusions. So was the concentrate technology—that cutback potion—responsible for these leveled acres, or was it the sheer will of the behemoth Simply Citrus corporation, its eye on unused "empty" acres, that commanded the relentless march of the technology? These oranges and grapefruit here, Isaac knew, would never match river fruit for quality, but quality was up against competing variables these days.

After a while, Isaac entered more naturally verdant, shadier acres dappled with countless small lakes. He glimpsed weathered fishermen here and there casting their lines from shrunken metal boats. For whatever reason, it hadn't occurred to him that Lakeland might have been named so, accordingly. He'd have to tell Ted about the area, he thought, before thinking better of it. Surely Ted knew already about the lakes in Lakeland.

The increasing congestion and businesses along the roadside told Isaac that he had reached Lakeland, proper. He wasn't sure what he expected the Florida Department of Citrus building to look like, but it wasn't quite the establishment that greeted him just alongside the highway, a squat unprepossessing office building with a few bashful sabal palms and tidy square shrubs out front. He pulled over to the shoulder, turned off the ignition, and gazed toward the entryway. He wasn't in any hurry to meet the commissioner. FLORIDA DEPARTMENT OF CITRUS read the marquee above glass doors. The only other appointments smacking of officiousness were the two flags waving in the east breeze from their steel posts, one for the state and one for the nation. He was pleased—and somewhat surprised—not to see a Confederate flag fluttering alongside. He exited the car, finally, leaned against the Pontiac's scalding frame, and gathered his courage. The state flag seemed to wave from somewhat higher on its pole than Old Glory. No citrus on the seal. Palms instead, a steamboat in the sunny backdrop, a dark-skinned Indian woman in the foreground either gathering or distributing flowers of an indeterminate specie. Hibiscus?

He took a few steps up the concrete walk. A young Negro man with a dark keloid scar at his throat mowed the already short St. Augustine carpet beside him. Isaac raised his hand upon the fellow's next pass to gain his attention. He didn't seem annoyed when he reached down to shut off the loud, odorous machine. "Excuse me, is this the Citrus Commission building?"

The Negro glanced back at the Florida Department of Citrus marquee, turned back toward Isaac. "Yes, sir," he said. "Sure enough is." His voice was surprisingly faint and raspy. The wound at his throat had likely damaged his vocal chords. He mopped his wet face—not just his brow, but his whole face—with a once-white rag he seemed to have brandished out of thin air. He wouldn't start the mower again, Isaac knew, until Isaac gave him the go-ahead.

"Just making sure. Grass sure looks nice," he offered by way of apology for wasting the worker's time. "Appreciate your help."

Isaac heard the starter cord crank behind him once, twice, three times, until the engine chortled its response.

The harsh fluorescent lighting inside was an ocular insult, the illuminated air vibrating somehow, nervous. But it didn't seem to perturb the lovely receptionist, seated behind a desk, itself behind a high protective counter. A fragrance buffeted the shoreline between them.

"How may I help you, sir?" she greeted him at an elevated southern register. One of her hands lifted, seemingly of its own accord, to check her copious shock of blonde hair, assembled neatly above her tiny ears. Her lips were full and painted red. She seemed too neatly scrubbed for a state employee. She was one of those women who would never dream of leaving the house without putting her face on, a woman who spent her waking and sleeping hours in Florida shuttling between frosty climate-controlled interiors. While Melody wouldn't go to *shul* or town without applying her foundation and at least a lipstick layer, she wasn't truly one of these women. Never had been. The Florida heat and her outdoors grove stand responsibilities only bolstered her more natural tendencies.

Isaac announced his appointment with the commissioner, told the woman his name. She nodded, then lifted her telephone's enormous handset, which dwarfed her head. The handset had some additional fixture attached so that she might rest it more comfortably against her shoulder's narrow ledge.

"A Mr. Ike Golden to see the commissioner," Isaac heard. So, there was an additional line of defense back there, he gathered, a personal secretary, maybe a whole line of secretaries, guarding direct access to the commissioner.

"The commissioner will be with you in just a moment, Mr. Golden," she advised him, raising manicured eyebrows. The flesh beneath seemed painted to compensate for the wispy follicles. "You can have a seat right over there. Can I get you some coffee? Danish? Glass of fresh concentrated orange juice, perhaps?"

Isaac had already consumed his thermos of coffee in the car, devoured the salami sandwich on rye with Gulden's mustard that Melody had packed for him in foil. He declined the concentrate, raised a palm in surrender as he retreated to his seat. So even the commission now foreswore fresh chilled for "fresh concentrated." He swallowed down the bile rising in his stomach. Garish oil paintings of Florida landscapes featuring Royal Poincianas, Jacarandas, various palms and sedges festooned the wood-paneled walls. An ocean scene too, the sun melting beneath a salmon sky, coconut palms leaning in the foreground. Sunset. But would Melody see a sunrise in the painting? A magazine accordion—*Life, Sports Illustrated, National Geographic, Time*—spread across the Formica coffee table, the day's *Orlando Sentinel* face up beside it. Isaac considered reaching for a magazine, then reconsidered, not caring quite enough to upset the fastidious design. He plucked the *Orlando Sentinel*, instead, scanned the headlines above the fold. *Kennedy Furious with Rogue CIA Operatives. Castro Seethes in Bellicose Radio Address, Denounces "Gum-chewing" Imperialists. Krushchev Decries "American Planes, American Bombs, and American Bullets."* At least one American military pilot killed during the Cuban invasion, apparently. So much for Adlai Stevenson's efforts to deny US involvement. Isaac shuffled absently through the rest of the paper, hoping to distract himself with other headlines. What a mess!

While the commissioner might have been busy, Isaac couldn't help but suspect the theater in all this, making him wait here. The commissioner was the one who pulled the strings. The man. The boss. The one for whom people waited. He had taken pains to reinforce this impression from the outset, sending his suited goons in their aviator glasses and lacquered hair and useless shoes right out to Isaac's grove on Sunday to do his bidding when he might have simply used the rotary, making him cool his heels now before offering him his audience. He was probably just sitting back there behind his desk counting down the minutes.

"You drive from quite a ways?" the receptionist asked without looking up from her duties. Her typewriter issued sharp little blows in the background. She didn't seem a particularly skilled typist, given the cadence. "I don't think we've yet enjoyed the pleasure of your company."

Was she flirting with him? Isaac told her where his grove was located and left it at that. He wasn't used to gentile women flirting with him, having avoided them his whole life.

"Ah, one of the river men."

Now what did *that* mean? "I suppose," he said. He curled his thick fingers before him and inspected the nails, self-conscious now of the stubbornly encrusted dirt from yesterday's labors with Ted. He would have to take a coarse brush to them this evening. Maybe use some Ajax.

An older woman with an unfortunate chin retrieved Isaac without warning and guided him through labyrinthine linoleum hallways past closed office doors. The building didn't seem large enough from the outside for such an interior commute. A hallway opened up, finally, into a square meadow of five office desks, spaced equidistant from each other like grove trees. The male employees, wearing thick ties with short sleeves, paid scant attention to his presence, pored over reams of mysterious documents instead. They all faced away from the wooden door behind them, the commissioner's lair. It surprised him when his officious escort opened the door without knocking, gestured for him to enter, then retreated, closing the passage behind her.

A besuited man of average size stood up from behind his walnut desk and walked around to the front. Taking in Isaac's heft, he froze for a moment, seemed to reconsider his choreography, but there was no turning back for the commissioner now.

"Ike Golden, I take it?" He extended a hand, which Isaac consumed in his own.

"That's right." He held the commissioner's hand in his firm grip somewhat longer than usual. Isaac was aware of his imposing size and wasn't above using his simple mass to his advantage, he supposed.

"J. P. Shepherd. Like the astronaut, no relation."

Isaac nodded. The quick way Shepherd said *Like the astronaut, no relation*—the words stumbling over each other—told Isaac that the commissioner was used to introducing himself this way. Shepherd's expression seemed frozen in a nascent smile, as if he were anticipating the punch-line of a joke, his complexion preternaturally tanned to a curious nut-brown hue, his thin lips nut-brown, as well, their borders difficult to discern. Tiny asterisks pocked his sunken cheeks, the remnants of adolescent acne, Isaac guessed.

"Smoke?" Shepherd finally inquired, retreating behind his walnut desk, flipping open a gleaming cigarette case.

"No, thank you."

"Each his own." The commissioner gestured for Isaac to take a seat in one of the two chairs facing him. The chair was too small for Isaac, the metal arms uncomfortably cool to the touch.

Shepherd, seated now in his larger chair, plucked a cigarette from the case, lit up with a silver lighter, extinguished the flame with dramatic flicks, as if the lighter were a silver revolver on one of those Wild West shows Eli watched. He issued a thin jet trail out the side of his invisible lips, smoke-squinted eyes fixed on Isaac. The commissioner's power seemed restored now from behind his desk. It occurred to Isaac, squirming some in his too-small seat, feeling underdressed suddenly in his pressed trousers and shirt sleeves, that Shepherd knew how uncomfortable these shrunken chairs were, that he wasn't someone who cared to put his visitors too much at ease.

"So, Goldens are Here," Shepherd finally burst the silence. "Shrewd piece of marketing." He wagged his cigarette at Isaac in mock—or actual—admonishment.

"I suppose." Isaac didn't like Shepherd's *shrewd*.

"We checked that out you know."

"Huh?"

"Got some complaints. Tourists. Other growers up the highway. False advertising and such. We don't cotton to it. You river boys can thank us too. Back in the day, before we got a handle on things, every grower St. Augustine to Miami bought their budwood from your stretch, then stamped Indian River Fruit on their crates, upped their prices. Thought themselves right clever. Not anymore, though. You know why?"

"No. Why?"

"The commission. Rules and regulations. Official river boundaries state law since '41."

"Okay."

"But in your case, see, you're free and clear. 'Cause Golden's your name. Jewish name I take it."

Isaac nodded.

"But your first name. Ike. Never met no Jewish fellow name like Ike."

"It's Isaac. Ike's for short."

"Still." The commissioner didn't care to concede his point, let his *still* hang there in the air between them a few moments before proceeding. "Not that I have anything against members of the Jewish faith."

"I'm sure."

"Just you don't much *look* Jewish is the thing."

"Oh, we come in all shapes and sizes these days." Shepherd's face flashed venom—an unchecked expression—its amiable plasticity, its nascent smile, restored the next instant.

"Now don't take offense. Just making conversation here." Shepherd lifted a hand and scratched his scalp above his ear, as if troubled by a louse. The brown strands had been gathered together into thicker discrete cords under the influence of a thick-toothed comb and some hairdressing or pomade. VO5? Brylcreem? Isaac harbored what he realized was an unreasonable prejudice against men who fussed with their hair. "Like I said," Shepherd continued,

"I've got nothing against members of the Jewish persuasion. Always admired y'all, tell the truth. Great minds. Give you that."

The old *Yiddisheh kopf* canard. If only Shepherd saw the flatulent *nudniks* at Isaac's Philadelphia *cheder* after regular school.

"That Jaffa orange, say," Shepherd persisted. "Know much about them?"

Isaac shrugged. He didn't. Not really.

"Sub-par orange, Florida standards. Finicky devil comes to setting and bearing. Seedy as a Sicilian in a sharkskin suit too. But a man grows anything edible in a godforsaken desert, A-rabs running amok on top of everything, got my respect. It's that drip irrigation. Know much about that?"

Shepherd's eyelids narrowed again, eclipsing pale irises.

"A little. Not much. Just starting in with it on some acres, matter of fact."

Does he think I'm in cahoots with the Israelis? Isaac wondered.

"Y'all think of things. Give you that. You know why orange juice took off in the first place, don't you, back in the day?"

"Spanish flu?" Isaac proposed. The worldwide epidemic, he knew, killed nearly a million Americans right around the time of the First World War. But nobody talked much anymore about its ravages—the flu's dead or the war's dead for that matter—the pain, suffering, and atrocity index rising steeply in its wake. Few knew, or remembered, that frantic mothers over breakfast plied their knickered children with orange wedges and that newest innovation (thanks to pasteurization), mass-market orange "juice." These mothers didn't know that its tonic effects resided in its ascorbic acid, which scientists would later dub "Vitamin C," nor did they know that its salutary properties stopped well short of warding off viruses, but they knew that citrus protected British sailors from scurvy, and so between stewed prunes and newfangled orange juice they put their faith in orange juice.

"Spanish flu, well, yes," Shepherd allowed. "But how do you think they got it in their heads to drink orange juice, rather than doing the hundred-odd other things that mothers might have done to make believe they were doing something useful? Garlic. Vapors. Leeches." Shepherd flicked his glowing cigarette like a baton, summoning these examples.

"I don't know."

"Albert D. Lasker, my friend. Jewish fellow. Like yourself."

The commissioner spread thumb and forefinger of both hands before him like a goalpost to summon a newspaper headline, "Drink an Orange." Shepherd's eyes shifted from his goalpost to Isaac, seated behind in the bleachers. "I see that expression on your face."

Isaac hadn't meant to express anything.

"Drink an Orange. Those apple bastards one-upped us with their Apple-a-Day campaign, but Drink an Orange wasn't too shabby, either. Maybe seems like a silly slogan now, orange juice taking up so much grocery store shelf space these days, frozen, fresh chilled, what have you. We're practically bathing in it now. Ubiquitous. That the fancy word?" Shepherd waited a beat for Isaac's confirmation, which he withheld. "Point is, you think it was easy going from *eating* oranges to drinking the juice? No siree Bob. Apples were pretty much always juiced, worm-eaten as they were, individually. Spoilage and whatnot. Juiced mostly for cider and applejack. Cheap alcohol. But not oranges. It took imagination. It took vision. It took *advertising*. That's where your Albert D. Lasker came in, my friend. Advertising. Wasn't even on our own dime. Sunkist out west he was working for. But no matter. Drink an Orange. Three words strung together just so and, *presto*, we go from podunk operation to worldwide industry. Center of it all right here in Florida, not that godforsaken desert, California. Our oranges the only ones worth drinking. Not Mexico or Brazil or Texas quite yet, we have anything to say about it. But here. Florida." Shepherd tapped his fingers against his desktop, the glowing cigarette jutting like an erection between them. His frozen smile had thawed. "My state. And you ain't seen nothing yet—"

"So you were born here?" For whatever reason—Shepherd's sudden stridency, perhaps—Isaac sought to shift the topic of conversation.

"Indiana. Moved here when I was in knickers, though, so native all intents and purposes. PhD from Gainesville, so my horticultural bona fides are in order, 'case you're interested."

Isaac remained expressionless, listened.

"Point being, I've been commissioner better part of five years now and I've got plans, you see. Big plans. My predecessors"—here Shepherd snuffed out his depleted cigarette in a crystal ashtray—"they lacked ambition. Half-assed lot, pardon the French." He swiveled in his chair and glanced at the framed black-and-white photographs of his four predecessors, who couldn't have been too pleased by Shepherd's speech. "Now they were alright fellas, but they saw themselves mostly as caretakers, referees, settling squabbles between the bird dogs and the growers, the growers and the packing houses, the packing houses and retail. Sure, they regulated the market, set the excise tax, the fertilization and insecticide schedules, cracked down on the thieves and black market with the help of state law enforcement, stayed a step ahead of the latest blights. But they lacked vision. And vision's what we need now if we expect to survive in this state."

Isaac felt his eyes roll of their own accord and instantly regretted the slip. The gesture wasn't lost upon Shepherd, who swiveled back around in his seat, brandished and lit a second cigarette, glowered at Isaac for a protracted moment through the stinging smoke.

"I know how all this might sound. Melodramatic, right?"

"A little, maybe. I'm just wondering, frankly, what this all has to do with me, commissioner. Why you've summoned me. It's budding time and I have a grove to—"

"What you got to understand, Ike, is this state's up for grabs now. Secret's out. We got in early, citrus. Thanks to Jesse Fish up near St. Augustine, your own Captain Dummitt, the Carney Grove in Lake Weir, Speer's Grove in Sanford, Hart Grove in East Palatka. Even after the 1895 freeze, we rebounded, expanded operations. So that's the upside. Holdings are solid enough. For now. Got sympathetic ears in Tallahassee. Our lobby knows how to keep the wheels greased. Doesn't hurt we send our honeys from the Miss Orange Blossom pageant with gifts every other month or so. But all sorts of interests horning in on our state. Agriculture and livestock alone: Cattle. Pigs. Strawberries. Tomatoes." The commissioner itemized the litany with derisive flicks of his slender fingers against the thumb of his same hand. "Even sugar cane now, you can believe that, least till we take care of business in Cuba. Mining interests keep finding phosphate every gosh-darned hole they dynamite. Besides that, we got that space business going on your parts. Movie and television industry. They film that *Sea Hunt* show with Lloyd Bridges right up at Silver Springs, you know?" Isaac shook his head. "Word is that cartoon fellow from Hollywood wants to turn over millions of acres smack middle of the state for another amusement park." Shepherd bent the "u" in *amusement* to deride the frivolity of the enterprise. "Sending spies to sniff around so the state won't spike the per-acre price. Thinks he's right clever. But when a bunch of proxies from Calif*orrr*nia"—Shepherd extended the state name into a slur—"start asking about fifty square miles of real estate, we find out who's behind the curtain. As if the water ski shows at Cypress Gardens, the mermaids at Weeki Wachee, and the glass-bottom boats at Silver Springs aren't enough. Those Seminole gator wrastlers in the Glades too if you count them. Know how they do that?"

Isaac shook his head. He wasn't prepared for the question.

"Gators can barely open their jaws. All their power's in the clamping shut." Shepherd held splayed, curled fingers of both hands before him and clamped them shut. His clean fingernails shone beneath the fluorescent lights. Some sort of polish? Isaac wondered. "Twelve-year-old can keep a gator at bay long as they keep the snout shut."

"Interesting."

"We need another theme park 'bout as much as a bull needs tits, pardon the French again. Golf courses too now. You realize how many acres, not to mention water, it takes for an 18-hole course?" Isaac shook his head, again. "Everyone thinks they're Arnold Palmer all of a sudden. Never took to the sport myself. And you can't forget the Seminoles. They'd grub out every grove and grow coontie, hunt panthers, and Lord knows what else we turn over any more land to those shiftless bastards."

Here was Walt, it suddenly occurred to Isaac, Walt, but all cleaned up and with a formidable collection of university degrees to bolster his greater ambition.

"No time for resting on laurels, point being. We're right around 700,000 acres now. I'm shooting for over a million this time next year. And I don't just want oranges at the groves. I want oranges on every license plate in the state, not these plain blue plates. Every city seal. State flag, too, we get the good ol' boys in Tallahassee to take another look. State letterhead. Mascots for the new state universities cropping up like kudzu. One starting up in Boca Raton now. But we need to have everyone on board. Hear what I'm saying?"

"I suppose." Isaac sensed that the commissioner was circling around his most valuable nugget, circling nearer and nearer.

"You're a family man, two children I hear." Isaac nodded, glanced down at his dull gold wedding band. "I have three children myself."

Isaac didn't like that the commissioner knew about his family, that he didn't hesitate to disclose that he knew about his family, or that he seemed to feel superior on account of siring three, rather than a mere two, children. "Our industry is something like a family," Shepherd continued. "Like any family, ours is only as strong as its individuals. You don't have skilled growers on board, all working toward the same goal, you don't have a darn thing. One weak member and the whole family suffers."

Isaac's thoughts drifted toward Eli—his weak family member—which filled him with remorse. He didn't like feeling this way, labored to turn the feeling into something else, something like anger. He didn't appreciate this lecture from the commissioner. What did Shepherd truly want with him, anyway?

"Now you're a big part of this family, got yourself some choice acres there, not too many acres but choice, swooped right in like a duck on a June bug and bought up Hawley's whole grove, didn't you?"

Isaac felt his temperature rise. His hands curled into fists in his lap. Isaac had always considered himself slow to anger. But for years now, since taking over the grove—no, earlier, he knew, since Eli was born—he increasingly found himself in the grip of emotions he could barely keep in check. It was only yesterday, after all, that he felt his dander rise across the irrigation ditch from Walt, that he entertained notions of leaping across the divide and throttling another human being. The commissioner must have noticed Isaac fuming, because he raised a pale palm to defang his words, then proceeded. "Don't mind me. I'm just talking here. Word is, though, you're not keeping up with the spray schedule . . ." *Walt!* Isaac thought. Walt had informed on him.

"Just one large grower like yourself offers safe harbor to some scourge, we all find ourselves in a heap of trouble. Flies, scale, weevils and such don't exactly respect property lines. Don't even get me started on your fungi and bacteria. All we need is another canker infestation."

"I've got things under control." Purple scale, in truth, seemed to be gaining a purchase along Isaac's acres. He had planned on asking the commissioner about those new wasps. But pride got the better of him now. "Sesame and fish oils work just fine."

"That's not the main concern."

"No?"

"Main concern is that hocus-pocus you're up to on all those acres." Shepherd paused here to let his words sink in with Isaac, scattered seeds seeking purchase.

"Hocus-pocus?" Isaac finally asked.

"Your propagation experiments. We'll never certify for market those crosses or hybrids you're up to, those bastardized scions, 'case you're wondering. Even if they pass Brix muster."

"Okay," Isaac uttered, tentatively. The statement seemed to surprise the commissioner, who opened his eyes wider, cleared his throat, leaned forward in his chair and rested his elbows on his wooden blotter.

"So what we're talking about, just so we're crystal clear, is a whole grove of young trees that'll never be tagged, never bear fruit, so to speak."

"Not the *whole* grove. Not even a quarter."

"Squandering choice acres. Now of all times." Shepherd shook his head and twisted his mouth in distaste. "Just after Simply Citrus outfits three separate processing plants on their own dime for concentrate. We need to harvest every last orange nub that sets to keep those boys happy. To keep them *here*. They might just as well set up in Brazil. Field-worker rates. Taxes. Labor Department breathing down everyone's necks. Darn feds. And now of all times I've got a grower squandering choice acres. You looking to go under, Ike? That what you're after? I've reviewed your balance sheet on the co-op's ledger. Public record. Might as well turn over those acres now to that Disney fellow. Jewish fellow like yourself, I'd hazard to guess."

"I don't think—"

"I'm sure that Hollywood fellow's itching to grub them out and plant carousels and what have you middle of Dummitt's Island, instead. Bulldoze Dummitt's castle out there without thinking twice."

"I'm not planning on going under, commissioner."

"Out with it, Ike!" The commissioner pounded his small fist against his blotter. "What are you up to all them acres? Chimeras? A new fruit? And who's funding you? The Israelis? Where are you getting your budwood? Boys say they just look like ordinary oranges to them."

"I'm not interested in chimeras. No one's funding me. I'm not smuggling in any foreign budwood." He regretted these disclosures. Why tip his hand to Shepherd?

"Listen, Ike"—the scaffolding of the commissioner's face relaxed as he pursued a softer, more congenial tack—"I appreciate your moxie and all, but we have experimental stations set up every microclimate in the state. Enclosed orangery too. Labs, state-of-the-goddamn-art. Smartest minds with the university, the commission, State

Department of Agriculture—scientists, engineers, economists—all working round the clock on citrus improvement, innovation. Every facet of the operation. Seed to store. Tree-shakers, for example."

"Tree shakers?"

"For harvesting. Been using them on those pecans up in the panhandle for years now. Engineers working on the necessary modifications. Uppity Negroes won't be giving us any more problems once they're replaceable." The embers of Shepherd's cigarette flashed orange as he inhaled a thick cloud of smoke, released it through his nostrils. Isaac knew that he was thinking over his next words, that he was about to say something important.

"Heard about your troubles, Ike. Someone cutting up your trees." Isaac tried to conceal his surprise that Shepherd had heard about the vandalism, but failed. "Don't act so surprised," the commissioner said, his pale eyes twinkling, clearly pleased to broadcast his omniscience. "It's my business to know these things. You sure it's not a colored? Disgruntled field-worker? They've been getting riled up here and there. Causing problems."

"I keep good relations with the field-workers. We all do, pretty much. My foreman is a colored man. Negro. They wouldn't bother my trees."

Isaac wouldn't tell Shepherd that there was a new besuited Negro in town, who didn't conform to the co-op fellows' expectations of male Negroness, who had the co-op fellows worried.

"Hope you're right. Anyway, we're close to something big at the lab, too. I'll tell you that much. You'll know more in good time. Now you may have read your Swingle, but do you really think you're gonna come up with something better, something we haven't already tried? Secure a patent?"

"I don't know," Isaac answered. "Probably not." He tried hard to steel himself against the commissioner's bluster, but his disclosures deflated him, as intended. Still, he couldn't offer Shepherd such an easy victory. He screwed up his courage, gathered his hefty frame higher in his too small seat so that he looked straight across at the commissioner. "Is this all you brought me here to tell me? Am I free to go now?"

"Yes, that's all. For now. You're free."

Eight

MELODY WAITED SEVERAL DAYS, hoped the urge might pass like inclement weather. Yet she couldn't shake her new knowledge. A week passed. The taste of Mary Beth's pie-crust still coated her tongue. So Melody summoned the courage—if it was a matter of courage—to pursue her errand in town. Sarah had nodded off in her perambulator by the time Melody reached the glass doors of the Piggly Wiggly. Another pram was already parked outside the grocery beneath the glossy magnolias, advertising pie-sized white blooms here and there. Its infant passenger squeaked mildly inside its blue swaddling cloths. She didn't recognize the baby. Melody parked Sarah beside this other, younger child and set the brake. She would only be a minute and the weather was mild today, last gasp of temperate spring. Some rain wouldn't hurt, her mind drifting toward the grove. Plenty of yearly rainfall here for citrus. Too bad it tended to come in clumps. That's why Isaac needed those drip lines. She pulled the loose-knit pink blanket down slowly from Sarah's face so that it just covered her bare legs and feet below the snaps of her onesie. The child exhaled loudly and turned her face to the side, but her eyes stayed closed like clamshells. She hated to deprive Sarah the comfort of her blankie, but her child, the scamp, had cultivated the unfortunate tendency to pull her blanket clear over her face while she slept. Melody feared that she'd smother herself. "There, there." She fitted the mesh net around the canvas opening to ward off the mosquitoes, sand gnats, and no-see-ums. The whole region used to be known as Mosquito County. Years ago, Erma told her, men stuffed newspapers down their trousers and women wore veils to ward off the insatiable airborne pests. That was before all the building and the drainage and the chemical spray-clouds of DDT behind slow-moving trucks, which the town boys chased after on their Schwinns. All the same, it was still pretty buggy.

As soon as she slipped inside the curtain of mentholated air, she swept the visible aisles with her eyes, as if she was a bank robber gauging potential complications. She wouldn't have bet on herself going through with this today. Yet here she was. She ought to just pick up the tub of pig fat, pay, and leave. Not bother with a basket, even. She didn't truly need anything for the house. She stood on the gleaming linoleum, frozen.

The automatic sliding glass doors slid open behind her, jolting her to. She lifted a hand to her heart and glanced back to see Luke, the young stock boy, returning with an empty cart. "Sorry to startle you, ma'am. Cart, Mrs. Golden?"

"No thank you, Luke." She smiled. "I just came in for a few things." She plucked a basket from the counter beside the carts and strode off. She could feel Luke's gaze trained upon her for a protracted moment, even though he was behind her now—the molecules of too-silent air between them, perhaps. It was something she was used to and didn't mind, the attention men paid her. Might as well mind the sunrise. Men admired women, and women sensed when they were being admired. But silly Luke, Melody thought. He should stare at girls his own age. Unmarried girls. Christian girls. Tamping down that cowlick of his wouldn't hurt, either.

She made a swift pass through the refrigerated aisle, registered peripherally the location of the green and white metal tin as she plucked a tub of Mazola, instead, then scurried off toward the dry goods. She picked up a dusty package of "no-sift" Gold Medal flour, a Charmin bathroom tissue four-pack, a golden Dial soap bar, a Hershey's Syrup tin. Then, glancing up, she spied Frieda Krupnick down the aisle, scrutinizing the label of a cardboard box. *Gott im Himmel!* Melody thought. Curious, to think in Jewish, now of all times. Thank heavens she hadn't already seized that *treyf* object of her desire.

Frieda, her eyes trained on the cardboard box, hadn't spotted her yet. Melody considered trying to sneak away, but reconsidered—poor form, in case Frieda *had* noticed her—and strode briskly toward her elder. "Fancy meeting you here," Melody seized the initiative, congratulating herself for striking this splendid nonchalant chord.

Frieda jumped a bit in her heels, held the cardboard box close to her barren chest as if it were a shield. "Oh, you startled me dear," Frieda frowned. A mild frown seemed her default expression, exacerbated by the stern bun with which she whipped her mousy hair into submission. Melody was certain that Frieda's graying strands were beginning to recede at the temples under the constant strain.

"I'm sorry I startled you, Frieda." *Betty Crocker*, Melody read on the box. Was this what was in store for Melody, a too-stern hairdo, a default frown . . . cake mix!? Frieda seemed to notice Melody noticing the cake mix.

"I usually bake from scratch, of course. But once every blue moon, now that it's just Meyer and me . . ."

Melody appreciated the latest advances as much as anyone. More. But she drew the line at baked goods and those TV-brand frozen dinners. Who didn't have time to roast a chicken, to bake a cake? What was the world coming to? Here she sounded like her husband, she realized, shuddering. Well, you couldn't live with someone fifteen years and remain unscathed.

"I've tried the Honey Spice," Melody lied. "It was super," she compounded her lie—*why stop now?*—which seemed to bolster Frieda, her frown supplanted by an expression of cautious enthusiasm.

"This Angel Food is brand new." Frieda loosened her clench on the *Betty Crocker* box. "Only one step. You should try it," she suggested, hoping to enlist a co-conspirator. "Busy homemaker like you."

Busy homemaker. A phrase straight from the television, it seemed to Melody. All of a sudden they were all busy homemakers.

"Yes, I should try it," Melody answered, more tepidly than she had intended. Frieda's face fell, returned to its default frown.

"Well, dear, I really must get back to the store. I won't keep you any longer. We'll see you at *shul* soon?" Melody assured her that they would, and Frieda was off. She hadn't asked after the baby. Or Eli. The only other Jews for miles, it seemed a pity to Melody that the Krupnicks couldn't be fifteen years younger so that they might relate to one another as contemporaries, or ten years older so that Frieda and Meyer might assume the role of surrogate parents. Their inbetweenness threw Melody ever off-balance in Frieda's presence, struggling to locate the proper frequency. She took vague comfort that Frieda seemed every bit as disappointed in them. The Krupnicks had invited them to their *Pesach* seder the first year they moved down, but Eli had behaved poorly, outright refusing to recite even the first of the four questions, fidgeting in his seat during the plagues, and, worst of all, spitting up the Manischevitz Melody had allowed him to sample on the Maxwell House haggadah, a few dribbles tattering the fabric chair beneath him, sending Meyer Krupnick on a frenzied, unsuccessful search for Club Soda. Since then, the Krupnicks enacted their own exodus each year, escaping the obligatory invitation, decamping to family in Savannah for the holiday.

Melody loitered amid the baked goods aisle, giving Frieda time to clear, then made her way quickly toward the front of the store to check on Sarah through the glass. Still sleeping. She spied Frieda on the way to her fancy Cadillac, Luke trailing behind with the cart, his white socks flashing at his ankles below his too-short slacks. Enough dawdling. Melody screwed up her courage and returned to the refrigerated aisle, where the meat and dairy commingled shamefully close. To be Jewish, it seemed to Melody, was *not* to do any number of things that lesser humans did. *We are the people who don't do this thing that you do. We are the Chosen. You are not.* It just didn't sit right. Not anymore. Not here.

ARMOUR PURE LARD, she read on the green-and-white tin. She plucked it by the wire-bail handle and dropped it into the basket, as if the paint-can handle scorched. Heavy, she thought. Heavy for such a modest tin. She walked briskly toward the cashier, checked herself (*slow, slow*). She was nervous, toting this *treyf* tin. But more. Her skin tingled. The wispy sun-bleached hairs on her forearms stood on end. The blood rushed to her face. She lifted her fingertips to her cheek, gauged the sudden heat. Exhilaration, more so than nervousness. She felt her nipples against the modest padding of her brassiere, which took her breath away. The rabbis weren't dummies, she supposed, gleaning the connection between food and sex. *We are a people who do not seethe kids in their mother's milk.* By which they truly meant: we don't sleep with our mothers. The incest taboo.

"How do you do, Mrs. Golden?" Thadeus Simpson, the avuncular store manager greeted her at the register. He stayed close to the money.

"Very well, Mr. Simpson. Thank you." Melody fanned her face with her fingers, hoping to keep the moisture from pearling through the foundation she had applied for her errand. She watched as the manager inspected the stickers on each item, as he punched the black keys. She held her breath as he reached the green and white tin, which he rang up without commentary, sliding it down the metal-wheeled ramp for Luke, who bagged it. Melody breathed. Could it be that neither of them noticed? That they didn't even notice?

"You saw your friend, I hope?"

"Uhh, yes. Frieda and I spoke."

Melody sighed. They were the town Jews, and so they were friends. This was one thing she missed about Philadelphia—the luxury of so many Jews about that she could afford to dislike a few.

"Have a joyous day," Simpson said, handing Melody her change. It was his routine closing line, or maybe only routine for Frieda and her. The Christian Lord seemed frequently to be invoked in casual conversation among the citizenry here in Florida, peppering salutations and goodbyes, especially.

"Help you to your automobile, Mrs. Golden?"

"That won't be necessary, Luke. It's just a small bag, dear." She was too young to be "dearing" people, but she felt compelled in this instance.

"You sure, ma'am?" Luke seemed deflated. His cowlick danced under the ventilation with incongruous whimsy.

Melody was sure.

"How's my big girl?" she greeted her daughter outside. Sarah was awake, but unperturbed, thankfully. She seemed to have been studying the mysterious mesh net ceiling of the perambulator, shifting her focus immediately toward her mother's voice, then to her face, the sight of which made the baby smile, flashing a wet tooth at the bottom. Quite something, to elicit such a smile. Quite something to be a mother. Pity it seemed different for fathers. "Isaac," she heard herself say.

She placed the paper bag in the pram above Sarah's head (plenty of room), unlocked the brake, and made her way to the Pontiac, pleased with herself. "Now don't look inside that bag, Sarah-le," she chided. "Don't you even look." Sarah chortled. "You won't tell on Mommy, will you, will you?" Melody lifted her gaze above the magnolias along the sidewalk and the low storefront toward the blue sky. A noisy flock of blue-black birds with tails like boat keels flushed from a sagging electric wire, swirled in a vortex above, then alit again on their perches. Above the birds, meringue dollop clouds drifted westward from over the ocean, heading toward Orlando. They didn't have these dark iridescent birds with boat-keel tails in Philadelphia; they didn't have these glossy magnolias with their pie-sized white blossoms, springtime; they didn't have these clouds, this expansive sightline above modest storefronts. She lay Sarah down on the front passenger seat in the plastic laundry basket, folded the large perambulator into the trunk and rushed to the driver's side, sealing herself and the baby behind the heavy door. A smile dawned across Melody's face as she fired the ignition.

She knew exactly where she would hide the Armour tin in the GE. No one would know. Not a soul.

Nine

MELODY COULDN'T TARRY. The bus would drop off Eli by three. And who knew when Iz would stumble in from the grove? Not that he'd much notice, anyway. He seemed more distracted, lately, ever since returning from his meeting with the commissioner in Lakeland. She had asked him what the man wanted after they repaired to the bedroom that night, whether it had something to do with whoever was attacking their grove trees, whether everything was all right. He had told her tersely, not altogether convincingly, that it was nothing, that everything was fine. "Concerned about our yields," he had finally divulged beneath the sheets, the bedsprings complaining as he sought out a more comfortable position. Melody had considered pressing, but reconsidered. She wouldn't nag her husband about business matters. She wouldn't be one of those long-suffering, screeching wives, like that Alice Kramden on the TV show that everyone liked, but that Melody didn't like. Because of that long-suffering, screeching wife.

She fastened Sarah into her high chair and scattered formula-softened cereal oat rounds about the tray like jigsaw puzzle pieces, hoping to keep her busy for a while. The baby batted at the tray with both hands, issued a hearty squeal, which betrayed a curious blend of excitement and exasperation.

"Now be good for Mommy, Sarah-le."

Melody washed her hands at the sink with Palmolive under torrents of scalding water, then meted out and mixed the no-sift flour, sugar, and salt. She used the plastic *flaishik* bowl she usually reserved for preparing burger meat. She didn't dare use her metal baking bowl. Not today. She paused to put a small glass of water in the freezer for later, then returned to the bowl and mixed the dry ingredients with her fingertips, not wanting to retrieve the butter from the cold refrigerator until absolutely necessary. Let your butter warm and you were done for. She always kept a stick for pie-dough in the fridge, pre-sliced twice, lengthwise, then cross-wise every quarter inch or so. Having mixed the dry ingredients, she retrieved the butter, dropped the cold butter rectangle-bits into the mix individually, coated them with the flour to keep them from sticking to her pastry cutter. Wielding the cutter like brass knuckles in her small fist, she issued sharp twisting jabs into the bowl. Ten jabs . . . twenty . . . thirty. “Now or never,” she muttered under her breath. “Now or never, Sarah-le,” she declared more audibly. The baby was busy pinching her thumb and middle finger around a soggy oat round. She looked up at her mother for the briefest of moments, returned to her own baby labors, knitting her wispy eyebrows. Melody retrieved the green and white paint-can tin from the farthest recess of the GE and set it down with a thud on the Formica countertop. She glanced out the bay window past her vegetable garden and wild tamarind, past the scruffy palmetto and lantana patches, their live oak triad and cabbage palms toward Eli’s grove. Through the screen she could hear one of the towhees singing, *drink-your-tea!* She spotted the rusty bird atop a clump of wax myrtle. So alert and alive, the creature! No sign of her husband. Or Eli. She had initially mistaken the tamarind for a sumac—its sharp clusters of leaves slicing the ground with dagger shadows every gust—before Clay had set them straight. Tamarind, not sumac, it was called. He and Pearl had brought a plate of divinity to welcome them to the grove. Melody had prepared a pitcher of lemonade, floated round rafts of Meyer lemon on top. Clay had obliged them by walking the circumference of the house, pointed out and identified the plants, the ice in his lemonade clattering against the glass. “That tamarind doesn’t usually grow so far up here,” he said, “but you have to give it credit for its gumption. That’s why Hawley let it be.”

Melody, marveling now at the thought of her tamarind—only tamarind in the county, its seed deposited by some storm-blown bird for all she knew—pried the lid of the pig-fat tin open with the flat side of her metal can opener. The can issued a hollow pop upon its breach. The fat was shiny like lacquer at the surface and tawny colored. It didn’t gleam white like vegetable shortening. She wasn’t quite sure what she had expected it to look like. The smell reached her nostrils, quivering rabbit-like. Crisco didn’t smell like anything. But there was definitely an odor emanating from the Armour tin. Not bacon smell or ham smell, exactly, which wouldn't have surprised her. Mild and nutty, rather. Like cashews. She punctured the oil-sheen surface with a *flaishik* dinner spoon—less solid than Crisco—and dispatched three rough tablespoons quickly into the mix, glanced back at the tin. The gelatinous fat struggled to return to its former shape, approximating the surface of a troubled foamy sea, instead. She ought to pound down the lid, stash the green and white tin back behind the jams and kosher dills on the low shelf and be done with it. As long as she had gone this far, though. In for a penny. . . . She dabbed at the troubled surface with her pinkie, pierced the skin, and reached down, deep, wetting her knuckle. She lifted her pinkie from the tin and held the small digit before her eyes, as if surprised that it was still attached to her hand. The pinkie gleamed with pig fat, excess tawny waves lapping up from her flesh and licking the air. Melody reminded herself to breathe. With her clean hand, she smoothed the cool lard over her other fingers and palm until the whole hand gleamed. She could see tiny fat stars twinkle on her flesh under the bright kitchen lights. She rubbed the nutty, oleaginous concoction into both hands, insides and backs, savored the feel of flesh riding over flesh. The lard warmed quickly under her blood's influence, seeped into her tendons and bones as she rubbed. Quite an emollient. She gazed out the bay window once more. She considered dipping another finger, kneading the fat into her wrists, her forearms, her chapped elbows. But Sarah's uncharacteristic sneeze—*Ha-thrrrrb*—jolted her to.

"Well *Gesundheit,* Sarah-le." Funny, you had to learn how to *achoo.*

"*Ha-thrrrb.*"

"*Gesundheit* again." Heavens, Melody thought, the butter will warm!

She strode quickly to the sink, squirted an ample dose of Palmolive into her hands, scrubbed. Then she sprinkled Ajax across them and scrubbed again until her flesh prickled. She rinsed her hands thoroughly, dried them with a dishtowel, then washed with dish soap once again to remove any last trace of the caustic Ajax, returned to her mixing bowl. She covered the fat with a dusting of the flour, butter, and salt and then had back at it with the pastry cutter, pounding even more vigorously this time as if to settle matters. She pounded until the mix was caramel yellow, cornmeal coarse, fat-flour bits the size of small peas here and there. She retrieved the ice-cold water from the freezer, splashed a few spoonfuls into the bowl, and folded the dough into a ball with practiced spiral-flicks of her wrists. Retrieving the ball—she wouldn't overwork the dough—she coated it with flour, wrapped it in plastic and deposited it into the GE.

She'd let the dough relax for an hour before rolling. Mary Beth, despite her obvious competence, probably didn't relax her pie dough for a full hour. "Let's go in the family room and play, Sarah-le." She removed Sarah's tray, unbuckled the sprout from her chair. It had only been a few tablespoons of *treyf*, she rationalized as she rinsed the baby's fingers under the kitchen sink. Sarah squealed with delight as Melody moved on to splash her mouth clean, a favorite activity for Sarah.

Melody's thoughts drifted toward Eli just before she heard his feet pound the porch, the whine of the front door swinging open, the thunk of her son's book satchel against the pine floor.

"Eli!" she called.

"I'm going outside, Mom!"

"Eli, wait! Tell me about—"

But he was gone. No use racing after him with the baby. She leaned out the bay window to catch a glimpse of him skirting around the waist-high eggplant and okra in the garden, slipping between two palmetto islands—the towhee lit into the cover to clear way, flashing rust—disappeared into his grove. Probably flitting off to meet his playmate, that unkempt Boehringer urchin next door. Her son thought she didn't know. Didn't he realize? A mother knew everything.

❦

"Here, *you* thwack for snakes, Jo." He handed her a live oak stick. "My arms hurt from PE. Mr. Merrit made us do pushups." There was something boastful in the complaint. Eli had done pushups. He did better than chubby Peter King did, anyway, who sat out PE with a doctor's note, like usual. Eli rubbed his freckled biceps. He wouldn't tell Jo that he could only do one pushup to the "Chicken Fat Song" exercise album, and only after his stern teacher—Eli's classmates called him Mr. *De*-Merrit—let him put his knees on the ground. Hunter Newell had made the suggestion to Mr. Merrit after their teacher lifted the needle from the record to stop it, leaned over Eli's defeated frame on the hot macadam, and scolded him for not trying. Hunter was much nicer to Eli than Dean Chapman, Hunter's rival, who wasn't nice at all. But they weren't exactly friends, Eli and Hunter. Shortly after they arrived in Florida, Eli's father had encouraged him to look out for the Newell boy at school—related somehow to one of his father's co-op partners—told him to "make friends." Eli had nodded and said okay, because how could he have explained to his father that Hunter, a year older than Eli and strong, who could kick the yellow rubber ball clear over the six-foot-high chain-link fence in the outfield during kickball, who didn't have to wear a floppy shade hat during PE, lived and breathed on a different plane, like one of those parallel universes in Eli's comic books. Eli might as well "make friends" with a bear or a walrus. Maybe *that's* what he should have said to his father.

"You're lucky, you ask me. PE is sooo boooring with Mrs. Whitesell."

"Where are you up to now?" Eli had seen the girls earlier that day at PE walking their laps around the painted track.

"I don't know," she uttered. "Ocala," I think.

"Where's that?"

"You don't know where Ocala is?" Jo shook her head. "You huckleberry."

It had been Mrs. Whitesell's idea to "walk across the country" with the girls at Woodrow Wilson this year. All without having to leave the macadam yard. She had hoped to incorporate US geography into their daily regimen—*We're now approaching New Orleans, girls, founded by the French in 1718,* that sort of thing—until the know-it-all, Madison Chapman, athletic like her brother Dean, and willowy (their mother, Joan, had been a Miss Orange Blossom finalist ten years back or so), informed her in front of the whole class that her calculations were all wrong, that it took *eight* laps around the track to make a single mile. The upshot: they'd never get out of the state at the pace they were going. So instead of teaching her charges all about the big important cities—New Orleans, St. Louis, Chicago—she settled on nuggets, Jo told him, like *Leesburg was home to the biggest watermelon festival in the country before they stopped growing watermelons . . . Apopka is an Indian word that means "Potato-Eating Place" . . . The first thoroughbred horse farm in Florida was located in Ocala, girls.*

"Hold up a second, young man!" Eli heard Mr. Ted shout at him across two rows, freezing him in his tracks. They had ventured past Eli's shrunken grove of hybrids and crosses and had entered the acres of taller, gnarly Valencias. Eli had thought they'd scamper past the crew, invisible.

"Let's keep going," Jo said, somehow shouting and whispering at the same time. "You don't have ta listen to him."

"But he sees us."

Jo groaned.

Eli made his way toward the foreman beneath the ancient Valencias, dragging his feet across the lupine grass, wax bean, and cowpea cover crop, warning away snakes. Jo lumbered hangdog behind, thwacking the grass with the live oak stick. Eli heard the stick crack behind him. "Aw, shoot!" she cried.

"Don't miss that shiner in there, Percy!" Ted shouted into the air, standing beside the flatbed truck. "To your left. Your *left*, you hear?" Ted was overseeing the last of the Valencia harvest with a diminished crew, the main harvest weeks behind them now. Empty wooden field boxes were stacked in pairs off to the side, beneath the shade of a tree. The two Negro field-workers on top of their stacked wooden ladders, roped together, seemed a mile high to Eli, big brown bushel sacks around their shoulders. They wore thick boots, long sleeves and pants, even though it was hot. Consumed by their labors, they didn't look down at their visitors, and maybe didn't even notice them. One worker in the tree just behind Ted had abandoned his ladder at the tree's spine and clambered amid the branches for the fruit that remained. The great tree rattled when he moved.

"Pecker-bird got it, boss!" the worker, Percy, shouted down about the big orange, the shiner, casting the worthless fruit to the ground. Eli knew Percy.

"Hi, Mr. Ted."

"That you I see the other day, Mr. Eli Golden, pitching last of my Valencias at the rabbits? Think they grow on trees, oranges?" The foreman's toothpick bobbed between his lips as he laughed at his own joke. Mr. Ted usually addressed him by his whole name—Mr. Eli Golden—as if the entire name were important. He was only pretending to be mad, or else he wouldn't have made a joke. Something about the way he held his hands on his hips, also, his elbows jutted wide to the side, told Eli he was only playacting. Mr. Ted liked him. Because he called him by his whole name. And because Eli liked to fish too. Jo didn't like to fish.

"Just a couple oranges, Mr. Ted. They weren't no good ones." Eli knew that Ted was concerned about the oranges, not the rabbits, which Ted hunted and ate.

"Weren't no good ones, Eli Golden?" the foreman repeated. He removed his toothpick from his mouth this time before he spoke. "*That's* how they teach you to speak at school now?" He jabbed the toothpick back inside. Eli wondered how he didn't poke himself.

"No," Jo uttered. "It's *not.*" Eli didn't like the way that she talked to Mr. Ted.

"They were mushy ones," Eli said. "Already on the ground. Honest Injun, Mr. Ted."

"Honest Injun, eh?" Mr. Ted warded off a dragonfly with a slow backhand wave in front of his face, shiny and black with sweat. Dragonflies were good, Eli knew. They ate the mosquitoes. "Why on God's green earth you need to pitch oranges at the poor rabbits, anyway?"

"We never hit them," Jo said.

"Then why carry on like that in the first place?"

Silence. Neither Eli nor Jo had an answer for this. He could say things to them, Ted, things that other Negroes would never say. Because Ted was older. And Ted was the foreman. But Jo didn't seem to think that Ted should talk to them this way. It was such a struggle for Eli to figure out where everyone stood here. Where *he* stood. Jo was white, but she was a girl. Eli was a boy, which was better, but he was Jewish, which wasn't quite as good as Jo's white, but better than being Negro like Ted.

The big tree behind Ted shook as Percy clambered above, barely visible now within the foliage. An orange landed with a thud near the trunk.

"Watch out below!" Percy called down in jest. Ted walked over to the orange and plucked it from the ground. It had started to re-green, Eli noticed. His father had taught him about that. Cold weather turned them orange. The late spring heat made them turn back to green if they didn't pick them in time. The foreman turned the greenish orange in his hand to inspect the stem. A long piece was still attached with floppy leaves.

"Careful up there, Percy! For Lord's sake! We want to kill the tree we can just get ourselves a tree-shaker." Ted made a clucking sound with his tongue, a sound which Eli didn't think that he could make even if he tried. The stem seemed to particularly irritate the foreman. Eli marveled at Ted's hands, as he always did. The insides were so pale, the outsides so dark.

The foreman turned his attention back toward Eli and Jo. "Let me teach you how to harvest an orange, Mr. Eli Golden, long as I have you here." He's bored, it occurred to Eli. That's why he stopped them. He didn't really care about them chucking oranges at the rabbits.

"Now you pull too hard and forget to twist, you plug the stem with the rind. Orange'll rot before you get it to Nevin's. We used clippers back in the day to make clean cuts, keep from plugging." Ted affected a scissors-snap with his two-toned fingers. "But that takes too long now. Everything has to be done fast, fast, fast, these days. No matter. A bit of care with your hands all that's required. You turn the orange this way and that, see, before you try to free it." Eli watched as Ted turned the orange at sharp angles from the stem. He didn't know to do that. He wondered whether Jo did. "Then you twist. You don't never pull an orange straight from the stem. Not never. Not on my grove. You twist." The *don't never* wasn't proper English, Eli knew, and sounded funny coming out of Ted's mouth. He usually spoke better, scolded Eli time to time, too, for his sloppy English. Ted twisted the orange fast on its axis now and it seemed to float right off the stem without even a snap. "Comes right off clean." Ted did something funny as he spoke, side-stepped back and forth upon uttering especially important words, planting his feet fresh, as if to command their attention through the dance. "See?"

Eli nodded. "I didn't know about the turning part. Twisting I knew."

"Huckleberry," he heard Jo say.

"Percy and Fred can fill a hundred of these here two-bushel boxes a day." Ted side-stepped, pointed to the stacked wooden field boxes in the shade. "High rollers, Percy and Fred. They're just helping old Ted out today, because I give them the best rows come high season."

The foreman brandished his budding knife from out of thin air and, twisting the orange more so than the knife, sliced off a single ribbon of peel from the stem end, exposing the fruit's white scalp. Eli watched as he gouged out a small circular chunk at the cap, flicked it away with the blade, then poked at the orange's insides with surgical strikes. "Here," he handed the orange to Jo, who took it without saying thank you. Juice welled up at the cap, Eli noticed. "Drink some juice. Good for you."

Jo drank. "Blossom end's sweeter," she said, wiping her wet mouth with her freckled forearm.

"Right you are, child. How did you get so smart?"

Jo shrugged.

"You two learn to pluck an orange proper you can come to work for me."

"It's the *Golden's* grove. Isn't it?"

"Manner of speaking, young ma'am. That's all." Ted lifted a hand to tip an imaginary hat. The workers wore old baseball caps with indecipherable advertisements above the brims. Ted wasn't wearing his hat. He carried one, though, the bill tucked inside the waistband of his trousers. Eli noticed the bare islands on top of his head, lathered with sweat, where his hair didn't grow anymore. He wanted to ask him about his head, but it was impolite, his mother had warned. None of his bee's wax.

"Can we climb one of the ladders?" Jo asked. She sounded nicer now. Ted exhaled, chewed his bottom lip, making it disappear, making salty bristles jut out from his chin. He was mulling it over, Eli could tell.

"Percy! Fred! Come on down a second." They watched the men descend. Percy reached the ground first. The skin on his face was smooth except for a broad, barely raised mole like a sliver of chocolate on his cheek.

"You see any wildcats from up there?" Eli asked.

"During the day, Mr. Eli? Naw."

"Children want to catch a glimpse of the view. Help them up if you would."

"Sure, boss?" Fred uttered, who had just made it down. He was older than Percy and had lumbered down his ladder, making heavy footfalls on each rung. Fred was missing a tooth in front, which made him seem like he was always smiling. "What if something happens to the young miss? You know Mr. Boehringer well as I do—"

"Think we're better off saying no to a red-headed white girl?" Percy asked. He wasn't smiling.

What were they talking about? Eli wondered. Why did grownups have to be so confusing all the time? They had taken off their hats, Eli just noticed, probably as soon as they reached the ground.

"Just make sure nothing happens to them, we got no problems," Mr. Ted said, which seemed to settle matters. He was the boss. But Eli's father, he knew, was the *real* boss. Like Jo had said.

The workers checked the sturdiness of their jerry-rigged ladders, bracing them more squarely against the tree spines, then ushered Jo and Eli up ahead of them.

"Last one up's a rotten egg!"

"Go slow girl, hear—"

⁂

She floured the counter sparingly before rolling out the tawny dough. Too much flour made a tough crust. She started in the middle, worked her way outward, gently. She wouldn't overwork the dough. Mary Beth was gentle with her dough, too. She could tell. Melody liked the feel of the wooden pin beneath her hands as she rolled, coaxing it toward flat, little by little. It would be a fine crust.

⁂

It was only thirty feet or so to the top, but it seemed much higher than that. Only ten feet up or so, Eli looked down and a shiver seized his spine. He hugged the ladder. The floppy brim of his fisherman's hat folded down against a wood rung, shielded his eyes from the view beyond the tree. He could feel his hot breath against his cheek.

"You all right, bossman?" Percy asked from below. Eli glanced over toward Jo, who was almost at the top. She advanced only her right leg up each rung, bringing up her left one behind, ascended at a quick, staccato pace all the same. Fred scrambled to catch up.

"I'm fine," Eli insisted. He couldn't stop now. Why was he suddenly afraid? He was fine climbing trees. But he had never been so high. And out in the open on a ladder, rather than within the protective canopy. He screwed up his courage and headed up again, imitating Jo's staccato technique, right foot first.

"Don't look down, you be okay. I catch you if you fall, bossman. Can't be more than fifty pounds soaking wet."

⁂

She fluted the edges, middle finger from the inside making small curves in the crust rim, thumb and forefinger of her other hand braced on the outside. Now the apples. Green ones. Granny Smiths.

⁂

Jo beat him to the top. She didn't act like a big shot, though. She hadn't yet said anything, in fact. Finally, Eli's head rose above the canopy. The sea breeze licked his face. The air, cooler. He could see the mangrove-lined river and the Haulover canal across, built by slaves, Mr. Ted once told him, which steamboats used for freighting oranges before the trains and trucks; he saw the smaller lagoon on the far side where fishermen in shallow boats caught the most sea trout and snook; and he saw the ocean beyond stretching to forever, a cottony chop at the surface, a few ships so far away they seemed motionless, pinned against the hazy backdrop. He looked closer by at his father's acres, the grid of dark green trees clearly discernible from the scruffier, duller green land bordering the river, dotted with cabbage palms and buttonwoods and privet. He looked north toward Jo's grove across the irrigation ditch. Their trees had ceilings and walls. He hedged his grove, Mr. Boehringer. What was here before their groves? Eli wondered. The land was a bit higher here off the coast a piece. Oaks and longleaf pines, probably, saw palmetto and switchgrass beneath the canopy. Just like the other side of the highway. Sure must have been nice. But weren't for the grove, his family wouldn't be here. And the grove was nice too. He considered turning his head to look back for his house, the palmetto and lantana and wax myrtle islands, the few live oaks with their shaggy beards, the towering tamarind with its tiny PEZ-candy leaves, but he was too scared to twist his shoulders on the ladder.

"You can see the base!" Jo finally uttered. "You see the rocket base, Eli!?"

He hadn't thought to look for the base to the southeast. He was more interested in their groves, the Haulover canal, the lagoon, the ocean beyond. This was what it must feel like to be Superman, he thought, but only briefly, as Mr. Ted was already clamoring for them to climb down.

"Been up there long enough, Mr. Eli Golden! Two of you come down now, hear?"

She deposited the pie in the oven, closed shut the door, and wept. Not because of the *treyf* pie. But because of the empty rack below the pie that she couldn't help but notice. And because the empty rack made her think of her mother. So preoccupied had she been with the apple pie that she hadn't thought to prepare anything to accompany it in the oven. Her mother would roll over in her grave had she glimpsed this empty rack in a three-hundred-fifty–degree oven. The waste! Noma Herskowitz would occasionally commingle inharmonious morsels for the sake of efficiency. Baked apples and brisket. Chicken paprikash and blueberry crumble. The lard would have been so unthinkable to her that Melody couldn't quite conjure up visions of her disdain. But to heat up a whole oven and leave an entire rack empty, without even preparing so much as a noodle kugel or a tray of mandel bread, some kichel twists at the very least? A disgrace. "Oh, Mother." Melody blotted her eyes with a tissue as if stanching the flow of blood. She laughed mildly at the memory of her mother's brisket-infused baked apples, tasting them on her tongue. "Silly Mother."

"Now come on down you two. And careful! Climbing up's the easy part. Most accidents happen on the way down. Come down now, you hear, Mr. Eli Golden?! You got him, Percy!? You got him!?"

Ten

ISAAC SPIED THE FRENZIED PARTY once they reached the live oak canopy, rushing in from the grove. He had been tending Melody's garden, salvaging the last of the okra and eggplant for the stand, culling pokeweed, beggarweed, hawksbeard, and torpedo grass. Ted was almost unrecognizable to Isaac, un-Ted, hewing to a strange labored trot, his face shining, Eli cradled before him. Frederick and Percy brought up the rear, hangdog, along with that red-headed urchin, Walt's youngest, Isaac was pretty sure. Now what was she doing on their grove?

"It's not broke, Isaac," Ted said straight away, before Isaac could ask what happened. "I'm pretty near certain it's not broke. We loosened the laces."

"Should have *tightened* them, Ted." Isaac reached for his son, performed a quick scan. Pinprick pearls of fresh blood on a raspberry knee. Swollen tube sock. "I'll take him. What happened?"

"Accident," his foreman declared as he relinquished Eli. "Took a tumble off the ladder," Isaac heard behind him. "Not too high, though. Not broke, I'm near sure. Like I said. Just sprained."

"It's okay, Dad," Eli uttered, his pitch even higher than usual. "It's okay," Eli insisted. His butterfly rash was inflamed across his bird nose, the zinc oxide having evaporated. Isaac noticed remnants of tears, clean trails across the otherwise dusty terrain of Eli's narrow face running back from the outside corners of his eyes past his protuberant ears.

"Should have tightened his shoes, not loosened them," Isaac uttered again to the salty wind as he loped toward the house, right through the tall wispy rows of gone-to-seed asparagus.

"Sorry, Isaac. Mr. Golden. Need anything, give a shout," Isaac heard Ted behind him. "I'll wait here. Right here."

Isaac sat Eli down in the kitchen and retrieved a five-gallon paint bucket from the carport, filled it halfway with water from the outside spigot and four trays of cubed ice from the freezer inside, removed his son's dusty sneakers and downright filthy tube sock and lowered the injured foot into the bath.

"*Owww,*" Eli cried. "It's . . . freezing . . . Daddy." He puffed up his cheeks, started to lift his leg, but Isaac clamped a hand on his bony knee. "Sorry, Elijah-le. It won't hurt after a bit more. It'll numb up. You'll see."

"Be brave, sweetie," Melody said, bobbing Sarah in her arms, deep worried dashes visible between her fine eyebrows. "Your father knows best." She had already retrieved the amber vial of Mercurochrome for Eli's raspberry knee, smeared the ochre fluid over the abrasion with the glass rod after dabbing it clean with a washcloth.

Eli's ankle, however, was the least of their problems. The shock from the injury—or perhaps the shock of the ice water cure, Isaac couldn't dismiss this possibility—triggered Eli's pulmonary distress. He began clutching quick fistfuls of air into his lungs as Isaac and Melody watched. A croupy seal bark escaped his throat. It had been a long time. Isaac looked up toward his wife, a pregnant glance that she understood.

"Oh Isaac."

"Now Melody."

"What?" Eli asked, clutching another fistful of air, seemingly unaware of his predicament, distracted as he was by the burning cold water.

"You can take your foot out now," Isaac said, kneeling by his son's side, folding his hand around Eli's small calf, helping him lift the foot, marbled with cold. The water from the bucket plashed on the kitchen's lemon linoleum. He folded a towel over the cold wet leg, patted it dry.

"That . . . feels . . . good," Eli uttered through labored breaths. "My . . . chest," he said, lifting a hand to his heart. "Daddy?"

Eli's lips had lost their blood. The musculature of his face grew rigid as he struggled for air, his lower jaw slid forward.

"Shhh," Isaac said. "I know. Just breathe, Elijah-le. Don't talk. Melody. Melody?" he uttered at a practiced tenor, calm and fraudulent. *Where had she gone!?*

Eli barked again, scaring himself with the noise. "Daddy?"

"Shhh, Elijah-le." Isaac rubbed his son's thigh. "Melody!" he cried, louder now.

"Coming! Here!" She handed Eli his inhaler. Eli looked into Isaac's eyes, still kneeling at his feet. Their son had always been fearful of his inhaler, reluctant to use it. He had been warned by Dr. Olivet that if he abused the device, relied upon it like a crutch, it might lose its potency. And what would happen if it didn't work, suddenly?

"Yes, go ahead, Eli," Isaac urged. "Use it, Elijah-le."

Eli took a deep breath of the medicine, swallowed a few shallow breaths.

"Again," Isaac ordered.

"Isaac?" Melody asked. Sarah began to cry. A mucus balloon inflated at her nostril. Melody bobbed her in her arms.

Eli inhaled the medicine a second time, but still labored for breath, jutted his jaw, flexed the muscle cords in his cheeks and neck. His jugular bulged blue.

"Daddy?"

"Don't cry," Isaac ordered, stern now. "Crying will make it worse. You have to be brave, son. Brave!"

Eli nodded, his eyes wide.

"Get my bag," Isaac declared with adamantine calm. "My bag, Melody." He folded his son in a loose hug, stroked his back, felt the tender buttons of his spine beneath his dusty shirt, his labored gravel breath. "*Shhhh,* Elijah-le. *Shhhh.*"

"Do . . . I have . . . to have . . . a shot?" The tears spilled from his eyes, marking fresh, clean trails down his dusty complexion.

Isaac leaned back and placed his large hands—dirty still from the garden—over the bony knobs of Eli's shoulders. "It'll only sting for a second, Eli. Promise. Just a second. And then you'll be able to breathe better."

Melody returned in a flash, having deposited Sarah somewhere (her playpen?) and handed him his large black leather bag with its looping handles. "Call the hospital, he said. Tell them we're on our way."

He heard the phone stir from its cradle as he fumbled through the bag for an epinephrine vial—found it!—as he sterilized his syringe with an alcohol wipe, twisting his thick torso to shield the needle from Eli's view.

"Uhhh," Melody uttered, nonplussed. Someone at the Boehringers was on the party line, Isaac could tell. Probably Glory, Walt's wife.

"Tell them to hang up, Mel," Isaac said with the same adamantine calm. "Just tell them to hang up."

"We need to call the hospital, Glory. It's Eli. . . . Yes, thank you."

He heard the clack of the receiver on its cradle, then its retrieval once again, the long whir of the rotary after Melody's brisk command with her index finger. Good, he thought. A dial tone.

"Yes, operator. The hospital please. Thank you."

"You're . . . not . . . gonna-make . . . it-hurt . . . right? You'll-make . . . it . . . not-hurt . . . You'll-do . . . your-trick."

"Yes, Elijah-le. Don't talk." As Isaac tamped the air out of the syringe, he glanced at his son's exposed legs, the knees crusty with grove dirt, hoping to locate an ounce of subcutaneous fat on his thigh. He held the syringe out of view behind his back as he wiped a patch of flesh with the same alcohol wipe (no time to spare) high above Eli's soiled knee, as he pinched a crest of flesh at the center. Eli hid his eyes beneath the crook of his freckled elbow. Isaac held the crest of flesh for just a moment longer between his thumb and forefinger pincers, scratching at the flesh beside with the dirt-encrusted nails of his free fingers as he plunged the needle down, hoping to confuse Eli's pain receptors with the added stimulus of his scratching. His trick.

"*Owww!*"

"It's all over, Elijah-le. You're going to be okay. Now relax." Isaac rubbed his son's thigh, hoping to stimulate the delivery of the dose. Eli lowered his elbow. Fresh tears welled in his eyes, but he sniffled them back, exhaled. A long exhale. Deliberate. Good, Isaac thought. "Good, Eli," he said. "Very good." The inflammatory response had abated. The bronchial passages had begun to dilate.

"This is Melody Golden, the mother of Elijah Golden," Isaac heard. "We're registered at the hospital. You'll find his file. Our son's having a . . . uhh . . . reaction. His breathing is labored. We're bringing him in now. Please call Dr. Olivet. Tell him we're on our way. . . . No, we can't wait for an ambulance."

"It's working, Mel. You can relax. We're out of the woods. Out of the woods for now. . . . Something burning?"

"My pie!"

Melody lunged for the avocado oven and flicked off the heat. She opened its frothy mouth with care, standing to the side, dodging its scorching breath, which permeated the room in an instant.

"Let's go to the other room, Eli," Isaac said.

"Oh sugar!" Melody cried, lifting the charred corpse from the oven with a thick mitt. Standing over the trash, she shook the pie off its ceramic plate and into the receptacle. She should take the fragrant trash out now, but there was no time.

They were out of the house within minutes. Eli's overnight bag was always packed, at the ready beneath his bed. A toothbrush and Pepsodent. Superman pajamas. An extra blanket. Some old comics, the corners distressed from his oily thumbs. Isaac scanned Eli's room quickly and stuffed a couple other items in the bag too. Thankfully, they hadn't used Eli's overnight bag for several months. But the pajamas would still fit, Isaac knew. His son grew by centimeters, not inches. He'd be lucky to reach five feet. Isaac kicked open the back door and a different quality of light greeted him. The sun had tucked itself between the westward pines, casting long shadows about. Ted's silent form, at the border of Melody's garden, startled Isaac, who halted for a moment. His foreman stood with his hat in his hands, exposing his patchy pate under the last light of day. He worried the threadbare visor with his thumbs. The field-workers, and Walt's urchin, were gone. How long would Ted have stood there, Isaac wondered, if they had stayed inside for the night?

"Y'all taking Mr. Eli Golden to the hospital?" Ted had noticed, surely, the overnight bag in Melody's hands, the baby in her synagogue clothes. Worry lines erupted on Ted's still shiny forehead. His concern was genuine, it seemed to Isaac.

"Yes, Ted. Ankle's not broken, though. That's not why we're taking him in. He had a reaction. Breathing issues."

Ted nodded his head, slow.

"Thanks for carrying me home, Mr. Ted," Eli said as Isaac bounded past toward the Pontiac around the side on the long pebbly driveway. He was calm now in Isaac's arms. Depleted. Wispy strands of his son's hair were coal-dark at the edges, pasted to his temples with perspiration. Isaac could feel Eli's birdcage ribs riding against his splayed fingers, his son's inhalations and exhalations within, the static thinner now, but still there, the passages still constricted. He would need a breathing treatment. A nebulizer within a tent. Penicillin drip just to be on the safe side, likely diarrhea and skin rash be damned. Overnight hospital stay, at the very least. Careful monitoring.

"That's all right Eli Golden. You just get yourself better, hear?"

"Thank you, Ted," said Melody, inflectionless, bringing up the rear.

"You can head home now," Isaac called to his foreman, behind them now. He could have struck a kinder chord, he realized. Yet he just didn't have it in him. He certainly wouldn't thank Ted for his part in all this. It irked him that Melody had done so, however mechanically.

"I'll see to things tomorrow," Ted shouted. "Erma too at the stand. 'Case you're held up. God bless."

They took Eli to the hospital together. All four Goldens. Isaac knew it would be futile to suggest that Melody stay behind with the baby. His wife had set the terms long ago. They were all in it together, Eli's health battles. Even Sarah was conscripted to the cause now—Isaac could hear Melody snapping the snaps of the baby's navy-and-white houndstooth synagogue outfit in the backseat—as if the four of them together, and dressed appropriately, stood a better chance of warding off any opportunistic pathogen.

"You're-not . . . gonna-be-mad . . . at-Mr.-Ted . . . right-Daddy?" Eli asked, his breath still noisome with static. He sat in the front seat so Isaac could keep an eye on him. The blood had mostly returned to his lips. His jaw had relaxed. His jugular had tucked itself down beneath the pale flesh. Good.

"That depends, Eli."

"Depends . . . on . . . what?"

"On exactly what happened." Melody, he noticed, didn't say anything, when she might have supported her husband. All he heard was Eli's raspy inhalations and exhalations, then Sarah's fuss-bucket groan in the back, punctuating everyone's displeasure with him.

"Fine. No."

"No, what?"

"No, I'm not going to be mad at Mr. Ted. Happy now?"

Isaac gazed over his son's head toward the western horizon, the twilight bruise beyond the slash pines impossibly, infuriatingly, beautiful. The palmettos flashed silver along the roadside, bathed in the headlights, not unlike snowdrifts.

He was a physician, Isaac. A pediatrician. Yet he didn't consider himself a physician, anymore. He had given all that up. Renounced his hard-earned profession, his successful Center City practice. Because there was nothing he or any other physician could do for Eli. During those first months of fatherhood—no, years—Isaac had lumbered about town, *shul*, his practice on Chestnut, the hospital, in a protracted daze. He tended to his duties, filial and workplace, but with perfunctory diligence. *Here you are*, he thought to himself every so often, as if to wake himself to the real. Sometimes he uttered the words to himself aloud as he made his way the few blocks from the station to Chestnut, as he walked the fewer blocks from the practice to the hospital to make his rounds. *Here you are.* Dr. Isaac Golden. Father of sick sick sick Eli. Small Eli. Painfully small. His Golden features forever disguised behind his bird nose, his protuberant ears, his butterfly rash. Chronic lung diseases, asthma, bronchiectasis, and various dermatological maladies would fester. Leukemia, lymphomas, or carcinomas, likely before his twenty-fifth birthday. *Here you are, Isaac Golden!*

He thought that he would grow to accept his lot, Eli's lot, that he'd keep things in perspective. There were worse tragedies. It wasn't even a tragedy, quite. Yet things only grew more troublesome for him at the practice as the months passed, as Eli's seal barks continued to herald new bronchial infections. He found himself welling with tears as he loomed over his healthy new patients in their hospital incubators, bursting with life, their clamshell eyelids splitting to take in their first dose of light through nascent rods and cones. Their perfect hip bones. Their clear lungs and melodious cardiac rhythms. It was worse at the office. He found it increasingly difficult to treat his young patients with the tenderness on which he had staked his reputation. "A big teddy bear," the mothers had once referred to him in the waiting room. He'd overhear their banter. "A great big teddy bear of a doctor." Not anymore. The children came in with their sinus infections and low-grade fevers, their contact dermatitis and swimmer's ear, their chicken pox and strep throat and three-day flu. And they would be healed. They would get on with their perfectly ordinary lives, while his son would never heal. He didn't wish them harm, quite, but he resented their resilience. Parents, sensing all this, or perhaps only their doctor's unfortunate and unabated malaise, began to flee the practice. Guiltily. Silently. But fled nonetheless, abandoning their charts rather than calling to retrieve them. The Levins. The Pinskers. The Fleishmans. The Dinners. The Waldens. The Scheinbaums. The Plaskows. There were other Jewish groups in town. Isaac hadn't the courage to explain the precise contours of his predicament to Melody. His own wife. How would it sound coming out of his mouth, the precise reason he could no longer practice? That he begrudged his young patients their vigor. He simply couldn't administer care, anymore.

After the briefest triage with an emergency room nurse, who refused to show her teeth, a more affable candy striper appeared and ushered the Goldens through various gleaming halls to the elevator. Random phrases drifted into the corridor like an angry wind. *Over my dead body . . . You can't make me . . . Won't you please, Mother, listen to the* . . . These wide linoleum halls. The chlorine-rich cleansing agents not quite masking the undertone of bodily effluvia. The mutterings of geriatrics in various states of distress echoed off the hard surfaces. The overchilled air. The oracular assault of the florescent lights overhead. The cavernous gurney-ready Otis elevator. Patients and relatives of patients loping about half-dazed, misty-eyed, arms crossed. The more purposeful strides of doctors, nurses, and orderlies in their scrubs. Hospitals, Isaac reflected, were not unlike those McDonald's restaurants cropping up all over the highways. All pretty much the same inside. A certain comfort in that, maybe. As they waited for the elevator's broad maw to open, Isaac glanced down the hall and noticed an elderly black woman at the far west end crouched over her metal walker, an incongruous church hat (Isaac presumed) covering her head. The colored ward was on this first floor, probably so everyone would know (especially the Negroes, themselves) that Negroes had no business riding the elevators. They hadn't admitted Negro patients at all here until a few years ago. Before then, Negroes had to drive all the way over to Sanford if they needed a hospital.

It wasn't quite a large enough hospital for a separate pediatric ward, per se, but they reserved the east wing of the second floor pretty much for youth admits. "Up you go, Elijah-le." Isaac grasped his small son beneath his underarms and lifted him up onto the examination table, covered with diaphanous crinkly white paper. He helped Eli off with his shirt, exposing his chicken chest, forced convex from his fierce bronchial battles over the years, his pale nipples barely visible on either side of the gentle slope, two bloodless eyes gazing off in separate directions. They didn't have to wait long inside Eli's room before the attending rapped his knuckles on the open door and crossed the threshold. It was the young doctor, Taylor Brock. Good. Stronger bona fides than most of his peers. Residency at Chapel Hill. And he had examined Eli once before. His small, soft hand, Isaac noticed, dusted with blonde hair, already held Eli's manila folder, thick with ditto sheaves.

"It's been a nice long while since we've seen you, big fella." Brock extended his small hand toward Eli, who shook in one steep pump, smiling. "Dr. Golden," he extended his blonde hand toward Isaac.

"Dr. Brock," Isaac said, accepting Brock's smaller hand in his own.

"Mind if I listen inside you, Eli, hear what's what?" Brock exclaimed at a higher pitch. He reached into his deep coat pocket at his hip and grasped his stethoscope, affixed the earpiece around his neck with the practiced pincers of one hand, never once taking his eyes off his small patient. "See?" Dr. Brock said, holding up the two-sided chestpiece, diaphragm and bell, for Eli's inspection. "You can touch." The wispy strands of hair at Eli's temples were still dark with perspiration. Isaac could still hear the static as he breathed. "Just a stethoscope, big fella."

"Sure," Eli said, lifting his bird nose, waving off the opportunity to inspect the instrument. His son seemed pleased with this opportunity to act brave. Quiet permeated the room as the young physician placed the broad diaphragm side of the chestpiece on the left slope of Eli's trunk. He placed a blonde hand on Eli's shoulder. Isaac wanted to tell Eli to sit up straight, but swallowed his words. Even Sarah quit her fidgeting. Isaac could hear the faint ticking of a clock now in the background along with Eli's breath.

"Just breathe normally, big fella," Dr. Brock exclaimed, his pale eyebrows knitted in concentration. "Good. Now how about a deep inhale . . . then let it out slow . . . now another . . . one more time." There was something glorious about an examination with a stethoscope, Isaac thought. This laying on of hands. This reverent silence. Nothing else mattered for this spec of time. Not the schoolyard or the grove, your sister or your brother or your wife or your husband. Nor the doctor's own harried life. All that mattered for this spec of time were the soundings of your heart, your inhalations and exhalations, the lifeblood and oxygen coursing (with any luck) through your vital machinery. Here was the real, Isaac thought.

Soon, in all likelihood, they wouldn't need stethoscopes. A more technologically impressive contact-free scanner or doohickey along those lines would render the ancient stethoscope, this laying on of hands, obsolete. A new standard of sterile care. Well, it would be a loss, Isaac thought. On both sides. Physician and patient.

"Good," Brock declared one last time, his rising timbre indicating that he had heard enough. He held a broad wooden tongue depressor before Eli's mouth, wielding it from out of thin air, it seemed. "Now open, partner. . . . You've been coughing a lot lately?"

Eli shook his head.

"Some," Isaac said.

"Not a lot," Melody countered from the hard plastic chair, bouncing Sarah on her lap.

Isaac shrugged. Brock nodded his head slow, noncommittal. "Big *ahh,*" he instructed, gazed down Eli's throat with a silver penlight.

"There's a bit more mucus in the sputum here than I like. Inflammation. Lungs somewhat occluded. You're just a tough-as-nails fella, that's what this is all about, isn't it partner?" Brock poked Eli's arm gently with his blonde fist. Eli smiled. They all did. "Can't hold out forever, though."

A needle, these last words, puncturing a distended balloon.

"Okay, you can put your shirt back on, Eli." Brock turned toward Isaac, still standing behind him. "If Eli were just presenting like this off the street it would be one thing," Brock said. "Probably just his asthma. Might be viral. Doubt it's an infection. We'd let it run its course, normally. But given his history . . ." Brock glanced toward Melody on the hard chair now, including her in the discussion. "I don't think we want to monkey around. I say we give him a breathing treatment, run a line of antibiotics, have a sleepover tonight, see where we are in the morning. All hands on deck, just to be on the safe side. Those lungs have been through the ringer. So let's not monkey around. Once they're scarred—"

"Yes, yes, Dr. Brock," Isaac interjected. "It's the best thing."

"We can wait until Dr. Olivet gets here, see what he thinks?" Brock replied, as if he weren't expecting such fast accord.

"No, no, let's get started."

"Mommy," Eli finally uttered, "do I have to go inside the tent all night?"

He seemed more exasperated than fearful, Isaac noted. Brock was right. Eli was tough. Tougher than any child should have to be.

"It's okay, sweetie pie," Melody said. "I'll be right here, Elijah-le. We'll bring in a cot."

Isaac exchanged a pregnant glance with Dr. Brock. It was against hospital policy for parents to stay the night with their admitted children. Best for all concerned, the common wisdom, to offer the doctors and nurses a wide berth to tend to their wards.

"Or I'll be here, son," Isaac proposed, partly to preclude any protest from Brock's quarter. Isaac was a physician, after all. "Mel, you should really take Sarah home. I'll stay with Eli."

"No Isaac. No. For heaven's sake." She lifted a tissue to her eyes.

"Now Melody."

Silence permeated the room. Isaac could hear the ticking clock, then Melody's exhale through her fine nose, her surrender, it seemed to him.

"It'll be like a campout. Right sport?"

"Sure, Daddy."

Melody stayed until the nurse entered with her rattling stainless-steel tray. She inserted Eli's IV as Eli hid his face in his elbow. She set up the nebulizer inside the translucent tent. Melody unzipped the tent after the nurse departed and kissed Eli on his butterfly rash beside his nasal tubing, withdrew and zipped up the tent again. "Have a good night, Golden men," she said as brightly as she could muster. Her eyes were wet. Isaac handed her the keys to the Pontiac. "See you first thing in the morning, Elijah-le. First thing."

"Maybe we can go on a real campout after this," Eli uttered once they were alone. It was quiet again, like it was during Brock's stethoscope examination. Isaac could hear the slow ticking again, looked up at the wall for the first time to locate the clock.

"Sure, Eli. Want me to slide you one of your comics? *Superman* maybe?" Eli shrugged. The atmosphere inside the tent was misty now from the nebulizer.

It had been a long while since Isaac had taken Eli camping overnight, it occurred to him. Even on the grove. He'd have to make it up to him. He fumbled through Eli's overnight bag and pulled out a comic. He unzipped the tent and put it on Eli's lap. "Here you go, sport." His son said thanks but didn't seem up for reading. He turned his head to his side on the thin pillow. They had forgotten to bring Eli's own pillow. Darn it.

Isaac searched Eli's bag again and took out another item he had stuffed inside just before leaving the house.

"Here," he said to Eli. "Your coonskin cap. Want to wear your coonskin cap?" Eli's eyes brightened some. He lifted his far hand from the starched sheets, the one without the IV, to retrieve it through the tent. He didn't put it on, but stroked the fur on his belly, as if it were a live pet. Isaac would get Eli a dog if it weren't for his lungs.

"There you go, sport. You want to lean back a bit more so you can sleep? It's okay to sleep now, son."

Eli nodded. He raised his arm without the IV from the starched sheets into the misty air and pointed a limp finger toward the foot of the bed. Isaac's throat thickened at the gesture; he cleared it to fight back untimely tears. The bed was a standard single-crank Hill-Rom. And Eli knew its specifications, the crank's locale at the bed's foot.

He turned his back to Eli as he worked the crank, lowered the incline, glad for the moment that the translucent tent, the mist within, further concealed his tears from his son.

"It's okay, Daddy," Isaac barely heard. The plastic muffled Eli's thin words.

"Huh?"

"I feel better now, Daddy. Honest Injun. Don't be sad."

Isaac rose from the crank at the foot, opened Eli's tent and stroked the wispy strands of his son's hair from his forehead, tucked them behind his ear. "All right. Deal. I'm not sad, son."

"Promise?"

"Promise. Just sleep, Elijah-le. Just sleep."

Melody, true to her word, appeared at Eli's bedside not long after daybreak. She had left Sarah, Isaac presumed, with Erma. Eli had slept fairly well, not even waking when Dr. Olivet poked his nose in, affirming Brock's course of treatment (though upping the fluids, as long as they were running a line, anyway). Isaac wasn't certain that he had slept at all. Concerned as he was over Eli, he couldn't quite bring himself to lie down in the cot, but leaned back, rather, in the cushioned vinyl seat, drifting off into a drowsy not-quite-sleep that approximated the half-lidded state of the weirdly vibrating hospital, itself.

"Might as well tend the grove, I'm thinking," Isaac greeted his wife.

"Fine. Tend the grove," she said, not taking her eyes off Eli, asleep still within the tent. She brought a dark mood in with her, which Isaac had failed to recognize at first.

"You'd rather I didn't go?"

"No no. By all means. See to your oranges."

"They're *our* oranges, Mel. Eli's. And Sarah's."

Melody's fine jaw dropped, her eyes rolled.

"What, Melody?"

"You can breed the best orange in the world, Isaac. The perfect genetic specimen. Seedless. Sweet as honey. Call it whatever you want for posterity. It's not going to change anything."

"What do you mean, Mel? What are you—"

"You're still going to have a sick child, Isaac," she uttered low, keeping her eyes on Eli to make sure that he was still asleep.

"I know that. You think I don't know—"

"Because that's what we have." She turned toward Isaac. "A sick, sick child." She said this as if trying to convince herself once and for all. The tears came. She wiped them with the sleeve of her dress. The edges of her nostrils were rigid and wet. Eli had been well for so many months now that it was quite a blow, all this: his staccato breaths and fearful eyes, the seal bark, the antiseptic hospital, the sterile florescent lighting and translucent tent. Melody had allowed herself to forget, maybe, how sick Eli was.

"I know, Melody. It's okay."

"And it's no use blaming God, or anyone else, or thinking how unfair it is. One in a million. Any of that malarkey. Because others have it worse. That's for sure. And besides, it just *is*. That's all."

"I can stay, Mel. I'll stay."

"No. Go. Take the keys. I want you to go. I *do*!"

"Okay. I'll go."

BOOK TWO

SPRING BUDDING

Eleven

MELODY COOLED countless glass goblets of chocolate pudding over the next week. Eli loved to pierce the dark skin layer on top with his spoon to reach the creamy-sweet goodness beneath. She plied Eli's chest at bedtime with VapoRub. She stuffed towels beneath his bathroom doorframe to keep the steam in during his showers. She trailed after him to the toilet to monitor his digestive processes, complicated by the antibiotics ("Don't you dare flush!" she warned from outside the door); she kept him hydrated with chicken stock and that new sugary drink he favored, Tang, which Isaac allowed past the threshold as actual orange and grapefruit juice upset Eli's bacteria-stripped stomach.

Isaac, meanwhile, labored in the grove.

Isaac could finally breathe out in the grove, released from the ammoniac hospital halls and their over-chilled home. There was something shameful in this great clutch of salt and citrus air he gathered into his lungs, while Eli's embattled machinery could gather only modest clutches of air, indoors. Even so, he couldn't deny the great relief he felt walking the grove, past the oaks and tamarind—tiny catkin clusters now on the oaks—past the spicy wax myrtle and lantana, the first rays of natural light bathing his face between the trees.

Isaac felt something in the hip pocket of his field trousers and pulled out what appeared to be a letter. Yes, Sam Luckman's letter from a week or so ago. *Drop me a line when you get a chance, okay Thomas Jefferson?* That's how his former partner closed his latest missive. The trousers had been washed with the letter folded inside so the ivory stationery was handkerchief soft, but stained still with some barely legible ink. Sam closed every one of his letters in this general way, referencing famous American gentry. Isaac passed his eyes over the crumpled letter once again on the way to Eli's grove, crammed it back into his hip pocket, glanced up above the row at the cloudless sky for relief. A dragonfly trio—a small iridescent green variety—danced against the blue relief, then darted beyond his field of view. Glorious day on God's green earth. That's how Clay would put it, and Ted. Maybe even Mr. Jefferson himself.

It was always intriguing to see which great American names Sam came up with in his letters, many of whom weren't even farmers. *Be well, William Bartram. Give our best to Melody and the kids, Thoreau. Don't take any wooden nickels, Cotton Mather. Enough for now, William Bradford.*

Fucking Sam.

What was Sam doing but calling him nuts, if only tacitly? Who did he think he was—this Hebe like the rest of them from West Philly—raising oranges and grapefruit in the middle of godforsaken Florida? Isaac was the odd ball, the *meshugener*, the crazy person, the loony tune. Not Sam, who commuted half an hour each way now from Radnor to Center City, who chomped down on calcium tablets like candy to keep his ulcers from flaring, who knocked a stupid white ball around a manicured lawn for pleasure, who struggled to keep pace with the manifold material demands of three grasping daughters.

There was just enough time before their budding conference along Walt's nursery rows to walk Eli's grove and take care of some business. His latest propagation efforts should have taken, little green beads arising from the developed ovaries at the base of the stylar canals. He would replace the paper grocery bags of these specimens with mosquito-net sacks. There might yet be about-to-burst flower buds on some of the late-bearing scions to emasculate and pollinate too. There wasn't a flower to waste. He had brought his dried flowers and pollen in their vials (35-millimeter film canisters, in truth), his surgical equipment, and paper bags. He had secured the folded paper bags inside the waistband of his pants, clumps of net bags in his oversized front pockets for the further-along specimens. He worried after Eli's every breath while he was home, so it offered him great solace to concentrate fully on this one fine thing now. These trees. This up-close work with his hands. The gone-to-seed cowpeas crackled beneath his boots as he reached the first tree.

Citrus improvement was a complicated affair, mostly on account of their randy miscegenate embryos and protracted juvenile periods. W. T. Swingle, at the behest of the U.S. Department of Agriculture, had already ventured the obvious crosses and hybrids some sixty years ago. But the industry had stagnated since Swingle's day. Commissioner Shepherd wasn't wrong about this. Each generation should improve on the former, yes? Here they were, though, still harvesting pretty much the same old Parson Browns, Hamlins, Pineapples, and Valencias. An early season cultivar with high-colored juice, fewer seeds, or both, sure would be something, or a later-bearing variety to round out the season. Might have to pay the field-workers a bit more in the July heat, but it would be worth it. Or, finally, Isaac's most ambitious, pie-in-the-sky undertaking, which had nothing to do with juice at all. Navels! A navel to compete with the California market. His Florida predecessors and peers had given up too soon, had all but ceded the navel to California. That was their failing. Giving up too soon, when there was still some hope for a worthy scion. *That's* what Isaac was up to, to answer the commissioner. Not chimeras. Just meat-and-potatoes genetic selection. The perfection of fruit!

He paused at his "improved" Valencias, later-bearing, he had hoped, with juice every bit as sweet. The buds of definitive and promising true crosses he had topworked (to accelerate production) onto these bearing trees before him two springs ago. So here they were. "Improved" Valencia scions stretching this way and that amid the scaffolding of over-the-hill Hamlins. His Dr. Frankenstein trees, he bitterly recalled Walt's remark. But the fruit had ripened too early. They'd gathered the moldering orbs up from the ground weeks ago to grind into cow feed, Florida's orangeade milk. No improvement. Ted was right. They should have grubbed out these acres, already.

Isaac walked now between his several Valencia rows toward the protected interior of Eli's grove, where the commission men hadn't ventured, his Summerfield, Surprise, and Washington crosses. The navels. A hundred small scions budded on trifoliate orange stock (more resistant to CTV and hard freezes than sour orange stock) stood like sentinels, several of them festooned with white paper bags. The bud unions didn't look so hot at the base, the trifoliate outperforming the scions and swelling over the border like molten lava. Yet the scions took, after all. What Isaac wanted, what the Florida fresh-fruit market needed, was a navel with a thicker, more durable peel for transport, one that nonetheless could be punctured readily enough by human fingernails, flavedo and albedo (the bitter white rind) peeled from the juicy endocarp beneath in meaty hunks. Somewhat thicker membranes would be good too, between the ovarian locules, more distinct, delectable segments for consumers to transfer from their sweet sticky fingers to their mouths.

Isaac started in on the first tree, removed with care the opaque bag to examine the flower within. It had been two weeks since he had emasculated and pollinated this specimen. Ah, yes. Dropped style. Green pea ovule. The fruit had set. He replaced the paper bag with net mesh to protect the fruit from insect incursions, while allowing the entry of light and heat and water. He performed the same exercise on the several other bags up and down the row, never tiring of the up-close work. It was good work, he felt. Necessary and clear. And the day was fine. There were still a rare few terminal flowers on a promising Washington that hadn't opened, likely candidates for the variant of Surprise pollen in one of his vials, so he pried open the first corolla and calyx, reached for his tweezers. He was pleased to observe the stigma at the proper stage, slightly above the anthers, its surface viscous with ooze, ripe for Isaac's pollen. He pulled off each filament and its associated anther with the tweezers, carefully lifted each one off the flower, wiping them on his pantleg. Once all the anthers were removed, he traded his tweezers for his small camel-hair paintbrush and pollen vial. He dipped the brush into the vial of dried Surprise flowers and pollen, swirled it around as if it were a witch's brew. He lifted the brush from the vial and dabbed the golden pollen on the sticky bulbous stigma.

Rapt in his up-close work, the encroachment at the periphery of his field of view, vague rustling amid greenery, startled him. Isaac raised his eyes from the snow-white corolla. It took a few moments for his vision to adjust to the deeper field, the darker human form before him. Ted. He wore a backpack outfitted with a twin-pack of pressurized metal canisters, canisters that had contained DDT and malathion, Hawley's day. Now, under Isaac's command, fatty acids, sesame and fish oils to spot treat foliage and stem that the ladybeetles had neglected to scout.

"Morning, Isaac," Ted uttered, showing his toothpick but not his teeth. Isaac lowered his eyes again and took care to finish what he started, covered his corolla with a white paper bag, secured it to the branch with a precut measure of twine. "Eli Golden feeling better today?" Ted asked.

"Yes. He'll be fine, Ted." *No thanks to you*, Isaac thought next, but didn't say. "He'll be fine."

"Praise the Lord."

"Shouldn't you be overseeing the crew at the Valencias?" Isaac placed both hands at his lower back and arched his shoulders, as if he were a much older man. It irritated Isaac that Ted had joined him here. He'd been more irascible lately, as a general rule, and didn't much like it. But what was he to do? Poor Eli. Fucking Walt. The commissioner now. His meager harvests. Hadn't he chosen a leaner, simpler life, stripped of extraneous confusions? Confusions like Ted?

"Percy and Frederick all right by themselves for a time," Ted insisted, growing bolder, his toothpick dancing between his lips now. "Figured I'd walk the rows for scale and such. Bad news, I'm afraid. Purple scale all over the Hamlins now inside the Hammock Road elbow."

"Oh?"

"I gave 'em the once over, but I don't think this sesame oil's gonna do the job all by itself. Aramite sure would knock 'em out."

Isaac breathed in hard through his nostrils, as if seeking wisdom from the grove air. "There's a new wasp I've been reading about," Isaac proposed. "A parasitic *Aphytis* that's supposed to work. I'll have to go to Lakeland to get them, though."

Ted nodded his head, slowly, doubtfully.

"Aramite sure would do the trick, is the thing," Ted said, looking at the ground, cleared his throat. "These oils and such might be safer and all, I suppose."

It was difficult for Isaac to gauge Ted's level of disappointment with him. Did he simply prefer Old Man Hawley's more conventional grove management style, or did he consider Isaac an outright buffoon with his Dr. Frankenstein experiments, his weedy cover crops between the rows now, his biological pest controls. It wouldn't be good if Ted lost utter faith in the grove. Who knew what the field-workers thought?

Isaac suddenly remembered what Shepherd had said about riled-up field-workers.

"Everything's okay with Percy and Fred and the other men, right?" Isaac never called the field-workers boys, savvy as he was to its denigrating implications, cranium-size lies. Ted kicked at the ground, looked up at Isaac, squinted against the sun that just now peeked over the rows.

"Okay?" Ted asked, lifting the blade of his hand to his forehead now to shield his eyes.

"You know what I mean. On the grove. You don't think it could be one of them bothering the trees, do you?" Ted's caginess irritated Isaac afresh, irritated him more than was warranted, probably.

"No," Ted answered, frowning. "Can't imagine it could be one of our workers."

"I mean, I can only pay co-op rates." Isaac reflexively spat out a gnat that had invaded his mouth, a dry series of spittings. "It's a collective decision," he regrouped, wiping his mouth. "Set rates. Out of my hands." This wasn't entirely true. There was nothing stopping him from paying his field-workers a bit more if he chose. The other co-op fellows sprinkled sweeteners around some. A couple extra dollars end of the week to the best pickers to keep the wheels greased. Walt, he knew, plied the workers with cases of Pabst and Schlitz cans Friday afternoons during peak harvest, claimed to enjoy watching the boys tottering off his grove, happy and garrulous.

Ted nodded, slowly. "Just hard times is all. Hard times all around."

Isaac bit his lip. This wasn't the answer he was looking for. Hard times. "Yes," Isaac agreed. "Tell me about it." He had hoped to curry sympathy, or at least the expression of sympathy. But Isaac's response didn't yield the desired effect. The brightest of dawns seemed to rise on Ted's face.

"I'll buy some acres, you willing to sell. These acres right here, maybe, ready to be grubbed out and turned over, I'd say. Ten or so. Ten or so acres I can afford. Now Levi up on his feet."

A woodpecker laughed from somewhere in the nearby foliage. Maybe two birds, Isaac suspected.

Levi was Erma and Ted's eldest son, who had suffered ambiguous brushes with law enforcement after Korea (petty theft, from what Isaac gathered), but had been working steady for several years up north, in New York City if memory served. Last Isaac had heard, anyway. Isaac didn't quite know what to make of his tribal name. Levi.

"Well, you know, Ted, that wasn't what I had in mind, is the thing. Selling off land."

Ted nodded, sucked on his cheeks. "I best mind what I came here to do. Just something to chew on is all." Ted disappeared into the next row of trees. Isaac could hear a few long breaths of Ted's sprayer before his foreman was out of earshot.

People, Isaac thought, moving on to a new specimen. He teased open a terminal flower, exposing unripe anthers and shrunken stigma. No good, this one. People just didn't do what you wanted them to do. That was the crux of it, Isaac was convinced. If Isaac had it his way, Ted would be happy with his weekly pay, the perk of Erma's employment at the stand to boot. He'd just be happy, period, and run interference with the field-workers. But, of course, if *Ted* had it his way, Isaac figured, white men wouldn't have the run of the place. They wouldn't arrange auctions of whole lots, rather than parcels, designed precisely (if not advertised as such) to keep Negroes from gaining a toehold. Northern Jews with their money and fancy degrees would stay in the North rather than descend on acres Ted had broken his back over near forty years. Ted had the greater complaint, Isaac allowed, which only exasperated Isaac further. What was Ted doing on these acres a moment ago, anyway, but scouting out his future property? On Isaac's dime!

The problem of other people.

People exerted all their force to get other people to see things their way. Walt and his noxious pesticides and herbicides, Shepherd and his citrus fantasies, Melody and her summer ambitions for the stand, Ted and his landowning aspirations. Perhaps he ought to adopt his father's way of seeing things. His father wouldn't have had much of a problem with Ted.

"Listen, I'm not my brother's keeper," his father liked to say on the phone when talking business. Isaac always knew when his father was talking business, because he spoke standing up, the slack in the cord wound up in his fist like brass knuckles. It was a phrase Isaac's father used often enough that he remembered its many utterances. Or maybe it was on account of its strangeness—its biblical derivation unknown to Isaac as a youngster—that it imprinted itself in Isaac's memory. *Listen, Sollie, am I my brother's keeper? It's nishta here nishta there, Herbie, we're not our brother's keepers. You want to be a schlemiel and give him your share of the commission, fine by me, but I'm not my brother's keeper.*

Isaac couldn't quite adopt his father's no-nonsense credo vis-à-vis other people. Fathering Eli had somehow made him more susceptible to complaint. Softer before others, if strangely harder, steeled, at home. He found himself brooding over Ted as he lumbered down his row toward the house, his nostrils drenched with pollen, the glimmering sunlight blinking against his brow in between the shade of his experimental Hamlins and Valencias and Parson Browns. Here was this person, Isaac thought. Ted. What does this person want from me? What shall I give? Or maybe this was the wrong way of looking at it. Maybe it wasn't the person himself who wanted something. To think of it this way was to miss the point, entirely. There was a want, to be sure, a demand even, but not a demand arising from the individual. A grander source, rather. A person stood before him, a person like any other person in his life—Melody, Shepherd, Walt, his struggling scion Eli, the baby—and existed in Isaac's life, purposively. Not at random. Isaac had only failed to anticipate Ted. Had failed, utterly. Every person a test, of sorts, delivered by . . . who? Here on the sunbaked row, his wet face pasted with the grove's effluvia (pollen, salt, unwary insects, dust), his half-moon fingernails encrusted with dirt, Isaac found himself contemplating the eye of God.

Twelve

IT FELT UNCOMMONLY GOOD to send Eli off to school this first morning, to walk her son down to the highway with his backpack, glimpse the yellow bus approach from the dusty distance, hear the oyster shells crunch under the tires, the brakes whine, the whoosh of the hydraulics, watch Eli scale the two steep steps to board.

"Welcome aboard, young fella, we missed ya," Mr. Langford saluted her boy, his sausage fingers gripping the metal lever to the accordion door.

"A blessed morning to you, Mr. Langford." Melody was feeling so expansive that she deployed a bit of the local patois.

"Ma'am."

It was just like one of those Mercury rockets, Melody contemplated, a school bus. You climbed onto the ship and it could take you anywhere. It really was a super country. So why did she feel this pang in her stomach as the bus rumbled on its way, as she bobbed Sarah in her arms? She wouldn't wave at Eli for fear of embarrassing him. It wasn't anxiety over Eli's first day back. Rather, a faint but palpable envy inspired that visceral twinge, she realized, making her way back to the small house, shifting Sarah back to her other hip, the loose river rock giving beneath her slippers, Eli heading off, Melody heading back indoors. She walked around the side of the house to the back to look about before going inside. Isaac must have weeded the garden. Good. She wondered what Iz was doing out there in the grove today, and where he was, exactly. Standing in this one perfect spot, she could see past the feathery tamarind, the triad of oaks with their shaggy beards and the scruffy shrubs right into the grove between two rows of twenty-year trees, a clearing that went down so far—clear to the river and Dummitt's Island beyond, practically—that she couldn't see to see where it ended. She inhaled the spice air from the wax myrtle and lantana to take some of the outside in with her before climbing the back porch.

She fed Sarah a breakfast of mashed bananas and prunes (to offset the bananas) by the kitchen bay window and then sat her down in the playpen in the family room. She'd tend to her correspondence, she decided, sliding up the tambour on her father's Amish roll-top desk. She liked the sound of the wooden curtain riding along its track, smooth still thanks to Isaac's occasional treatments with the everlasting tin can of 3-IN-ONE Oil. The desk was one of her father's few extravagant purchases, picked up on a lark during one of their otherwise frugal long-weekend vacations in Lancaster. The wood was aspen, purportedly, though it seemed like ordinary oak to her. Not a particularly practical configuration, too many small square compartments scaling the walls rather than proper drawers, as if it were designed for an apothecary. But Melody supposed that her father—an accountant who savored clean calculations—must have found all these tidy little drawers enticing.

Sarah mewled and chortled over her Yuban coffee tin in the playpen beside her, worrying its ridges with her tiny fingers, her brow knitted, her lips pursed over her gums. Such determination over this plain old tin can, Melody marveled. Sarah had just started to sit up, and this new perspective on the world had inspired her earnest inquiry on whatever came under her gaze. Soon she'd be crawling, off to the races, and then it would be harder to look after her. She was unusually smart, it seemed to Melody. Or else all babies unburdened by their own breath behaved this way. In any case, Sarah's gainful employment with the Yuban tin afforded Melody the time to savor Dottie Gelb's letter. She had received it in the mail yesterday, but deposited it inside the cocoon of the roll-top so that she might appreciate it in the morning, when she wasn't so beaten down by Sarah's grasping and pleading, and Eli's grasping and pleading, and Isaac's complaints about the grove, and that horrible Walt Boehringer with the creepy red mustache. She gazed for a moment at Dot's fine cursive on the Crane's envelope (she used such nice stationery), the four-cent Boys' Club of America Movement postage stamp, its hundred-year anniversary, apparently. Amazing country. That you could send a first-class letter anywhere in the country for four cents. The stamp featured a crimson profile of a handsome youngster, a copious shock of wavy hair and full lips. Did Dottie select the stamp with Eli in mind?

Retrieving the letter opener from the desktop (it was too long to fit in one of the useless compartments) Melody sliced open the seal of the cotton fiber envelope and unfolded the thick leaf.

Dearest Melody,

Sorry it's been so long since I've written. Time does fly, doesn't it? Carol, Barbara, and I (the girls!) sure do miss you. How's Eli-le? No lung problems, I hope. We still can't believe that you've been gone so long. I feel bad saying this, but we thought you'd be back by now. That's what Carol said: They'll be back before Tish B'Av. We thought you both (Iz mainly) just needed to work through some things. Eli. And your poor parents, may their memory be for a blessing. But you showed us, didn't you? I don't mean to sound like a snot. That's not how I mean. You know I'd never hear a harsh word about you. I wish you'd come up to see our new house in Bryn Mawr. Carol and Irv and Barbara and Sam live just down the street in Radnor. You know we all joined the country club there, right? It really does feel like the country here. Such big trees and lawns! Maple and sycamore and elm and chestnut and ginkgo. We had cardinals nesting in the forsythia out back. Sandy and Laurie watched them every day. I know it's only a half hour away or so from the old neighborhood, but it seems like a different planet. America! You drive down Montgomery and the trees canopy the whole road, and there's a babbling brook on the left. A real babbling brook! What was that Longfellow poem we had to memorize in school? A big rock juts out too and the trucks have to swerve around it. I asked at the children's school why they didn't dynamite it and you know what they told me? George Washington himself camped under that rock back during the Revolutionary War. Aaron Burr's headquarters, too, are right there, although he did something bad, right? Stupid me. I don't know anything. It must really feel like the country where you are, even though you said there aren't too many tall trees. Hard to imagine no elms. Or maples. But you have oaks, right? And palms trees of course. Not to mention all your oranges and grapefruit. We're still eating the grapefruit from the last crate you sent! So super, it must be, picking your own fruit from the tree. How's Iz doing with his experiments? We read in the papers about the rocket tests at the base. How close are you again to all that? Can you hear and see those tests? Next we'll be sending a man to the moon, they say. Are they serious, you think? Imagine that, Melody. In our lifetimes. Well, enough already. Genug, shoyn! as your dear parents would say. Please write, soon. You don't write to us, enough. All the girls say so. And send another polaroid of the baby.

Your friend,
Dottie

Melody pressed Dottie's words to her chest and took a deep breath, sighing as she exhaled. For whatever reason, she barely breathed while she read letters from her friends and needed to take a few deep breaths afterwards to restore the oxygen to her lungs. There was something glorious about receiving and reading a letter. She could hear Dottie's voice so clearly in her ear, her growls and clicks, the snap of her Doublemint against her silver fillings. She might as well have been right there next to her in the family room, reading the words she had written. Reading these words scrawled several days ago was more intimate, somehow, than hearing Dottie's muted voice over the long-distance wire, seasoned with salty static. Who could stay up late enough for the Bell rates to go down, anyway?

Melody considered writing back, even started the first lines of a letter—*Dearest Dottie, So super to receive your latest letter and hear how well you're all doing in the new neighborhood. Things here*—but stopped when it occurred to her that she'd have to mention the worrisome attacks on their grove trees and Eli's latest crisis. She was simply no good at withholding vital information, so she decided to wait a few days until there was something else more hopeful to report on the Eli front: a good grade on his arithmetic, maybe, his bounding once again through the grove, a mangrove snapper mess in her kitchen. She would shower, instead, and head out to the stand to join Erma. Her pulse quickened at the thought of this small escape from the house. Just yards from the front door, but an escape, nonetheless. Contact with grown-ups. Actual people. Thank heavens for the stand.

Melody grasped Sarah beneath her underarms and headed to the master bedroom and shower. She disrobed first, then removed Sarah's onesie and drenched diaper on the bed over a changing pad, rolled the bloated diaper like a rug, and taped Sarah's urine shut inside. She'd discard it in the nearly full kitchen trash and take the bag outside on the way to the stand. Brand new invention, these thick throwaway diapers. Just hit the Piggly Wiggly shelves a few months ago—nick of time for Sarah—and there would be no turning back for Melody. Impossible for her to believe now that she had folded and pinned countless cotton diapers for Eli, that she had scrubbed heaps of them by hand in the washroom sink under torrents of scalding water after emptying as much of the putrid waste as she could into the toilet. Whoever invented Pampers deserved a medal. A Nobel Prize! Those rocket scientists on the Cape could wait in line as far as Melody was concerned. The time alone restored to her!

Melody, bracing the baby on her hip, scrubbed Pepsodent over her teeth. She'd put Sarah down on the bathroom rug, but the baby enjoyed watching the strange spectacle in the vanity mirror, her mother lathering up the toothpaste foam, then spitting it out into the sink. Sarah flashed a wet tooth and batted the air with her free hand. The ritual complete, Melody carried Sarah with her over the high lip of the porcelain-frosted cast iron tub and sat her down at the end. She closed the curtain, adjusted the water's heat under the faucet, then pulled the lever for the shower head and aimed it so the perfect volume of water ricocheted off her body to sprinkle, but not douse, Sarah. Creases upon creases circled the baby's plump arms and legs like planetary rings. Fat dimples winked like stars from the wet flesh between. Melody lathered copious Breck suds into her hair, rinsed carefully to keep the soap from splashing into Sarah's eyes below, then smoothed the Camay bar over her flesh, pleased on the whole with her restored figure. She hadn't let herself go, like some of the other girls back home. Zaftig Dottie for one. The cabbage leaves beneath Melody's brassiere had stanched her milk and her modest breasts had returned to their essential geometry. Her tummy too had mostly tightened and cocoa butter had smoothed, if not erased, the four pale fingers that still splayed upward from her navel. Oh well. It was the navel itself that smarted some. It had popped during both pregnancies, but never quite withdrew into her abdomen after Sarah. She pressed down on the soft bulb now, her back to the shower head, rivulets of water coursing over her shoulders down her fine clavicles, over that navel bulb to her dark sex below, then down the inside of her thighs to the tapered ankles Melody couldn't help but admire. As much as she pressed on her navel, though, the soft bulb just wouldn't stay put, poking its head back up immediately to breathe. Isaac didn't seem to care, or even notice, just as he didn't care a whit about her fine ankles. Sarah chortled below and flashed a wet tooth, having spied her mother's silly poking and prodding of her extruded navel.

"You think Mommy's awfully funny, don't you?" Melody cooed.

This utter lack of bodily privacy was one thing that she somehow hadn't anticipated before having babies. Yet she wouldn't leave Sarah alone in her crib or playpen when she showered beneath the deafening stream. What if the baby got her hands on some stray object and choked on it, or smothered herself with her blanket? And Sarah was a merry companion in the shower, in any case. The baby relished her bath time, clapping now, enjoying the *plashing* sounds of the water smacking against her palms.

The stand. Sarah down for her morning nap in the perambulator beneath the whirring fan, Melody culled depleted produce with Erma—shrunken citrus globes from their grove, parched peppers, their skins riding loose and wrinkly over the softened pulp, shriveled green bean fingers from Deland, Plant City strawberries in their fuzzy jackets exuding their cloying breath.

"Mr. Eli back at school today?" Erma inquired.

"Thank heavens."

The pair continued turning over fistfuls of beans, nodding their heads, thoughts of Eli and heaven inspiring their protracted silence, save for the barely audible growl that seemed to emanate from somewhere deep within Erma.

"Must worry about that poor child something awful," she finally uttered. "Mmm-mmm. Something awful."

"We count our blessings," Melody heard herself say, shocking herself. Her mother's words—although her mother would conclude with a *kine-ahora* flourish. Melody had resented the frequent refrain.

Whenever Melody dared express an emotion bordering on self-pity, heaven forbid: *You should count your blessings, kine-ahora.* There was something hard and impregnable and not quite human in her mother's stern counsel. Sweet as sugar to Eli, Noma Herskowitz, but not so sweet with her daughter, as if she feared softening her when Melody truly needed some toughening. Good intentions aside, Melody would have appreciated some unalloyed sympathy now and again. She liked to think that her mother would have come around had she lived long enough.

"Life sure is a strange thing," she heard Erma say. "Never know. Ones you lose sleep over now might turn out right fine. Your pride and joy today runs into trouble tomorrow. Lord works in mysterious ways. Eli might grow up big and strong."

"Maybe. We can hope, anyway, right?" Melody tried to keep the tone bright.

"Hope and pray," Erma added. "Sure does have spirit, that child." Melody glanced toward Erma, her amused mouth flashing silver now. "Way he runs after mischief in his grove. Gracious."

Melody found herself contemplating Erma's words as she headed back to check on Sarah in the perambulator. Did Erma mean to offer hope for Eli or was there a warning about Sarah there to be gleaned? Or both? How much was Erma revealing about her own children? That bad one, Levi, their eldest, whom Melody had never met. Had he turned out all right, after all? Or was there some golden scion who had disappointed her?

Sarah still slept peacefully, sucking on her lower lip as if it were a pacifier. It was good that she never took a pacifier. One less habit to break her from down the road. Melody considered returning to the vegetable bins to take up these questions with Erma, but decided against it. She hadn't memorized the names of most of Erma's children for one thing, and it was really none of her business to pry. They weren't quite intimates, Melody and Erma. Partly because Erma was her employee, and there should be certain boundaries. And partly because of their ages. Erma's children were long out of the house, which made her very life seem past tense to Melody, thick as she was in the business of Eli and Sarah now. Plus, Melody was Jewish, after all, while Erma was a Negro. A strong current of sympathy flowed, but they didn't swim in the same waters, exactly. It sure would be nice to have just one of her people down here. Someone like Dottie. There was Isaac, of course, but he didn't so much listen to her words lately as withstand them, his own problems on the grove—those embattled acres—weightier concerns by far.

The first car pulled up, which impelled Melody to man the antique register behind the counter. She opened its mouth to check on her change (*got it*), then shut the tray and sighed, glanced down at her reading material. She should really start the novel by that Harper Lee everyone was talking about—she had splurged on the hardcover—but she didn't want to think so hard this morning. She flipped through an old issue of *McCall's*, instead. Wasn't it about time Eleanor Roosevelt gave up her silly column and relax? *Flip.* A royal lemon pie filling ad gave her an idea. She'd try her hand at citrus pies to complement pecan and apple. Isaac's sweet Meyer lemons. Having pretty much figured out how to bake lard-crusted Florida pies after several doomed attempts, Melody still hadn't quite mustered the courage to put out her *treyf* pies for sale. But she had brought out a pecan and had placed it behind the counter, from which she had decided to offer free samples to willing taste-testers. Mary Beth sure would be frosted once she found out that Melody was baking and selling her own pies. *Flip.* She had dog-eared the sewing pattern for a smart waist-length jacket she never got around to attempting. She could wear it during the dry season here. She would teach Sarah to sew one day on the Singer. The thought made her smile, and the smile felt good on her face. She lifted a hand to feel her mouth.

The first customers were milling about now.

"Morning, praise Jesus," the husband greeted Erma.

"Morning, praise Him," Erma returned the greeting, flashing her silver mouth, sifting through the black-purple eggplant gourds with somewhat greater energy, as if mention of their Lord was a mild stimulant. "Praise Him," Erma repeated. This was one thing that Erma and Ted shared with the white gentry, the locals and the tourists—even the unabashed bigots with their confederate license plates, ball caps, and chewing tobacco—that Melody could never share. Jesus, that special Him to whom they all constantly, casually referred. These Christians always seemed so happy with their salutations. She envied them their easeful camaraderie.

These two were midwesterners, Melody could tell, because they drove a sensible boxy sedan and superfluous r's kept stampeding over the vowels inside their words, and the husband had asked Erma next where he could discard his bottle of "pop." Plus, Melody noticed their Illinois plates when their sedan pulled to a crunchy halt on the oyster-shell parking strip. The midwesterners tended to stay on the Gulf Coast, but increasingly they crossed the I-10 to poke around this new space coast. And so here these two were, loitering up and down the aisles of vegetable and fruit pyramids, orchids and honey. It wasn't a planned stop, she could tell. Tourists rarely planned on coming across the stand. But something about the woman's affect, trailing after her husband—she clucked her tongue at the signage above the thick tangle of beans, she crossed her arms above the Valencia pyramid, refused to cradle even one of the gleaming waxed fruits in her palm—told Melody that this woman wasn't one to diverge from her plans. She eavesdropped on the pair from behind the counter, flipped absently through the photographs in *Life*. Elizabeth Taylor. Friskies dog food. Inside the White House with JFK.

"Now Carl, let's think," the wife brayed over the Valencias. "We can't just spend money willy-nilly. We already bought a fine gift for Catherine, the orange blossom perfume and key lime bathroom soaps in Jacksonville. And nothing for the boys. Not a thing. Now how will her brothers feel when we give her a crate of oranges, in addition? On top of the perfume and the soap?"

"It's just she enjoys oranges so," the husband replied.

"To spend money willy-nilly."

They were close to the age her parents would be, Melody thought, and it made her sad to hear them quibble. The Depression must have hit these midwesterners hard. Or else it had to do with their received version of Christianity. Lutheranism? Or their Scandinavian stock, perhaps? Whoever said Jews were cheap, anyway, didn't spend sufficient time in the Midwest with these gentiles.

"I can give y'all three crates for the price of two," Melody finally heard herself utter, her down-south dialect issuing naturally somehow from her person. She'd offer them three crates for the price of one were she not worried that they'd grow suspicious. (It was almost the rainy season. Every day she and Erma sifted through the crates and replaced softened oranges with fresher ones.) It pained her to think of their poor daughter denied—a pretty name, Catherine—all over the mother's careful calculus to enact an unimpeachable distribution of parental affection. There was something bloodless about the woman's logic that made Melody recoil. It was simply no use trying to dole out one's affections like pie in perfectly equal slices. Pretty soon it ceased to be affection, at all, slicing it up in sharp angles. If mothering Eli and Sarah taught her anything, it was that nothing was equal or fair, anyway. The thing to do was love your children truly, which wasn't the same, quite, as equally.

"They're a Golden variety?" the husband asked. "We saw the sign."

"No. Sorry. That confuses everyone. They're Valencias. Sweetest orange there is. *We're* Goldens. It's our name. There's no Golden orange. 'Least not yet. Husband's working on it." Melody bobbed her head eastward toward the grove. "Here, try."

Melody halved a Valencia at the counter with a budding knife, then sliced each half into three equal segments with decisive strokes of the blade, then teased peel from pulp quarter-way down each segment by curving her wrist tight, taking care to slice off as much of the bitter white albedo as she could. She enjoyed performing this simple surgery for visitors. The couple, for their part, didn't seem to notice.

"Germanic origin?" the wife inquired.

"Helen," the husband said.

"Hmm?"

"Your name, dear."

"Oh. No. Jewish," Melody said, handing a prepared segment to the woman, then to the husband, who thanked her.

"My lands, of course," the woman replied, focusing her eyes afresh on the raven-haired southerner before her, jostling her head atop her frame in a reflexive spasm as if to clear a separate image from her mental screen. "I'm so sorry, dear." Her whole mien was softer now, creases of heartfelt worry between her pallid eyes.

"Sorry?" Melody asked. Erma, she noticed, was elbow deep again in the beans behind them, culling shriveled fingers.

"Now Helen," the husband said at a higher, exasperated pitch.

"I mean about that Holocaust over there, dear. That's what they're calling it now, I'm fairly certain?"

The woman's rising pitch suggested that this was a question.

"Yes," Melody said. "I suppose so."

"We saw that *Exodus* movie last year with Eva Marie Saint and that handsome young actor, what was his name?" She furrowed her brow and rubbed her thumb against her fingers to summon the actor's name, but couldn't quite remember.

"Newman," the husband said. "Paul Newman, you mean."

"Yes, Paul Newman. Anyway, it's all over the news now. The Holocaust. That Eichmann devil's going to get what's coming to him now that you finally captured him."

"The Israelis," Melody said. "The Israelis captured him."

"Of course," the woman uttered, her mouth descending into a confused frown.

"So is this where that Project Mercury . . . pilot—"

"Astronaut, Helen. They're called astronauts."

"Is this really where that pilot launched a few weeks ago?" The woman wrinkled her nose and glanced dubiously west across the small highway at the scruffy land, the flowerless foliage. "From here?"

Melody didn't like the way the woman said *From here?* as if she couldn't imagine that anything significant could actually transpire in such a dusty benighted place. She wouldn't offer her a free sample of her pecan pie from behind the counter, after all.

"Well, not here exactly. Across the river. On the Cape. Few miles south."

"Ahh, a few miles south," the woman said, as if she had won an argument.

"We'll take those three Valencia crates," the husband offered by way of charity, reaching deep into his right front pocket.

The rest of the day took its time. Customers, mostly locals, drifted in with the breeze—a less common west breeze today, more menthol from the pines than salt from the sea—taking pit stops on their way back and forth from Daytona, mostly to divert themselves. They made small obligatory purchases. A couple of the girls from Junior League, useless small purses dangling from their arms, bought juice and eggplant. That recipe from the new *Better Homes and Gardens Cookbook*, eggplant parmigiana, was popular now with the girls, and the Piggly Wiggly didn't even carry eggplant. Clay's wife, Pearl, purchased a small jar of honey, which Melody knew she didn't need—they used the same beekeeper for their groves, after all—though Melody didn't attempt to deter her. It was kind of Pearl to buy their honey and there wasn't enough kindness in the world. She had offered Pearl a generous slice of pecan pie in exchange, which Pearl devoured with a plastic fork. It wasn't so smart to offer Pearl a slice before giving Mary Beth fair warning. This only occurred to Melody after Pearl's sedan grumbled off, leaving a fragrant exhaust wake. Before the day was out, MB would know all about Melody's pie. Pearl wouldn't be able to help herself. Oh well.

Come lunchtime, she strolled Sarah back to the house in the perambulator to feed her a lunch of peas Melody had mashed, apples she had sauced. (It was just easier feeding the baby indoors and not *shlepping* the food and cutlery to the stand.) Back at the stand, behind the counter with the baby, Melody licked the salty wet beads above her plump upper lip. Sarah in her onesie didn't seem fazed by the heat. She chortled in her makeshift E. Bean crate-bordered playpen as she worried the ridges of an acorn squash with her tiny fingers. Summer was pretty much here. Besides the heat, there was the light that was different, a whiter light with shorter shadows, the sun tracking higher in the sky, almost directly above the corrugated metal stand roof as it made its impossible journey from the waters over the Cape all the way behind the slash pines to the west beyond their managed acres. A miraculous thing, a day in the life. A long hot day in the life. Not something that would have occurred to Melody up north, miraculous days a Florida thought.

It was then that she spotted him, her mind on miracles. He was a colored man, a Negro, wearing a smart suit with a slender yellow necktie. He must have pulled the car up quietly at the north end beyond her field of view. She scanned the aisles instinctively for Erma, seeking her out as if for protection against this besuited Negro. A shameful reflex, maybe. Yet she couldn't quash the habit. Negro women or whole families didn't inspire the same trepidation. Only individual Negro men somehow raised a red flag. On the rare occasion a Negro man by his lonesome crossed her threshold, her eyes darted about to perform a quick scan of the premises—the baby, her employees, the cash register, errant stock—gauging vulnerabilities, lines of defense, avenues of escape. Silly. They'd never had a problem. The Negroes around here knew better, especially after what happened in Mims to that poor school principal and his wife, firebombed in their sleep. A Negro wouldn't dare attack a white woman, Jewish or otherwise. Not in blackest night, and certainly not in broad daylight. In any case, there was no sign of Erma all of sudden. Probably in their small stockroom.

"Morning ma'am." He lifted a small hand to an imaginary hat. Melody remembered when men wore hats as a matter of course. Now they mostly gestured toward imaginary ones. Who knew how long they'd keep that up?

"Good morning." She offered a toothless smile, welcoming but not too welcoming.

"You serve Negroes, I expect?"

"Of course." Melody knitted her fine dark eyebrows to feign offense, though it was a legitimate question. None of that crude *White* and *Colored* signage about town, but everyone knew the rules. Negroes sick enough to seek out the hospital knew that the small wooden door at the west wing was their entrance and exit, that their soiled linens and serving ware would be scrubbed in separate machines; Negroes still sat upstairs only at the Magnolia Theater beside the hot clacking projector; Negroes only ate at the black-owned restaurant on Hopkins, not at Janisse's; after dusk, Negroes didn't dare venture west of Hopkins and the tracks into the center of town. Everyone knew the rules. Which was why there was no need for signage.

From a pure business standpoint, Melody couldn't imagine ever turning away perfectly good money. More and more Negro families ambled down the highway on weekend trips from as far away as Atlanta. There was a green guidebook they seemed to consult, Melody noticed, which helped them navigate Jim Crow, just starting to founder hereabouts. (Goldens Are Here was far too rinky-dink an operation to merit mention in any guidebook.) From what Melody gathered, their stretch of Florida had never quite been as bad as Groveland, or Live Oak, or Sanford, or Apopka, inland. There weren't quite enough people here, period, to set up race hatred in earnest. Not even a White Citizens' Council, far as she knew.

"Shucks, ma'am, I meant no offense."

She liked the way he said "shucks." He was much smaller than she originally suspected now that he was standing directly before her across the counter. He smelled vaguely of talcum, she thought, and looked like that handsome Day-O singer from the *Carmen Jones* movie with the high broad forehead like a porpoise, which advertised the active mind inside. Only this Negro seemed lighter, like milk sweetened with Hershey's syrup. Lighter than Erma and Ted. His pasting of tight curls, like that Day-O singer's, stopped well short of where his porpoise forehead started its downward slope, except for in the middle, where his hairline dripped farther over the broad precipice, pointing the way toward a fine aquiline nose that didn't have that flared Negro look at all.

"I was only teasing," he continued.

"Oh. . . . I see."

It was awfully nervy of this Negro fellow to tease her at her own place of business. She had never been teased by a Negro man before.

Something about the way he looked at her—*that* he looked at her, right in the eyes—unnerved Melody.

"Something I can help you with? You're here for the oranges, I presume."

"Oranges. Yes, the oranges," he declared, as if the thought of oranges just occurred to him. What was his *shtick*? Melody wondered. Where was Erma, already? It wasn't that she felt threatened. He couldn't seem less a threat. He held his small hands before his yellow necktie in a peaceful clasp, like a rabbi giving a sermon. His nails were pared short, revealing only the slightest moon-slivers. They were unusual for Negro hands, small and clean and uncalloused—hands that didn't pull fruit or fix engines or dig trenches.

"Goldens carry the finest oranges on the river. That's the word."

"Well, the word's the word," Melody replied, taken aback by her own brighter tone now, as if she had just caught on to the tune this Negro had been humming. "Let me offer you a sample." She performed her simple surgery with the budding knife and Valencia before him. She sliced each half into three equal segments, teased peel from pulp quarter-way down each segment, sliced off practically the whole bitter white albedo this time.

"Mm-mmm, the Mrs. sure knows her way around a knife. Husband best be careful."

"Melody," she told him her name. "He is." This last bit might have been a warning, but not the way she said it.

The man didn't offer his name in return. Instead, he lifted an orange wedge to his mouth below the fine dusting of a mustache. Melody turned her eyes away, toward sleeping Sarah, as he teased the orange flesh from its rind with his teeth, freed peel from pulp. He consumed the sweet fruit with hardly a sound. She could scarcely hear the kiss of his mouth bursting the juice vesicles as he chewed and swallowed. It never ceased to amuse Melody the way different sorts went about the business of eating an orange wedge. Some left the peel on as they chewed, worked the small wedge at their mouth with two hands as if it were a harmonica, while others freed fruit from peel as quickly as possible; some wolfed down the bolus of pulp in a single swallow as if they were in it for the quick calories, while others nibbled gingerly, rodent-like, licking their lips all the while; some chewed with their mouths open, smacking their lips, chewed up remnants of fruit visible within the moist cavern of their mouths, while others pursed their lips so tight as they chewed that they couldn't much enjoy the exercise of eating; some growled audibly as they savored the sweet nectar, while others ate so quietly you'd hardly know they were breathing. She liked the way this Negro ate, quiet but not too quiet, neat but not too neat.

"Napkin?"

"Much obliged," he said, dabbing the sticky corners of his mouth, leaning forward some so the juice wouldn't dribble on his yellow tie. Melody waited for his appraisal of her fruit.

"Delicious," he finally said. "I'll purchase one of those red nets you've got there on the counter." He reached into his pocket and pulled out a fistful of silver and copper. "Boys all through with the picking for the season?"

"Nearly so," she said. It was sort of an odd query, but Melody didn't think much of it. Just making conversation, she supposed. It wasn't always easy to think of what to say to fill the air.

Melody was just about to offer the Negro a slice of pecan pie when Luke approached. She recognized the towheaded, cowlicked Luke at an instant, cleared her throat, stood up somewhat straighter. Her Negro customer must have noticed young Luke's approach too, because he didn't look into Melody's eyes anymore as he accepted his small change back.

"I'll just be getting on my way, ma'am," he said to the cement slab floor. "Good afternoon." He tipped his imaginary hat before pivoting on his heels, then walked clear around the Plant City berries to offer the young white man a wide berth. Luke, for his part, didn't seem to notice the Negro fellow at all, young white men not having to notice Negro men much in the course of their day, Melody supposed.

Luke stopped by the stand once a week or so, flirted harmlessly with her as he made his small purchases, miscellaneous fruits the Piggly Wiggly didn't carry, fruits he probably didn't eat. Melody was no fool. She knew Luke drove the few miles each week mostly to see her, and she made no attempt to dissuade him. Truth was, his attentions flattered her, offered her a pleasant diversion, and she knew how to deflect his harmless advances. She wouldn't let things get out of hand. Soon enough he'd have a steady and that would be that.

But she navigated Luke clumsily today.

"You sure are a sight for sore eyes, Mrs. Golden," he said first thing, grasping a straw basket. "My my," he shook his head over the overripe berries.

"Those are awfully pretty words you're wasting on me, young man."

Here he looked up at her. "I only meant to pay you a compliment, Mrs. Golden. That's all I meant."

"I'm a married woman, Luke."

"I know that. Hell, you think I don't know that? What do you take me for?" Now Luke seemed downright angry, and older. A furrow she'd never noticed before emerged on his scarlet forehead.

"Nothing. I mean, I wasn't suggesting, uh"—Melody fumbled for the right words—"I shouldn't have said anything. I apologize. Can I offer you an orange?" Her hands trembled as she reached for the budding knife.

Her encounter with the Negro fellow was to blame. It had taken her some effort to strike the right key with the smartly dressed Negro, and now here was Luke singing an altogether less subtle tune that eluded her harmony.

"Naah. Your fruit ain't no good, anyway. And it costs too much." He dropped his straw basket where he stood, glanced over toward where the Negro had fled.

"Luke! Luke, please!" The utter change in his manner stunned her. "Wait!" But he was gone.

The baby sat stock still within her E. Bean crate fortress, clutching her squash, her eyes fixed on her mother, anticipating her next syllable. Sarah had somehow intuited the awkward adult cadences, her mother's discomfiture.

"Oh Sarah-le," Melody declared, gazing down at the sprout. "Looks like Mommy went and made a mess of things." She crouched to pick up the baby, if only to garner some selfish human comfort. Sarah raised her arms, eager for the attention.

She had overreacted to Luke's schoolboy flirtations. Melody wondered whether she had let her vanity get the better of her, after all. With all the lithe giggling fair-haired girls in town, what would a young man want with a tired Jewish mother of two? He had said so himself. Her fruit was no good. So what had gotten into her? It was that Negro fellow. But how had he thrown her so far off course? Was she drawn toward him? She couldn't fathom carrying on with a Negro. The very strangeness of his body. The dark skin, that lamb's wool hair, dark as her own, but curly. All over his body, surely, that dark lamb's wool hair. His bottom lip was curiously pink and pale compared to his dark purple upper lip. Those lips pressed full on her lips. His dark flesh against her olive flesh. His deep talcum powder smell drenching her nostrils as they lay entwined, her tapered ankles wrapped inside his lean calves. She couldn't fathom it, until it dawned upon her that she *could* fathom such a thing, that it was precisely the vision she'd conjured while she licked the salt from above her swollen upper lip. A sudden bout of hiccups seized her, almost painfully. She felt the hair rise at her nape, her nipples pressed sore against her brassiere.

"Oh my, Sarah-le. Oh my."

Thirteen

All the river growers except for Isaac—where was he? Clay wondered—knelt before Walt's rootstock as if in prayer. Spring budding. Hard for Clay to believe they used to grow bearing trees from seed back in the day. So many years till first harvest—frost, fungus, foot rot, pests or pestilence of some other ilk didn't kill your tree in the meantime. Plus hardly true to type, most citrus seed. Confused little bundles, most seed. Plant a seed from inside a Hamlin orange and any number and variety of shoots might spring up from God's green earth. Kumquat, Key lime, Duncan grapefruit. They must have culled a crapload of worthless mystery trees back in the day. But must have appreciated that first true harvest. A single orange, no small miracle.

To get around those mixed-up seeds and get to first harvest faster, the old salts, a couple generations older than Clay's daddy, moved on to grafting first: splice graft, tongue graft, whip graft, American whip graft, cleft graft, saddle graft. Now they budded, ever since Captain Dummitt's day, that tomcat, splitter of black wood, as Walt liked to joke, which made Clay's stomach roil. The quickest process, budding. Rather than set whole branches on full-grown rootstock, which didn't always take, Dummitt propagated single buds to year-old sour orange stock, when he wasn't busy shooting up the Seminoles or carrying on with his Negress in that big ole heart pine castle of his out on the island. A good budder, like Clay himself, could set over a thousand buds in a day. Bud didn't take, a second one could be set on the same stock. Clay, like his daddy, had experimented with several different budding techniques over the years. He wasn't entirely uninterested in experimentation, innovation. Shield or T-budding, reverse shield budding, annular budding, chip budding. All worked okay, but the inverted-T shield method was superior, he had decided. (Clay's daddy had preferred plain old T-budding.) Most efficient trade-off between successful setting and manual effort. Inverted-T shield method you cut the bud from the scion in an oval shield just the same as plain old T-budding, but you carved the T upside down. Something about the coordination to make the upside-down T was easier and faster, and this way you shoved the bud up into the cut from below before taping over it, which felt better to Clay's hands.

The other co-op fellows weren't so much interested in budding. Except for Ike. Edwin, bored apparently, took a swig from his RC Cola bottle and swished it in his mouth, as if it were Listerine. They'd work down the nursery rows together, maybe bud a thousand trees if they didn't tarry while they convened (taking stock as they budded stock, as it were), if Ike ever got here, thought Clay. There was the matter of those laminate-tagged suits from the commission, tromping out on Ike's grove. Walt had mentioned them at Janisse's few weeks ago. What was it they wanted with Ike, with the rest of them?

"I just can't get up and over on fifteen," Edwin complained. "That's my only gosh darn problem the whole course. Can't get up and over on fifteen. Have to lay up before the crick every time. Would have broke eighty."

"Your hips is the thing," Walt cried over Clay to Edwin. "You gotta break the barrel during your follow-through, Win." Walt put a fist down in the loamy earth and stood, groaning. The muscle cords in his forearm rippled beneath the pasting of red fur. He flicked his glowing half-spent Lucky to the dirt and snuffed it out with his boot, then took a mock swing with his phantom club, thrusting his hips forward at the end. His belly protruded, but there was something strong and solid about Walt's belly, the way he carried it proud out in front, like it was a muscle. He shooed an airborne insect from the vicinity of his face. "See? Break the barrel."

"Barrel? What the heck you mean?"

"Like a cooper's barrel."

"Cooper?"

"How old are you, Win, twelve? It's just a way of looking at it. An image, or a . . . whatchamacallit?"

"A metaphor," Clay declared, the corners of his mouth rising. Mrs. Pritchard would be proud. Whole poem by Longfellow he could still recite too, even though it didn't make much sense in steamy Florida.

The day is cold, and dark, and dreary . . . Clay sighed and began whittling his first Hamlin bud from its stick, felt the gratifying give of the tender wood under the influence of the sharp rounded blade. The slender ivory haft tapered to a spatula at the end for teasing open stock bark. It felt smooth and good in his hand, the ivory haft. It had been his daddy's knife, Old Man Griffin, Clay thought. His mouth creased into a broader smile at the memory, his dry-cracked bottom lip smarting some. That's one of the reasons Clay insisted on these budding conferences every season, while the others (except for Ike) would just as well have the Negroes do all the budding, to feel his father's ivory-hafted budding knife warm beneath the seashell of his aching fist. But more, he knew that it was important that they all keep a hand in every stage of production, except maybe the picking. Taking things a bit far, that would be.

"Like Arnold Palmer, Win. Get on your feet and give it a try. Like that Arnold Palmer."

Clay remembered when they used to talk about citrus. Oranges. Grapefruit. Lemon. Else snook and sea trout. Bobwhite, turkey, and wild boar too, which they used to take regular. Boar they'd hear at night from their windows snorting and snuffing out in the grove. Not much around, anymore, the bobwhite and turkey, or even the boar. Their neater plowed rows, their newfangled chemicals. Now here they were, about to bud new Hamlins on sour orange stock along Walt's row, talking about golf. Win's hips for goodness gracious. Could Walt hear himself? Wouldn't be so bad if he'd cottoned to the activity. But Clay was too old to pick up this new sport at the new country club, Whispering Pines. He had taken a lesson at the range from the part-time professional from Daytona, but couldn't even get the darned dimpled ball off the ground. Fishing the lagoon in his skiff was frustrating enough, seemed to him. Didn't hardly seem right, anyway, sawing down all those slash and longleaf pines to make room for the fairways, chasing off every last one of those special woodpeckers with the white cheeks (near as he could tell), then naming the club after the tree-ghosts.

"Now don't start in yet, Clay," Walt demanded, having just noticed Clay's whittling. "You're making us do our own budding all morning we're waiting on Ike. Can't squirrel out of everything."

"That's not fair, Walt," Doyle said from the end of the row without turning his head, his fingers interlaced at his lap. An ancient baseball cap, a barely visible Texaco star at the brim, protected his depleted scalp. He looked like one of those A-rabs, Clay thought, sitting back on his haunches all peaceful-like, the sun bathing his red neck, not so much creased but crevassed with deep tannic rivers. "Ike's as hardworking as they come," Doyle continued. "Fool, maybe. Jew, maybe. But hardworking as they come. Gotta give him that."

"Palmer's stroke doesn't look so pretty on the tube to me, anyhow," Clay said, shifting the topic from Ike's tardiness, Ike's Jewness. "Too flat or something. Just plain ugly. Miracle it works for him."

"Came back six strokes at last year's Open," Walt declared. "Six strokes! Who should Win watch, instead? Charlie Sifford?"

"Could do worse," Doyle answered. "Taught that palooka Joe Louis to play, anyhow."

"He's mediocre what he is. Won't win a single tourney up with the big boys. Not a single tourney. Couldn't even take the Whispering Pines trophy from Hugh King. He were smart he'd stick with the Negro Open, not go muddy up the waters. Boxing's one thing. Football. Even baseball. But golf? Just not in the genes. Thinking man's sport."

Ike appeared on the horizon just then, lumbering toward them. Great big bear of a man, Ike. All his brethren cut like him, Clay thought, they wouldn't have had no problems with that wormy Eichmann fellow on the television. He was glad they had gotten the golf talk out of the way before Ike's arrival, as they couldn't exactly ask him to the club. There wasn't any policy against Jews, per se, no Jews to speak of in town other than the Krupnicks, now Ike and his family. It's just people wanted to stick together. 'Least socially. Stuck in the craw some, cause people, both sides, didn't always want to stick with their own. Wanted to mingle. And then what? But Clay couldn't see himself standing against it, cause that's what most people wanted, seemed. To stick together, social purposes. Besides, there must be a Jew club in Orlando. Daytona maybe, not too far off. Now Sifford in the pros was another matter. Competition. Best player should have out, white or colored. That's what Clay thought. But socially? Most people wanted to stick together, seemed. Mostly.

"As I live and breathe," Walt uttered, sounding like his more proper wife, Glory.

"Sorry I'm late," Ike announced. Yet he didn't seem sorry. If he was sorry he'd have hurried down the row. Or act like he was hurrying. That's what Clay had half a notion of telling Ike right then and there. But there were countless little things just like this that Ike didn't do natural. It would take a school marm like Mrs. Pritchard to point out for him every time he said or didn't say, did or didn't do, what was right and proper. Hell if he'd be Ike's school marm. He traced his partner's deliberate progression toward the liner at the end, far away from Walt as possible, next to Doyle. Still slow, still unhurried, as if the whole wide world was waiting on him. Ike kneeled on his Dickies like the rest of them, sighed. His eyes seemed rimmed with red, as if he hadn't slept. It wasn't quite that he felt superior, Clay knew, knowing all the while that the rest of the co-op didn't know, that they wouldn't offer Ike the benefit of the doubt. It wasn't quite arrogance. More like he was distracted. He seemed to think a lot, Ike. That was his problem. Well, with a sick child like that. Plus a pretty wife. Neither easy to truck in this world.

"Everything Jake on the grove?" Clay asked, hoping to strike a mild chord. Ike really should grub out those experimental acres of his by now. But heck if he'd tell a grown man how to manage his own affairs. Now if Ike asked, that would be one thing. If he asked.

"Yepper, Clay," Ike answered in a sigh. "Everything's Jake." Clay watched as Ike reached into his hip pocket for his budding knife.

"At home too?"

"Sure, Clay." Ike glanced over at his partner and flashed a brief smile, expending great effort to carry off the gesture, it seemed to Clay. His eyes were definitely rimmed with red, the lids just inside his lashes inflamed.

"Boy of yours feelin' better?" Doyle asked. It was good of Doyle to ask, Clay thought. Most of the time, people didn't say the one thing most in need of saying.

Ike lifted a shoulder, as if to say, so-so. "Oh, he's fine," he finally uttered, plucking a leaf from the sour orange stock before him, as if to release some pent-up pressure. "Shall we begin, gentlemen?"

"Damn straight we'll begin. Just you we've been waiting on," Walt said, patting his hip pockets as if for loose change to find his budding knife.

"Begin boys," Clay said. "Good clean cuts. Let's not rush the first few. Not a race."

Clay carved an inverted T on the rootstock about eighteen inches off the ground. He glanced around to make sure the fellows were adhering to the same best practice. They were. Optimal height to discourage foot rot. He felt the bark slip cleanly from wood. Those dividing cambrial cells accounted for this nice separation of the thin bark from the wood beneath. Spring. Best time for budding. He glanced over toward Ike, who seemed to be doing okay. Not a natural budder, physically speaking. Thick mitts like his weren't any advantage, that's for sure. But he concentrated proper on what he was doing. Something about the way Ike braced the slender stock trunk with his left hand while he whittled with his right, his meaty fingers splayed, as if he was cradling his sick child's neck or something, leaning the tyke's head back down in bed. Something tender in it. Quiet. The other boys were noisy budders, fidgeting and groaning and cursing and complaining the whole way through this very first liner, the stock leaves rustling against their clumsy efforts. He wished Walt would just clam it. It was just a chore to them, budding, as if they thought they'd be better occupied being somewhere else, doing something else, when Clay knew perfectly well that they had nowhere better to be, and nothing better to do.

Here was the problem with the country in a nutshell, seemed to Clay. The great mass of men thought they should be doing better things, or maybe just more things. No one cared anymore to hunker down over one simple fine thing. That was the trick to budding proper, or doing anything proper, to know that you were doing precisely what the good Lord intended you to be doing at that very moment. What was so meager, anyway, about setting up a whole new generation of trees?

His stock carved, Clay picked up again his slender Hamlin bud stick, inspected its contours, eyeballed that first bud he had already started to whittle before Walt stopped him. Doyle seemed to be laboring still over his rootstock incision, muttering wicked oaths under his breath. The rest, like Clay, had begun to shave bud shields off their sticks.

"Need help there, Doyle?" he called down the row.

"I got it. Shit-ass stock I'm dealing with."

Clay didn't like the way Walt beside him appeared to have wasted a perfectly good bud, having carelessly carved an ill-shaped or too-deep shield with his knife, then discarding it in the dirt before moving on to the next bud on his stick, issuing an *Ah, hell.* Just because the commission's Citrus Budwood Protection Program distributed subsidized cut-rate CTV-free budwood—Commissioner Shepherd knew how to work those good old boys in the legislature, Clay had to give him that—didn't mean that Walt should just squander perfectly good buds as if they were nothing.

Clay slid the half-inch bud shield beneath the bark's incision from below. The shield was near paper-thin so he took special care to slide it in clean, without folding it over, teased open the narrow slit in the bark with thumb and forefinger.

"Ah, yes," Walt uttered. "Just like a pink canoe."

"Goodness gracious, Walt," Doyle said.

Win laughed, his hand braced on the stock, burying his towhead in his underarm. He had started already to wrap the bud union of his liner with plastic tape, cheaper than the wax strips they had used just ten years ago. "He's not too far off, though," Win said. "You have to give him that. Just like a little twat."

"You boys must be awfully hot and bothered," said Clay, "a cut in a piece of wood gets you to thinking of a woman's lady-business." Clay looked past Doyle to Ike, concentrating still over his incision and shield, carving out a deeper split up in the T with his knife so that his shield might fit better, teasing open the wound with the ivory spatula haft. His shield was a bit too long, it seemed to Clay. But if he could give Ike any advice, it wouldn't be about his budding. He'd tell him to laugh at Walt's joke, or at least say something. React. Did he have to act so highfalutin? Or not quite highfalutin, exactly. What was the word? Aloof. That's how he seemed. Aloof.

"Now don't cover any of my buds with the tape," Walt warned, starting to wrap his own union above and below the actual bud. "You hear, Ike, you greenie? Might start growing in a week or two, late spring and all."

"I hear you, Walter," Ike responded.

Good, Clay thought. At least he said something.

"Anyone mess with more of your trees?" Walt asked. He was always the one to broach the topic of the vandalism with Ike, Clay noticed, as if broaching it cleared him from suspicion.

"Nope. I've been keeping an eye out."

"That just ain't right," Doyle said, shaking his head. It swayed like a pumpkin on top of Doyle's Ichabod Crane frame. "A man's trees. His livelihood. Just ain't right."

"Must be kids," Win remarked. "Bored kids. Only kids do something so . . ." Win groped for his next word.

"Criminal," Clay said.

"Yeah, criminal," Win said. "Probably ruttin' in your grove too. Ruttin' like the hogs. Now we cutting the stocks too, Walt? That what you want us to do? Might as well."

"Let's just leave 'em for now. Boys'll do it later."

"Don't you trust us?" Doyle asked, his fresh Camel bobbing between his lips, a smoky plume shrouding his face. He had just finished wrapping his bud.

"Not as far as I can throw you," Walt answered, his shoulders bobbing in a chuckle. They all walked on their dirty knees to the next liner, just one stride or so, only twelve inches down the row.

"Sure can use some rain," Doyle said, apropos of nothing. The comment seemed to stir something in Walt.

"So you gonna make us ask, Ike? Is that it? You're gonna make us ask?"

"Huh?"

"He's talking about the commission boys," Clay said.

"Hell yeah I'm asking about those commission boys. That's who they were, right? Let's get down to brass tacks, Ike. What did those suits want?"

Clay paused over his rootstock; they all paused over their stocks, gazed toward Ike. Ike was the only one who continued his whittling. He wasn't in any hurry to answer, but something about his expression told Clay that he was about to say something, that he just wanted to taste the words in his mouth first.

"Commissioner wanted to see me." Ike bobbed his broad shoulders. "So I went."

The disclosure left the co-op dumbstruck.

"You ain't shittin' us?" Win finally asked. "The actual commissioner? J. P. Shepherd?"

Ike nodded, began whittling the second Hamlin bud off his first stick.

"Quit your whittling a second and talk to us, Ike," Walt commanded. "What did he say? What did he want?"

"He's got his knickers in a bunch about our yields, don't he?" Doyle said. "Son 'bitch, he wants us to switch to rough lemon stock, don't he, don't he?"

"Like those Simply Citrus fuckers out on the ridge," Walt added. "Don't he? Bird dogs finally got to him, yeah?"

"Not exactly," Ike said, his hands resting on his knees. He was being cagey, Clay thought. More cagey than usual.

"The feds then?" Clay asked. "The feds after our property for their outer space business? Is that it?"

Ike shook his head. "I don't think we have to worry about that with the commissioner. He's pretty gung ho about expanding citrus holdings. Pretty gung ho about that."

"Well then?" Walt uttered. "Out with it, Ike. For Jesus' sake."

The men sat on their haunches waiting for Ike to speak. They gripped their budding knives in their clamshell fists, the blades on their dusty thighs glinting beneath the strengthening sun. Clay watched as Ike contemplated his next words, tasting them again in his mouth.

"He mentioned labor problems. The field-workers." Soon as he said this, Ike began whittling his bud off the Hamlin stick again.

Clay took him in, the slits of his eyes narrowing. He wasn't lying, Clay thought. He just wasn't revealing everything, maybe the main thing. Even so, Walt jumped on Ike's morsel like a duck on a June bug.

"I knew it!" Walt cried. "That nigger in town. Stirring up the tree monkeys. That *is* what he's doing! I knew it!"

"Now Walt," Clay said, mostly so Ike wouldn't have to say anything. "It's just us out here, but mind your tongue."

"Ah hell, Clay, don't get so sensitive. I don't mean nothing by it. You telling me they don't look like monkeys, all up there in the trees picking shiners? That what you're telling me?"

"The nigger part too, I mean. Not just the tree monkey stuff."

"I don't mean nothing by it. We're all Christian gentlemen here."

"Yeah, we're all Christians," Win agreed.

"Not all of us," Ike said.

"Well, uh, of course . . ." Win fumbled for words, ". . . but you know what I mean, anyway. Right, Ike? You know what I mean."

"Not really," he answered, without heat.

"Just that we're God-fearin' men," Doyle came to Win's rescue. "That's all. God-fearin' men. Servants of the Lord."

"You're a God-fearin' man too, right Ike," Walt stated more than asked.

"Sure," Ike said, shaking his head, tending to his rootstock. "Sure I am." The response seemed at least half sarcastic to Clay. He wondered what it felt like to be a Jew like Ike. He didn't seem so different from them in most respects. Never know there was Jew in him. Was it just inconvenient happenstance, then, like being left-handed? Didn't seem hardly fair in this world the way it was, being left-handed. Or Jew. But it was more than just that, certainly. Being Jew. More to

Ike, anyway, who drove with his family all the way to Orlando for Saturday church, or whatever they called it.

"It's awful soon to start speculating about the fellow anyway," Clay said, wrapping his second bud with the tape. "Is he really stirring the pot? What do we know about him?"

Clay would have to do something about the new Negro, who he recognized straight away. Soon. Before things got out of hand. He would talk with Ted, he decided. He'd have to talk with Ted.

"Just a colored man in a suit," Doyle said. "Not a zoot suit, anyway. Walks uppity all about town like he owns the place, though. Don't wear no hat. Staying up in Mims at the motel, Janisse thinks. And not teaching at the school. And not a preacher."

"Negro in a suit, and not a preacher or a teacher? Well that's a problem, ask me," Walt said. "Don't have to be one of them rocket scientists at the Cape to know that's a problem."

The men walked on their knees to the third liner, whittled their inverted T's into the fresh bark.

"Who does he think he is in his starched suit, that raisin-in-the-sun fellow?" Doyle said, his attention fixed on his stock.

"Poitier," Clay said. "Sidney Poitier, you mean."

"Ladies took a real shine after that movie played at the Magnolia."

"Put anyone up on that silver screen," Win sighed, shaking his head, turning his attention from the stock to his bud stick. "Even a colored."

"All dressed natty-like," Walt said, sliding his bud into the stock-slit. "And his voice. Hear him talk, that Poit-i-*ay*? He's not even American. He's a foreigner. Jamaica or something."

"Born in Miami, I think," Clay said, taping his union. "From Miami, matter of fact."

"Now you're splittin' hairs," said Walt. "Miami," he uttered with derision.

Doyle laughed. Win laughed. Ike concentrated on his budding. What was he thinking? Clay wondered. About that Negro actor, about that new Negro about town who Clay alone recognized. The Jews and the Negroes were pretty tight. But Ike was an orange man. Like them. Right?

The fellows walked on their knees to the fourth liner. They had hit their budding stride, picked up their speed.

"Just you wait, boys," said Walt. "Miami be overrun with those Cubans now that Kennedy botched things up. They'll all be speaking

Spanish down there this time next year. Dollars to donuts you voted for Kennedy, didn't you Ike? Feeling proud of yourself now? Dollars to donuts you voted for that fisheater."

Everyone looked toward Ike.

"Nope," Ike said, teasing open his bark with the haft of his knife. "Actually, no. Melody did, though." Here, they all knitted their brows. Ike surprised Clay and the rest of them on two counts here: that he had voted for Nixon and that his wife had voted for someone different than he did. Whoever heard of a wife voting against her husband? What was the point of that?

"Well who cares about Miami or the president, anyway?" Walt said. "We got problems closer to home. Everyone knows those N-double APC—"

"N-double A*CP*," Ike corrected Walt, slicing his bud off the Hamlin stick. "It's N-double ACP. For colored people."

"You bird brain," Doyle teased Walt. "Don't you never watch the news?"

"Sure. I know. National Association for *Collard* People. Sure. Point is, those rabble-rousers been up and down the state, trying to organize." Walt wrapped his bud union with exaggerated fury. "We're all just scraping by is the thing. Can't all be Joe Buck Wilson, run our own packing house and concentrate plant. Pickers get uppity with us, demand day wages or something—"

"Overtime!" Win joked, making quick revolutions with his tape around the stock. "Imagine that! Overtime."

The fellows walked on their knees to the fifth liner.

"Piecework's the only way to go," Doyle said. "Can't budge on that. Only way to get a decent day's work out of those lazy fellas, pay by the box. Besides, we all pay our foremen an honest wage. We're Christian men. But the field-workers? Gotta be piecework. Otherwise we gotta ride herd every one of them to get an honest day's work. Can't budge on piecework."

The fellows muttered their general consent, carved their inverted T's.

"Maybe we can just up our rates per box," Ike suggested. "I can run some numbers." The co-op fellows lifted their eyes from their stocks to look toward Ike, who felt the heat of their gaze. "I mean if it comes to it, we might want to consider the possibility. Beats an all-out strike or something."

"Someone get to you?" Walt asked, one of his woolly red eyebrows raised. "That's what this is about, Mr. N-double A-*CP*? Someone get to you? The commissioner? This Sidney Poit-i-*ay* fella about town? Maybe Ted?"

"No. No one got to me, Walt. I'm just thinking out loud here."

"Well careful," Walt said, pointing his budding knife at Ike like a finger. "You just be careful, partner. Was a time folks around here knew what to do with Sidney Poit-i-*ay* Negroes. Knew what to do with their friends too. Not right here. Not us, mind you. But just yonder in Apopka, Winter Garden, Sanford, Groveland. Sheriff McCall and his boys. Groveland wrecking crew the ones who drove in through the fog and stuck dynamite underneath that troublemaker's cinder blocks Christmas night in Mims. No secret there."

Clay was about to intervene, to keep the peace, but Ike spoke before Clay could think of what to say.

"You don't have to tell me about that sheriff, Walter. I trust he's not a personal friend of yours, that McCall. I trust you don't know too much about wrecking crews. Is that what you call them, wrecking crews? Aren't y'all supposed to love the stranger, suffer the children, turn the other cheek, all that good stuff?"

Now here even Clay bit his lip to keep from taking offense. He had brass balls, Ike, he'd give him that. Brass balls talking that way. Hardly masking that Jew sarcasm at all. Something must have happened, Clay suspected, for Ike to talk this way, like he was itching for a fight. Something had happened with the commissioner. Or at home. Eli. Back in the hospital? Or that pretty wife. It was like he had nothing to lose.

"You tellin' us about our Bible?" Walt cried, standing now and turning his shoulders toward Ike, thrusting out his powerful paunch, his knife gleaming in his clamshell fist. Ike, thankfully, didn't rise, didn't even look over at Walt, but kept his attention on his liner. Clay and Win and Doyle rose instead to subdue their partner.

"Let's just finish up this budding for now, gentlemen," Clay said, raising his hands as if in surrender. "It's been a tough season. We're all just a bit hot under the collar. Right, Ike? Right?"

"Right," Ike allowed. "Sure."

"We're orange men," Doyle said. "Orange men. We're not fighters."

"Christian gentlemen," Win said. "God-fearing men."

"Hallelujah," said Clay, lifting the day's first Winston to his lips, which trembled until his lips steadied it. He sparked the cigarette with a match inside the protective cavern of his palms and took a deep pull of the frothy smoke. It tasted good, but provided no counsel. Yes, he'd have to talk with Ted as soon as he could about the new Negro in town, whom Clay had recognized straight away. No time to waste. He stretched his arms to both sides and arched his back to exercise his aching spine. Then he dropped forward on his knees before his sour orange liner, the soft earth yielding some to his weight. The sun was already high over the grove trees and the river. He could feel the heat on his liver-spotted hand-backs as he carved his inverted T on his stock, as he held the true Hamlin stick before him, eyeing its most promising buds. It would be hot as blue blazes in a couple hours. And it wasn't even summer yet. But hot as blue blazes already. Clay didn't know how long he could stand it.

Fourteen

Mr. Langford pulled the giant lever and the bus door exhaled, releasing Eli into the slate gray Florida afternoon. His mother didn't like these days—"for the birds," she said—but Eli liked it when the sun hid itself. He peered up and to the west to locate the normally bully-bright orb wrapped up somewhere in the sky's iron sheet, above the pom-pom pines, but he couldn't find it. Days like this his mother didn't schmear that white paste all over his face after school, didn't even make him wear his fisherman's hat. That's mostly why he liked these slate gray days. The loose river rock gave and crinkled beneath the rubber toe-caps of his Keds. He tried to walk gingerly on the driveway, like Tonto, so the stones wouldn't give beneath his sneakers, making a game of it, but eventually he gave up and walked along the harder, packed dirt at the edge, which was easier. He walked around the side to the back porch, took the measure of the outdoors a while longer before leaping the steps and heading inside to check in with his mother. When the sun was bright, like on most days, all the green looked different, the green on the ferny-looking tamarind tree he was looking at now different from lantana green and wax myrtle green and cord grass green and cowpea green and citrus green. But days like today all the green looked the same, sort of like the canned peas with the French name his mother boiled in a saucepan. Hospital light was the worst kind of light.

Smack! He slapped at his neck where the mosquito's needle stung. All manner of bugs were out days like this. He could hear mysterious insects—cicadas? crickets?—sizzling in the grove trees, tempting him outdoors.

"I'm goin' outside, Mom!" he leaned his head across the threshold, bracing the screen door open with his foot, dumped his backpack inside on the pine floor. He'd take a pee outside. He liked peeing outside in the privet and wax myrtle before he disappeared inside the grove. It seemed like you always had a better pee outdoors. Too bad for girls.

"Wait!" he heard his mother call from the kitchen. He wouldn't escape so quickly. He stepped full inside the house and sighed. The house smelled like lemons. His mother appeared cradling her heavy yellow bowl with the white insides. An inky lock of hair twirled down from her bun to lick her cheek, dusted with flour. He could hear his sister padding about on the lemon linoleum inside her playpen beyond the pocket door. Probably playing with her Yuban can or wooden blocks. He hated the wooden blocks, which hurt like anything when he stepped on them by accident. "You don't have homework?" his mother inquired, stirring whatever was inside the bowl with a wooden spoon.

"Just a page of 'rithmetic. I can do it after supper." She nodded, her eyes narrowing to almonds.

"Will you pick off some of those scales for your father while you're out there? You can take an empty Kodachrome container from the junk drawer. Here, I'll get you a couple. Stay there. I don't want Sarah seeing you if you're just running outside. You'll get her started."

His mother disappeared and returned in an instant, handing him the two black plastic vials.

She placed the vials in his outstretched palm. He felt one of her nails against his softer skin. "You're a little gentleman out there with your friend, right Eli?"

"Mo-om."

"Right, Eli?" she insisted. "I know she's older than you, but she's still a girl. And girls are different than boys."

"I know."

"Now you have your Timex on. I want you back by five." His mother tapped at an imaginary watch on her thin wrist. The knob of a bone jutted there. A slender vein streaked across the rise. "We're having meat loaf tonight."

"What about pie? We're having pie tonight too, right? Lemon? I smell it."

"No, my little man. I'm making it for the stand. You can have orange sherbet. And don't forget the Watkins on the counter. It's horribly buggy out there."

"Aw, really? Okay." Eli hated sherbet. He hated the sticky Watkins.

"And remember," he felt both her palms on his shoulder bones. "A little gentleman. We don't need any more trouble from that Mr. Boehringer."

Jo was waiting for him at the dry ditch by the time he pasted on his bug lotion, peed in the wax myrtle, and made his way there. She'd already crossed to his side. She always beat him to their meeting place. She didn't have to check in with her mom, he knew, who was older than Eli's mom and worn out with mothering, Jo said, by the time Jo came around. Except for church she could do whatever she wanted. Lucky Jo.

"Took you long enough, slowpoke," she teased, not looking up at him, thwacking at something invisible with her live oak stick in a thick tuft of brownish cord grass, acting like she didn't care whether Eli was there or not. No skin off her nose. Her hair, Eli just noticed, seemed shorter and poofier, like a Raggedy Ann doll. That's how Dean Chapman sometimes teased her at school when he didn't tease her by calling her Red, and when he wasn't busy teasing somebody else. *How's Raggedy Ann today?*

"You get a haircut or something?" Eli asked.

"Nah, it's just the close air makes it curl up terrible. Can always tell how wet the air is by my hair. *You* know that, Eli."

"Yeah, sure. I forgot."

"I better use my Prell tonight." She lifted an upturned palm to bounce imaginary curls below her actual ones, opening her mouth as if to say *Ahh*, imitating some TV commercial Eli hadn't seen. "It makes my hair radiantly alive!" she sang. Eli laughed. "Radiantly" sounded funny coming from Jo's mouth.

"My mom uses Breck," he said.

"Prell's better."

Eli shrugged.

They made their way toward the clearing, Jo swinging her live oak stick at the limp cowpea, peanut, and wax bean plants between the tree rows. Eli, walking beside, waved the black lovebugs from his face. Something about the wet gray days brought out these lazy bugs.

Least they didn't bite. He made sure to walk with his mouth closed, even though it was harder to breathe.

"Icky day," Jo said, just to say something, it seemed.

"I like it." He looked down at the cover-crop plants at his feet as he walked, at the unknown weeds mixed in, then up at the experimental Hamlins and Parson Browns and Valencias to each side, branch ends here and there covered with mesh bags, as if they were windswept litter from the highway that got stuck there. Then Eli looked higher above the branches at the slate gray sky. His eyes felt less strain on dark days like today, only one quiet green color about. Here was another reason he liked days like today. More quiet on the eyes.

"What's your daddy doing again with these trees?" She noticed the queer mesh bags too, apparently.

"I don't know." Which was true. Jo nodded.

"Dean's sweet on me you know."

"Nu-uh. All he does is razz you."

"*That's* how I know, Eli. Gee, don't you know anything? Mom says that's a sure sign he's sweet on me."

Eli couldn't imagine that Dean Chapman truly liked-liked Jo, whose hair never seemed brushed like the other older girls, the ones with straight blonde hair tucked tidy behind their ears. The ones who wore barrettes. Mary Lou Simpson or Kelly O'Flanagan. That's who Dean probably liked, Kelly O'Flanagan, whose tiny freckled nose twitched like a rabbit. Her father owned the Furniture & Electric store in town, too, so they were rich.

School had been particularly mortifying for Eli the past several days since he'd been back. His lungs had yet to fully clear—it was impossible for him to disguise the sound of his breath—so his mother insisted that he turn in Dr. Olivet's note to Mr. Merrit excusing him from even *Moderate Physical Activity*. The only thing more humiliating than struggling through the calisthenics of the "Chicken Fat Song" regimen—Mr. Merrit still played the song on the record player out on the macadam track—was sitting out the exercises on the sideline along with fatty Peter. There was no one to supervise them in the classroom during physical education, so all week Mr. Merrit made them sit Indian style on the hot pebbly ground that made his butt itch, doing nothing, while their more able classmates performed their calisthenics to the silly song.

Nuts to the flabby guys.

Go, you chicken fat, go away.

They reached the clearing and, after checking for snakes, set about lying in their straight line across the soft lupine grass. "Scooch farther down," Jo said. "I don't wanna be in the dirt."

Eli complied, tried to act the gentleman like his mother told him. "So you'll help me pick off some scale like you said, right? We don't have to take too long. I'll split the money even-Steven like I promised. Penny a scale, my dad says."

"Sure. Now if your daddy just sprayed you know . . ."

Silence. Except for his breath through his nose that came easier the longer he laid still, and the sizzling insects all about, and a frog that kept belching somewhere, which was odd for the afternoon. The frog must have thought it was night already, gray as it was.

"We should keep our eye out for enemy planes now too."

"Huh? You mean the Russians?"

"Heck yeah, the Russians. And the Cubans. All the Reds."

"Reds?"

"The communists," Jo declared, then exhaled in a deep exasperated groan that seemed to come directly from her stomach. "They're called Reds. Jeez, don't you know anything, Eli?"

He didn't protest as he could tell that Jo had more to say.

"There's gonna be a war soon, Daddy says. That's why they're doing all those rocket tests. And now that we went and attacked Cuba."

So that's what his parents were upset about over the news the other night, before he fell out of the tree and got sick and had to go to the hospital, which made them even more upset.

"My mom's saving up tuna cans and water bottles in the shed, 'case they do it before we do. We're gonna build our own fallout shelter soon, buy one of those Castro Convertible beds to put inside. You know about the fallout shelter underneath the theater in town, right?"

"Right," Eli lied.

"'Cause this is where the Reds'll do it, you know."

"Do what?" He wasn't exactly certain what she was talking about.

"Drop their H-Bombs!" She was nearly yelling at him now, but not in a mean way. "What do you think all those drills are for in class, ducking under our desks, hands behind our heads? We'll be the first target, rocket base nearby."

"Kingfisher!" he declared, pointing up at the sky, the medium-sized bird giggling overhead, banking east. In the poor light, he couldn't discern any color at all on the bird, but he recognized its chattering, the cadence of its wing beats. He saw lots of them at the river, where this one seemed to be heading.

"Turpentine," Jo said, hangdog. "That's luck. Hardly see any right over the grove no more."

"How'll we tell, anyway?"

"Huh? . . . Mourning dove!" she cried, pointing one of her stubby fingers toward the phantom that darted in and out of their field of view. Its telltale bleating had given it away.

"How'll we tell which planes are the bad ones?"

"We'll just know it when we see them, I bet. They'll seem different than the others we see from the base."

They lay for several minutes, but no more birds appeared overhead. "Used to see ospreys all the time," Jo said. "Pelicans too."

"It's those chemicals. They said so on TV."

"That's not what my daddy says."

Eli knew better than to argue the point when it came to her father. "Better get going," he said instead. "Le's get at least two hundred scales each. Then I can buy a new cast net."

They rose and made their way toward the tagged, harvestable five-year and ten-year Hamlins beyond Eli's experimental grove, closer to the river near Hammock Road. The grove seemed so different amid these taller rows. Darker, especially today. He usually didn't dally here, or along the more ancient Valencia rows, but walked fast to get to where he was going—the river to fish the deep pools and mangrove edges for snapper and flounder. There was a job to do here today, though. He paused in the middle of a row once he noticed a stricken tree, the soft spring flush foliage limp and tattered with dark-red sesame-seed dots.

"Might as well start in on this one," he said. They were still a few rows away from Hammock Road. "See all this scale?"

Jo nodded. "Look," she said, pointing to the tree's base. "It's dropped some of its leaves too. That's real bad. Means it's suffering something terrible when it can't hold its leaves this time of year. This whole row. For crying out loud." Jo pointed down the row, toward the river beyond. "Critters suckin' the juice right out of them. Like that Dracula movie."

"You didn't see that Dracula movie." It irked Eli to hear Jo run down their trees. As if Eli's dad was to blame. As if *her* dad's trees were better. "No way your parents let you see that movie. It's for grownups."

"So."

Eli looked back up at the tree. "Hasn't dropped much fruit, anyway," he defended the poor thing. He searched harder inside the dense foliage and was relieved to make out even more dark spheres, camouflaged within the uniform green, big as ping-pong balls almost.

They began picking off scales and dropping them in their Kodachrome vials. Jo suggested that they work side-by-side and work their way counterclockwise around each tree. Eli said okay. Being a gentleman, far as he could tell, pretty much meant letting girls do things how they wanted. They'd make five dollars easy, Jo said. It was tedious work, and Eli kept having to wipe the bugs off his brow with his shoulder. Some were stuck to the sweat on his forehead, he could tell. Here's how his father could offer a penny a scale. He knew that they wouldn't have the patience to keep at it very long, what with the heat and the bugs and all the other things they'd rather do in the grove. "*Darn it!*" Eli said, removing his hand from the foliage to smack the sand gnats from his neck.

"My daddy drinks beer to keep the bugs away," Jo said. "Schlitz, mostly. When we're old enough we can drink beer."

"I have Watkins on."

"Lot of good *that's* doing."

Eli shrugged.

Most of the new leaves along the stricken stems were crinkled, Eli noticed, streaked with mucus trails. Probably the floppy swallowtail caterpillars camouflaged just like bird poop, Eli thought, but didn't say. He knew that Jo's dad didn't like their butterflies. Finally, Jo stepped back and took a breath. He knew she was getting ready to say something. She had to say something to justify taking it easy like this while he still worked.

"Thing we have to decide is whether we do each tree like real good, take our time on each one, or if we just take off a li'l bit on each one and cover more trees." Eli stepped back from the tree too now and looked at Jo. She seemed to be contemplating the dilemma, a hand placed on the ledge below her waist that wasn't quite a hip yet, her teeth chewing the corner of her bottom lip. Her face was hot and red already, disguising her freckles, even though it wasn't really too hot outside under the iron-cloud sheet, just thick and buggy.

"Probably better if we cover more trees," Eli proposed.

Jo nodded. "Right," she said. They resumed their efforts and worked in silence for a while.

"Next tree!" Jo finally announced.

They noticed the inscription on the smooth bark of the next tree at the same time, both knowing that they both noticed by the way they paused there on the soft earth, hands at their sides. A fresh attack on one of their trees. But this one was different. A word had been carved into the tree.

"They misspelled it," Eli said.

"No they didn't," Jo said.

"Sure they did."

"No. They didn't. It doesn't say what you think it does, Eli."

"Well what *is* it, then?" He looked again at the word, studied the bark. The strange four-letter word sounded bad in his head. It must have been carved recently. Eli could still see the green of the cambium at the inside edges of each letter that hadn't dried up, especially inside the first K, which was carved out much bigger than the other letters as if the vandal started out with greater artistic intentions but couldn't muster up sufficient energy or patience after that first K.

"It's a nasty word," Jo said slow, almost sad. "For people like you and the Krupnicks. Jew-folk."

Alien voices suddenly vibrated low in the thick air.

"*Shhh. Get down,*" Jo somehow managed to whisper and shout at the same time.

Eli dropped to his knees, then to his bony chest, and they both scooted back away from the voices between the rows on top of the cowpeas where the ground was lower. He tried to quiet his raspy breath. He tried making himself small. Invisible. Sometimes it was good to be small. Like now. He knew this from synagogue. *Tzimtzum*, it was called. How before God even made the light that made the world, he made himself very, very, very small, an invisible pinpoint of energy, Rabbi Klein said. Only when the time was perfect did God burst into light. Eli wasn't sure he believed in God, but he liked the story. He liked to think of himself as small but mighty. Ready to burst at any time.

"Come on," Jo nudged Eli's shoulder. Eli had curled himself into a ball.

They crept up toward the top of the rise and leaned their chins on their forearms. The voices seemed to be coming from at least five rows over toward Hammock Road.

"*There,*" Eli uttered softly, pointing toward the tangle of trousered legs and boots mixed in with the citrus trunks. One pair of legs didn't end in boots but in brown leather shoes. Not grove shoes.

"Negroes," Jo said. How did she know? Eli couldn't recognize any of the voices, or even make out any of the words. All he heard was the rumble of the lowest bass notes and highest trebles. He crab-crawled a bit more to his right on his elbows and knees and suddenly he could see more of them through the thinner patch of foliage. Jo was right. They were Negroes. Who else would be in the grove besides Eli's father, who was at the commission today getting those wasps?

There were just three of them. Not Ted, whom Eli was looking for, because then they wouldn't have to hide any more. But Fred. His mouth flashed black where his tooth was missing. And Percy, his chocolate mole clearly visible on his shining cheek. They looked down, mostly, at something in their hands. He would come out of hiding for Fred and Percy too. But there was that other person, the one attached to the not-grove shoes, someone Eli didn't recognize at all. His yellow necktie flashed through the dull green leaves like a grapefruit and he carried a brown clipboard, the edge of which he braced against his lean stomach. He was smaller than Percy and Fred. He must have been talking about whatever Percy and Fred were studying in their hands, narrow paper rectangles. Percy chewed his lips and nodded a lot, while Fred mostly stood still, but Eli couldn't hear what they were saying.

"*He work for your daddy?*" Jo whispered.

"*Guess so.*"

Eli knew the man didn't work for his father. What would he be doing with a yellow necktie and not-grove shoes out in the grove? Yet he didn't want to admit that someone who didn't work for his father was out tromping on their property without his father's say-so, that his father would let something like this happen while he was away. The Negro with the tie, it occurred to Eli, might have known somehow that his father would be away today. Now he'd have to tell his father about two things that would make him angry—the nasty word on the tree and this strange Negro with the yellow necktie and not-grove shoes.

Jo nodded. Slow. Doubtful. "*Le's get out of here,*" she said. They rose to their feet and tip-toed several yards down the row away from the voices, a clean getaway almost, until a covey of birds flushed northward in a flurry of bleating wingbeats, flashing gray for an instant before vanishing. Eli's heart leapt to his throat. Bobwhites.

"*Run Eli!*" Jo shouted.

Eli ran, not looking back, but couldn't quite keep up with Jo. His Keds kept getting stuck in the soft earth and his breath felt heavy in his lungs. "*Come on!*" Jo implored, at least ten yards ahead now. She finally stopped and waited for him when she reached the broader access road between the rows, where his father and Ted drove the groaning freight trucks.

"They're not coming," Eli said, gripping his knees, clutching fistfuls of air into his lungs in staccato breaths, his shoulders rising and falling. His throat burned. A viscous thread of saliva descended from the corner of his mouth to the weed-choked earth. He retched to clear his scalding throat. He considered using his inhaler, reached for it even, but was ashamed in front of Jo so left it alone.

"Cheese 'n' crackers, you okay, Eli?"

Eli nodded, his head lowered still, hands still gripping his knees.

"Easier to breathe, maybe, you pick your head up. Like this."

Eli stood straight and locked his fingers behind his head, like Jo. She leaned over to look down the row, making sure they weren't being followed. Eli felt his breath slow, his throat cool.

Jo's face was flushed and strands of sweat-soaked hair were pasted dark and not-red to her temples and forehead. But she wasn't breathing heavy. She stood there, silent and still, looking right through Eli now. The weight of her stare didn't feel good. He looked away, toward a squadron of dragonflies stripped of their iridescence in the dull light, flying helter-skelter for mosquitoes and other airborne morsels.

"Come on," Jo said. "We're all this way to the river. Let me show you something. My side." She began walking north on the access road toward her own grove. Eli followed.

Eli had never been on her grove. She claimed she liked his side, their cowpeas and lupine and their clearing. But Eli also suspected that Mr. Boehringer probably wouldn't want to see him on his grove, and that maybe he had told Jo as much even though she never said so.

"You're taking me to see a wildcat aren't you? You know where they are," Eli said more than asked.

"No. It's something different."

They walked northward in silence for several minutes toward Jo's side, covering a good bit of ground. It was easier to walk on the broad access road. The heavy truck tires ground two rock-hard tire paths in the dirt between the grassy weeds. Jo took the left tire path and Eli took the right one. It was cooler here too, the south wind gaining momentum along this more open stretch of air. He could feel the almost cool breeze tickle the back of his sweaty neck.

"Sure are neat birds, those quail."

"Yep."

"Wish my daddy didn't shoot 'em. It's sad the way they just plop out of the sky."

Eli nodded as he walked, but didn't say anything. He couldn't imagine shooting a bird out of the sky. Fish were different.

His father's trees yielded to the tall wiregrass, patches of palmetto, and the dry irrigation ditch. They were farther east along the irrigation ditch border than their usual meeting point. The ditch was wider here. An irrigation pump sat idle, its rusty tongue lowered to the bottom, waiting to lap up the rains that hadn't come yet. They climbed down and then up the dusty ditch sides over to the Boehringer's grove and continued north. The Boehringer's bigger trees were hedged like rectangles and Eli didn't much like them. He couldn't even distinguish between the trees as they walked down the row, thirty-foot walls of green on either side. But he didn't say anything about their monstrous trees. Or about the smell. Sweet, but in a bad way. Chemicals. Jo didn't say anything, either. It was a long walk and they both needed to concentrate on their breath. Eli could even hear Jo's breath now. Her breath sounded lower than his breath.

"How far is it?" Eli asked, careful not to whine.

Jo froze in her tracks, forcing Eli to stop too. "You feel okay? Wanna go back?"

"No, I'm not complaining. I'm just curious." He took the lead. He shouldn't have said anything. "I'm not complaining," he said again.

"Cause if you feel sick—"

"I'm fine!"

Jo took the lead and turned right to head toward the river.

"Boy, your dad's grove sure is big."

"Yeah."

They finally reached the end of the rows and a narrow band of wiregrass and palmetto before another ditch. Jo looked up and down along the band of wiregrass and then told him to follow her again. She headed north until she reached a wood plank holding a white metal sign.

TRESPASSERS WILL BE SHOT, Eli read the black letters. Bad people, Eli had heard, boated in on the river and stole oranges time to time. Jo must have noticed Eli reading the sign.

"That's how I know where I am. The sign."

Eli followed after as Jo hopped across the narrow ditch. Dense forest canopied the ground after another small band of wiregrass and palmetto. Mr. Ted had told him about this dark finger of land just before the Florida East Coast tracks and the river. The first settlers cleared most of the pines, palmetto, scrub oak, wiregrass, and cabbage palms to plant oranges, but the water was too high in the ground here and salty from the nearby river so the trees died. They let the pines and palmetto and scrub oak and wiregrass and palms grow back but cut the pines to use them for houses and citrus boxes when they got tall enough. The pines sort of gave up after that and without the pines to attract the lightning and catch fire now and again, the palms sort of took over and canopied the ground, which couldn't grow palmetto or wiregrass anymore. Eli could smell the salt and sulfur from the nearby mangroves.

On Eli's side, the dense canopy just sort of petered out into smaller windblown scrub before the tracks as the land slowly descended into the sulfurous mangrove shoreline. But here they reached a slight rise just as the palms thinned, the gray sky peeking down at them once again. The plants were mostly strange to Eli on this slight rise. Instead of wiregrass and patchy stands of palmetto, the vegetation was greener and thicker. The shiny wrinkled leaves and red berries of the coffee shrubs were the only plants he knew by name. They stood taller than most of the other plants, which carpeted the ground in round white berries and yellow flowers. One other shrub with leaves broad as cow tongues grew taller than the coffee, its small white flowers curving up into the sky like rocket trails from the base. The ground cover lapped up at this strange cow-tongue plant and the coffee plants. He couldn't even make out the ground below.

"That's marlberry," Jo said, tracing Eli's gaze, pointing toward the cow-tongue plant. "And that's snowberry," she pointed to the white-berry groundcover. "And that's wild coffee."

"I know coffee," Eli said. Jo nodded.

The air smelled good here. Sweet from the flowers, but not chemical sweet. There lingered, too, a not unpleasant undertone of salt and fish from the nearby mangrove shoreline.

"It's called a midden. With a d, not a t. A kitchen midden."

"Why?"

"Here. Look." Jo bent on her knees and cleared away a patch of soft snowberry with her dusty hands. Then she dug with her fingers till her hands were wrist deep and scooped out a handful of earth. Eli expected that the earth would be sandy so close here to the river, like it was near his grove. But Jo's scoop of dirt was dark with pale shell shards like jigsaw puzzle pieces mixed in.

"See that?" Jo said, pointing to the loose troubled earth. Her hand was dark with dirt. Rich earth, he knew. Good for planting. If it stained your skin like that. That's how you knew the earth was good and rich.

"That's oyster and clamshell," Jo said. "That's why the dirt's so black, why the snowberry and marlberry and coffee grows here. The Indians ate the oysters and clams, conch too, sometimes you can find conch, and piled the shells right here. Leftover fish-bits mixed in. Way back before there was a town. Before Columbus even."

Silence. They took their time to breathe the air, to drench their lungs in the salt and the sea and the sweet flower smells. Eli heard the rattle of a kingfisher far off to the east, over the river, probably. Maybe the same kingfisher he spied earlier.

"So don't worry about nothing, Eli," Jo finally said. "Indians were here way before all of us. Before the Negroes too. Indians the only ones have something to say about who lives here or not. That's what I really think."

Eli nodded.

"Used to be thirty feet high, Daddy says. Probably had human sacrifices up on top or something like that. The midden just keeps going too, over a mile." Jo pointed northward. "You can tell how far from the bushes. Far as the snowberry grows."

"Why isn't it thirty feet tall anymore? Erosion?"

"'Rosion," Jo groaned. "You and your erosion. Nah, they brought diggers in and shoveled it off to make the highway. Shells are good for highways. You can see those shell bits right in the road still. Just have to look."

Eli wasn't sure how to feel about diggers carting off a thirty-foot hill. It would have been pretty neat to play on a thirty-foot hill. Could see forever from a thirty-foot hill. But he liked that some of the shells were still here, and the plants. He'd pluck a sample of the snowberry to make a rubbing for his bedroom. It seemed a miraculous thing. The actual shells the Indians plucked from the river, cooked under a wood fire and lifted to their savage mouths to eat, right here still in the ground. He bent down and scooped up a fistful of rich dirt, rubbed a pale shard between his thumb and forefinger. Last person to hold this shell was an Indian, Eli thought. An actual flesh-and-blood Indian. Like Tonto from the TV. More Indian, seemed to him, than the Seminoles who supplied their orchids and dressed just like everyone else and weren't even much darker than his mother.

"Let's rest here awhile," Jo said. "Snowberry's soft."

They lay on the carpet of snowberry and looked up into the open sky. Jo reached her hand up above her face and made a snatching motion.

"Sort of feels like you can grab the sky when the air's thick like today, don't it?"

"Yes," Eli said. And then: "Will you come get me?"

"Get you?"

"If the Russians come. So we can go to the fallout shelter at the theater."

"Sure I will, Eli. You know I will. But I sort of think we'll be safer here. Right where we are now. Seems like nothing can touch us here. Or middle of the grove. In your clearing, maybe. Nothing could touch us there, either. No H-bomb, no mean people, no nothin'. We can live forever on the grove. Friends forever. Like I said before."

Eli wanted to believe her. That word, though, carved deep into the cambium of their scale-stricken Hamlin.

KIKE.

"Okay, Jo," he said.

"Better tell your dad about the tree, though. About that Negro with the necktie."

So Jo hadn't forgotten about the tree, or about the Negro with the yellow tie. "I know," Eli said. "I will."

An invisible woodpecker picked up a beat against a cabbage palm inside the canopy just behind them. Eli could hear gusts of the east wind thwacking the nearby palms. Then jet noise to the south—the rocket base, likely—silenced the woodpecker and the wind. Another test, maybe. A few days ago at school, Eli had stood with all his classmates out on the macadam yard to watch Alan Shepard's louder rocket flash up into the sky, then disappear.

The jet noise finally petered out, the wind continued its barrage against the palms, and the woodpecker resumed its beat, tentatively at first, then upped its tempo. Eli liked the sound of the palms and the woodpecker better than the jet noise.

"Thanks, Jo," Eli said. "Thanks for bringing me here."

Fifteen

SONNY'S GOOD FOOD. Formerly Good Food. Formerly Food. Clay Griffin's seen it all on and around Hopkins, where the Negroes lived. The Negro restaurant was plain old Food when Ben Norwood was running things. Clay always liked that. The humility. He liked old Ben. Food. Why get all highfalutin about it. Then Junior Norwood had to go and add the Good to it after his daddy dropped dead of a heart attack over the fryer. Junior just didn't cook as good, seemed to Clay—the Good only so much bluster in shinier red paint on the plate glass above the Food. Then Junior went off to the war, got a taste of the big city and never came back. Ben's old whist partner, Sonny Green, finally unshuttered the place and put his own stamp on it without having to strip off any of the old paint, just painted SONNY'S on the plate glass left side of the door. So now it was Sonny's Good Food. The meat-and-threes were better than they had been under Junior's brief reign—the macaroni less dry, the greens less salty—but Clay still liked it best when Ben ran things, when it was just plain old Food, when you just told him what you wanted and picked up your plate at the counter when he called. Maybe that was the way of the world. Things were always better before.

He parked his Buick on the street where he could see it, cut the lights. Night's hot breath. Crickets chattering up a storm, even here in town, up there in the oaks and fewer magnolias. Negroes out on their stoops rather than roasting inside. Summer, all intents and purposes.

Most growers didn't visit these few blocks across the FEC tracks, smelling distance of the river. The white citizenry appreciated that the Negroes stayed east of the tracks and North Palm, especially after dusk. They left the Negroes to tend to themselves along Hopkins, Ulee Wright's Negro deputy, Samuel, their only regular visitor from law enforcement. A certain deference obtained both ways, seemed to Clay. But he was no stranger here. The co-op depended upon these men and their sons to work their groves. While Walt and the others sent their foremen to pick up the crew at the Save-a-Lot, corner of Hopkins and Main, Clay himself pulled up in his flatbed at least once a week during season to collect the men, and he always made it a point to take a meat-and-three every month or so at Food, or Good Food, or Sonny's Good Food. Hell if Walt or Doyle or even Win would step foot inside. But Big Ike joined him on occasion, even if he ate like a dyspeptic, keeping to his Jew ways. Not even the greens he'd eat 'cause of the fatback. "Just for flavor," Clay had reasoned with Ike. "Hardly no fatback at all." But no use.

Clay was no better or worse than these Negro folk. That's what he meant to say by breaking bread here. Plus, Clay liked Negro food, even if he paid for it on the crapper now that he was so old. Smothered pork chops with yellow rice and gravy. Chicken and waffles. Okra, shrimp, and sausage. Fried catfish. Oxtails in gravy. Collard and mustard and turnip greens in fatback. Sweet peas. Fried cabbage. Sweet potatoes doused with orange and molasses. Red velvet cake for dessert. Better on the whole than Janisse's mild meals, or Pearl's. A good Christian woman, his wife, his salvation the way he saw it, even if she couldn't cook or give him children. Poor girl.

He walked straight across the threshold, the glass door ajar to let some of the heat out. The metal fan buzzed at the ceiling, pushing hot air around. He paused for a moment on the sawdust floor, scouted out a seat, tried not to notice the few patrons noticing him. "Anywhere you like," a young waitress called—waitresses they had now. Clay wasn't so pleased to be at Sonny's Good Food tonight. He didn't roam Hopkins at night. He only took the occasional lunch here. But he knew Ted played whist Wednesday nights at Sonny's Good Food. And he needed to speak with Ted. And so here he was.

He sat against the wall and waited for service. And waited. The young waitress would make him wait longer than necessary, maybe without even realizing it, just to let him know that he was in a place where he'd have to wait his turn just like the old Negro men there in the corner. That was okay. He folded his hands on the table and waited. Ted, he noticed at a glance, worried his cards with the other codgers at the round table, their menthol plumes enveloping them in fog. Ted had surely noticed Clay's strange nighttime presence, as they all did. He'd come over eventually, Clay knew. A young couple nearer by were obviously courting, the buck wearing a thin tie and leaning over the table as he spoke, the gal smiling soft and nodding, lifting a hand to her teeth when she laughed every so often. The young fellow cleared his throat when Clay sat down, spoke more softly across the table. It seemed to Clay that they liked each other well enough, these two. He hoped, for whatever reason, that they'd make a go of it.

"Yes sir," the waitress finally said, as if it wasn't *Yes, sir* at all she meant to say, setting down a glass of water without ice, lifting her pad above her small breasts like a shield. Her hand trembled around the paper pad. Her nails were unpolished and pared short, like the schoolgirl she was. She wouldn't look him in the eye. Now couldn't they just be friendly? He'd been coming to this establishment once a month, daylight hours, from before her mama was a glint in any fellow's eye. That's what he wanted to tell this scowling girl. Too pretty to make such an ugly face. "Chicken and waffles," he said instead. Then, as she scribbled, "Shouldn't you be doing your homework gal, getting ready for school in the morning?"

"Already done it," she said, refusing to defrost. Then: "Two sides you get."

"Macaroni and whatever greens are in the pot today will be fine, young miss."

"Mustard."

"Sounds right nice."

More scribbling.

"Corn bread comes with it too, right?"

"Corn bread's extra with the waffles."

"Oh. Okay."

"Okay you'll pay the extra, sir, or okay you don't need the corn bread?"

Clay smiled. The gal had moxie. He'd give her that. She seemed to gain courage with this last sentence. Looked him in the eye, even, if only for the briefest instant. Girls, white and colored, used to like looking him in the eye. That was before he was so darn old.

"Okay, I'll pay the extra, child."

She nodded, scribbled again in her pad and spun away on the sawdust floor in her Mary Janes.

Ted also made him wait longer than he felt was reasonable,

finishing his whist hand. Clay wondered how long things could go on like this. He didn't have too many good years left in him. Ten. Maybe twenty. But if he could unravel himself out into time, fifty, sixty, a hundred years from now, what would this place look like? There'd be orange and grapefruit groves, he was pretty sure. No matter what they did out on the Cape with those rockets. No matter what the Simply Citrus frozen people did out there on the ridge. No matter how many Weeki Wachis they opened up to amuse the northerners with mermaid shows. A comfort in that. River fruit the pride of the state. Pride of the whole dang country. But who'd be owning these groves and who'd be working them? Who'd live west of the tracks and who'd live east? Would the races finally mix into mud? Maybe, Clay thought. If those Kennedy boys had their way. And maybe that would be a good thing, all said and done.

"Clay," Ted said through his toothpick, groaning into the seat across, finally. Not Mr. Griffin, but Clay, because they'd known each other all their lives, and because Ted was old like Clay, and because Clay was here on Hopkins at Sonny's Good Food at night, and because of something else too.

"I seen him back in town," Clay said, once Ted stopped shifting in his seat.

"I expect." Clay watched Ted, waited for additional words of explanation that didn't come.

"Others have too. Haven't recognized him like I have. But they took note, new Negro poking around in a suit. Not something that goes unnoticed."

Ted nodded but didn't say anything.

"Figured he'd stay in New York like Junior Norwood. New York, I figured, ruins the South for a young Negro fella."

Still nothing. The toothpick just bobbed in Ted's mouth, in lieu of words.

"Well, what's he doing here?" Clay asked. "He's staying with you and Erma up at the house, I suppose."

The mention of Erma's name seemed to trigger something inside Ted, who looked more intently at Clay before uttering his next words.

"He's got business to tend to, I suppose. Like the rest of us. Not my place to say where he lays his head at night."

"Aw hell, Theodore. Fine. I don't want to know, anyway. But if he's here to cause trouble, trouble with the workers, I won't be able to protect him. Not anymore. Gets his neck broke it's his own fault.

He's a grown man now. A grown Negro man in Florida. You realize that, Ted, right?"

"Sure enough I do." Here Ted looked Clay straight in the eye. His toothpick stopped its bobbing. "He's his *own* man is the thing. Near forty years old, Clay. Maybe *you* should speak with him yourself, you have concerns."

"Don't be outrageous, Ted. For Lord's sake. Don't be outrageous. Me. Talk to him."

Sixteen

HETEROZYGOSITY. Protracted juvenility. Sealed inside the Pontiac, off to Lakeland for that new *Aphytis* larvae just to hold the line on the grove, Isaac contemplated the obstacles that stymied his more ambitious efforts. Those meddlesome miscegenate citrus embryos. You just never knew what was in a single seed until you invested all sorts of precious time waiting for that first fruit set. Plant a sexual seedling from a lemon tree and you're just as likely to wind up with grapefruits, limes, or tangerines, after waiting five years for first set, anyway. It was no easy thing—did he think it would be?—to encourage improved somatic hybrids in citrus. No surprise that propitious bud sports, pure chance, had thus far accounted for most of the commercial crop.

Lovebugs spattered and oozed against the car's windshield, smeared viscous inky rainbows under the influence of the wipers Isaac supposed he should replace. The Krupnick's Cash Store sold them fairly cheap. The very air an insectival minestrone, iron gray day like today. He hoped that Eli would lather on his Watkins after school before he lit out for the grove. Melody would remember, he hoped, if she weren't too preoccupied with her pies, with their grasping baby. He shook his head in vague resentment. Pies. Didn't Mel already have enough to do taking care of Eli and Sarah? Asinine lyrics and a tinkling tune reverberated from the Delco. Something about itsy-bitsy swimwear. He pressed the Wonderbar to call up a new station and exhaled upon hearing the more mellow timbre of Elvis pleading with some girl that time was short, better seize the day.

He'd grub out his experimental acres by next spring, maybe, plant tagged Valencias and Marsh grapefruit from registered budwood for harvest like the rest of the co-op. He'd give it until then. But maybe Walt was right. Maybe his old partner Sam in Philly was right, too. Who did Isaac think he was, Thomas Jefferson? He had no choice but to up his yield if he planned to keep afloat—simple math, really—if he didn't want to sell off the meaty middle of his grove to Ted, or to Walt, God forbid.

The modest urban gestures of Orlando gave way to scruffy cattle pasture, citrus groves, and dribbly lakes all competing for real estate en route to Lakeland. The drive seemed shorter this time. The Department of Citrus. The same young Negro gardener from Isaac's first visit to the commission, the keloid scar at his throat, stood like a sentinel at the front walk, edged the randy St. Augustine grass with a triangle-toothed implement that looked not unlike a medieval weapon. Pasted across the fellow's wet forehead was a galaxy of darker gnats that seemed not to bother him. Isaac tipped his imaginary hat to the young fellow as he approached, hoping only for a look of vague recognition in return. But the Negro withheld the gesture, lowering his eyes and giving way, his hands clasped reverently at the broom-handle tip of the edger. Isaac supposed that the Negro encountered plenty of white scientists, growers, bird dogs, and packing house executives every day and didn't have time to parse the fine distinctions between them. Else he recognized Isaac but didn't care to complicate his day with strange people.

The receptionist's station. The walls festooned with garish oils. The air vibrated under the harsh fluorescent lights. Four women congregated there before the Formica counter in a tangle of mismatched limbs and dress patterns, looming over the comely receptionist. They nearly shrouded their associate, who remained seated behind the counter, assailed her in falsetto tones.

"Knock me over with a feather," he heard. "With a feather!"

"We'll sure miss you, sugar."

Isaac stood behind for a moment, waited to be recognized, then cleared his throat, finally. "Pardon me."

"Mr. Golden," the toothsome receptionist declared, her register more sober than that of her allies. "Yes, the commissioner is expecting you. Fresh frozen concentrate?" she asked at a higher, practiced timbre.

Isaac warded off the offer with an upraised hand. He thought he noticed something in her eyes as she lifted the receiver to her ear to check on the commissioner. She had neglected to darken her fair brows today. But that's not what he noticed. He had seen these leaden female eyes often at his practice in Philadelphia.

The women decamped toward their proper stations. "Patty's getting married!" This verbal wake.

The receptionist ignored the remark, nodding instead at whatever she heard on the other end of the line. "Milly will be right here to walk you down," she announced, looking up at Isaac now, raising her fine eyebrows. She clutched her stomach, then removed it just as fast, cast her eyes downward at the gleaming linoleum.

The eyes always gave expectant mothers away.

"Well best wishes I suppose are in order. Best wishes to you, young lady," Isaac said, as if he were a much older man, or the pretty blonde secretary were a much younger woman.

Isaac sat and read the headlines from the day's *Sentinel,* the thin gray paper still crisp, untouched. Exiles from Cuba arriving by the thousands on Miami's shores. Mostly wealthy, this first wave. But some unaccompanied minors too. Operation Pedro Pan. Refugees, the word. Isaac wondered about this. Jews from Europe had been the truer refugees, it seemed to him. But both Cuba and Florida turned its back on the *St. Louis* and most of the Jews on board had perished in the camps. What about them? Was it fair now taking in all these mostly well-heeled Cubans and their offspring just because things hadn't gone their way on the island? Was this bearded fellow truly as bad as Melody and others feared? He wasn't Hitler, was he? Isaac exhaled through his nostrils, sifted through his first thoughts, his stingy feelings for the Cuban refugees. Well, he reconsidered, Hitler wasn't Hitler, either. Until he was.

Other headlines. *President Kennedy Announces US Intentions to Send Manned Flight to Moon and Return Safely by Decade's End.* Apollo, the new initiative. So all the rumors were true. Smart, Isaac thought. Anything to deflect attention from the fiasco in Cuba. Send the nation's thoughts skyward, having botched things on land. *NASA to Expand Operations on Cape.* Tensions with the Air Force, however. Considering potential future sites for primary base of operations. The Bahamas. The barrier islands of Georgia. Hawaii. Merritt Island. Interesting, Isaac thought. Joe Buck Wilson owned most of the managed acres on the island, proper. Too big a fish to join their ragtag co-op, Joe Buck. But Clay owned a small holding over on the island, too. He knew Clay was worried about NASA's expansion plans, the possible federal incursions on his woolly island.

After a few moments, the same weak-chinned woman from his first visit, Milly, he gathered, retrieved Isaac and guided him silently through the vibrating light of the labyrinthine halls to the commissioner's office. An enormous man carrying a white ten-gallon hat in his frying-pan hands was just leaving the suite as they approached, the commissioner trailing after him, painting a solicitous tableau, slumping his already shrunken shoulders. Milly fled without warning, as if she knew this man and didn't much like him. The big fellow's face, bracketed by gray lamb-chop sideburns, seemed rubicund with rage. He turned back toward the shrunken Shepherd, raised a bejeweled finger.

"I wanna play patty-cake with 'em," Isaac heard. "I'll just set one of your Orange Blossom Queens in your seat, you hear!?"

He set his ten-gallon hat down hard on his red pate, as if to contain the anger beneath. The male workers manning the desks in shirt sleeves and ties sat frozen in their seats, gazing up slack-jawed at the outsize fellow, who stamped his silver-toed cowboy boots on the hard floor as he strode out, clacking them on purpose, seemed to Isaac. He was only a shade taller than Isaac, but broader, and ignored him altogether, which Isaac appreciated. An acrid olfactory wake lingered in the air. Chewing tobacco.

"That, my friend, is Joe Buck Wilson," Shepherd declared, raising his shoulders. "Last of the great citrus barons."

"Doesn't seem too happy."

"He's not. Simply Citrus putting the squeeze on, set up those big concentrate plants and packing houses on his turf, not too far from Joe Buck's smaller plant. Poaching his field-workers out on the ridge. His foremen too."

"Really."

"Joe wouldn't budge on his field box rates, stubborn bastard, so bushels of tangerines and oranges went unpicked. Too busy politickin' in Tallahassee to keep tabs until it was too late. Getting ready to run for governor, word is. Anyway, shiftless son-in-law of his let things slide and fruit just rotted on the trees."

Shepherd exhaled audibly in a sigh, still gazing after the citrus baron's invisible trail. It seemed as if it were his first full breath in quite a while. "Well," he said, "come on in, Ike Golden."

"I'm really just here to pick up those *Aphytis*."

The commissioner descended wearily into his seat, didn't seem to hear Isaac's words, or didn't care to acknowledge them. He lifted a hand to smooth back his lacquered strands of hair, which complied.

"Shut the door." Isaac shut the door. "Have a seat." He sat. "Offer you a smoke?" Shepherd asked as he opened his slender silver case of cigarettes above the desk. Isaac raised a palm and Shepherd shut the silver case like a clamshell. "That's right," the commissioner said, remembering.

"Brave new world, Ike Golden. Single grower just can't compete against a corporation, even if his name *is* Joe Buck Wilson." Shepherd shook his head mildly in his chair now, gazing off at something over Isaac's shoulder, his small hands interlaced at his chest, from which his unlit cigarette protruded like a snorkel. He hardly seemed the cocksure commissioner. His skin was paler than before—had he been wearing makeup at Isaac's first visit?—the asterisk pockmarks in his sunken cheeks more pronounced. It seemed to be a truer Shepherd before him, as if Joe Buck Wilson's assault had stripped away his veneer.

"Know what they should put on my job description, Ike?" He fixed his eyes on Isaac now. "Tightrope walker. That's what I feel like half the time. Packing house owners. Bird dogs. Field-workers. Simply Citrus. Joe Buck. Small grower co-ops like yours. The feds and the scientists. Everyone's got their own agenda."

"What was that patty-cake stuff all about?" Isaac asked, hoping he wouldn't regret it.

Shepherd's eyes widened. "Oh, you heard that." He lit up his cigarette with his silver lighter, forgoing the flourishes from last time, inhaled deeply, the ash winking at Isaac from across the desk. The commissioner exhaled out the side of his mouth, squinting a pale eye against the smoke. "The field-workers, he meant, who do you think? He longs for the good ol' days of debt peonage. Before the war. You know what that is, right, debt peonage?"

Isaac shook his head.

"Wild times here back in the day. Sheriffs Jacksonville to Palm Beach combed the colored neighborhoods for roustabouts, arrested them for vagrancy, slapped them with fines they'd never be able to pay, then sent them off to the turpentine camps, cane fields, and Joe Buck's orange groves." He pointed with his cigarette over Isaac's shoulder, as if Wilson's groves could be located just outside the door.

"Four cents for a two-bushel box of oranges to work off the fine. Debt peonage. Still on the books, those vagrancy laws, but we don't enforce them."

"We?" Isaac asked.

"The state!" Shepherd barked. His nostrils breathed dragon smoke. "Not the commission. Not me. The state, I mean." Shepherd fixed his gaze on Isaac, who sat silent, his wheels spinning. Here he was, Commissioner Shepherd, revealing to Isaac how things once worked. Maybe still worked in some counties. Revealing more than he had intended, perhaps. A complex network of power brokers drove the industry, loosely united by their common interest in accumulating wealth and keeping it out of the hands of the Negroes. The growers, the sheriffs, the commissioner, the legislature, the governor himself, for all Isaac knew.

"I know what you think, gentleman of the Jewish persuasion like yourself. Probably think we're *all* backwards. *All* redneck crackers." Isaac was about to protest, but Shepherd waved him off with a hand trailing tobacco smoke. "Well we're not. Claude Neal. Willie Howard. Ocoee. Rosewood. Groveland. What happened more recently your neck of the woods, that poor school principal and his wife. Outrages, all." Shepherd tapped the ash worm from his cigarette into a crystal ashtray, as if to punctuate his point.

Claude Neal. Willie Howard. Ocoee. Rosewood. Groveland. Isaac had only heard about the Negro school principal in Mims, firebombed in his bed Christmas night, and the Groveland shootings a few years before—Sheriff McCall gunning down two handcuffed Negroes in his custody along the highway.

"Florida depends upon the right treatment and education of the Negro field-worker," the commissioner continued. "Citrus is to survive, we need a loyal cadre of Negro laborers, high rollers in the trees." He lingered over the word cadre, stretching each of its syllables. *Ca-dray*. "They know it, the field-workers, and we know it. Except for Joe Buck Wilson. That's why he's a dinosaur, Joe Buck. Thinks we can go back to the good ol' days before the war, horde all the profits, cheat hardworking high rollers out of an honest day's pay. But those days are over. It's a moral issue, way we treat our brethren, white and colored, like our new president says. He's right as rain about that. Bet you voted for the fellow."

"No. Actually no," Isaac said. "Wife did." The commissioner nodded, pensive.

"Hell, I wanted Smathers. Would have voted for *him*. Johnson even. Kennedy just wants to move too quick, my concern. Honest day's pay is one thing. Fair's fair," Shepherd uttered at a lower tone, his words slowing to a trot. "But field-workers have to be reasonable too. It's all about risk and reward. Growers take all the risk, they deserve the lion's share. Sure *you* can appreciate that, all people."

Isaac nodded. He wasn't sure what Shepherd meant, exactly, by *all people.* Because he was a grower who'd taken these risks? Or because his risk wasn't panning out?

"Any trouble your way, yet?"

"There's been someone hanging around in a tie," Isaac heard himself reveal. "Negro fellow. Co-op's worried about him." *What was Isaac saying?*

"Just be smart about it if he starts organizing your workers. Don't do anything rash. I'll trust you to be the smart one. Let me know about it."

Isaac said all right, that he would let Shepherd know. He pondered whether he should tell the commissioner about his more immediate concern, the vandal hacking up his trees time to time. Yet the words wouldn't come. He wondered why, troubled with his tongue the filling of a molar, as if he'd find his answer against its smooth contour, its shiny taste. Shame, it occurred to him. He was ashamed that someone had targeted his grove. That he couldn't protect his trees better against a possible Jew-hater, had allowed himself to be the victim. And there was something else, too, he realized. He was afraid of what Shepherd might do if he told him, what forces he might unleash on Isaac's property to set matters aright. While he hoped that Sheriff Wright would capture the culprit or culprits, he didn't want things to get out of hand. Shepherd was the type, he feared, to set a whole house ablaze to kill a mouse. Walt too.

"What we're working on here, see, will be good for everyone, the commission, growers like yourself. The field-workers too. Good for citrus, is the thing. What's good for citrus is good for everyone." Isaac felt himself being drawn ever so slowly into a dubious alliance. "Come on. I'll show you." Shepherd rose and snuffed out his cigarette, strode around the desk and opened the door. What was Isaac to do but follow? He needed his wasps.

"I need those wasps!" he called after the commissioner, who bounded ahead. "Scale's thick, I'm afraid." He was embarrassed, suddenly, to acknowledge his stricken trees, which he refused to spray with chemicals on account of Eli's lungs, but Shepherd seemed uninterested. Isaac struggled to keep pace down a separate network of labyrinthine hallways.

"Where do you think we keep the critters? My desk drawer?"

The commissioner halted at a solid unmarked door and withdrew a large set of keys from the breast pocket of his suit. "They're from Israel, you'll be pleased to know."

"Huh?"

"The new wasps. Shared their new bug with us, anyway, your Israelis. Far as effectiveness versus scale, they beat the tar out of the *Melinus* variety from India. You'll see. *Cohenis,* they're called, these new *Aphytis.* Jewish wasps." Shepherd stopped shuffling through his keys, slapped Isaac's back and howled, as if the irony of the phrase just occurred to him, having uttered it. "How do you like that, Ike!? Jewish WASPS!"

"Funny," Isaac said, but didn't laugh. "So where are we going?"

"Roof."

The roof? Did they breed and store their beneficial insects in rooftop warrens, Isaac wondered, like homing pigeons?

He followed after Shepherd, who finally found the right key, up a narrow dimly lit stairway. The commissioner swung open a metal door at the top to reveal the iron gray sky and something else, something Isaac hadn't anticipated at all.

"I'm not getting on that thing!" Isaac cried as soon as he saw the chopper. Somehow he knew that Shepherd intended to take him somewhere on that rickety contraption, that he had anticipated and planned for this dramatic reveal from the very beginning. It looked like an overgrown mosquito to Isaac, the two swollen panes of glass for the windshield its bulbous eyes.

"Where's your spirit of adventure, Ike Golden?" The commissioner removed his suit jacket as he spoke, folded it over his arm. No moons beneath Shepherd's underarms. He wasn't one to perspire, the commissioner. "You want to know how things work, don't you, Ike? It's something I knew about you from the very start. Swooping down here and buying up Hawley's acres—fancy MD in your back pocket."

Isaac's eyes widened, which Shepherd noticed.

"Think I didn't know about that, Dr. Golden? I know everything about my growers and their trees. It's my business to know."

Shepherd sounded more like his old self now, Joe Buck Wilson having departed. A more southerly cocksure commissioner. Isaac preferred the glimpse of that different commissioner back in his office.

"Now the other river growers," Shepherd continued. "They don't care a whit about how things work. Which is fine. I've got nothing against them, 'long as they mind their p's and q's, 'long as they keep an eye on the spray schedule, our frost warnings, see their product from bud set to packing house with due diligence. But you're a different sort. Hell, I feel a kinship I don't mind saying. Not a go along to get along type. Not satisfied with the current best practices. No, Ike Golden wants to see how things work, doesn't he?"

Yes, Isaac wanted to see how things worked.

"You'll want to put these on." Shepherd handed Isaac a pair of black headphones as he set about flicking innumerable switches on the helicopter's dashboard.

"Safety belts too." He could hear the commissioner's voice through the headphones, equipped with small microphones. The commissioner demonstrated how to throw the black canvas belts over his shoulders, clipping separate shiny buckles at his hips. The restraints somehow made Isaac feel less secure. He gripped a vinyl loop at the door. When he looked back at Shepherd, he was wearing silver-rimmed aviator glasses with dark lenses and a blue baseball cap over his lacquered hair. He had placed his suit jacket on the hard floor between them. It seemed like pure theater to Isaac, this helicopter business. He expected, hoped, that at any moment the commissioner's facade would shatter under the strain of these protracted shenanigans. *Joke's over!* He'd lead Isaac back down the stairs to their *Aphytis* laboratory. But after Shepherd flicked another toggle switch, Isaac heard the whine of the engine, like a giant blender, then saw the blades above begin to whir until he couldn't see them anymore, and then they were off. It felt at first as if someone were holding them precariously above the solid tarmac, a lopsided field box of oranges. The tenuous buoyancy unnerved Isaac. His gastric juices roiled. He could taste the pungent vapors in his mouth.

"Relax, Ike. For Lord's sake," Shepherd said. He smiled as he banked right, northward Isaac thought, more dramatically than required. The commissioner relished Isaac's discomfort, he knew, so he exhaled through his nostrils, loosened his grip from the vinyl strap and settled himself in his seat. Better. An auditory assault, all the same, traveling by helicopter. He hadn't anticipated the deafening roar of the whirring blades, which penetrated the headphones. It seemed to Isaac that engineers should do something about the insufferable interior noise. Perhaps they should put NASA on it. The only solace was that he needn't make small talk with Shepherd.

The land looked different by air, greener. Less human and more vegetal. Rolling hills shrouded in broccoli floret oaks. Manicured citrus groves along the flats. Occasional lakes like mud puddles beneath the dull light. Insignificant two-lane highways bisected the land in places, insectival automobiles crawling slow. The sun split through the clouds and painted the earth in lighter green as they buzzed northward. It was curious and hopeful seeing the land from high above. They hadn't made a total mess of things yet with skyscrapers or amusement parks, housing developments or phosphate mines with those eerie aquamarine lakes. Perhaps that Disney fellow wouldn't make an incursion, after all.

Forest thickets and grove land gradually gave way to crumpled carpets of pastureland buffeted by postage stamps of oak woods and more narrow oak bands between the clearings.

"*Ocala!*" the commissioner shouted. Isaac strained to hear through the whirring of the blades, the insulation of his earmuffs. "*Horse country! Almost there!*"

Isaac could see the black and brown beasts below, motionless against the clover backdrop. Horse country gave way to dense oak woods and then Isaac saw the spherical structure straight ahead, rising from within the canopy like a transparent eyeball. Sun glinted off its innumerable panes. But for its spherical shape, it reminded Isaac of a photo he'd seen of the Crystal Palace in England, burned down by a suspicious fire before the war, if Isaac remembered correctly.

"*Nice thing 'bout Alachua County!*" Shepherd shouted through the microphone. "*Old oaks around give us our privacy. . . .*" Isaac couldn't quite make out all of Shepherd's next staticky words, just sporadic ones. "*. . . spies from Brazil and Texas and Cali' . . . Sunkist bastards . . . off the scent!*"

As they drew closer, Isaac noticed the blurry green inside the glass dome—an orangery, of course!—a humble brick building beside with a cement landing pad for the helicopter. The commissioner set the mosquito down with surprising gentleness and set about flicking off the toggle switches. The blades slowed, their whir lowered in pitch. "Haven't lost one passenger yet," Shepherd boasted, flashing white teeth.

The cement pad felt unusually solid and heavy beneath Isaac's feet, as if he were one of those astronauts returning from space orbit. He lowered his head instinctively beneath the slow blades as he followed after the commissioner. Was it something he'd seen on television, this dance? Indoors, the chopper echoed strongly now in Isaac's skull. He opened his maw wide to clear his ears. No luck. Shepherd led him down the narrow metal stairway and into a broad fluorescent laboratory, which reminded Isaac of his med school days. Centrifuges. Microscopes. Bunsen burners and glass beakers. Graduated cylinders and Erlenmeyer flasks. Long stainless-steel counters. Anonymous bespectacled men in white lab coats. Curious lead ovens like bank safes, too. Isaac wondered about those heavy ovens.

"Afternoon, Dr. Shepherd," the nearest scientist rose and greeted them. The scientist sported thick black-framed eyeglasses and a flat-top hairstyle so recently graded that it recalled the helicopter pad above. The other scientists, most of them flat-topped and bespectacled too, looked up from their labors, then back down just as quickly, unfazed by Shepherd's visit. The commissioner visited regularly, Isaac gathered.

"What's the good word today, Dr. Davis?" Shepherd fairly shouted.

"Coming along," the scientist answered, stingily. "Can I be of any assistance?" He cast brief stabbing glances toward Isaac.

"He's okay," Shepherd assured the scientist, still too loud. Then, lowering his volume, the commissioner told the scientist that they were just visiting the orangery, that he was sorry to disturb the team, that they could carry on with their good work. He didn't actually introduce Isaac to the scientist, which Isaac appreciated. He was anxious to see the enclosed orangery. The commissioner had alluded to the facility during their first encounter, but Isaac hadn't anticipated the sheer size of the thing. The Russians, he figured, must have spotted the structure by now from one of their high-altitude spy planes or satellites. What must such a structure look like to them, this enormous glass eye smack in the woolly middle of America's big toe?

Isaac trailed after Shepherd toward a separate door at the other end of the lab, which opened into a narrow unadorned vestibule, dark but for the halo of light in the distance. Isaac's flesh tingled. He admonished himself silently for his schoolgirl excitement, which he tried to disguise.

The orangery's mouth. There wasn't a door. Strips of transparent rubber sheeting sealed inside from out. The electric roar of conditioned air. Isaac followed the commissioner through the sheeting into the orangery.

Glass-encased orangeries in chilly Europe dated from the fourteenth century, but this was something else, entirely. The sheer scale. He looked up before looking out. The glass ceiling wasn't quite as high as Isaac might have guessed from the chopper, but plenty high, all the same. Fifty feet up or so. And the expanse! Looking down, finally, straight across the eye's pupil in between a tree row, the structure stretched farther than Isaac could clearly make out. Room for at least two hundred trees down the row. The nearest trees seemed about five years old and especially robust, the foliage dark green, bursting with nitrogen, iron, and magnesium. The ammoniac chemicals burned in Isaac's nostrils. Orange fruit hung down, odd for this time of year. It was cooler than in the vestibule, but wetter. The atmosphere felt different in his ears, too, a shift in altitude. He hummed a bar low to hear the sound vibrate in his skull, which he didn't think Shepherd would hear over the electric hum.

"It's the climate control," the commissioner said, either reading Isaac's thoughts or hearing his own hum. "Noisy as a stuck pig, I know. But the glass roof"—Shepherd pointed skyward—"allows us to control the temp, humidity, and such. Keeps the pests out too. Completely controlled environment, except for the light." Isaac nodded, but didn't say anything.

"Impressive, huh?"

"Yes," Isaac conceded.

The commissioner led Isaac across the short expanse to the trees. It was difficult to make headway. The soft earth gave beneath his feet like pure sand. Ridge earth here, Isaac gathered. Not as rich as river dirt. That's why they doused it with ammoniac fertilizer. The electric roar of the climate control dissipated some as they neared the grove.

"See 'em yet?" the commissioner asked.

Isaac did see them, the oranges to which Shepherd obviously referred. Isaac couldn't believe his eyes, expected the picture to adjust as they lumbered forward, to come into new focus. But the original appearance of these strange fruits only grew sharper.

"Square oranges?" Isaac asked as they drew close to one cultivar, wincing. He looked down at the trunk base toward the bud union, rootstock spilling liquid over this mutant scion. Trifoliate stock, he gathered, which tended toward this strange growth at the union.

"Now don't turn up your nose. Go on and pick one. Here." Shepherd plucked one of the square fruits from its stem and handed it to Isaac, who almost dropped it like a hot potato.

"Why?" Isaac asked, staring down at the miniature monstrosity in his hand, four inches across, he'd guess. Same general size as a Valencia.

"Shipping. Why do you think? Standard box of three-and-a-half-inch sweet oranges, we pack four layers, four rows, six across, as you well know." Isaac pursed his lips, nodding. "Ninety-six per box, par for the course. Now most people look at that and think, if they think anything at all, *Okay, we fit ninety-six oranges in a packing crate to New York. So be it.* But a man like me—a man like you too, Ike, I have a notion—looks at that same packing box and thinks, *Look at all that empty air, that wasted space all on account of simple geometry.*"

Isaac hadn't entertained any such notion.

"Now a square orange takes care of that problem," Shepherd continued. "Same size square fruits'll pack an orange extra every row. That's sixteen additional oranges every box. You know what something like that adds up to, shipping costs?"

Isaac shrugged. He didn't like the feel of this square orange in his hand. There was something singular about a perfect round orange nested in one's palm. Something inviolable. The human hand just wasn't shaped for these square fruits.

"Taste it."

Isaac pierced the thin pericarp membrane, exposing the snowy albedo cap, dropped the peel ribbons to the ground. He'd been waiting for permission, anxious to inspect the fruit's innards with his eyes more so than with his mouth, really. The pulp seemed encased in eight or nine ovarian locules of haphazard size and shape, belying the tidy exterior geometry, as if the segments didn't quite know how to grow up inside their unusual confines. He plucked one of the smaller segments from its neighbors and, after the briefest hesitation, placed the entire morsel into his mouth. The skin melted away under the slightest influence of Isaac's incisors, the juice vesicles burst, releasing an acid mouthful. Isaac spat out the bitter oyster, which landed in a clump between their feet.

"See?" Shepherd said. "That's the only problem. Can't seem to get that damn TA level down. Solids just won't take over like normal. Outside color breaks okay, but insides won't ripen proper."

"Thanks for telling me."

"Folks at UC Davis out in Cali' are having the same problem with their tomatoes. Square's not the problem. Getting them to taste like tomatoes . . . well."

Isaac spat again, jettisoning the acid remnants to the earth. A tiny spark from the acid ignited at his lower gums, where he'd probably flossed too aggressively.

The commissioner laughed, slapped Isaac on the back. "Oh, come on now, Ike. Be a big boy." Isaac, wiping his mouth with the back of his broad hirsute hand, couldn't help but smile. It was the first truly human moment between them, and it frightened him.

"Hope that's not all you're up to out here."

"Nope. Follow me."

They lumbered down the row on the sandy earth through the grove of square oranges. There was something strange about all these trees, something other than their square oranges, their too-green leaves, the ammoniac effluvia. The stillness, it finally dawned on Isaac. Not one leaf trembled beneath the glass panes. No wind. Not one bird sang or skittered across his visual screen. No jet noise. No butterflies. No dragonflies. No marsh rabbits. Only the faint hum now of the climate control units, these motionless too-green trees.

It took a lot of things, countless large and small things, to make up a world, even a small corner of the world. You never realized how much stuff it actually took—how full the world!— until these features were culled, one by one.

They reached a gap in the tree rows, a broad irrigation pipe, then a separate grove of trees, grapefruit. Big fruit. Round, at least. They hung stock-still in grape-like bunches, looking like the berries they and all citrus truly were. Hesperidia.

"Big fruit," Isaac said, stupidly.

"That's not the half of it. Let's open one up." The commissioner brandished an ivory budding knife from his back suit pocket—"Never leave home without it," he said—and sliced open a yellow globe. The knife was too small for the project so it took a bit more carving than it might have, juice dripping onto Shepherd's small hand from the severed sacs inside.

"Texas pasting our behind of late with that dang Ruby Red,"

the commissioner said as he sliced. The Ruby Red developed in McAllen, Isaac knew, singlehandedly vaulted Texas into the citrus industry. Isaac didn't like the sticky sweet juice, not nearly as complex as Isaac's river fruit, his Marsh and Duncan cultivars. Yet the American housewife, evidently, thought otherwise. Plus, the Ruby Red was seedless. "Well," Shepherd said, handing Isaac half of his sloppily shorn sphere, "Texas can stick that Ruby Red where the sun don't shine." The pulp was deep red, redder than the pinkish Marsh insides of Isaac's river fruit, rivaling the crimson interior of those Ruby Reds. But that's not what captured Isaac's attention. He stared down hard at the exposed pulp as if he were reading tea leaves.

"You see it, don't you?"

Isaac nodded.

"Could tell straight away you noticed. Can't get one by you, Ike Golden. Real fart smeller, as my daddy would say." Isaac counted the ovarian locules, his thumb on top of one segment so he wouldn't lose track. A mere eight segments instead of fourteen. "You know how long it takes your average housewife in New York to slice up two halves of a grapefruit every morning?"

Isaac didn't.

"Well I do. Three minutes, forty-six seconds. Family of four, two grapefruit, that adds up to over seven-and-a-half minutes that the American housewife wastes on carving up breakfast for her family. Lord knows she's got better things to do. Laundry. Ironing. Dishes. Those Jack LaLanne exercises. Fewer segments to labor over the better." Isaac could feel the weight of Shepherd's stare as he continued to gaze, nonplussed, at the shorn fruit.

"You're not impressed," Shepherd stated.

"No, no, Isaac heard himself say. It's quite something, I'll give you that. I don't know how you did it. How *did* you do it?"

"Irradiation. X-rays."

The ovens, Isaac thought.

"Amazing what kind of useful havoc you can stir up in a simple seed, irradiate the embryo. Hard to take too much credit. Never know how you'll tweak the profile. Just irradiate enough seeds, take enough time waiting for them to bear fruit and something worthwhile's bound to come down the pike."

Isaac winced. He hadn't realized that the scientists were irradiating seeds, forcing propitious mutations. It seemed to him that a line had been crossed. *Behold,* God commanded in the Tanakh, *I have given you every herb yielding seed, which is upon the face of all the earth, and every tree, in which is the fruit of a tree yielding seed—to you it shall be for food.* Isaac believed in seeds. He believed in the improvement of fruit, the careful winnowing of natural, mixed-up citrus seeds. But these terrific new human powers. How small a step, he considered, between H-bombs and irradiated seeds. These freakish oranges and grapefruit.

"Might as well taste it at least." The commissioner placed the ivory haft of his small knife in Isaac's broad palm. Isaac carved out one of the large segments, lifted it to his mouth along with the knife. Bright. Sweet. Tart. A superior fruit.

"Quite something, isn't it?" The commissioner seemed rather subdued under the circumstances.

"It's a fine fruit," Isaac admitted, matching Shepherd's tone.

"Know what keeps me up at night, Ike? Besides those Russians blasting us to kingdom come? I close my eyes some nights, Ike, and you know what I see?"

"What?"

"I'm looking down from the chopper, just like we were just doing." Shepherd splayed his small fingers toward the fortified, ammoniac earth. "Except I can see the whole peninsula, not just a patch of it. But I don't see orange groves or lakes or even cattle pasture. All I see is miles and miles of cane grass stretching clear north of Okeechobee, the whole state a furry green arm ringed by concrete and steel on the coasts. You ever seen a sugar cane field, Ike?"

"No. I haven't."

"Biggest dang waste of perfectly good land you're likely to see. Not even a respectable plant, ask me. Just an oversized thicket of sawgrass. Have to burn it all down, throw up thick plumes of stinking black smoke all over creation to get at that little bit of cane inside. Propped up, though, by the US federal government just to keep those dang rich exiles on our side. Politics. But there ain't nothing you can put in that ground to grow"—here the commissioner stabbed a bejeweled finger down to the earth—"nothing compares to the majesty of a citrus tree. Miracle enough to make a grown man come back to the Lord, an orange tree, he 'least stops to think about it. Now I truly believe that, and I think you do too, Ike, even if it's different Lords we might have in mind."

The commissioner's words threatened to move Isaac.

"Thing is, I need your help, Isaac. Texas is pasting us in grapefruit, like I said. All they got is land over there, the fuckers. Endless supply of wetbacks across the Rio Grande work for a song. Unlike our new Negroes. Simply Citrus threatening to pull stakes." Ike's eyes widened, which Shepherd must have noticed. "There, I said it. I'm worried about keeping Simply Citrus happy."

"So what do you want from me, JP?"

"Orangery's one thing, Ike. But how'll these scions perform in the field? The river, site of our finest grapefruit holdings. That's where we make our stand. Ridge'll never hold a candle to the river far as grapefruit's concerned. Hundred scions, I need you to bud. Whole crate in the lab just waiting on you. I can make it worth your while too, Ike Golden. Lord knows I can make it worth your while."

Isaac exhaled through puffed cheeks, pursed lips. He believed in the improvement of fruit. But there were boundaries somewhere. Blasting a simple seed with gamma rays? Isaac gazed about at the lush grove, the too-green trees. The fumes from the fortified earth burned in his nose.

I have given you every herb yielding seed, which is upon the face of all the earth, and every tree, in which is the fruit of a tree yielding seed.

Still, something about Shepherd's plea moved him. Here was a man, Isaac thought. A man not unlike him, who only wanted to succeed. Under great pressure, this man, as they all were. Like the earth itself, its tectonic plates beneath their feet shifting and grinding this very moment. It was hard to deny such a man.

"Come on. Let's go and get you those *cohenis*, anyway. Your Jewish wasps."

Isaac trailed after the commissioner on the sandy earth, glanced up at the crystal roof. He had forgotten all about the wasps.

Seventeen

"RELAX, MEL, even the Negroes like Sheriff Wright well enough," Eli's father assured Eli's mother.

Sheriff Wright would be climbing their porch any moment, which, for whatever reason, caused his mother to pace about the kitchen, wiping her hands on her apron, over and over. GOOD HOUSEKEEPING, the apron said. Eli made himself useful with Sarah's tiny spoon, trying to corral her saliva-soaked cereal oat rounds back into the tiny cavern of her mouth from her cheeks, where they adhered.

"Now just relax, Mel. He's not like that good ol' boy sheriff from Groveland. Probably voted for Kennedy just like you."

Eli liked the sheriff. He honked his horn in town and sometimes flashed his red light. All Eli had to do was lift his fist and pull it down hard. *Honk! Honk!*

They heard the scrunch of the loose river rock beneath the sheriff's Tasca, the two car doors clapping shut.

"You won't mind if Samuel joins us," Sheriff Wright uttered at the threshold, something tugging down at the vowels in his *you*, as if other people might mind the Negro deputy joining them. But not Eli's father. Not *yoouu*.

"Of course not," his father answered, swinging his shoulder open to the house. Something about having the sheriff and his deputy here this morning didn't feel right to Eli. It felt like they were in trouble, that *he* was in trouble, even though Eli knew that he didn't do anything bad, that someone else had done something bad. That's why Eli's father phoned the sheriff in the first place.

Eli had told his mother about the bad word on the tree, and then told his father when his father got home last night from Lakeland carrying a crate he didn't want to talk about. Eli, however, didn't tell his mother about the strange Negro in the grove wearing a yellow tie, and he didn't tell his father, either. He didn't know why he didn't tell his parents about the strange Negro. The words just never came.

It was already bright in the house as they made their way to the kitchen. Eli would be late for school. *That* was nice, anyway. (His mother had put on her thin nightgown and went outside to warn Mr. Langford at the bottom of the river rock driveway.) Sheriff Wright and Deputy Roosevelt seemed to take up a lot of room under the roof. Noisy too, their stiff shiny boots clackety-clacking on the pine floor, a bit softer on the lemon linoleum. Something about their crisp brown uniforms, their silver badges, their broad cowboy hats, seemed loud too in the house, even though they didn't make any noise, even though they held their hats in their hands. And their guns! They were big and heavy-looking and Eli didn't like them in the house. Deputy Roosevelt's scalp was shiny and black beneath the kitchen light, except for the orbit of dusty hair above his small ears. Eli had always thought that Deputy Roosevelt, who never honked his horn in town, had more hair underneath his brown hat. He thought that he was younger.

His mother had set the table with their good china. She offered them coffee from the percolator, and offered them pie too, even though it was morning, which Sheriff Wright accepted, but not Deputy Roosevelt, who didn't even sit down but stood near the pocket door, setting his hat down on the counter, gripping his belt with his black hands, his heavy silver gun drooping over the linoleum. He smelled like aftershave and leather and stole glances at Eli time to time, wondering about his weird rash across his nose, Eli figured. Lots of people he didn't know stole glances at him, wondered what was wrong with him.

They didn't talk about what they were here for even now, which Eli thought was strange. Strange, too, that Sheriff Wright's thick gray hair still held its part on the left, even though he had been wearing a cowboy hat.

"Hot as blue blazes today," Sheriff Wright said as he sipped his coffee.

"Summer's coming on," his mother said, bobbing Sarah in her arms. She reached behind the counter and unplugged the percolator.

The sheriff smelled like aftershave too, but more orangey, less spicy than Deputy Roosevelt. The fancy china looked funny in the sheriff's leathery hand, even though his nails were clean. "That's good coffee that is, Mrs. Golden. Much obliged."

"Not at all," his mother said.

"This Maxwell House?"

"Yuban."

"Yuban. I'll be. Have to tell the Mrs."

His mother wore a dress now and her hair was in a bun, which Eli didn't like. It made her look old. Eli saw tiny beads of sweat above her plump lip. She was still nervous, it occurred to him, even though they were just talking about coffee. He could feel the wet in his own palms beneath the kitchen table, the hot blood pumping through the butterfly across the bridge of his nose. He lifted a small hand to feel its heat, the swollen ridge of skin. His father didn't look scared, anyway. He sat beside Eli and just breathed, as if he were waiting for something to happen.

Sheriff Wright, across from them at the breakfast table, carved a small triangle from the spearpoint of his pie and took a bite. "*Umm-umm,*" he moaned. "Warm."

"I wouldn't serve you cold pie, Sheriff." His mother's face was blotchy with red all of a sudden, as if only part of it would blush.

"You're one lucky man, Ike Golden." Sheriff Wright wagged a finger toward Eli's father. "I'd watch out if I were you."

Now what did *that* mean? Eli wondered. His father didn't seem to like the comment, or the wagging finger, because he didn't say anything, just nodded his head slow and hid his teeth behind his lips. He wished that his father would say something. The sheriff seemed to expect some words from his father, because he kept his eyes on him until it was clear that no words would be coming out of his mouth, after all.

The sheriff took another bite, then washed it down too fast with his hot coffee, brushed his hands off as if they were dusty and said, "All right then," as if he needed two slurps of coffee and two bites of pie before saying what he really needed to say.

"Eli," his father declared, "now tell Sheriff Wright exactly what you saw on the tree. Then after we finish our pie you'll go out and show us. You can find the tree again, correct?"

Eli nodded. He told Sheriff Wright what he saw. Deputy Roosevelt groaned low, then cleared his throat as if to erase his groaning.

"Well that's a good boy, keeping an eye out on the grove for your daddy. That's what we need more of these days, Russians, Cubans, and all, more citizens like you, Eli, keeping an eye out. Thinking about organizing a Citizens Patrol. You'd help us out with that, right Ike?"

"Of course," his father said. He seemed confused though. His eyebrows narrowed over his nose.

Sheriff Wright sighed. "I suppose that's a pretty bad word, Samuel, yes? That word on the tree?" He didn't look back toward his deputy when he spoke. He swallowed another piece of pie, instead, his eyes on his plate, as if the bad word weren't quite as important as pie, anyway.

"Sure enough, Sheriff. Hateful as words come, I'd just about say."

"It's quite a slur," his father added. Sheriff Wright nodded. Eli expected his parents to shoo him out of the room at any moment. Most times his parents shooed him out of the room the rare occasion other grownups were over. Mr. Clay and Mrs. Griffin. The Junior League mothers.

"It's an extremely hateful word," his mother assured the sheriff, then wrapped her arms around her chest, as if from a sudden chill. "Vicious."

"Now Melody." Eli's father.

"So what we're talking about is a pretty bad word. That's the thing of it." The sheriff took another bite of pie.

"Yes," his father said.

"Mmm-hmm," Deputy Roosevelt said. Why wouldn't he sit? Eli wondered.

"An awful word," his mother said. "Just awful."

"You have to understand, we're just not used to this sort of thing around here." His father nodded his head, made a listening noise. "Anti-Semitism." The sheriff said the word slowly, tasting each syllable, which sounded strange to Eli from the sheriff's mouth. "Miami, one thing. Jewish churches dynamited and whatnot. But just the Krupnicks in town here all these years, Meyer and Frieda, who we all like well enough, running the . . . store"—the sheriff hesitated before saying store, as if he were used to calling it something else—"hardly any Jewish folk for people to think on. Just the funny ones on the TV. I'm surprised dumb clucks around here even knew that awful word to begin with. Can't say I'm too familiar—"

"You'll understand that we just can't wait around for things to get worse," his father said, his temperature rising. Eli saw the blood in his cheeks. "I hope you plan to investigate now. In earnest."

The sheriff inhaled deeply, wiped the corner of his mouth with the cloth napkin, raised his paler palms as if to surrender, displeased that he wouldn't be finishing his pie. "All right, Ike Golden. I hear ya. Let's just go take a look."

Eli's mother smeared the white lotion across the bridge of his nose. It was sunnier today. He led his father and the officers past his mother's vegetable garden, the triad of live oaks with their shaggy beards, pinpricked with tiny acorns now, the wild tamarind. He liked leading this party of grownups. He knew something, something important that the grownups didn't know.

"Now what kind of tree is *that*?" Deputy Roosevelt asked behind him.

"Tamarind," his father said. "No business growing here, really. Too far north."

"Could cut it down," the sheriff proposed. "Looks like a big weed to me."

"I suspect we'll just let it be," his father answered. "Like Hawley."

Eli led them past the islands of lantana and palmetto and privet and wax myrtle and into the grove, proper. He walked faster than he usually walked when he wasn't running. His throat started to burn, but he didn't slow down. It felt good to make the grownups keep pace.

"These peas we're walking on?" The deputy inquired. "Okay to stomp on them like this?"

"Cowpeas. Wax beans. Few peanuts. You can walk right over them, deputy. They're not for harvest."

"What are they for then?" asked the sheriff. Eli looked back. The sheriff's shoulders were narrow but he held them high. Deputy Roosevelt was broader all around and taller but he walked with a stoop.

"Cover crop. I turn them over after the rainy season. Fixes nitrogen in the soil—"

"Fixes?" the sheriff's voice seemed to reach up high. "What's wrong with it?"

"By fix I just mean that the cover-crop roots capture the nitrogen from the air and sort of put it in the soil for the trees. That way I don't have to use chemical fertilizer. Can't just douse the earth with chemicals. Works short-term but sooner or later the ground gets angry. Keeps weeds down too, my cover crop. Pokeweed. Pigweed. Beggarweed. Hawksbeard. Goatweed. Pepperweed. Cudweed." Eli's father always got more talkative, too talkative, when their grove was the subject.

"Alrighty then," the sheriff said, as if he weren't really sure it was alrighty. His alrighty seemed to stop the conversation for a while.

"Quite a ways," Deputy Roosevelt finally said.

"Maybe we should have driven a spell down Hammock first," Sheriff Wright said. Eli looked back in time to see the sheriff tilt his hat up high on his forehead, mop his wet brow with a white handkerchief. His face was pink like Porky Pig on the color TV.

"Slow down, Eli," his father warned. "I can hear your breath. Just go slow, Eli. You'll make yourself sick."

They reached the five-year Hamlins. It wasn't far now. Nearing the scarred tree, Eli worried suddenly that it wouldn't be there at all, that someone or something might have plucked it straight out of the earth overnight just to get Eli in trouble. But there it was. And there was the nasty word. It looked older now, the wound of letters, hardly any fresh green now visible in the sliced cambium.

"Aw phooey," the sheriff said, as if he was disappointed by the discovery.

"Sure 'nough," the deputy said, removing his hat, lifting his hand to mop his wet dome. "Who'd they expect would see this tree way inside here?"

"Us," his father said. "Us."

Eli didn't like the quick and harsh way his father said and repeated the word *us*, like he didn't like the sheriff's question.

"Still think this is kids, Sheriff?" his father asked.

"Probably. Not exactly professional work. Sloppy as all get out, these last three letters." The sheriff crouched under the canopy and ran his fingers down the scars, as if he might smooth away the hateful letters from the bark. "Won't kill the tree, scarring like this. Am I right, Ike?"

"Yes," his father said. "Right. Tree itself should be fine. Now if they'd sliced through the cambium clear around the whole tree—"

"Because then we'd really have something. Property damage with a price tag on it." He stepped back from underneath the canopy. "Scale pretty bad on these trees," he said, as if he hoped to change the topic of conversation.

An east breeze rustled through the grove. It felt good on Eli's sweaty neck, the mild breeze that penetrated the canopy. The breeze brought the salt and sulfur river smell with it, which made him think about the Indian midden and its snowberries. He wondered if Sheriff Wright knew about the midden.

"Property," the sheriff uttered again. "Some property you got here. Choice acres." He leaned away from the tree, arched his back, planted his hands on his hips.

"Yes, I know."

"You have to understand, Ike, the way some folk think around here. They take the southern way of life real serious. Samuel'll tell you better than anyone. Almost lost the election after I appointed Sam here deputy to round out the crew."

"Mmm-hmm," the deputy muttered.

"Your case, it's one thing to have the Krupnicks set up shop in town, modest storefront and all. But land. Land's different. Old Man Hawley owned these choice acres long as most folk can remember. Then a Yankee swoops down, fellow of the Jewish persuasion—I'm just telling you straight here, Ike, I won't stand on ceremony—and folks see the change coming. Change to the southern way of life. This ain't *me* talking, hear?"

"I know. It's all right," Eli heard his father say.

"Folks around here don't like change is the thing. Who knows what this Yankee's got planned on these acres down the road? Sure, he seems interested enough in the grove, family man too, that helps, but how long before he sells out to some corporation, the Cubans, the Feds, some other real estate concern? How long before he turns over these acres and plants Miami-style condominiums instead? Or a golf course? Who knows?"

"That's not going to happen, Sheriff. I only want to grow citrus."

"Hell, I believe you. Don't get me wrong. But people see you and they see all sorts of other things. They see change. Now change is good, I say. That NASA business. Breathe some life into this sleepy town. Tourists. Money. Progress, in a nutshell. I'm all about change. I'm all about progress. Would I have a Negro deputy by my side I weren't all about change?"

"I suppose not."

"Trouble is, plenty of folk around here, white folk anyway, just assume roll *back* the clock. Southern way of life under attack on all sides, way they see it." Sheriff Wright glanced toward his deputy, who nodded.

What was the southern way of life he kept mentioning? Eli wondered.

"So what do you suggest that we do?" his father asked. "About *this*"—he gestured toward the scarred tree. His voice had that hard-edge sound back again that frightened Eli.

"Tree'll live is the thing," the sheriff said. "Like you said. No property damage to speak of. That's the thing of it."

"So you still think it's a harmless prank. You won't investigate. Fine. But if I find out that Walt—"

"Careful now."

"Pardon?" Eli didn't like his father's *pardon.* It sounded like too fancy a word for the outdoors, especially with his father's hard-edge voice.

"That Walt business. Just giving you fair warning. Walt wouldn't carve up a perfectly good orange tree. He may be a mean son of a gun, but Boehringers go back a ways in this town. Back before the freeze in '95. That still counts for something."

Eli could tell that his father's dander was up the way he scratched at his tawny hair above his ear, the way he swallowed a quick fistful of air and shot it out his nostrils, hard. He knew somehow that his father was about to say something bad to the sheriff. Eli winced even before his father's words escaped his lips.

"I suppose I pay my taxes like everyone else around here, Sheriff Wright. Taxes that pay for your salary. I suppose my money's just as green as Walt's. That ought to count for something too."

Eli held his breath. Sheriff Wright stood frozen, as if he were listening to the words a second time. Deputy Roosevelt groaned low, as if his stomach were upset by the pie he didn't eat.

"Well I'll be," the sheriff said, shaking his head. "My salary. Your green money." The sheriff locked eyes with Eli for a moment, as if to make sure he was still there. Then he looked away again, toward one of the trees. His lips were pursed to keep words from spilling out, seemed to Eli. He raised his hands to his hips, his elbows making triangles. "I'll be."

Eighteen

BIOLOGICAL CONTROL. Beneficial insects. Parasitic Wasps. *Aphytis coheni.*

Come evening, Isaac set about distributing with Ted the new *Aphytis*—his Jewish wasps—throughout his scale-stricken acres. They waited till evening, because the day was too hot to release the tender bugs late morning by the time Sheriff Wright had departed. Isaac had made a mess of things with the sheriff. And why? Because he was tired of taking things in stride, tired of his forbearance, which was just another word for obsequiousness, maybe. Because he had rights like everyone else, as he'd argued. Because Isaac, also, had been anxious to get the too-comfortable sheriff out of his kitchen and off his grove so he could get started with the *Aphytis* application, anxious because every hour mattered. And because he wished to share some words with Ted, actual words he'd been reluctant to broadcast into the air between them, as if actual words (as opposed to most words people shared) were potent seeds from which something alive and dangerous might spring.

"Okay, stop," he ordered Ted, who drove the flatbed slowly over the legume cover crop between the rows. A patina of dust coated the windshield; the pump for the wiper fluid had long ago failed. His foreman struggled to downshift the enormous lever for the gears between their knees, finally located the groove. The engine growled. The brakes squealed. Isaac uncharacteristically took the lead, because he knew more about distributing beneficial insects than Ted knew, the ever-expanding arsenal of chemical agents—aramite, malathion, DDT, arsenic, ovotran, parathion—vastly preferred by the co-op fellows, including Old Man Hawley, over biological control. Ted knew more about tending the nursery row, and budding the liners, and culling the year-old trees, and harvesting the fruit, and staving off decline, drought, and frost. Ted knew more about pretty much everything practical. But he didn't know more about lacewing and *Aphytis* and ladybeetle and *Aschersonias,* the friendly fungus that kept the whitefly in check. It felt good to know more about a single grove matter than Ted knew, biological control, even though it would have been better had they not needed these parasitic wasps to begin with.

"Now we need to distribute about three cups per hectare along these forty acres," Isaac declared in the cab. "A release point every thirty yards or so, then we'll skip a couple rows. I plotted it out last night." He reached in his front pocket and took out his crude pencil sketch of his trees on graph paper. Overhead view. He held it between them above the cracked vinyl seat. The late afternoon sun cast orange light through the rear window, making the dust particles shimmer in the still air above the sketch. Ted nodded his head over the drawing, said "Mmm-hmm."

"We'll stop every sixty yards, distribute both sides of the row, then head over a couple rows and stop at release points in between the first row's release points." Isaac pointed to an X on his drawing beside one of the dots demarcating a tree. "We've got just enough for that."

"Sounds good," Ted said, leaning his shoulder into the sticky driver's side door to open it.

They met at the bed. Isaac jimmied up the heavy metal gate and dropped it inside. It felt good to do the heavy lifting rather than rely upon Ted. He grasped the first cardboard box just within reach—there were only five—ripped it open and removed two small paper cups, handing one to Ted as if it were coffee. "Let's just check," Isaac said, opening the first cup gingerly, peering inside. Several tiny yellow sparks rose and disappeared into the failing golden light. "Oh well." He went ahead and peeled off the perforated lid, entirely. A few of the creatures clung to the honey-pasted inside. Isaac tapped the outside of the lid to release them. Most of the tiny yellow bugs, only a centimeter long or so, crept within the shredded paper insides of the cup like mites invading a bird's nest. They seemed perfectly content where they were. Isaac would hardly identify these winged creatures as wasps had he not known that they were wasps. He jostled the contents with a flick of his wrist. A few more sparks rose into the humid atmosphere. Curled at the bottom were just a few desiccated specimens.

"Most of them seem alive, anyway," Isaac said.

"That's good," Ted said. "After all your trouble."

"Good bugs sure are something."

"I suppose," said Ted, unconvinced. "Parathion take care of this right quick, though. I know we've got Mr. Eli's wind to consider. Something about it, though. Doesn't hardly seem natural, spreading these strange critters around. Ladybeetles, one thing. But these bugs?"

Isaac contemplated Ted's words as he sifted through the shredded paper. He plucked a small measure between his meaty fingers as if it were a tobacco plug, tossed the paper shreds up into the thick evening air to shoo the reluctant wasps.

"They're just as natural as the orange grove, Ted," he said as he pulled out a new cup of wasps. "Here, let's go. We don't have much time." Isaac led his foreman to their first release point in front of the truck. "These *Aphytis cohenis* from Israel—have I mentioned they're from Israel?—they have just as much claim here as these Chinese trees, way I see it. Or *us*," Isaac added.

Ted frowned. "I don't know. These trees been here an awful long time. Sour orange grows all by itself in the Glades. After a spell, doesn't something sort of earn its rightful place?"

Isaac thought about this. Were they still talking about orange trees and wasps, he wondered? "I see your point," he heard himself concede, which caused Ted to release a sort of satisfied listening sound. What people and plants had a right to this place? Clearly whoever carved KIKE into their tree wanted the Goldens gone. But on what grounds? Was the culprit's claim on this patch of Florida land any greater? What mattered most, Isaac liked to think, was the *way* you lived where you lived, not how far back you could claim ancestry. Whoever'd been carving up their trees wouldn't have much patience for this view. Nor would Walt. But Clay would agree. Even Ted, maybe.

"So, anyway, this is how we release them," Isaac changed the topic. "We tap the lids to encourage the ones up there in the honey to fly out into the foliage" (Isaac opened his lid and tapped it); "then we'll place the lid under the canopy and let the others take their time" (Isaac placed the lid under the canopy); "then we'll jostle the cup itself to encourage the bulk of them inside to fly off" (Isaac jostled the cup and sparks flew); "then we'll place some of the shredded paper with the bugs right up on a branch" (Isaac removed a plug of paper and set it in the crotch of the Hamlin); "then we'll set the cup with the rest of them on the southeast side under the tree's canopy, since it's still hot" (Isaac set the cup down). "That's five release points, Ted. Capisce?"

"Capisce," Ted said, smiling. He had learned some of Isaac's funny sayings.

"Beautiful. Let's get to it, my friend." It felt good to call Ted "friend." But there were other words he wished to share with Ted. He was biding his time. "I'll have Eli come back in a couple days and pick up the containers and lids. Earn his allowance."

They went about their business for several minutes without words. Tended to the release points across from each other along the row. Drove on. Ted kept his sticky door ajar. Tended to the next release points across from each other. Drove on. There was something beautiful and simple about performing this necessary chore to heal the trees. Isaac placed one of his big hands on each trunk he visited before setting down the cups in their designated locales. The trunks felt warm and alive on his palm, strangely warmer than the air, having absorbed the full heat of the sun earlier in the day. "We'll fix you right up," he uttered to one scion, as if it were a child. It had shed some of its leaves (a bad sign), but it still held its small dark green fruit. It truly was a glorious thing, an orange tree, just as Commissioner Shepherd claimed. There was something especially true about a citrus tree, something that most people took for granted. That it continued year after year upon the proper encouragement to advertise fragrant white blossoms, then set its pebbly fruit, which reliably matured into Hamlins or Midsweets or Parson Browns or Valencias or Marshes, year after year after year, when it might have produced anything at all, or nothing at all, in a different world.

Here Isaac was, thinking these thoughts that his parents, and most all the Jews he knew, for that matter, would find strange. Pagan, in a word. Marveling after these sublime trees. Yet the Lord took pains to protect trees—didn't he?—forbidding his chosen armies from destroying the trees of cities they conquered. *Is the tree of the field man that it should be besieged by you?* Or something like that, Isaac recalled. The rabbis, too, prayed for the health of trees. *Grow, grow, grow!* they prayed before their fruiting trees. What about all that? Isaac wondered.

Ted drove on. Isaac placed his thick mitt on a new warm trunk, tended to the release points. A definite comfort in a proven tree, he thought. The comfort of constancy. Isaac wished that his old friend Sam could see him now while he performed this simple but useful work with his hands. Sam probably thought he only sat around all day waiting for his trees to grow, the oranges to ripen and break color as the sugar overtook the acid. But there was always something useful and important to do on the grove.

An hour nearly passed without Ted or Isaac exchanging fresh words, the words Isaac would speak before long. But there was nothing awkward in their silence. The atmosphere was full enough with the buzz of their necessary labor. The light began to fail. The frogs began to chirp. Something buzzed, its pitch ascending to a crescendo. Insect, probably.

"Parula," Ted said from across the row.

"Oh?"

"One of those warbler-type birds. See a bunch of them in that tamarind by the house chasing all the insects. Should be up around the St. John's to set up housekeeping by now."

So it wasn't an insect.

Ted drove on. A jet engine, or maybe a pair of jets, tore through the eastern sky, above the Atlantic.

"They just get louder and louder," Isaac said, the jet noise too piercing to ignore.

"Mmm-hmm," Ted said. "That's the truth. Wonder who they'll send up next."

Isaac found himself thinking again about Ted's remark about the trees, their longstanding tenure on Florida's soil, their parasitic wasps that just didn't seem quite right to him, the fresh KIKE scar on a nearby tree, which Ted had tarred over as soon as the Sheriff Wright left. "You knew that fellow, didn't you, Ted? The one who got murdered in Mims before we came down. '51 or so."

"Of course I did. We all did."

Isaac felt himself closing in on the words he truly wished to share with Ted.

"Schoolteacher, right?" He tapped the lid of his cup to release the yellow sparks.

"Started out that way. Then principal. Then got himself fired when he started making a ruckus about equal pay for teachers at the Negro school. Worked for the association after that."

"Association?" Isaac looked across toward Ted. He seemed to be taking out too much of the shredded paper, but Isaac didn't say anything.

"NAACP."

"Oh. Of course."

They met at the truck. Ted drove on. "Upped the dues from one dollar to two dollars overnight. Wasn't too popular, that decision." Isaac looked over at Ted, who flashed a silver smile and shook his head as he recalled his friend with affection or nostalgia, or maybe both, his eyes straight ahead beyond the windshield. The patina of dust on the glass wasn't visible anymore now that the sun had set behind them. Soon they'd have to put on the headlights.

"So what was he like?" Isaac asked. Ted looked over at him now as he downshifted.

"Why are you so curious all of a sudden, Isaac Golden?"

"I don't know." They exited, walked to their trees and tended to their release points. "Just seems like I ought to know something about the fellow," Isaac called from across the row. "Local history and all."

"Serious man," Ted answered from beneath his tree's canopy, tapping the lid of his cup, setting it on the ground. "They were younger than Erma and me so we didn't socialize too much. And they didn't live in town but in a shotgun house on a young grove up in Mims. That's what I'd say first off, though. Serious man. Sharp dresser. Always wore a tie. Small fellow, but plenty of pluck. Strict with his baby girls. Played whist for keeps."

"So what'd he do? For the NAACP, I mean."

"Progressive Voters League he started up. Got over half the Negroes this part of the state registered." Ted sifted through the shredded paper in his cup, extracted a large clump and placed it in the tree's crook. "As Democrats too. That was the main thing. No Republican ever won any local election these parts. Not registered Democrat, there's not much point voting in the first place. Till Horace came around we weren't allowed to register Democrat. Changed things right quick after that."

"That was his name? Horace?"

"Horace Manning, yes sir."

They returned to the truck. Ted pulled the lever for the headlights, which illuminated the cowpea and citrus foliage, and darkened everything beyond the headlights' gaze. He started the engine and drove slow, slower than he had been driving between the release points. Isaac could smell their ripe human smells mingle in the close air of the cab, maybe because there wasn't so much to see anymore now that it was nighttime, practically. Ted was still thinking about Horace, Isaac could tell. The truck seemed to rock and buck more at the slower speed. "That's what got him and his wife killed, ask me," Ted uttered. His voice was softer now. Almost a growl. He nodded his head and frowned. "Horace and the league came out strong for Pepper over Smathers in the Senate race back in '50. Smathers held on but the white folk saw the change coming, change to the southern way of life. He really started something, Horace, rest his soul."

"Started," Isaac said more than asked.

"Mmm-hmm."

There was something about Ted's *started*, something about Ted's *mmm-hmm* that Isaac didn't like, not liking that he didn't like it but not liking it all the same. Maybe the way Ted uttered the words, uttered them in a manner that excluded Isaac somehow. And then Isaac heard himself speaking the words, finally, the actual words he had hoped to share with Ted this evening.

"This new Negro fellow around town. The fellow with the suit and necktie that has Walt and the others so hot and bothered. Sure you've heard. I suppose you know him too, Ted. Am I right?"

"Yes. You're right, Isaac." Ted stopped the truck, but didn't step outside. He leaned back against the cracked vinyl seat, instead, laced his ashen fingers in his lap, waited for Isaac's next question. His eyes were glassy against the ochre dashboard light, but there was something bold about the way he just sat there, waiting for the conversation to run its course.

"Well, who *is* he then, Ted?"

"He's Levi, Isaac. He's my boy."

BOOK THREE

SUMMER

Nineteen

SUMMER RESTED on its haunches along the river and made itself too comfortable. Melody's blood would thin in time, Pearl had assured her. And Mary Beth had assured her. And Erma had assured her. She'd perspire less. Only August to truly fear, they claimed independently, the Negro and white citizenry having reached an apparent consensus on this point, as if to persuade prospective tourists and residents, or maybe only themselves. Otherwise they were simply insane. For a body couldn't get used to heat like this—June, July, August, *and* September, seemed to Melody. This dragon's-breath heat. Not normal heat that most Americans knew. But unnatural heat. Unearthly heat. Perfect for the mosquitoes and no-see-ums and sand gnats, but heat a human body could barely endure.

Yet the Goldens remained, because the nomadic age was over. Because you couldn't just up and leave a grove, your livelihood hanging precariously from the stems. Because they wouldn't get chased off by a Jew-hating vandal. Because summer months were the worst months for weeds and brown rot and foot rot. Because the copious summer flushes brought on by the rains and long days attracted any number of pests like leafminer, bird grasshoppers, aphids, and root weevils. "You turned your back for a second . . ." said Isaac on countless occasions, leaving Melody's imagination to construct the rest of the sentence. Because more and more motorists from the North were taking their Florida vacations during the summer, the children off from school, Miami hotel prices at record lows, the turquoise ocean bathwater warm. Because she couldn't just shutter up the stand now, her pecan and lemon pies having caused something of a sensation

New Smyrna to Palm Bay. Because the window-hung air-conditioners in Eli's room, and Sarah's room, and the family room rumbled on and made life indoors bearable, anyway. (They truly were "Living Better Electrically," just like that handsome television actor named Reagan boasted on the *General Electric Theater*.) And so the Goldens, like the rest of the small river growers, like the summer heat itself, hunkered down and made the most of it.

Here was Melody in summer.

She rose especially early these summer days to start her pies before the big bully sun rose. Hot oven in a hot house made little sense, maybe, but the townsfolk and tourists alike craved summer pies that they weren't forced to bake in their own homes, and the extra summer income—modest though it was once she factored in the cost of ingredients, the electric bill and whatnot—was welcome indeed during these lean months between harvests. "Got to hand it to you," Isaac had encouraged her. "You knew what you were doing, what the market will bear," he said. Melody didn't quite understand what that cryptic phrase meant. Her father had used that phrase too. What the market will bear.

Pies in the oven, Melody set the egg timer and brought it with her to the family room. She savored these warm dark mornings on her very own, the frogs and insects still chanting outside, a louder mockingbird picking up the nighttime tune from its perch somewhere on the wax myrtle or lantana. There just wasn't much daylight time to herself, especially summer, Eli off school now and tromping about, Isaac retreating to the kitchen table indoors half the time with his ledger to concentrate on the business end, Sarah requiring even more strenuous supervision, toddling about now and putting everything she scavenged—everything!—directly into her mouth. Sarah rose later in the morning now, at least. That was something, anyway.

Before the RCA, having toted a wooden chair from the kitchen, Melody raised hands to her shoulders and felt her diaphanous nightie slip to the pine floor. She performed her exercises nude each morning in the near dark, at first so she wouldn't soil her nightclothes, answering the call of frugality. But now because she liked the way it felt to perform her calisthenics in the nude. She dialed down the volume so that Jack LaLanne's instructions and the grating accordion music wouldn't stir her slumbering family. She dialed down the brightness on the tube too so that the blue glow just barely illuminated her flesh. Not out of modesty, exactly. Who would see her? She liked the way her nude body looked in this faintest glow. In a word, new. The fingerprints from her pregnancies across her stomach and breasts, invisible. The tender bulb of her extruded navel, flirtatious and winsome, somehow. A curious little man, that LaLanne fellow, standing there in his jumpsuit and ballet shoes. He somehow seemed small and strong at the same time. She had to hand it to him. He had convinced her, and countless American housewives, that it was their duty not just as women and wives but as American patriots, also, to keep "fit as a fiddle." An American flag loomed in the backdrop. This battle against flab seemed important to the president too, that Americans not go soft while the communists loomed, sharpening their knives.

"*One-two-three-four*," she followed the man's chirpy instructions, thrusting skyward on toe-tips to shape her calves and ankles, her finest feature. "*One-two-three-four . . .*" If her mother could see her now. She wouldn't approve, Melody knew. These strange calisthenics. Wasting time and effort over something so trivial, her body. *Narishkeit*, her mother would say. Foolishness. A body was for holding up your *kopf*, your head. That was all. Well, where was her mother's body now? In the earth, Melody contemplated, angry of a sudden at her mother, leaving her here to fend for herself. Had her mother taken better care of herself, maybe . . . Melody wiped her eyes, bit her tender lip to punish herself for her disrespectful thoughts. "*One-two-three-four . . .*"

"Now this little exercise will improve your bustline," LaLanne promised without the slightest trace of embarrassment. "*One-two-three-four,*" Melody followed along, seated now on the wooden chair, crossing her raised arms before her to please LaLanne, anyway, if not her mother.

Sarah began wailing before the half hour was up. Heaven forbid Isaac rise to change their daughter. He must have heard the cries! Melody let Sarah carry on for a moment, if only to give her husband ample opportunity to offer her a pleasant surprise by retrieving their child. He was awake by now, assuredly. But no luck. She wouldn't get to LaLanne's face-sculpting routine, those exaggerated expressions. She slipped the nightie over her moist flesh (she'd have to wash it now in the sink with Sarah's Dreft detergent) and made her way to the baby's room.

After serving breakfast, after shooing Isaac and Eli out of the house, she took Sarah into the shower with her and lathered herself with snowy Camay and Breck suds, then applied Tea Rose to her pressure points on her neck and wrists before slipping on her sheer store-bought dress with the smart collar, trying to convince herself all the while that she wasn't lathering herself with snowy Camay and Breck suds, then applying tea rose to her pressure points, then slipping on her sheer store-bought dress with the smart collar because it was the second Wednesday of the month, when he'd likely stop at Goldens Are Here on his way to his regular meeting in Jacksonville.

He was Erma's son. Erma's and Ted's. Their eldest child. Levi. He had told her his name weeks ago, even before Isaac crept in from the grove in his sour mood, having set out those wasps with Ted.

"Ted's own son!" her husband had declared, incredulous. "This new Negro with the suit and tie! Levi! *Their* Levi!"

The blood had rushed to Melody's face. Isaac's tired body just in from the grove exuded an acrid odor to match his mood. Melody implored him to use the shower, if only to be free of Isaac for a time while she collected herself, composed her thoughts. He'd feel better after a shower, she said. They'd hash this out after he bathed. But Isaac continued to berate her over the bed, as if she were responsible.

"It's his own son here to cause trouble, Mel. Field officer for the NAACP. Didn't have the decency even to deny it. Up to something with the field-workers, I bet, harvest right around the corner. A rabble rouser. Somehow Ted doesn't see anything wrong with that! His own son! And *him*, our foreman!"

"You sound like one of them," she told her husband.

"One of them?' he asked.

"Like Walt."

Here's what else Melody had learned about Levi, which she hadn't shared with her husband. He liked books, unlike his siblings or parents. Steinbeck. Upton Sinclair. And someone Melody hadn't heard of who sounded foreign. Dos Passos. He convinced Ted and Erma to send him off to the Normal School at Florida Memorial College somewhere in Suwannee County. He rented a room at an AME minister's house. He wanted to be a lawyer, but the university in Gainesville still wasn't taking Negro students. When the Korean War broke out he enlisted in the more Negro-friendly Air Force so he wouldn't be drafted by the Army or Navy. He serviced bombers on a base in Japan. After some New York tomfoolery (his ambiguous characterization, which Melody didn't press him on), he joined up with the Association, because he didn't see why life for a Negro should be better during wartime on a base in Japan than it was at home in Florida, or New York. "Niggers to the left, whites to the right," an officer greeted him just off the gangplank in the New York harbor. He never wore a hat, even on full-sun days. This way, he didn't have to take one off his head in the presence of whites. He liked her Borden's peppermint milkshakes. He liked eating unsalted pecans straight from the shell. He barely seemed to perspire, even on these hot-as-Gehenna summer days.

That's all she knew so far about Levi, which maybe was a lot. How much did you really know about someone, anyway?

The stand. Orchids. Honey. Pecans. Postcards. Seashells. Dixie cups of ice cream with wooden spoons stacked in the small chest freezer. Nonperishable specialty items now, too. Jacksonville supplier. Curious canned and glassed goods. Hot pepper jam. Four-bean salad. Bread and butter pickles. Hot chow chow. Sweet baby beets. And that brand-new tomato dip from Mexico called salsa. Increased inventory to compensate for vacant fruit bins. Peaches from Georgia still, anyway. Plus her pies. Shoo-fly she just introduced, bringing some of Pennsylvania to the subtropics. She didn't much care for the cloying syrupy sweet shoo-fly, so wasn't tempted to sample a fattening wedge.

Loud, these summer days at the stand, the six overhead fans pushing the hot air and mosquitoes out from underneath the corrugated roof. Pretty bearable under the shade, but she didn't like that she couldn't hear the nearby towhees, who picked up their *drink-your-teaaa* song during summer, or the crimson cardinals the citizenry (and Eli) insisted on calling red birds, as if cardinal were too complicated a name, a bird that actually went *tweet*. One nice thing about summer, anyway, these lovestruck towhees and cardinals still chirping away, even if she couldn't listen under the buzzing fans. Plus, the greener thickets of cord grass and wiregrass on account of the rains, the afternoon thunderstorms pounding the stand's metal roof, tongues of water lapping at the oyster-shell ground.

Melody tidied up the displays, checked the inventory while Sarah busied herself with her alphabet blocks. Her blocks could now occupy her for half an hour or longer, even though she couldn't know what the letters meant. She arranged them in meticulous rows and columns and towers, which somehow worried Melody, the fastidiousness of the architecture. Could it be a good thing, these uncompromising right angles and parallel lines? Sarah now seemed to be fixated on one block in particular, setting it down along its row, then picking it back up and inspecting its sides, setting it down again, then picking it up again, inspecting its sides once more, as if half expecting its constitution to have changed in between.

Melody moved along slowly through the aisle, moved her arms and hands slower, and even pivoted her head slower atop her shoulders. That was the trick to coping with summer, smothering them all on its fat haunches. You couldn't move about normally. You had to take it slow. It would help to drink more water too. Erma, who Melody only kept on weekends during this first summer they kept the stand open, was better about drinking water. Sometimes she even lifted up the hose behind the stand for a metallic mouthful. Melody, by contrast, didn't like water, which drove Isaac crazy. She didn't even drink Tab on account of the gassy carbonation. Tired, thirsty vehicles sputtered up and down the highway. Most motorists slowed as they passed the stand, taking the measure of the place, its strange marquee, GOLDENS ARE HERE. A few stopped. Melody usually heard the pitch of the engines shifting down, the scrunch on the oyster-shell berm and parking strip, before she looked up to notice her visitors. But her eyes were drawn first now to the southern approach of the gleaming new El Dorado as she reorganized and wiped clean the thumb-smudged postcards in the display. She liked this new Cadillac, its more restrained tailfins and headlights, its cleaner lines. Elegant. She could almost smell the lush leather interior from the stand. Virginia, the license plate read. Melody observed the curious couple while trying not to appear that she was looking. The woman applied a fresh coat of lipstick in the rearview mirror while she waited for her husband to retrieve her. He walked clear around to her door and opened it for her. His lips moved as he uttered silent words—"Careful," or something like that, Melody guessed—which she couldn't hear over the whir of the fans overhead. The woman planted a short heel with great care on the uncertain oyster-shell ground, gripping her husband's arm for ballast. The fellow placed a soft hand on her back, ushered her toward the shade of the stand. They were only slightly older than Melody, but seemed older than that. An attractive couple. She felt a pang of envy for this well-heeled couple, probably on their way back home from their cruise ship debarkation portal in Miami. (The Port at Canaveral would be open for cruise liners any year now, they said.) Her envy quickly passed. She liked to think that she traveled a greater distance these two hundred yards from her kitchen to GOLDENS ARE HERE than this elegant Mrs. from Virginia would travel her entire lifetime, no matter where her husband toted her in Cadillacs or cruise ships.

She'd let them mill about a while at their leisure. There was something conspiratorial about these two. They loitered along the specialty item aisle and talked in hushed tones Melody strained to hear over the impossible fans.

"I simply must have one, Wallace?" Melody thought she heard.

"Yes, darling. We'll see what we can do."

"But I don't see a single one? Where are they, for heaven's sake? Do you see any, Wallace?"

They've heard about her pies, Melody gathered. Probably in town. Rather than approach the couple, Melody walked in the opposite direction to retrieve Sarah, who raised both arms from her blocks. "All right, Sarah-le. Up you go." Melody often lifted Sarah up before approaching customers, partly because the presence of her vivacious toddler, her very Sarah-ness, disarmed visitors, offered Melody a curious edge, whereas poor bird-faced Eli—why deny it?—tended to repel visitors.

Levi, suddenly. Melody noticed his Harry Belafonte forehead and thin tie a split second before the husband noticed his presence and spoke.

"You there! Young fellow! Can you fetch us an orange tree? Yea tall, maybe?" The husband placed a level hand beside his shiny alligator-hide belt.

"We don't see any," the wife complained, "and we simply must have one. We've come all this way."

Melody wouldn't count these two among the terrifically bigoted. Only sheltered. Only presumptuous. And none too bright, evidently. Did they truly think a field-worker would be wearing a tie and thin-soled Florsheims, middle of summer?

"Excuse me, that gentleman doesn't—"

Melody was about to set them straight, but Levi intervened.

"Sho', I'll go fetch you a Valencia in a jiffy," he said, affecting a voice that wasn't remotely his own. Melody bobbed Sarah in her arms but didn't say anything. She smiled awkwardly instead at Levi's curious playacting. What was he up to?

"I'll show you which one," Melody heard herself call, leading Levi toward the nursery row outside. She needn't lock the register. "We'll only be a minute, folks."

"Mr. Golden out on the grove with Pop?" Levi asked, scanning the horizon.

"Yes. Don't worry." She nodded toward the empty five-gallon plastic pot and spade behind the stand, which Levi retrieved, and they walked the short distance between the greener palmetto fans and cord grass thickets to the young tree rows, the air redolent with spice from the nearby wax myrtle. It seemed especially quiet beyond the reach of the overhead fans. And hot. She felt a bead of perspiration trickle down between her breasts. The very air seemed thicker, waves of heat almost visible between them in the soupy air. "What are we doing, Levi?" she asked once they were out of earshot. She liked saying his first name out there in the open. Levi.

"*Drink-your-teaaa!*" a towhee sang from atop a wax myrtle shrub, piercing the quiet. She could see its rusty sides.

"Just play along, Melody. You saw that car of theirs well as I did. Way I see it you can name your price on your orange tree. Pop will likely cull half of these anyhow." They had reached one of the two-year rows. He leaned over to inspect the stake at the front of the line.

She shook her head. "You're terrible, Levi. Terrible."

"Maybe you should whup me, mistress." His coffee eyes twinkled.

"Oh, stop it. Don't listen to him, Sarah. Talk normal now, Levi, would you please?"

They seemed to be in a different place together, making this mild mischief. Strange and exciting and vaguely dangerous. Strange and exciting didn't come around much anymore, or ever, so she was willing to live with vaguely dangerous. She watched as Levi scooped a bit of dirt into the bottom of the plastic pot, then dug around the tree. Expertly. Disciplined strikes around a broad circle to extract the root ball—slender uncalloused hands, but they knew what they were doing. Yes, a son of Ted's, no matter how bookish, would know his way around a shovel, around an orange tree. Even though he was on the small side and trim, the muscles in Levi's hairless forearms rippled. She turned to shade Sarah from the mid-morning sun with her shoulders, and to avert her own eyes. The sun's heat penetrated Melody's sheer dress to scald her shoulders.

"There," Levi said, depositing the small Valencia into the pot. He shoveled additional doses of moist earth around the sides, gripping the shovel at its neck, the distended flesh at his knuckles almost white. He grasped the scion's slender trunk with his other hand, leveling it in its temporary pot. It was a nice cultivar. Ample summer flush. Pale green shoots at the axial buds, betraying robust roots and sufficient hydration. She felt sad, suddenly, for this poor Valencia, this casualty of their shenanigans, off to its likely demise in frostbitten Virginia.

"It's splendid," the woman said, lifting her hands toward her painted mouth, pressing them together under her lips as if in prayer. "What a splendid little tree, Wallace." They were anxious for their Valencia. Why else had they ventured out into the heat of the sun to settle matters? Levi was right. She could probably name her price.

"Now what do I owe you?" the man asked. He removed a gold money clip from his pleated trousers, flipped through the paper bills before his slender stomach in a manner that struck Melody as coarse, the bills making smacking sounds against each other as he collated them. A Jew, man or woman, could never handle money this way.

"Mr. Golden says twenty dollars, right ma'am?" Levi asked, holding the tree beneath his waist away from his trousers to keep the pants clean, the copious summer flush foliage shielding his expression from the Virginians.

"Uhhh," Melody groaned. It was a staggering price Levi had floated out into the air between them.

"Twenty dollars?!" the woman brayed.

"Fine," the man said, unfazed. "Twenty dollars." He lifted his shirt sleeve at his biceps to his wet brow, wiped. "What Evelyn wants . . ."

"You'll want to plant it in a large clay pot," Melody warned after the man placed two crisp ten-dollar bills in the hand that wasn't holding Sarah. "That way you can bring it inside come winter. Find a south-facing window for it. Otherwise it'll die, I'm afraid. Winters and even fall in the mid-Atlantic are too cold for citrus."

The woman's face—Evelyn her name—betrayed sudden discomfort, as if her stomach ached. A pot clearly wasn't part of her plan for her lovely tree. She probably already had a garden plot somewhere in Charlottesville or Richmond or Roanoke all staked out for the doomed Valencia next to her white dogwood or tulip poplar. In fairness, it was probably tough to accept the inexorable approach of a Virginia winter in the midst of a Florida summer; in fairness, a single orange tree in her yard seemed to mean an awful lot to this well-heeled wife (without children in evidence), and maybe wasn't so very much to ask for.

"Very well," the man said. "I can take it from here." He took possession of his Valencia, which Levi handed over without words. Perspiration archipelagos had risen through Levi's blue Oxford cloth shirt. It seemed strange to see him like this for the first time. Exercised.

"Good luck," Melody said. She and Levi stood there for a moment, watching after the couple as if half expecting them to turn back and ask for a refund. But they didn't. "Oh, I hope we didn't go and make a mess of things, poor tree," she declared once the couple was out of earshot. "It was such a happy tree in the nursery row, bursting out all over with shoots. And then we had to go and ruin things for it."

"Now look how silly you're being," Levi chastised her, his fine eyebrows ascending into a surprise, lifting ridges across his porpoise forehead. "Twenty dollars you just earned, Melody Golden. Twenty dollars! For a puny little tree." A vein swelled at his temple. "Pop culls near half of them anyway, like I said. You know that."

"Still. Virginia, for heaven's sake."

They walked silently a few paces toward the stand. Melody shifted Sarah's weight to her other hip. "Here, I'll take her," Levi said. Melody handed Sarah over, who immediately cried and stretched her arms back toward her mother, her tiny fingers splayed.

"Now Sarah, what's got into you. You know Levi. He's Erma's son."

"Better take her."

Melody took her.

After a few paces, Levi leaned a shoulder into her shoulder, which made Melody look up at Levi and smile just before she looked ahead and glimpsed Pearl and Mary Beth looking straight at them, their mouths making small o's, upon which she stepped away from Levi, careful not to break her stride, the heat rising to her face, glancing toward Levi's dusty Florsheims to notice that he too had stepped away, looking up to notice that he had noticed her noticing, and then Melody knew that the blood could rise to Negro faces too, or maybe only to lighter-skinned Negroes like Levi.

"Happy to be of service, ma'am," Levi uttered for the ladies' benefit as they reached the stand, keeping his eyes down, then walked clear around the perimeter toward his ancient Plymouth with the newer whitewalls. Melody nodded at Levi. He wouldn't get her into trouble, she gathered. Not purposefully.

"Hello girls!" she greeted her Junior League friends with fraudulent ease, turning her back to her visitors to set Sarah down with her blocks. She paused over her toddler for a moment, making sure the blocks would take. They did. "What can I do for y'all?" The *y'alls* almost came naturally now, sounded only mildly like playacting to her ears.

"Umm," MB said, gathering her wits—both women fanned themselves furiously with folded sections of the morning's *Star Advocate*—"is that him?" MB asked, her eyes trailing after the Negro toward his car as if to make sure that he hadn't circled back within earshot.

"Who?" Melody replied.

"The new sharp-looking Negro in town all the men have been talking about."

"Clay hasn't said anything about any new Negro," Pearl interjected, fanning herself even more furiously, her concern rising.

"No," Melody said to MB, ignoring Pearl. "It's not him." It frightened her how quickly the lie escaped her lips. Is this what Melody was, a liar? She heard the engine of Levi's Plymouth fire up, the crunch of loose oyster shells beneath the tires. MB nodded slowly across from her, fanned herself with her newspaper, slowly now like her nodding head, as if deciding whether or not to believe Melody.

"Still," MB said, "you should be careful."

Melody felt fiery pinpricks against her forehead, her neck, hoped a rash hadn't risen to betray her. She heard the tires of Levi's car gain greater purchase on the asphalt highway, the motor shifting into higher gears, then fading away to the north. It took all her will power not to look away from MB toward the car.

"Alone here with the baby, Mary Beth means," added Pearl. "Might want to make sure Erma or one of the field hands is around all times. You can't be too careful, right MB?"

"Yes," MB allowed, her thin lips twisting into an unflattering expression. "Right." She lifted a bony fist to her mouth and cleared her throat, which signaled the end of the discussion. For now, anyway. "Pearl and I came out here to speak with you some about the spaghetti dinner gala," she declared at a more friendly timbre.

"Oh, yes, the dinner gala. I'm sorry. I know I've missed a couple meetings. It's just been so busy at the stand. And with the children . . ."

It was discourteous, maybe, to mention how busy the stand had been, which was why Melody added the bit about her children. The stand was open and fairly busy, after all, on account of her pies. *Her* pies. Not Mary Beth's. To her credit, MB had been surprisingly magnanimous about it once Melody mustered the courage to warn her at Janisse's at one of the rare Junior League meetings she hadn't missed. *Oh, sugar, that's all right. I can see you're all tied up in knots over it.* That was the thing about these Christian women in town. They tended to be generous to a fault, it seemed to Melody. So self-assured. Chock-full of confidence. The right and wrong of things, crystal clear to them. They didn't agitate over the in-between. Or concern themselves at all with matters financial. That's what husbands were for. What did a few pies matter, anyway, eternal salvation on the line? Melody hadn't known Christian women in Philadelphia and was fully prepared to disapprove of them upon her southward migration. Their sanctimony. Their piety. But mostly she found herself wishing she could be more like one of these self-assured, civic-minded Christian ladies, putting on their twenty-ninth annual spaghetti dinner gala to upgrade the fallout shelter in town beneath the Magnolia Theater and outfit additional ones at heretofore undetermined locations.

"It's all right about the meetings, sugar," said Pearl. "We all understand. Can't be easy on you out here all alone, children to care for. Eli."

Pearl was barren. Or perhaps the problem was on Clay's side. In any case, Clay and Pearl were childless. So maybe adding that bit about her children to compensate for her gaffe about the stand hadn't been so tactful of Melody, either, Pearl-wise. It wasn't so easy, saying the right thing. It seemed to Melody that she was better at minding her words, and her deeds, in Philadelphia.

"How's our Eli lately, hon?" MB asked, scanning the cement slab floor for him, worry lines creasing her brow. Melody told her that Eli was doing well, that he'd bounced back nicely from his latest bronchial infection, that he was fishing the river today, the stand no longer able to contain him. She didn't like talking about Eli with people who furrowed their brows over him, so she wordlessly stepped behind the counter and retrieved the half-moon pecan pie from the fridge, carved two slices for the girls. She wouldn't make *chocolate* pecan.

Now *that* would be treading on MB's toes. *Chutzpahdik*, as her mother would say. She appreciated this opportunity to showcase her plain old pecan for Mary Beth.

"I sure remember what it was like out here," Pearl picked up her thread as she waited for her slice. "Clear out on the island, we set up housekeeping when we married. Clay insisted we light out for the island 'cross the water. Ten years we lived out there." Melody marveled at the faraway look in Pearl's eyes, a contemplative look she wasn't used to seeing on Pearl's face, her weak chin lifted eastward over the pyramid of honey jars and the grove toward the river and the island beyond. "I plum insisted after ten years that he move us to our Queen Anne in town. Darn crickets and frogs and growling gators alone. Couldn't sleep a wink. I was fit to be tied. Ten years," she repeated, as if she could hardly believe the broad span looking back. She lowered her gaze toward Melody, returning to the here and now. "Long enough, I told my Clay."

"Mmm," Mary Beth moaned, sampling her slice. "And not being able to use butter in the kitchen," she said. "Don't know how you do it."

"I can use butter," Melody corrected MB.

"Eggs is it then?" Pearl inquired.

"I can use eggs too, girls. Eggs anytime. You've seen me eat eggs at Janisse's. It's just the combinations we mostly have to worry about." She considered elaborating, but watched as MB and Pearl nodded slow, uninterested, their plastic forks and paper plates held high before their mouths, chewing.

"Just Spry for this crust?" MB asked, troubling the yeasty layers beneath a plastic tine. Maybe it wasn't such a good idea to offer them pie.

"Crisco," Melody lied, anxious to get on with matters. She wouldn't admit that she used lard. "About the spaghetti dinner. I sort of figured I'd just be on the decorating committee like last year. It's not till November, right?" She glanced northward up the highway, could see the heat dancing above the asphalt. The immediate crisis of Levi behind her, she now resented MB and Pearl for chasing him off. She wouldn't likely see him again for two long weeks.

"That's the thing of it," MB said, setting aside her pie on the counter. "The girls and I were talking—"

"Yes, we were talking," Pearl echoed her cohort.

"At the last meeting you missed at Janisse's—"

"Janisse really put out a spread for us this time. Her deviled eggs were out of this—"

"And we were hoping that you'd agree to canvas this year."

"I think she adds pickle juice and sour cream—"

"Pearl, would you quit your jabbering for one precious instant!"

"Oops," Pearl exclaimed, lifting a forkful of pie to her mouth to stuff it closed.

"You can drop Sarah off at Pearl's house or mine and we'll mind her. Eli too if you want."

'I don't know, girls. I've never—"

"You're the prettiest," MB interjected, which made Melody blush.

"Without a doubt," Pearl concurred. "The way the boys look—"

"No point being shy about it now. Everyone agrees. Who'll say no to you? You'll sell more fifty-cent tickets than the rest of us old hens combined. We want to try Cocoa and Deland and maybe even Sanford this year, main streets anyway."

"Town's depending on us for the fallout shelters," said Pearl.

"Not like the north," added MB. "Basements every domicile. They have to be dug out fresh for the most part. And carefully, water table high as it is."

"It's important we're prepared, rocket base now at the Cape. First place Russians'll bomb, my Clay says."

They looked her in her eyes, taking her measure, it seemed to Melody. She wondered whether MB, and even Pearl, doubted her patriotism, whether they wondered after her origins in some backwater of the Russian Pale. Did they think for an instant that she pined for the blood-soaked old country she'd never seen? Only dogs returned to their vomit. Israel for its part seemed a distant fantasy land to Melody, teeming with Jew-haters on every side, Arabs in frightening white robes sharpening their curved knives. That Paul Newman movie last year only made it seem more strange and forbidding.

"Yes, I know we must be vigilant," Melody said. "I know we can't let our guard down."

So it was settled. Pearl and MB would watch Sarah (Eli could fend for himself) and Melody would canvas a few weekends for the Junior League spaghetti dinner. Melody Golden, the pretty one. So that's who she was. Everyone agreed, apparently. Levi too. Why kid herself? At this point she only saw Levi at the stand every other week when he was certain that his mother and Isaac were otherwise occupied. Nothing had happened. Nothing, she assured herself. Yet his visitations seemed laced with sin, regardless. The unspoken but mutually understood surreptitiousness of their encounters, the way he had blushed just moments ago. He had no legitimate business to conduct there. Melody didn't think she would let things get carried away. But how far might she let things proceed? She certainly hadn't foreseen their mild mischief this morning, which thrilled her.

The risk was greater on Levi's side, of course, a Negro in the South taking liberties with a married, mostly white woman. Mostly white, but not quite. This seemed to be how the town saw her. Junior League, yes, but Whispering Pines, no. Grove owners, yes, but grudgingly. Nasty scars carved into their trees, putting them on notice. Would MB or Pearl say anything to their husbands about the sharp-looking Negro at the stand who bumped shoulders strangely against Melody, who sought out this intimacy and was not rebuffed? Pearl, she feared, was the type of wife not inclined to process a troublesome or complex thought without Clay's counsel. Yet she hoped that neither Pearl nor MB would say anything, that the three of them had reached an understanding, however oblique. They needed her for the spaghetti dinner, after all. It was just easier to dismiss what they thought they might have seen—the strange intimacy between Melody and that sharp-looking Negro, bumping shoulders and showing their teeth out there in the open, which made MB's mouth and Pearl's mouth make small o's. They must have been imagining things. So Melody hoped.

Melody sighed. MB's warning had been clear enough—*you should be careful*—but she wasn't certain that she'd heed it. Seeking separate counsel, she walked over toward Sarah and studied her handiwork with the blocks, her single row, hoping to glean what instruction she might. AIELKFRUSHMORGSYNDV.

Melody frowned, shook her head. Sarah's jumbled letters didn't say anything at all.

Twenty

BECAUSE HE PRETTY MUCH fended for himself these days. Because he'd already read the latest *Superman* three times in his air-conditioned bedroom. Because Woolworth's wouldn't have a new ten-cent copy for another week. Because Stan Lee's new comic book, *Fantastic Four,* wasn't realistic at all—*at all!* Because there was nothing on television during the day and his father would break every bone in his body if he burned out the tube. Because his mother didn't take him anymore, summertime, to the air-conditioned museum or theater for double features or Janisse's for egg creams ever since Sarah, practically, ever since she kept the stand open. Because the stand was boring as watching grass grow and he didn't like the way strangers from the highway looked at him, making him lift his fingers to his angry red cheek. Because his mother would only let him eat one slice of pie. Because she might make him watch his sister and now that she was bigger her BMs smelled something awful. Because the gators mostly stuck to the fresh water on the island, or further inland at the St. Johns and the lakes, and pretty much stayed away from their brackish stretch of river. Because the skeeters came in waves and might not be so bad today, especially if he lathered on his Watkins. Because if he could cast net a few brown shrimp trapped in the tidal pool and freeline them beneath the mangroves he might even catch a flounder. Which were near impossible to fillet, but tasted even better than snapper. Because his mother might prepare stuffed cabbage middle of the week if he didn't bring her home a decent mess of fish from the river, instead.

Here was Eli in summer.

Zebco in hand. Backpack holding his tackle box. Face and neck, ankles and calves slathered with stinky Watkins, pasted over with zinc oxide. Floppy-brimmed fishing cap scrunched tight over his scalp. Oversize bug-eyed sunglasses. Sheer long-sleeve shirt. Shorts, at least, bony knees barely exposed above high tube socks the skeeters bit clear through. Filthy canvas Keds with rubber toe-caps that never dried all the way on the porch these wet summer nights and felt clammy and gross through his socks when he first put them back on, till his feet warmed the wet shoes back up. Four-foot cast net crammed in a two-gallon bucket. Quite a spectacle, Eli Golden in summer.

He tromped quickly past the short unshaded stretch, his mother's weed-choked vegetable garden (defunct till fall), the wild tamarind, seed-pod tendrils visible now within the ferny foliage, the triad of shaggy-bearded live oaks beyond where a tiny gnatcatcher now wheezed, the mud-smelling path, finally, between the green patches of palmetto and lantana, the taller spice-smelling islands of wax myrtle and privet where the bigger towhees and scrub jays and red birds and mockingbirds picked up a ruckus, hardly at all bothered by the heat. Shade. Raised rows of his grove. Father's experimental, unharvestable acres. Eli's grove.

He had to check in with his father first. Else he'd be in trouble. Sheriff Wright still hadn't caught the *nogoodnik* (that's what Eli's mother called whoever it was) hacking up their trees, carving KIKE in that last one, so his parents liked to know his general whereabouts on the grove, just in case. They didn't think, and Eli didn't think, the *nogoodnik* would trespass clear light of day and cause trouble, but there's no accounting for people. That's how Mr. Ted put it the day he tarred over the bad word on the tree, *There's no accounting for people.* Today, his father was pruning the ten-year Hamlins and older Valencias near Hammock Road. Upright water sprouts were the worst. Those and useless rootstock sprouts. His dad could barely keep up with them during summer now, when he couldn't afford to pay for more workers than Ted and maybe one or two hands time to time.

There must have been a thousand different ways he could make his way toward his father and the river from here, beyond his experimental grove and the clearing, past the older Valencias and Hamlins and Midsweets, then past the even older Marshes, which the workers didn't like picking so much, Mr. Ted said, because the pay-per-box weren't as high for grapefruit. Yet Eli adhered day after day to the same zigzag of right angles across and along the same rows toward the river, the worn path between the cowpeas guiding the way. He'd never see a wildcat this way, he thought, but here he was still, zigzagging along his tired old path. A red bird tweeted loud and urgent from the top of a tall Hamlin. Eli took advantage of the distraction to stop, set his bucket and rod down, and look for the bird. And breathe. He couldn't breathe heavy when he got to his father or his father'd send him back home to the air-conditioning. The thick hot air was hard to gather into his lungs. Air-conditioning spoiled his body for the outside. Only thing he didn't like about it. He patted down his shorts pocket and felt the hard contours of his inhaler, just to make sure. Looking up, the red bird was easy to spot, like an apple on top of the dark green foliage. He wondered whether the red birds were actually louder during the summer or if everything else was just more quiet during these smoldering endless days. Lots of things weren't around at all. The warblers and vireos and gnatcatchers and their Morse code calls wouldn't return until September. Even the larger, louder brown sparrows seemed to be gone. Else they just stayed hidden with the snakes in the thick thatches of palmetto beneath the terraced pines off the grove, west of the stand and the highway.

He heard human murmuring as he reached the area near Hammock, where his father told him he'd be working. The murmuring made him slow down again, look up at a tree. It was one of the Hamlins he and Jo peeled scale from weeks ago before they came across the tree the *nogoodnik* had carved up. He recognized the framework on this particular tree, spiraling from its strong crotch as if it had been pruned more carefully than they pruned citrus. All the same, it had looked different weeks ago, tender somehow against the more shallow slant of spring light. Strange how light changed everything. He and Jo had only pulled off a few hundred scales before they were flushed by the nasty word and the strange Negro with the yellow tie and the bobwhites. His father's wasps seemed to have eaten up lots of the rest. Good thing. There wasn't any more fresh leaf litter on the ground—his father had sprayed the leaves with some kind of vitamin mix—and Eli could only spot a few of the little sesame seed pests here and there. No purple ones. Good bugs sure were something, though he didn't like the wasps as much as the ladybeetles. He walked down the row to check on the tree with the nasty word, as if to make sure the tree was still there. Yep. Tar still covered up the wound. Eli set down his rod and bucket and felt the black tar with his small palm. The black covering the nasty word was hotter than the rest of the bark.

He crossed the rows, leaving his well-trod path, to make his way closer to the murmuring. He began to make out isolated snatches as he neared. He knew it wasn't the bad man carving up their trees, because he wouldn't be talking if he was up to that sort of thing.

". . . want to play it close to the vest, fine," he thought he heard his father say. His father's voice made him freeze on the soft earth. He set down the bucket, but held on to his Zebco. His back felt hot and itchy beneath his backpack. Adults sounded different when they thought they were alone, talking amongst themselves. *Close to the vest.* What did that mean, anyway?

". . . only one person is the thing . . ."

It was a Negro voice, and not Ted's, talking with his father. That's all Eli could tell.

". . . only one person too. . . co-op . . . won't put Ted in that position . . . not fair . . . but you've worked for me how long . . . best rows . . ."

". . . sho . . . sho . . ."

". . . and we're all counting on this harvest . . ."

". . . that's the truth . . . always like working this grove, you and Ted . . . good people I say . . ."

". . . fair is fair . . ."

". . . not just me is the thing . . ."

". . . and not just me . . ."

"Dad!" Eli called, finally, not wanting to get in trouble for eavesdropping.

"There you are, kiddo," his father said, his father voice sounding somehow phony now, like playacting compared to his other voice.

"Hey, partner," the Negro worker said, hands on his hips. Percy.

"Hi Mr. Percy." Eli set down his bucket holding the cast net. He tried not to stare at the chocolate mole on Percy's cheek. Both Percy and his father wore moleskin gloves, Tuttle clippers holstered like guns in small leather pockets clipped to the waists of their field trousers.

"Too hot to fish, ain't it?" Percy asked.

"Fish still gotta eat," he heard himself say, pleased with the bold words he had learned from Ted. Percy seemed amused by his answer too.

"Right you are, partner." He wagged a gloved finger at him. "Never looked at it that way."

"Your mother pasted enough zinc oxide on you, I can see," his father said.

Eli nodded.

"Well, go on, I guess. Just be on the lookout. Go catch us some dinner, sport."

Eli grabbed up his bucket and fled.

He returned to his familiar row, headed farther east and finally reached the wiregrass and palmetto berm at their property line before the irrigation canal, higher now on account of the rains, but still leapable. He gazed northward up the ditch, considered trekking to Jo's side, sneaking over to the kitchen midden to see what the marlberry and snowberry was up to this summer, but he wouldn't dare get caught by Mr. Boehringer on his property. Jo's father carried a shotgun for turkey and quail and butterflies. And for the thieves, who sometimes snuck in at night on the river by skiff, people said. If Mr. Boehringer complained all red-faced to his father about Eli tromping on his property, his father would break every bone in his body, which only truly meant that he'd get awfully mad, but mad was bad enough. So instead of heading north, Eli disappeared beneath the canopy of sabal palms on their side, keeping his eye out for a wildcat, for the *nogoodnik*, too. He reached the Florida East Coast tracks and crossed them after looking both ways, then disappeared into the more narrow band of sabal palms, where the air was clammy and dark, which gave way to dense but shorter mangrove, which he'd never be able to cross if it weren't for the cleared stretch and the rickety raised wooden footpath that someone had built. Maybe Old Man Hawley. Small insectival crabs scuttled brown across the gnarly windswept branches. Eli yanked off a leaf and tasted its salt. Then he felt a bite on his neck. *Ouch.* The mosquitoes were worse here in the mangrove, even with his Watkins smeared all over, so Eli sprinted on the short wooden path until he reached the sugar sand beach and the river, a broad stretch of dry beach now that it was low tide. He gazed across the stretch of shallow water at the island and the Haulover Canal, built by slaves, Mr. Ted said. Some of his "own people," he said. The draw bridge was up, offered a big hazy ship passage from the river to the lagoon and the ocean. Not one of the Simply Citrus boats, Eli knew. They shipped out their sour fruit to New York in a bigger white ship they owned from the port farther south at the

Cape. He walked down the sugar sand toward the necklace of murky pools, some large and some mere puddles. A reddish egret danced above one big pool, batting its wings, corralling shrimp and baitfish. A funny thing, these reddish egrets, who didn't hunt patient as statues like the other herons or egrets, but found a different way. It was a good pool, probably, but the bird found it first so he'd leave it alone. He walked past toward a second large pool farther out, simmering with trapped creatures waiting for high tide to release them. Nameless winged insects flew whirligig above. Eli set his bucket and rod and backpack down in the moist sand from a distance and lifted out his small cast net. Mr. Ted had taught him how to gather the horn in his fist like an ice-cream cone, which he did now, how to dangle the lead line, separate the selvage, hold a piece of net between his teeth, then send it off like a flying saucer with his right hand, releasing the netting from his teeth just in time.

Poised with the net, Eli crept toward the pool. There was no reason to be too quiet—the baitfish and shrimp trapped as they were—but Eli crept over quietly, anyway, reading the water. The baitfish and shrimp seemed concentrated mostly in the frothing center, where it was deepest, so Eli would be getting his shoes wet. He used to take off his sneakers when he first started fishing the river a few years ago, but learned his lesson after he sliced his heel open on an oyster bed. The water was almost too warm, stranded here under the sun. He walked slow through the ankle-deep, then shin-deep, then almost knee-deep pool, lifting the piece of net to his teeth as he neared the simmering section. He twisted his torso counterclockwise, the net a secret behind him for a brief instant, then twisted back and released it into the blazing sky. The net dilated in the air like an enormous white eye, then plashed down in the pool. Eli tugged the nylon green line to close the lead-line maw. Silver dashes winked against the sun as he pulled in his catch, made him smile. He hustled with the quivering net over to the bucket on the sand. He had forgotten to fill it with water, though. *Gosh dang.* Straining on his toe-tips, he lifted the net above the bucket and pulled up on the horn to release the gleaming baitfish and browner shrimp, which thwacked against the dry plastic sides, a desperate sound that made Eli wince, even though they were just baitfish and shrimp. He dropped the net and scurried with the bucket to the pool, gathering up a dose of water, losing more than a few baitfish in the process. No matter. He studied the creatures in the bucket. Plenty of bait, mostly pilchards and greenies. He wouldn't need to cast the net a second time. He picked up his rod and swung his backpack around his shoulders. The net he wrapped around his shoulder too, the lead lines dripping down over his backpack. The bucket was heavier now, quarter full with water as he walked up the beach.

He looked down at his shins beside the sloshing bucket. His socks had fallen. The hair on his legs had changed. Once blonde and sporadic, like the hairs his mother plucked from the frozen raw chickens they got at the Krupnick's store, the hair on his legs now was suddenly darker and coarse. He didn't much like it. Next he'd have hair under his arms like Dean and Hunter, and on his thingy too. *Yuck.* But he felt stronger now. Definitely stronger, which he did like. Partly he felt stronger because he'd just caught his own baitfish, and partly because he didn't have to go to school now and be around boys like Dean and Hunter, who'd seem even stronger, diminishing any gains Eli had realized. Partly he didn't call Jo this morning to join him because even having her around would make him feel smaller today. And partly he didn't call her because she didn't like fishing as much as he did and he didn't feel like fending off her complaints about how boring it was when they didn't catch anything, how gross and slimy it was when they did catch something.

Sometimes it was good just to be alone.

He glanced out and read the river. It was just starting to gather momentum northward, tide coming in. The hazy draw bridge at the faraway canal was down now. He'd walk north of the wooden pathway toward the small spit of land at the end of the access road, walk past the spit toward the thicker mangrove shoreline. That was the best place to fish incoming tide. If the tide was high enough, he'd walk out into the current, then toss a freelined shrimp to drift down underneath the mangroves, pilchard if there were snook.

The spit. First thing he saw was the sagging canvas tent, right there on the leg of land closer to the tide line than Eli would have staked it. Then the makeshift fire pit with its metal grate, dented tin cans strewn about. Then the dilapidated jalopy with a frowning fender, higher up and close to the FEC tracks. Then he saw one of the bearded, shaggy-haired men, crouching out of the tent, fishing rod in his hand, then the other shaggy man, hip deep in the water several yards out, casting his line in a way that struck Eli as unpracticed, amateurish. What did he think he'd catch out there in the open water, anyway? A manatee? A dolphin? Were these sloppy men the bad men who'd been carving up their trees, the *nogoodniks*? He'd stay clear of them, that's for sure. That was the thing about being small. And sickly. And Jewish, maybe. Eli's antennae were ever alert for signs of danger. These sloppy grown men and their discarded dented cans. Their sagging canvas tent. Their dilapidated automobile with the frowning fender. He wasn't sure they were the anti-Semites (the word his father had used), but they just didn't seem right to Eli. *Shlumpy*, his mother would say. Running away from something, Eli felt certain, as if they hopped into their cruddy car and lit out as far as they could go before the river rose up and stopped them.

Skirting around grownups sure did take up an awful lot of Eli's time these days. He'd have to go inside clear around the spit to avoid these men and their fish camp. It angered him. It wasn't his private property, but still. What were they doing setting up a fish camp here, way outside of town on this spit of open riverfront?! And how long would they be here? Something about the makeshift fire pit suggested a few days, very least. He felt his butterfly rash flare up beneath the zinc. It wasn't fair that he'd have to walk inside to escape these strangers, who probably couldn't fish at all. They didn't seem to notice him yet, thankfully. He walked toward the high-tide mangrove edge where the mosquitoes were thicker and scooted north inside of the spit. Just after the mangroves yielded to the dirt road, though, the man from the tent saw him and shouted, "Hallo there, young fella!" Then, after Eli ignored him, "You there! Come be neighborly, why don't ya?" Eli wouldn't stop. Or look up, even. "Ol' Pervis got some baseball cards, hear?" The voice seemed laced with smarmy ill-intent, as if he thought Eli were younger—as his small body suggested—and wouldn't be able to detect his smarmy ill-intent. Eli scampered farther away from the man to the tracks and followed the railroad north, rather than walk back down to the shoreline. There was another rickety access bridge a ways up that would lead him back through the mangrove thicket to the river, far enough away and around a bend and without a road or spit so that the men wouldn't be able to see him, or easily find him.

Long-shanked hooks were best. Easier to pull out the fish's mouth with his pliers. Two-oughts plenty big. He poked the ten-pound monofilament through the two-ought eye, licked the salt from his new peach-fuzz mustache. Wrap, wrap, wrap, wrap. Poked the line through the gap at the eye, then through the second gap higher up, wet the loose knot between his lips, pulled it tight. Improved clinch. The one thing about fishing his father had taught him.

Tide still out. He couldn't freeline under the mangroves. Too shallow. He'd have to work a hole with a split-shot instead. There was a hole he knew close by. He plucked up a shrimp from the bucket. It tried curling into a tight comma to escape, a spasm of strong muscle. He pressed inside its tail to make it fan out, slid the shank of the hook in the open V between, then pierced the shell. The most natural presentation. He tromped out knee-high into the water with the Zebco, looking south every step, relieved he couldn't see the faraway spit around the bend. He looked down-current for the eddy. There. A bit farther out than Eli remembered, or maybe the tide had just come in farther than he thought. It was deeper under the eddy, twenty yards or so away. Perfect. He cast out the shrimp and kept the bail open, feeding line to the current, but the line went too far inside, missed the mark. He reeled in slow so he wouldn't shed the shrimp, droplets of water winking against the sun along the monofilament. He cast again, farther to the right this time, the blue line under the split-shot's influence drifting perfectly over the hole. The shrimp ought to be in the strike zone now, he thought. Now. NOW. *NOW,* he urged, softly.

Bingo! The tell-tale mangrove snapper tug. Not deep and steady like a redfish (which he always released because they didn't taste good at all) or lightning fast and violent like a snook (which did taste good but were scarce on account of the haul seine poachers), but herky-jerky like a snapper, tastiest of them all. He loosened the drag at the dial so the fish wouldn't snap the line. He couldn't horse in a decent-sized fish with ten-pound mono. He reeled it in all the way until the split-shot rattled against the rod's guide. "Shoot," he uttered. That's how you broke the guides. First the water he forgot to put in the bucket, now his clumsy retrieve. He grasped the flailing snapper with his bare hand, sliding his hand down from the head to smooth the dorsal barbs, and sloshed in to shore. Ten inches, this snapper, heavy in his small hand, more silver than red, its angry dark eyebrows rising. He didn't like seeing the eyebrows rise, this mere creature expressing a grievance. He grasped the hook with his pliers and held the fish by the pliers alone over the bucket to shake it loose. The creature plopped into the bucket after a few shakes. Eli looked at it for a moment alongside the smaller baitfish.

He plucked a second shrimp from the bucket and covered up the bucket with its lid to keep the birds away, returned to his hole for the rest of his dinner.

"Mom! I got fish!" Eli called, having swung open the wooden door, then retreating. He knew enough not to tread on the pine floor with soggy river-smelling shoes and a dripping bucket. His mother would greet him on the porch, gather up the fish in a dishcloth, then fillet them in the air-conditioned kitchen. He knew she'd be home. His mother closed the stand this summer at 3:00 p.m.

"I'm coming!" he heard her call. He heard the cotton flick of the dish towel from the oven handle, his mother's bare feet scampering on the lemon linoleum. She met him at the screen, Sarah in her arms. She was big now, Sarah, and made his mother seem smaller. His sister didn't smell poopy, thankfully.

"Hello Sarah-le," he cooed at his baby sister from the welcome mat. Sarah flashed her wet teeth at him—four teeth now, tops and bottoms. Eli was feeling expansive, having brought home six chunky snappers. (Three smaller ones and a catfish he let go.) He reached to kiss his sister as his mother inspected the contents of his bucket, as she drew Sarah away from his advance.

"Like a Torah, for heaven's sake, Eli. Kiss her like a Torah. You're filthy." Eli touched Sarah's cool forehead with his fingers, then brought the fingers to his lips and kissed them. "Quite a catch, Elijah-le. Here, take the towel and bring them in the kitchen for me. Shoes and socks off first!"

Eli deposited his catch on the counter and watched after Sarah as his mother filleted the snappers. She learned how to fillet whole fish from her big cookbook, *The Joy of Cooking*. It was the one thing about fishing that he didn't know how to do. His mother wouldn't let him handle a knife long and sharp enough to pierce snapper-scale.

"Well," his mother asked, making her first slice behind a pectoral fin—its angry brow had faded now that it was dead—"how was your day, Eli? Anything exciting happen on the river? Mosquitoes weren't too bad, I hope." She slid the knife under the meat, paused as she felt for the ridge of rib bone against the blade, Eli figured. Then she sliced.

"Umm . . . no Mom," he evaded her question. He knew she'd worry about the *shlumpy* men and their fish camp. Plus, Eli was pretty sure they couldn't be the *nogoodniks* carving up their trees. They were from somewhere else, he was pretty sure, so how could they know that Jews owned the nearby grove? "Nothing exciting. Just the fish. Skeeters were okay. Few bites, maybe." Eli pinched hard either side of the crimson welt at his neck, then rotated his pincers forty-five degrees and pinched again, harder. Jo taught him. That way it didn't itch.

He drummed his fingers against the top of Sarah's Yuban canister, trying to get her to imitate his simple rhythm. "*Bop, bop, bop-bop-bop.*"

"My oh my, I'll have to freeze some of these fillets."

"Come on Sarah," he implored. "*Bop, bop, bop-bop-bop.* You can do it, Sarah, can't you?"

Sarah gazed up at him, dumbfounded, her tongue resting on her wet lip.

"What a good brother you are, Elijah-le." His mother dropped the first stripped carcass back into the bucket, plucked out a fresh one.

After his mother finished filleting the snappers, she wrapped the carcasses in the large dishtowel and handed the makeshift sack to Eli. "You know what to do with them," she said, twisting open the hot water valve at the sink, pouring a copious dose of Palmolive and then Ajax powder into the cavern of her hands, scrubbing off the scale and fish slime. "Go. Get these stinky fish out of my kitchen. Sarah's fine with me."

Yes, Eli knew what to do with the fish carcasses, bury them in the garden, barren except for the weeds now that it was summer. He'd bury them deep enough that the raccoons and stray cats wouldn't sniff them out. The carcasses added important nutrients to the soil. That's how the Indians taught the pilgrims to grow corn, Eli learned at school, bury alewives and shad beneath the seeds. Shovel in hand, Eli looked about for signs of troubled earth. He had forgotten exactly where he had buried the last carcasses and he tried to bury them in a pattern so he wouldn't dig up his own half-decayed fish by accident. He noticed the fewer weeds and choppy earth near the gone-to-seed asparagus thicket and then he remembered. He'd dig his hole just beside the last one. The enriched earth in the garden was soft and easy to dig. His arms were skinny, but cords of actual muscle seemed to have developed overnight and a single green vein bulged now from his biceps. He emptied the carcasses into the hole, then shook the open bucket above, making sure to empty all the stripped skins too that his mother sliced off the meat. Sometimes the skins stuck to the sides of the bucket.

It felt especially good to shovel the soft heavy earth back into the hole to cover the fish, to pat down the top that looked like a pie crust. Because burying things also made them clean. When he used a *flaishik* knife by accident on the butter, his mother buried the knife overnight in the garden and said a prayer. The next morning—*presto!*—the knife was clean. *Kashered.* Eli, too, felt cleaner now having tucked the fish beneath the pie-crust ground. He didn't mind being filthy with the river. But the *shlumpy* men there had somehow left him feeling sullied. He had decided almost immediately that he wouldn't tell his mom and dad about them. *Nothing exciting,* he told his mother. *Just the fish.* He would just avoid the bad men. For if he told his parents about them, they wouldn't let him go fishing. They wouldn't let him go off into the grove at all. And then he'd never see a wildcat. And then he'd be bored all day. So he buried the fish, and the men, and his memory of the men, deep in the cleansing earth. And he felt better.

Here was Eli in summer.

Twenty-one

HERE WAS ISAAC IN SUMMER. He pored over the ingredients, active and inactive, at Clyde's Ag-Mart and Feed. *Guaranteed Analysis By Weight: Total Magnesium as Mg, 1.00%. Water Soluble Mg, 1.00%. Chelated Mg, 0.70%. Soluble Iron as Fe, 1.20%. Soluble Manganese as Mn, 1.20%. Soluble Zinc as Zn, 1.70%. Sulfur as S, 4.10%. Soluble Copper as Cu, 1.00%. Derived from: Magnesium Sulfate, Magnesium Lignin Sulfate Chelate, Manganese Sulfate, Manganese Lignin Sulfate Chelate, Zinc Sulfate, Zinc Lignin Sulfate Chelate, Copper Sulfate, Copper Lignin Sulfate. Ferrous Sulfate, Ferrous Lignin Sulfate Chelate. Chelating agent is Lignin Sulfate.*

Micronutrients. That's what Isaac's scale-stricken acres needed now, a supplementary micronutrient spray to buttress the nitrogen, phosphorous, and potassium potion he administered to the still-yellow leaves just after the *Aphytis* wasps established themselves. Grubbing out close to twenty acres and waiting five years for transplanted liners to bear a piddly three or four field boxes wasn't an option. Not one he could afford, at any rate, even with Melody's pies bringing in some welcome currency. So Isaac pored over the label of the micronutrient spray at Clyde's Ag-Mart and Feed, scrutinizing its contents against those of its cheaper competitor. If he were going to pay a dollar extra a gallon for their latest concentrated chelated concoction—now with copper and a .70% zinc kick, apparently—he'd darn well know what he was paying for. He wouldn't just take Clyde's word for it, even if Clyde did seem peeved behind his broad beat-up wooden counter. Soon as Isaac carefully untaped and unscrolled the book-length labels on the two plastic containers, Clyde made a snuffing sound from his nostrils and retreated from the cash register, crossed his plaid arms and leaned back beneath the sepia photo of Walt's father looking confused amid his frozen grove, his feet hidden underneath dropped leaves and fallen, frostbitten fruit. A conversation piece, the old photo. Beside the framed photo now was the makeshift FOR SALE sign for Clyde's used red Ford Powermaster 861 tractor out back that he wouldn't ever sell for the price he was asking. The steel fans seemed to roar in the sudden human silence as Isaac studied the labels. Isaac glanced up to see Clyde's farsighted eyes looking right at him, big and bloodshot behind the magnification of his black-framed spectacles. As if Clyde had anything else to do this long hot day. Heat was getting to Clyde. Getting to Isaac too, maybe, making them both irascible. *All the money I spend here*, Isaac felt like saying, *you'd think I could inspect a label or two without getting the stink eye*. Instead, after verifying the zinc and copper contents, after hearing his mother's favorite saying rattle inside his skull, *no use being penny-wise and pound-foolish,* after convincing himself that ten extra dollars would probably be worth it in the long run, he looked up at Clyde and offered his verdict:

"I suppose I'll take ten gallons, then."

Here was Isaac, next morning, the sun still tucked beneath the grove trees to the east. These hot dark mornings were curious, as if the grove didn't even need sun during summer to feel too hot. Here was Isaac, digging up the shallow eight-inch grave beneath the protection of the shaggy-bearded live oaks, looking about to make sure Ted hadn't arrived for work yet, as if it were an actual corpse he was exhuming. It wasn't, of course, but who wanted to explain to someone why he was digging up a pine box from a shallow grave in the near dark? It only took a few minutes to carve out the field box, wipe off the moist rainy-season soil with his moleskin-gloved hand and lift up the makeshift lid. The least Isaac could do for the commissioner was store his irradiated grapefruit bud sticks, properly. For free, Shepherd had given him the *Aphytis* that saved his scale-stricken acres. No denying that. So as soon as he had returned from Lakeland a couple months ago now, he removed the innocuous-looking bud sticks from the polyethylene bag and set about adhering to the best practice for budwood storage. He lined a field box with brown paper then damp redwood shingle tow. He spread the first layer of bud sticks like bedfellows down on the damp tow, then tucked them in under a moist layer of sphagnum moss. Then he laid another layer of bud sticks down on the moist sphagnum, and so forth. There were enough bud sticks for eight layers. He still hadn't decided whether or not he was going to bud these irradiated scions onto sour orange stock come October, but no point letting the bud sticks wither in the meantime. He hadn't checked the field box for a few weeks now so he was pleased to see that the moss and bud sticks were still moist, thanks to the rainy season and oak shade, the dormant buds—he peeled back the sphagnum layers gingerly—unmolested by pests and scavengers. It wasn't as if these were Eli's fragrant fish carcasses, dug up half the time by the feral cats and raccoons and who knew what else, those wildcats Eli was anxious to see, maybe. He replaced the cover and lowered the field box back down into its shallow grave, scooped a layer of soft earth back on top and patted down the dirt with the back of his shovel.

Just as he lifted his biceps to wipe his brow, he saw an airborne object streak down from overhead, so near it made him flinch, then heard the plaintive shriek from captured prey atop the oak canopy, a dove maybe, as the airborne object—probably a Cooper's hawk—streaked off and disappeared into the grove with its prize. The scarce light of dawn and dusk, stripped of shadows, tended to be the times when Isaac observed raptors snatching a meal. He wondered what to make of the vision now, having just buried the budwood. He couldn't help thinking there was a lesson in there somewhere—hoping, rather, there was a lesson he might glean about irradiated seeds, about Ted and his hovering son, Levi, about the unpromising experimental grove, about Eli, about his increasingly harried and remote working wife, if only to relieve him from the burden of thinking so hard about matters, grove and human. But there wasn't any lesson, he decided, tromping off to the greenhouse to retrieve his chelated micronutrient spray. Only a hawk doing its hawk business.

He spent a full hour spraying the chelated concentrate on the foliage of the recovering Hamlins before Ted joined him, his empty metal sprayer slung over one stooped shoulder. Isaac liked that he beat Ted outdoors this morning. *Here I am*, his presence said without words. *Here I am these many hours before your arrival, laboring over my grove.*

"Solution's over there, Ted," he said, pointing to the opaque bottle of the micronutrient concentrate beside the irrigation spigot. Ted nodded and headed toward the container and the spigot.

"This new, Isaac?" he asked.

"Yep. Same dosage, though," Isaac replied.

Ted nodded, twisted open the spigot.

They sprayed mostly in silence for the better part of an hour. Relations with Ted had grown more distant since his foreman had acknowledged his relationship with the new besuited Negro in town.

He's Levi, Isaac. He's my boy.

The insult, it seemed to Isaac, should properly be felt on his side, Isaac's side, so Ted's standoffishness bothered him all the more. It seemed to Isaac that Ted could try harder to be friendly. Heck if Isaac would be the one to bend over backwards under the circumstances. Isaac didn't at all like having strained relations with his Negro foreman. He considered firing Ted and being done with it, but hiring a new foreman was no small matter, and he didn't have the foggiest idea who else he would trust with his grove. Plus, Ted had overseen these acres so long that Isaac just didn't have the heart to turn him out on his ear. He feared that Ted's son might take special pains to persecute him come harvesttime if he sacked his father. He was a regional field officer for the NAACP, Levi. Isaac had teased that much out of Ted, anyway. Five counties he was responsible for, including Brevard. Labor issues just a small part of his purview. That's the very phrase Ted had used, *just a small part of his purview*—what kind of word was that for Ted, *purview*?—as if Ted had worked it out ahead of time with Levi what he'd reveal, and how he'd reveal it, after Isaac prodded.

Isaac was going to try to do right by Percy and Fred and the others, with or without the specter of Levi. But he wouldn't give Ted the satisfaction of disclosing his plan. His foreman would just report back to Levi, and then where would all the co-op's leverage be?

"Breeze picks up any more, might as well hold off till tomorrow," Ted finally said at the next spigot down the row, opening it up to release a frothy torrent. Both their metal canisters had run dry, but they'd each have a long drink before refilling their sprayers. "No point making expensive air," Ted declared, taking a stutter step sideways and opening his palms as he tended to do when making a point.

Isaac laughed here at Ted's little joke—*expensive air*—which made Ted laugh, showing his teeth for the first time this morning. They both watched as the hot water ran itself out onto the spoiled swatch of weed-choked earth. The small joke somehow cut through the ten acres Ted wanted and Levi's unignorable presence, cut through Isaac's big lumbering whiteness and Ted's unignorable

Negroness. "Expensive air, huh?" Isaac said, slapping his foreman's muslin shoulder. "That's a good one. Go ahead, have a drink first. Age before beauty."

Ted cupped his pale palm beneath the spigot now that the water wasn't so hot and splashed handfuls over his face and his patchy pate, then soaked the rag he tied to the back of his neck to keep it cool and to keep the sun off it. That was the trick to warding off the heat, Ted had told Isaac his first summer. Keeping the back of your neck cool.

Isaac waited for Ted to finish and duplicated his ablutions at the spigot. He splashed the not-quite-cool water on his neck but didn't tie a rag there like Ted.

"Might as well call it quits for the day, I guess."

Town. Intersection of Washington and Julia. Isaac parked the truck and opened the door without looking.

"Hey, watch it mister!" one of the town boys accosted him, swerving out of the way on his Schwinn with the banana seat and looping handles. A pack of his cycling brethren followed after on similar bikes.

"Sorry!" Isaac called down the sandy street, then shut the truck door. He thought he recognized the urchin with the blonde flattop. Dean Chapman, who seemed to be the leader of the local boys—him and Doyle's nephew, anyway, Hunter, who Isaac didn't see in the pack. One child he was surprised to notice was Peter, Hubert King's porky son. He lagged behind, which was why Isaac noticed him, his front tire zig-zagging inefficiently on the macadam with each labored pump of the pedal.

"Keep up, lard-butt!" Dean called back, which surprised Isaac even more than Dean's temerity in telling an adult to *watch it, mister!* Not so much that the Chapman boy called Peter a name, but that he did so within earshot of an adult. *Hey there!* he felt like shouting down the macadam. *Cut that nasty business out!* But Dean and the more agile members of his pack quickly disappeared down South Palm. It would hardly help poor Peter's standing, anyway, for Eli's father to fight his battles for him. Did Hugh know what was in store for his son when he dropped off Peter this morning in town with his bike?

Isaac sometimes considered trying harder to involve Eli in the daily goings on of the other local boys. Plenty of free time on their hands to raise holy hell now that it was summer: whooping and wailing down the streets on their bikes, terrorizing insects and any small mammals they came across, trading baseball cards or comics under the shaggy oaks at the park just up the slope, lighting their farts on fire inside RC Cola bottles. So Isaac guessed. Who knew what they did to fill these endless summer days? They were pretty much on their own, the town boys, summertime. It wasn't a good thing, he worried, that Eli spent so much time now alone in his room reading, or fishing the river, or out in the grove with a wild unkempt girl, Walt's girl of all people. But he realized now, standing before Janisse's on Washington and Julia, what he only vaguely sensed formerly, that he'd only be setting poor Eli up for the indignities that accompanied being a weak boy—a Jewboy to boot—among much stronger, gentile boys. Even that chubby Peter was much bigger and stronger. And even Peter they terrorized. Here these few children were, growing up in the middle of Nowhere, Florida. Seemed they all should stick together, very least. But it didn't work that way, amongst the children or the adults.

Janisse's. *AIR-CONDITIONED FOR YOUR COMFORT*, the white sign propped inside the window now advertised in fancy black cursive, summer heat in full force. Most stores in town were air-conditioned summers. Except for Sonny's Good Food. Except for Clyde's Ag-Mart and Feed.

His first year on the grove, Isaac had asked Ted how he felt being unwelcome at Janisse's and Ted had surprised him when he answered, "Oh, white folks getting on over there okay without us, I expect," showing his Wrigley's spearmint between his teeth, which made Isaac hear a corollary in Ted's answer: We Negroes getting on at Sonny's Good Food okay without white folk. Segregation was more complicated than Isaac had thought as a northerner. Not that it was right. Just more complicated.

The bells on the glass door announced Isaac's arrival to the co-op fellows, already slumped in their seats. Isaac breathed in the mentholated air. He couldn't help but notice Janisse's chalky concentrate shamelessly on display behind the bar, sheets of the ersatz juice recirculating along the sides of its fancy plastic bath perched atop the fountain dispenser. Beside the concentrate machine on the back counter was the small Zenith, projecting a nervous sepia screen despite its foil-tipped rabbit-ear antennae.

"Afternoon, Ike," Clay uttered for the group, twisting his stool to about three o'clock for just an instant. The co-op fellows, judging by their shoulders, were immersed in two separate conversations. Isaac said hello as he made his way to the bar, noticed Walt's crusty BVDs riding high above the sagging waistline of his trousers. He took his seat on the cracked vinyl stool at the far end from his cantankerous red-headed neighbor, set down the lined sheet of factors he'd been working on beside his water-stained butter knife. Someone else would have to tell Walt to pull up his pants.

"Angel food's angel food and pound cake's pound cake, that's all I'm saying," Win uttered beside Isaac to Doyle. Having made his point, he took a healthy swig of his RC Cola—fourth or fifth RC of Win's day, Isaac figured—then sucked at his Kent and offered a lusty exhale above the bar now that he couldn't turn Isaac's direction to expel his spent smoke. "Not sure what the difference is, exactly, but is it too much to ask my Connie to make pound, 'stead of that spongy angel food?"

"Mmmm," Doyle murmured. Isaac noticed the plastic-coated sheets of new stamps in front of Doyle, greens and blues.

"Looks like some nice stamps down there," Isaac said.

"Fort Sumter four cents just came in."

Isaac nodded. "Great," he said, trying to sound enthusiastic for Doyle.

"Club sandwich hold the bacon?" Janisse greeted him with this question, carrying a glass carafe of hot coffee. He wasn't sure he wanted turkey today, but he didn't want to disappoint Janisse so told her sure.

"Coffee?" she asked. Isaac declined, told her that water was okay.

"More coffee, sugar?" she asked Doyle next, who nodded.

Isaac could only hear bits of Clay and Walt's conversation a few seats down, but he could tell that it was more important, because Clay hadn't dipped one of his steak fries in the blue cheese since Isaac sat down, which he usually consumed with gusto, because Walt leaned his crossed arms over the Formica counter, his shoulders hunched, as if the conversation were a bone before him he was protecting from a rival dog.

". . . better have given you a decent price," he heard Walt utter.

"Eminent domain, not a thing I could do, anyway," said Clay, ". . . confiscated . . . Glad I got out with my—"

"Can't even chew it, it's so foamy," Win complained closer by, drowning out Clay. "The kids won't even touch it, that cruddy angel food."

"What are you boys talking about down there?" Isaac called over Win and Doyle to Clay.

"Janisse, what's the difference between angel food and pound cake?"

"Quiet, Edwin, for crying out loud!" Win's noisy blather over nothing was beginning to pester Isaac.

"Near fifty acres of mine they finally snatched up," Clay admitted, lifted his Winston to his lips, making it glow. He lowered the cigarette to the black plastic ashtray, tapped off the gray worm. "The Feds. For that NASA business. Chose the island, after all. Just like I thought would happen, remember?"

"Yeah. I remember. Son of a—"

"Expanding operations. Glad they didn't kick me clear off the island, the way I see it. Screwed Joe Buck good, they did. Confiscated his acres straight out. 'Least they didn't confiscate all mine. Can still tend my northern plot, just can't leave my big equipment on the grove overnight they say. For now, anyway. Tomorrow, who knows?"

"That's the truth right there," Doyle said, sliding his nicotine-stained fingertips over the few green stamps before him, squinting against the smoke of the cigarette that bobbed like a baton now from his lips. "Tomorrow, who knows? Life in a nutshell, that is."

"Angel food's made out of egg whites, mostly," said Janisse to Win, softly, in deference to the more important topic of conversation. "Pound cake's got butter and yolks, too. Pound each. Get it, Edwin?"

"That's why it tastes so good, I guess," he said.

"They better do something worthwhile out there," Walt declared. "That Kennedy thinks it's gonna scare the Reds shooting ourselves up into space just to drop straight back down in the ocean, he's got another thing coming."

"They're going clear to the moon is the plan," Win joined the conversation now. "You know that, Walt."

"The moon, huh." Walt shook his head, flicked the ashes off his cigarette, then lifted up his creamy iced coffee to his mouth with the same hand. Some of the milky liquid adhered to his woolly red mustache. "Darn fool Grissom near drowned the other day. And you're talking about the moon."

"Not his fault about that hatch," said Win.

"Jury's out on that," said Walt.

"Still takes brass balls, ask me," said Doyle.

"I guess it's good news all told," Isaac said, retrieving the thread. "Just those island acres, anyway. Not coming after our acres *across* the river. That's still true, right?"

"That's the word," Clay said, which seemed to satisfy everyone.

"One less thing to worry about, sure enough," said Doyle. "Now just those Simply Citrus bastards messing with our prices. And the field-workers, harvest around the corner."

"Time to open up a hotel in town, ask me," Janisse declared, refilling their waters. "Tourists we'll be getting. Open to the public, they're saying, the new rocket facility they aim to build on the island. I didn't have my hands full . . ."

"Just seems like pound cake now and again with my straw-berrs isn't too much to ask," Win muttered, fingering again the jagged grain of this small hurt.

The river men worked over their midday meals in peaceable silence until the Special Bulletin screen on the television captured Walt's attention. "Turn up the TV, Janisse, will you?" he called down the bar, which compelled Janisse to lift her head from her stack of tickets and the legal pad where she maintained her records. Her eyes looked bleary. She had been in the middle of a semi-complicated calculation, Isaac suspected, probably the week's receipts for her ledger.

"Sit tight," she said as she made her way to the TV. She twisted the volume up on the dial, fiddled with the rabbit ears to steady the picture until it held fast.

"There! Just like that," Walt said. "Hold it just like that."

"I'm not standing here all day, Walt Boehringer."

"Simple please wouldn't kill you, either, Walt," said Doyle. Doyle had showered with apparent purpose this morning, Isaac noticed, maybe for his visit to the post office to retrieve his new stamps, but maybe for Janisse. Isaac hoped so. Why not? Fresh pomade darkened his embattled strands of hair. The creases and fissures at the back of his sun-stricken neck weren't encrusted anymore with dirt.

"*Please*, Janisse," Walt said. "Satisfied, Doyle?"

"Thank you sugar," Janisse said to Doyle, then poked her tongue out at Walt, an unflattering amphibious expression.

The broadcaster, younger than Edwards, was mentioning a wall in Germany that the Russians were building. Isaac didn't recognize the young broadcaster at all, perhaps the only news man available in the studio to appear on camera so early in the day. Newsreel footage behind his shoulder showed a woman nearly garroting herself as she tried scurrying under what appeared to be barbed wire.

"My," Janisse said, lifting her free hand to her mouth.

President Kennedy has expressed his grave concern, the broadcaster declared, *but the United States will not interfere with the wall's construction.*

In other news, he continued, *the trial of Nazi SS officer, Adolf Eichmann, has finally reached its conclusion.* A file photo of Eichmann in his SS garb flashed now in the frame behind the man's shoulder. *Given the extraordinary amount of testimony and documentation, it is expected that deliberations among the three Israeli justices will carry on for quite some time. We return now to our regularly scheduled program.*

"Okay?" Janisse asked, releasing the antennae and returning to her labors down the bar.

"String him up, they oughta," Doyle said, glancing down toward Isaac.

"Yep," Win agreed. "Dollars to donuts that's just what they do." Win, too, glanced over at Isaac, then looked away just as quick.

There was something in all this coverage over Eichmann that unsettled Isaac. Something grotesque. Why all this interest now, when it scarcely mattered, the overtones of collective repugnance over the European horrors? The civilized nations hadn't earned the right to their interest, it seemed to Isaac, or their repugnance. Not at this late date.

"What's that scrap of paper you got there before you, anyway?" Doyle asked, leaning forward over his stamps to look past Win at Isaac's lined sheet of factors. Isaac had been waiting for the right time to broach the issue of his factors, or for one of his co-op fellows to inquire about the scrap of paper before him.

"I've been running those numbers, gentlemen. Our field box rates."

Walt rolled his eyes as he lit a fresh cigarette between the practiced cavern of his palms, necessary protection from the wind out on the grove, but an extraneous gesture here. "Isaac and his numbers," Walt said, fanning out his match beside his ear. A dig here. Bigoted, too, in a vague Walterish sort of way. Eggheaded Jews and their numbers. It wasn't quite pointed enough a remark for Isaac to protest, but he felt his hackles rise all the same. Fucking Walt.

"Anyway, I've run them against historic yields, factored in grove upkeep, pest and weed management, irrigation, tree replacement at five per acre every three years, which is conservative. We up rates to thirty cents per box for oranges, twenty cents grapefruit, we're still coming out ahead. Enough ahead, anyway. The way I figure it."

"Thirty cents a box!?" Walt cried, which brought on a coughing jag, forcing him to wheeze in great clutches of air every few coughs.

"Put your hands up!" Doyle advised.

"That doesn't do anything," Clay said.

"Smack him on the back," Win said to no one in particular.

Doyle smacked Walt on the back without enthusiasm, twice.

Walt wasn't choking, Isaac knew. If he were actually choking, Isaac wouldn't let Doyle smack him on the back, which would only make matters worse. Or maybe he would let Doyle smack Walt on the back.

"Leave me be," Walt uttered between coughs, batting Doyle's hand away.

"Glass of water?" Janisse asked from down the bar, where she was consolidating the condiments now into fewer glass jars. Walt raised a meaty palm in protest, issued a more violent single cough into his other fist, which seemed to settle matters.

"Thirty cents," Win uttered, then exhaled through puffed clean-shaven cheeks, troubled the swirled glass neck of his RC Cola bottle with his fingertips.

"Gracious, Ike," Doyle said. "Thirty cents?"

Clay dipped one of his steak fries in blue cheese, took a bite, chewed slowly. He wouldn't tilt his hand quite yet. It occurred to Isaac that he might have run all this by Clay first.

"Whose side are you on, anyway, Ike, thirty cents a box?" Walt's face above his ginger mustache was beet red, mostly on account of his recent coughing jag, Isaac thought, but partly on account of his anger at the proposition. He clutched in a fresh fistful of smoke, breathed it out his nostrils, coughed mildly again as if he were just clearing his throat. His actual mouth was invisible beneath that woolly red mustache. Pursed, probably.

"Ten cents a box our daddys paid the pickers, Ike. *Ten*!"

"Yep," Edwin uttered, then swished his RC around in his mouth. "Ten."

"Mmm-hmm," said Doyle, tamping down the few pomaded strands of his hair with both hands either side of his unfortunate middle part.

"And the workers didn't complain none about it," Walt continued. "Everyone was happy. That's when you could still make a dime owning a small grove. Hell."

"Good ol' days," Win said.

"We take all the risk," Doyle said. "Freezes, disease, pests like your scale, thieves off the river."

"Done with your plate, sugar?" Janisse stated more than asked, lifting up Isaac's ironstone platter.

Clay didn't say anything, but seemed to be stewing in his juices. He was quieter, lately, more contemplative.

"Between Simply Citrus and their concentrate driving down the prices with the packing houses and bird dogs," Walt complained, "now pickers ready to turn the screws, working man just can't get ahead no more. So, like I said, whose side are you on, Ike?"

It wasn't a bad question. Whose side was Isaac on? He liked to think that he was on his own side, his family's side, but that being on his own side didn't necessarily mean being against a network of deserving others. The field-workers. Ted. His co-op fellows. The commissioner. Why did there have to be only one side? With pencil and paper, he had labored over these numbers before him mostly to please these multiple parties, or at least displease them all equally, which amounted to pretty much the same thing, maybe.

"I just want us to be prepared," he explained. "In case it comes to it. We don't want to be blindsided. Commissioner warned me about labor trouble already on the ridge. I saw Joe Buck Wilson with my own eyes storm out of Shepherd's office."

Isaac wouldn't tell the co-op that he now knew the identity of the besuited Negro hanging around, that his name was Levi, that he was his own foreman's eldest son, that he was the new regional field officer for the NAACP. How could he? In any case, Isaac's mention of the commissioner, of Joe Buck Wilson, captured the co-op's more respectful attention.

"You saw Joe Buck?" Win asked, starry-eyed.

"In the flesh?" Doyle asked

"Big as they all say he is?" even Walt inquired.

"Little taller than me, I guess. More barrel-chested."

Clay still hadn't said anything about Isaac's proposal, but just sat there nursing his Winston, gazing straight ahead at the three columns of amber plastic water cups on the back counter. He knew something, Isaac thought. Something he wasn't sharing. Something about the field-workers. Or maybe about Levi. Maybe he knew, like Isaac, that his name was Levi, that he was Ted Lomax's son. Or maybe Clay had his own bundle of grapefruit scions from irradiated seeds, for all Isaac knew. When you knew a secret, like Isaac did, you just assumed you were the only one who knew it. It didn't occur to you that others might know your secret too, or might know other secrets you hadn't fathomed.

"Thirty cents a box," Clay finally pronounced. "Like Ike says. That's what we offer if it comes to it. Twenty for grapefruit. But we hold firm." He snuffed out his Winston in the ashtray to punctuate the terms, even though the stick was only half spent.

The river men, save for Isaac, groaned in their seats. But they'd listen to Clay.

A low chord of distant thunder vibrated at their elbows. Doyle twisted his stool to three o'clock and gazed out the plate glass. It had grown darker outside, a storm giving notice.

"Best settle up before the rain," Doyle said. "Farted around long enough, I'd say."

"Guess I won't be working on the tractor, after all," Win said. He didn't seem disappointed.

"Son of a gun, I just sprayed," said Isaac, feeling now the weight of perplexed stares. "Not pesticides," he clarified. "Don't get excited. Nutritional spray. For the scale."

Walt made a farting sound through his lips to register his displeasure.

"Weather might not get here," Clay offered Isaac some hope, reached in his hip pocket for his wallet. "Coming from the west. Might just spend itself over Orlando or the St. Johns."

"Bring on the rain, hot as all get-out," said Walt, unconcerned with the nutritional requirements of Isaac's beleaguered trees. "Hotter every summer, seems."

"Oh, hush," Janisse said, marrying the condiments again. "Fall's just around the corner."

Cooler weather? Could it be? Isaac wondered. The prospect of bearable outdoors just around the corner would only occur to someone like Janisse, who enjoyed the luxury of air-conditioning indoors all day.

Here was Isaac, this long hot summer.

Twenty-two

SUNDAY MORNING. Eli's feet sunk deep beneath the soil's thin shell as he trod across his mother's defunct vegetable garden, frosted with weeds. He didn't like his sinking feet, feared the several snapper carcasses below, feared they might feel his weight and nip at his ankles. Easier treading outside the garden. He paused beneath the fickle shade of the wild tamarind, its feathery foliage parting in the salt breeze to let the sun slip inside its canopy. The tree smelled good now. Almost orange-blossom sweet. He gazed up at the tiny white powder-puffs bursting all over the leaves. Bees and such, whirligig. Didn't the tree know it was too hot already for blooming? Some of its seed pod tendrils had gotten huge and flat and brown. Maybe this was what spring felt like wherever tamarind trees usually grew. He touched the smooth trunk. The skin felt hot and smooth with muscle cords beneath, like a dog's neck. He patted it. "Good boy," he said. He wished his lungs were better so he could have a dog. A dog sure would be nice out on the grove. He made his way across a blazing stretch to the sturdier canopy of live oaks and savored the refuge beneath their shaggy beards. He touched one of the massive trunks, ridged and rough, spurning his canine comfort.

Jo'd be mad if he was late. He leapt outside the oak canopy and followed the dusty path between the scruffy patches of palmetto and lantana, the taller spice-smelling islands of wax myrtle and privet. Iridescent blue and green dragonflies, small ones, hovered and zig-zagged all about the soupy air, snatching invisible prey.

The grove. Eli's acres first. His father's experimental Hamlins and Parson Browns and Valencias, and those others, the Navels. The hard green fruit didn't seem much different this summer than last, and the summer before. Still small. Neither the Parson Browns nor Hamlins had broke color yet, Eli noticed, which was one thing his father was aiming for, an earlier orange. He noticed a green inchworm climbing its invisible thread like a Slinky up toward the leaves of one of the Hamlins. They weren't good for the trees, he knew. He considered squishing it between his fingers, but that wouldn't be good for the worm, so he left it alone. The trees didn't seem much worth protecting anyway, he thought. Maybe his dad should give it up. That's what Jo said sometimes, repeating her father's words, he could tell.

Jo was already there by the time he reached their clearing, poking the tall lupine and peanuts and shorter cowpeas and wax beans with her oak stick, checking for snakes. Her shins and calves above her dirty socks were dotted all over with shiny orange Mercurochrome stains.

"What happened to your legs?" he asked.

"Nothing."

"Don't look like nothing."

"Just skeeter bites." She slapped at the ground cover, still looking for snakes. "They itch like crazy, 'specially on my ankles. I picked them till they bled."

"Better stop pickin' at 'em then."

"No duh."

"Just pinch 'em both sides like you showed me. It works."

"Don't always work."

Eli didn't argue with this. Her itchy bites had put her in a bad mood. Jo finally gave the all clear so they laid lengthwise on the ground cover, their heads almost touching.

"Lots of dragonflies today."

Jet noise peeled through the air so Eli had to wait to answer. Fighter planes from the base.

"Yep," he said. "I like them."

"Hardly no birds up in the sky, though."

"It's the chemicals."

"Just summer, I think," Jo sighed. They'd had this argument before.

"More birds last summer, though. And the summer before that. Doncha think? Ospreys and pelicans. Haven't seen hardly one pelican all summer."

"Grackle," Jo said, as if she'd proven Eli wrong with the sighting, her stubby finger pointing skyward at the inky stain.

Several silent minutes passed. Eli kept his mouth closed and breathed out his nose so he wouldn't swallow a gnat. A mysterious insect wheezed and rattled loud in one of the grove trees, complaining about the heat. But the trees, he thought, flush with floppy light green leaves, liked the heat, or at least the afternoon downpours that went along with the summer heat. Eli let his eyes relax so the green blurred all about his axis of vision, interrupted only by the scrim of white sky directly above. It felt good, somehow, to let his eyes relax, to court this blurry green. Sort of like drifting off to sleep without actually falling asleep. He heard Jo's stomach grumble, loud.

"Mom made birds-in-the-nest this morning," she uttered by way of explanation.

"I had Cream of Wheat." Eli liked to let the cereal sit for a while after his mother poured in the boiling water from the Revere Ware saucepan. That way it got thick and pasty so he could scrape teaspoon mouthfuls in a series of intersecting lines that gradually revealed the winterberry pattern on the plate.

"You know what birds-in-the-nest *are*, right Eli?"

"Sure. My mom makes them too. She calls them eggs-in-the-middle." Eli especially liked the foamy Wonder Bread patches his mother tore out to make space for the eggs, then cooked crisp in butter. He dipped the rough circles into the loose yolks. He told this to Jo, who told him that the Wonder Bread middles were her favorite part too, that her mother pressed the open side of a juice glass into the bread slices on the counter to cut out perfect circles. That was her secret. Eli wasn't sure why the circles had to be perfect, but didn't say anything about it, not with Jo in a bad mood over her itchy bites.

"Daddy doesn't eat eggs," she said. "Or anything from a chicken. Or anything that flies. He's superstitious about eating things that fly, even the quail he shoots. But turkey he eats 'cause they don't hardly fly."

"That's queer."

"Yeah, I know." Jo laughed, a deep laugh that rustled the cowpeas beneath her, and which gave Eli permission to laugh too. He was glad she didn't get angry that he called her father queer. Usually she got angry at this sort of thing, but Eli supposed she thought her father's fear of flying things was queer too, so it was okay.

"Mourning dove," Jo said, pointing at the sky. Eli's eyes were still lazy so he didn't see the bird.

"Okay," he said.

Melody relaxed and let Levi explore her private places. From behind the stand's counter. With words. He had stopped in on his way to church. They were alone, except for Sarah, napping in the perambulator. "Your boy," he uttered. "Eli. That rash and his . . . umm . . . size. Is that some affliction he has?"

She wondered only now why it had taken him so long to ask this question, a question that must have occurred to him, as it occurred to others, the moment he laid eyes on Eli. She appreciated his reticence. There was something askew in the child, he had realized, something serious that commanded respect, discretion, deference. She pondered these words, unsure that she had located the precise sentiment that governed Levi's reticence.

"A condition," she answered, not quite liking the word affliction that he had used. "Rare. Genetic. Bloom's disease, it's called."

"But he'll be okay," Levi stated more than asked. The creases in his usually smooth brow spelled out his concern. She usually didn't like these furrowed brows, which most times betrayed only counterfeit concern. But something about Levi's brow expressed more durable worry. Care, it occurred to her. Levi's simple care accounted for his reticence.

"It's chronic," she answered. "Mostly affects his lungs. We also have to watch for Leukemia. We test his blood regularly." Levi winced upon each staccato sentence, as if they were stiff little jabs. "But yes," she said, "he'll be okay. We hope."

"Why do you think it's the chemicals?" Jo retrieved their earlier thread. "Pelicans and ospreys don't eat the oranges. I don't get it."

"It makes their eggshells too soft. That's what they think. My dad read about it in the newspaper."

"Sounds like hogwash to me. They're just gasping at straws."

"*Grasping* at straws, you mean."

"Huh?"

"It's grasping at straws. Not gasping."

Jo, the elder, wasn't used to being corrected by Eli and didn't much like it. He could tell by the way she snuffed air out her nostrils and clucked her tongue.

"Why would you grasp at a straw, huckleberry?" she asked. "It doesn't make no sense."

"I dunno. Why would you gasp at one?"

Silence.

"As long as we're sharing," Melody said, "how about your name? Levi."

"Yes?"

"Why did Erma and Ted give you that name?"

"You're a member of the tribe," Levi said, showing his teeth below his dusty mustache. "You ought to know what it means."

Melody knew, of course, that Levi was one of Leah's many sons, progenitor of one of the twelve original tribes. But why had Ted and Erma given their son a Jewish name, of all names, rather than something African, or Christian, or just plain-old American? Few people seemed eager to glom on to the Jews' unhappy lot.

"But why a Jewish name?" she asked.

"All men are Jews, maybe," Levi said, his eyes twinkling with mischief, like they twinkled last time they were together, when they sold the Valencia liner to the moneyed couple from Virginia.

Now what did he mean by that? Melody wondered. All men are Jews.

"I'm bored, Eli. It's too hot. I'm going inside. I've got church soon, anyway." She lifted her shoulders from the ground, braced her weight on a palm. Eli rose too. The red flesh on Jo's elbow, he noticed, was indented in the pattern of the lupine grass, like one of Eli's rubbings, almost.

"Don't go, Jo. We can go fishing."

"I don't feel like fishing. It's boring." She rose to her feet, brushed the summer-soft landmines from her thighs.

And so he told her about the scraggly men on the spit, which was Eli's first mistake. He told her, because it was all he could think of to say to keep her outdoors. There wasn't much novelty to these long summer grove days. The birds weren't the only creatures to flee the grove. Hardly any field-workers, either. Only the frogs and bugs at night seemed livelier, issuing their urgent cries. Life seemed on hold, otherwise, braced for more bearable weather. A new fish camp on their spit—a dilapidated car, a canvas tent, a strange pair of men—counted as an exciting development.

"Let's go spy," she said.

"Okay," Eli said, which was his second mistake.

"Why did you come back? From New York?"

"I already told you, he said. The struggle. You should understand. Near half the Freedom Riders are Jewish folk."

"But why here? Right here. To live, I mean. Middle of nowhere. I know your parents are here, but still. You could live in Orlando, or Jacksonville. Then you wouldn't have to drive so far to your meetings. It's better being a Negro in the city, right?"

"I have business here," he said, his tone even, soft, and serious. His eyes weren't twinkling anymore.

"Personal business, you mean."

"Yes. Personal business."

He looked her straight in the eye when he said this, his porpoise forehead smooth and even like his words. Her eyes lingered over his eyes, as well. She didn't know what this personal business could be, but something about the way he said it told her that it was serious, serious enough that she lifted her hand to her chest, felt her heart beating within. It was her turn to speak, but she wouldn't say anything quite yet. She'd allow ample time, instead, for Levi to elaborate upon his disclosure. The metal fans whirring overhead sounded louder in her ears, deafening. He wouldn't share anything further, apparently. Maybe to protect her, she thought. All the same, his silence finally made her lower her eyes. And after all she had shared about Eli. She lowered her hand from her heart and placed it on the scarred wooden counter, as if to gird herself.

"Well I hope it works out all right for you, Levi. Your personal business."

"Thank you, Melody," he reached for the hand, covered it with his own. Sarah began to stir from her nap in the perambulator. The flesh of Levi's palms felt soft. She felt the gooseflesh rise on her hand beneath his, and even above, on her slender wrist and forearm. She wondered if he noticed, if he could feel her electric flesh beneath his soft hands, see the pinprick eruptions above.

A lattice-barked cabbage palm offered them added cover amid the mangroves just south of the spit so they could spy the fish camp. The jalopy with the frowning fender was still parked in the same place. The scraggly man who called himself Pervis last time was poking with a charred stick at his failing fire in the makeshift pit. Eli could smell the burning embers. He scanned the horizon for the other scraggly fellow and saw him out on the river, waist-high, fiddling with the weathered orange buoys of a net.

"They're using a seine!" Eli shouted and whispered at the same time, somehow. "That's not right! It's against the law!"

"Let's tell 'em!" Jo said. "It's *our* spit!"

"They'll take all the mullet and snook!"

"I'm gonna say something! Can't just set up on our spit and take all the fish!"

"No, don't!" he warned, grasping her arm, which felt loose and chunky in his small hand. Jo turned toward him, knitted her brow.

Boehringers lived on the grove as far back as Jo's great-grandfather, Eli knew. The name Boehringer meant something here, as Jo knew, maybe without even knowing she knew. And so nothing seemed to scare her, not even these scraggly *nogoodnik* men. Dangerous men, he sensed from somewhere deep. But he half-believed in her moxie, too.

"Are you sure?" he added.

Which was Eli's third mistake.

"Hey mister!" she cried, slipping from Eli's grasp, leaving the cover of the palm, treading along the blazing beach toward the spit.

"Yeah, gal?" The scraggly man at the pit lifted his eyes from his failing cook-fire, stood up from his driftwood seat and put his hands on his hips. Eli froze behind the palm. What should he do? He couldn't stay hidden beneath the canopy. That's what a sissy would do. Eli wouldn't be a sissy. He was about to run after Jo, but his hands felt too empty and small. He scanned the sand and marl beside his canvas Keds for a stick or a rock. All he could see beside the rubber toe-caps of his sneakers were some dry indeterminate seed pods mixed in with the browning fans of leaf litter. He gathered the pods up, scraping up plenty of sand and marl too, curled the pods and sand and marl into the seashells of his small fists. He wouldn't be a sissy.

"Wait up!"

"Look, it's the Ricardos," the man said, casting a bit of something into the smoldering fire as if to do something with his hands. It smelled like burnt fish now that they were closer. "*Babaloo!*" the man sang. He staggered a bit on his feet, then played it off as if he were dancing to the Cuban song. Eli puzzled over the reference, then figured that it was on account of Jo's red hair and his own darker hair that the man thought of that television show. He was older than Eli figured last time, when he only spied him from a safe distance. There was some gray in his matted hair and even more gray in his beard. The pores on his broad nose were big and visible, pockmarked with dirt.

"Hey, you're that kid from the other day," the man said. "What's wrong with your face, that paste all over it?"

"Nothing's wrong with it for your information," Jo snarled. "Mind your own bees' wax, why don't you!"

"Let's go!" Eli pleaded, noticing now the crunched red and white tin cans like leaf litter all about the fire. Schlitz, he read on one of them. He was drunk, Eli realized. A *shikker*, his parents would say. That's why he couldn't stand on his feet in one place for too long before checking his balance.

"You can't use those nets out there," Jo said, ignoring Eli, lifting her finger toward the orange buoys. "And you're makin' a mess with all these cans. You better pick them up or I'm telling."

"Who you gonna tell, Lucy?" the man asked, then belched, pursed his lips around his mossy teeth as he opened his mouth. A practiced belch. The man seemed more amused than angry, but he scared Eli anyway. His matted hair and mossy teeth. His broad nose pores, pockmarked with grime.

"Come on, let's go!" Eli pleaded again.

The other man was suddenly plashing onto shore to join them. He seemed younger. This wasn't good, Eli knew. Two against two. And they were grownups.

"Now let's all be nice," the first man said in a different voice. "I've got an ice-cold beer in the cooler for you, gal. Big gal like you old enough to enjoy an ice-cold beer now and again."

"I don't like beer," Jo said, scowling, a hand braced now on her uncurved hip. She wasn't scared yet. Didn't she know to be scared?

"Taste don't matter none, gal. Make you feel good inside, hot day like today. Ice-cold beer."

"Let's go, Jo!" Eli urged again, straining to keep his voice soft.

"Now don't spoil the party, small-fry, she ain't goin' nowhere." The man lunged forward and gripped Jo's arm, surprising Eli with his speed. He dragged her toward the fire pit, her feet skidding against the sand and marl.

"Oww!" she cried, her eyes wide. "Le'go! I'll call my daddy! *Daddy!*"

Now Jo was scared.

"Let her alone!" Eli shouted after them, but his feet remained frozen on the sand and shell bits.

Jo tried kicking the scraggly man in the shins, which halted their progress, but he was strong enough to keep her at a distance with his arms. He wasn't as drunk, maybe, as Eli first thought.

"Summer heat gettin' to you, Pervis?" the man's companion finally spoke. "She can't be all haired over yet, even."

"Now let's just be nice," the pockmarked man said.

"Let me *go*!" Jo cried again, her Mercurochrome-stained legs flailing at the air between them.

Neither man seemed to pay Eli any attention at all, having decided that his paltry presence wasn't worth their concern. Standing there on the sand, thinking these thoughts, Eli felt his fright turn into something else, felt his rash grow hotter across his nose, his jaw tighten.

"Let her *go*!" he shouted again, lunging toward the bad man, who turned toward Eli just in time to watch the fistful of seeds and sand make contact with his yellow eyeballs.

"*The fuck!*" he cried, letting go of Jo to rub his eyes.

"*Run!*" Eli commanded, which he didn't need to say. Jo was already ahead of him, halfway to the tracks.

"Get 'em!" Eli heard from behind, then looked over his shoulder to see the younger man make chase, his elbows swinging wide.

"Go right!" Eli commanded from behind just after they crossed the FEC tracks. Jo was faster than he was but heard him and obeyed, skittered off the dusty road into the dense cover. Eli looked back again and didn't see anyone running after them. But it was only a glance so he wasn't sure. This wasn't their usual trail. In fact, Eli hardly ever ventured into the brush on the Boehringer's side, up where Jo showed him the remnants of the Indian's kitchen midden. The dense foliage—palm fans and palmetto, privet and exotic underbrush Eli didn't even know—thwacked against his shins and his arms and his hands that he kept up high to protect his face, which also took its share of cat-claw thwackings. He was close behind Jo now. He could hear her crying as she ran. Or not crying, exactly. More like the whine of an ambulance siren, interrupted only by her heaving intakes of air.

"We can stop now," Eli called once they leapt over the irrigation canal and entered the cover of her father's towering, hedged rows. "They're not coming, Jo! You hear!?" Eli stopped and clutched his bare knees, his chicken chest rising and falling. He couldn't go any farther. He reached for his inhaler inside his pocket and pumped a dose into his throat, which felt cold and good. No use shouting anymore after Jo. She kept running up the row toward home, making her whining siren sound. Eli didn't like being alone all of a sudden. He sort of half walked and half jogged farther up into the Boehringer's grove before cutting over toward his own property. He peeked out carefully from the cover of the Boeheringer's last column of ten-year Valencias, chewed up some by the butterflies, then hustled across the more exposed cordgrass and wiregrass berm, leapt the irrigation canal to his own grove. It felt better to be walking along the cowpea and wax bean cover crop between his father's rows, to be home, all intents and purposes.

He made his way directly to the stand, where his story spilled out his mouth to his mother as if it were a liquid too hot to contain. She'd been talking to Levi, whom Eli had spied weeks ago in the grove, but never mentioned to his parents. His name was Levi, he'd learned since. He'd seen him at the stand before, a couple times now. He was Mr. Ted's son, his mother explained that first time, as if she needed to explain Levi to him. His father didn't like Ted's son, he somehow sensed, which was why he didn't tell his father when he saw Levi at the stand. After Eli told his mother the story of the scraggly men, she told Levi to go and he obeyed. Which was sort of weird, Eli thought. That she told him to go. Not that he obeyed. Of course he obeyed. Eli and his mother made their way together with Sarah back up the loose river rock drive toward the edge of the grove. His mother shouted after his father, who finally appeared, his eyes wide. They went inside to escape the heat while Eli told his story again, tears spilling from his eyes this time (*sissy!*) as he punctuated key details. The Schlitz cans. The mossy teeth. The seine net. The younger man's odd words, which he didn't remember to say to his mother the first time, *She can't be all haired over yet, even*, and which made his mother cover her mouth with her hand now.

The pounding at the porch door jolted Eli in mid-sentence. He feared that it was one or both of the *nogoodnik* men, that they'd try to get him into trouble for throwing sand in their faces.

"Don't get it, Daddy!" Eli pleaded.

"Now Eli," said his father.

It wasn't the *nogoodnik* men. Instead, it was Mr. Boehringer, who looked queer standing in the doorframe, probably because he'd never before darkened their pine porch with his shadow. Also because he was wearing a suit and tie—all ready for church, Eli gathered, before Jo came running inside with a flushed, tear-soaked face, a mucusy nose, and a story to tell. Also because both his woolly hands were thrust out before him, holding up two shotguns like football goalposts.

"You comin', Ike Golden, or'm I gonna have to take care of our business at the river myself?"

"Now Walter, we're just as horrified as you and Glory," his mother declared. "Eli told us everything. But it's a police matter. We'll call Sheriff Wright to take care of those two."

But Eli's father had already reached for the shotgun in Mr. Boehringer's left hand. Its walnut forestock made a slapping sound as his father grasped it. His father turned toward them to offer the briefest of instructions—"Lock the door behind, Mel"—then made chase after Walt past the vegetable garden and the wild tamarind with its powder-puff blooms, past the scruffy palmetto and lantana patches, the live oak triad and cabbage palms, kicking up a knee-high cloud of dust in his wake, disappearing into the grove. Mother and son followed after as far as the pine porch and watched the pair until they were gone, the blades of their hands shielding their eyes. The sun bore down on them from above the grove trees in the east horizon. Impossible, Eli thought. It was still only morning. And after all that had happened. Still morning.

After Eli locked the door, after Eli's mother called Sheriff Wright, they sat on the family room sofa and didn't say a word. His mother bounced Sarah on her knee to keep her quiet. The pine floor squeaked beneath the weight of his mother's feet.

Boom! they finally heard, after minutes that seemed like hours to Eli, braced as he was for the report.

Boom! he heard again. *Boom! Boom!*

"Shhh," his mother said to Sarah, hugging her close on her knees. "Shhh, Sarah-le, shhh."

"You don't think—"

"No, Eli. Now hush."

"But you don't think—"

"Hush."

BOOK FOUR

FIRST HARVEST

Twenty-three

FALL WASN'T SOMETHING TO SPEAK OF in late September along the river. Not outright anyway, for fear of scaring it off like a skittish bird. The citizenry tended, instead, to dismiss the cooler currents in the atmosphere licking their flesh, daring that skittish bird to draw nearer. But then there was Pearl.

"Not quite so close this morning," Pearl let slip at Janisse's, provoking worried stares from her Junior League sisters.

"Summer's not nearabout done yet," Glory checked Pearl's careless remark.

"Darn tootin'," Mary Beth concurred, which made Melody smile. *Darn tootin'.* Another phrase from MB's Michigan backwater. Unless it was a southern expression, after all.

"Can't even think of turning off the air-conditioning in the store," Frieda added, squeezing the juice of a Eureka lemon wedge into her steaming teacup. For Junior League meetings, Janisse broke out her delicate porcelain cups from beneath the counter.

"Not done by a longshot," Janisse added in a weary exhale, standing above the conjoined tables, the two Formica squares now a rectangle, filling their cups of Lipton with fresh doses of piping-hot water. "Near Halloween we can start talking."

"October all over!" Pearl sang, then sampled another of Janisse's deviled eggs, leaving a half-moon lipstick smear across the creamy yolk middle. The phrase, Melody knew, was part of a local adage signaling the boundaries of summer and the associated hurricane season. *June too soon. July stand by. August you must. September remember. October all over.*

"So, Melody, we'll cover town first is the plan," said MB. "Sanford can wait."

"Makes sense," said Frieda.

"Need some advice?" asked MB.

"Advice?" Melody asked, bobbing Sarah on her knee. "*The noble Duke of York,*" she sang softly as she bounced Sarah.

"On what to say, sugar," Pearl clarified. "Your script."

"*. . . he had ten thousand men,*" Melody continued her song, nodding toward Pearl to let her know she was listening.

"She won't need to say much," Glory declared, her painted lips curling into a smile.

"Oh hush, Glory," Janisse said, slapping at the back of Glory's hand. She had taken the seat beside the plate glass so she could face the bar.

Glory's remark turned Melody's olive face beet red. She had been careful since Pearl and MB had chanced upon her and Levi at the stand. MB had put her on notice none too subtly and she had been careful, mostly for Levi's sake. Neither Pearl nor MB had said another word about the sharp-looking Negro at Goldens Are Here that hot day, which seemed very long ago. Still, it unnerved her, given the events of that day, given the way her flesh rose even now at the thought of Levi, when one of the girls commented upon her beauty. She tried to concentrate on Sarah's song to make the heat go away before the ladies noticed.

"*. . . He marched them up to the top of the hill . . .*"

Glory herself was blonde and slender. An attractive woman in her own right, even if smoking all those Salem menthols had torn a row of comb-teeth wrinkles above her top lip. It was a pity that her youngest, Jo, favored Walt's shape and coloring. It helped a girl to be pretty, Melody thought. Looks didn't matter as much for boys.

"*. . . And he marched them down again . . .*"

"You okay up there, Clyde!?" Janisse called out to her single patron, owner of the Ag-Mart and Feed, where Isaac bought his fertilizer, his irrigation equipment and such. "Need more coffee, hon'?" Clyde waved her off.

"You see that new actress on *The Dick Van Dyke Show* other night?" Glory asked, apropos of nothing, seemed to Melody.

"Perky little thing," said Pearl. "Name's Mary Tyler Moore, I think."

"That's right," Janisse said, then groaned to her feet, cleared the empty platter, dusted with paprika still from the deviled eggs.

"Handsome couple, those two," Frieda declared. "Ah, to be young." She lifted her teacup to her thin, unpainted lips.

"They're not a real couple, you realize," Pearl said.

"You certain?" Frieda asked, her mouth forming a worried "o."

"Pearl's right," MB declared.

"Married or not, a lady just can't wear slacks like that on national television," Glory complained. "What're they called, those queer slacks?"

"Capri, I think," MB said. "Capri slacks."

"Least she has the figure for it," Frieda said.

"Sure enough," Pearl agreed. "Cute as a button."

"Mmm-hmm," Janisse added from above, having returned with a pastry platter. She plucked a bear claw before setting the platter down and devoured its big toe as she sat. "What I'd give for a figure like that."

"Gotta do your Jack LaLanne," Pearl advised, reaching for a cruller.

"You can practically see her lady business up there on the screen!" Glory continued, ignoring Janisse and Pearl. "What kind of example's that for our girls? My Jo Ellen? It's just not right and proper, ask me." Glory's fingers danced undecidedly above the pastries, then plucked half a cherry Danish.

"Anyway, I haven't given much thought to what I'll say when I canvas," Melody said, resisting the temptation of the sugary treats before her. She hadn't seen the first episode of that *Dick Van Dyke Show*, but Glory's priggishness unsettled her and she was anxious to change the subject. How did a woman like Glory marry a lout like Walter in the first place? It seemed to her that a man like Walt would wear away the sharp edges of Glory's piety over the years, but maybe the opposite was the case, that his boorishness only intensified her countervailing impulses. Or maybe Walt wasn't as boorish in the home as Melody assumed. He did chaperone his wife and Jo Ellen to church every Sunday, which had to count for something.

Sarah pivoted her head toward her mother and reached her sticky splayed hand to Melody's painted lips, hoping to turn the words of the song on once again. But no luck.

"I suppose I'll just start off by introducing myself: 'Hi, I'm your neighbor, Melody Golden—'"

"Good morning, I'd say first," Glory declared. "Not hi. Blessed morning, maybe. Or God bless."

"Neighbor part's good," Pearl consoled Melody. "Good instincts there. Tough to say no to a neighbor."

"Or to the good Lord," Glory said.

"Mmm-hmm," uttered Janisse, swallowing a sugary bear claw bolus.

Sarah whined, her voice rising to a falsetto screech, having just discovered this effective location on her vocal register, which made the ladies wince as if they'd bitten down on their lemon wedges.

"*And when you're up, you're up, and when you're down, you're down,*" Melody returned to Sarah's song, hoping to mollify her.

"You can say God bless, can't you sugar?" asked Pearl.

"Of course she can," Frieda answered for her. "What do you think we are, Hindus?"

A good humored rather than snappish retort, which inspired a chorus of laughter. That strange and funny word, Hindus.

"*. . . And when you're only halfway up, you're neither up nor down.*"

"Yaaay," Melody said. Sarah clapped her sticky, splayed hands and looked about. She had just learned to clap too.

"Yaaay," the ladies followed Melody's lead, clapped their hands like Sarah.

"All right then," said MB, once the clapping subsided. "You'll be fine, Melody." She unsnapped her small purse slung over the chair and retrieved a thick stack of blue tickets secured by a thin red rubber band, the kind the delivery boy wrapped around the *Star Advocate*. She slid the stack of tickets across the table toward Melody. "Just got these from the printer in Jacksonville. Now it's a dollar per ticket, remember Melody. And be sure to keep the stubs for the raffle."

"And if they decline a ticket," Glory said, "you can ask if they'd like to make a small donation, instead."

"At least get a quarter that way," MB said.

"Donations accounted for a good sum last year," Frieda added.

"Remind them it's for the fallout shelters," Pearl said. "Communists and all."

"I'll fetch you a large cup of water with a straw you can take with you," Janisse said, drumming the table with three little beats, rising to her feet. "September heat'll sneak up on you." She left this warning wake as she made her way behind the bar.

"Here," Pearl said, poor barren Pearl, holding out her palms, "give over that beautiful baby of yours."

Meanwhile, the co-op's first fall budding conference on Isaac's grove. The men, kneeling before their short sour orange stock, alternately deployed their budding knives and Tuttle clippers.

"What're we budding here, anyway, Ike?" Doyle inquired, squinting past the smoke of his Camel. "Sticks look funny. These just ordinary Marshes?"

Isaac's spine shivered at the question despite the climbing heat. He contemplated his own bud stick before answering as he whittled off his nub. The wood did look a bit different from their ordinary grapefruit sticks, redder, the buds slightly more protuberant. Still, he was surprised that Doyle noticed. Clay, maybe. But Doyle?

"Look normal to me," Edwin said from his knees, flicking the butt of his spent Kent to the ground, covering it over with loose dirt. He washed down the smoke with an RC Cola swig.

Walt didn't say anything. He concentrated the whole of his fury on his liner, making vigorous revolutions with his tape around his first bud union, working with far greater purpose on Isaac's trees than Isaac was used to expecting out of Walt. Things between them had gotten better since their business together at the river, since they ran off those roustabouts. Not friendly, exactly. But better. There hadn't been any recent attacks on Isaac's trees, either, which made Isaac wonder afresh whether Walt had been the culprit, after all. But he tried to put that out of his mind.

"Just ordinary Marshes, Doyle," he lied, feeling shitty about his lie, gazing down the row toward Clay, consumed in his labors like Walt—or maybe just distracted by other matters—slipping his first bud beneath the inverted-T slice in the stock's bark.

Isaac would bud Shepherd's irradiated scions from the commission, he had finally decided. He'd try, anyway, to live in the here and now, accommodate himself to the commissioner's version of the real. Whether he'd actually transplant these brave new cultivars from the nursery row to his grove was another matter, entirely. Buying time was mostly his intent. It would be easy enough to cull these few liners if he changed his mind.

"So we banking these liners?" Edwin asked, taking the last swig of his RC, discarded the bottle, stood tall on his knees now, pressed the backs of both hands into the small of his arched back while he awaited the response.

"Does the Pope shit in the woods?" Walt answered for Isaac, deploying one of his favorite expressions, which Isaac never fully understood. He was pretty certain there was a cheap anti-Catholic slur in there, but not so certain about whether Walt's play on words was still supposed to affirm whatever question it followed. The Pope, as far as Isaac knew, *didn't* shit in the woods. Thankfully, Walt elaborated. "What do you think these shovels are for, Win? Have we ever *not* banked new trees in fall?"

Banking new trees above the bud union protected them from winter cold. The co-op's choice river acres were far enough north along the peninsula that frosts were not uncommon, even though the last devastating freeze occurred way back during the winter of 1895. Overnight temps below twenty-eight degrees stripped doomed trees of their fruit and leaves as far south as Palm Beach. Fewer than 150,000 E. Bean boxes of Florida citrus survived to be shipped that year, from an estimated target of 6,000,000 boxes. Most of the survivors were grown down near the toe-tip of the state. Julia Tuttle, one of the few white settlers in the swampy backwater called Miami, dispatched a messenger with a garland of orange blossoms to Henry Flagler at his frozen redoubt north in St. Augustine. Her gesture lured Flagler, and his railroad, and a land boom all the way down the peninsula clear to Key West. That was the story, anyway.

The river trees weren't quite as lucky as Tuttle's trees down south. That small sepia photo in Clyde's Ag-Mart and Feed, Walt's father standing amid the bare ruined choirs of his grove, gazing dumbstruck at the camera, an eerily lush carpet of leaves and fruit shrouding his feet. It was quite a ways back, this last terrible freeze, but grove memories died hard. Ever since 1895, the river growers banked their new fall trees as close to the scaffolding of stock branches as they could pile the dirt, a secular ceremony of sorts to appease whatever powerful and capricious force governed the weather. The river men even scouted new liners during the season to fortify the weathered pyramids of soil, the bud union being the most temperature-sensitive part of the tree. Win really ought to have known better than to try to weasel out of banking.

"Jeez, just asking," said Win, hangdog, on his feet now like the rest of them, spearing the sand and clay soil with his shovel. "Still awfully hot," he said as he piled the dirt up the trunk, as if to explain himself. "Hardly even seems like fall."

"First harvest soon, any case," Clay finally uttered what was on all their minds, leaning against the worn wooden handle of his shovel, so worn and oil-coated from his hands that it glinted dully like iron in the still-hot sun. "First harvest."

Twenty-four

SOON, it was impossible to deny the cooler evening and morning air, the dew that frosted their painted pine porches and the greenery beyond, the longer shadows cast by the more bashful fall sun, arcing daily in shallow southerly parabolas toward the Gulf, the prettier pastel sunsets filigreed with amethyst clouds, the cleaner menthol aromas from the pines mostly west of the highway overtaking the rotten-egg summer smell of the river mangroves to the east.

Fall budding on all their groves complete, there was little for Isaac to do these last few weeks before first harvest of the early-bearing scions: Parson Browns and Hamlins and Marshes and Navels. Little besides scout the rows for insect insurgents—red mite, rust mite, bud mite, thrips, whitefly, blackfly, aphid, pumpkin-bug, wax scale, soft scale, red scale, chaff scale, mealybug, leafhoppers. Little besides scout for foot rot, tristeza, and decline. Little besides cull the goatweed, pigweed, pepperweed, beggarweed, and hawksbeard to keep them from clogging up the holes in the new drip lines. Little besides prune the too sharply angled summer flush stems from his trees with his Tuttles or his California saw for those larger branches that had eluded their attention last flush, or the flush before that. Little besides monitor the progress of his ripening experimental cultivars to see if they would bear fruit, so to speak, after all. Little besides walk the nursery row to check in on the commissioner's irradiated grapefruit scions he'd just budded with his fellows.

And so Isaac finally took Eli to camp out on the grove, even though they hadn't caught their tree vandal yet. It had been some time, anyway, since the last attack.

Father and son tromped around, not through, the vegetable garden—slender shoots now bursting the fish-rich soil to lick the salty air—then past the wild tamarind (hosting a colony of small tree snails now, apparently), the triad of shaggy-bearded live oaks beyond wearing their heavier acorns now like so many earrings. Once past the oaks, Isaac looked back toward Eli, lagging behind.

"Come on, sport, you can do it!" he encouraged his son. Eli kept bucking up his pack, searching in vain for the perfect distribution of weight between his shoulder blades. Isaac was sorely tempted to carry Eli's pack for him—in exchange, maybe, for Eli carrying the lighter naphtha stove—but resisted the temptation, chewed his lip. For one thing, Isaac was already weighted down with the tent satchel, plus the stove. For another, he wouldn't coddle Eli. Worst thing he could do for his son was do this thing for him that Eli ought to do for himself.

"Coming!" Eli answered, propped up his pack once again.

"Want me to adjust the straps?"

"Naah. It's okay, Dad."

"Thataboy."

They followed the worn path between the scruffy patches of palmetto and lantana, the taller spice-smelling islands of wax myrtle and privet where the towhees and scrub jays and cardinals and mockingbirds loitered, where the smaller sparrows, the painted and indigo buntings had returned just weeks ago for the season, singing their dizzy high-pitched songs. Father and son disappeared into the raised rows of the experimental, untagged, unharvestable crosses, hybrids, and chance seedlings of Eli's grove. Isaac tried not to look over at the damn Parson Browns and Hamlins and Navels, bound to disappoint him. The tree row was wider than the shrub-lined path. There was enough room now for father and son to walk side by side.

"Should we camp in your clearing?" Isaac asked, pleased that he could simply talk now and not shout behind.

"Naah," Eli protested. "That's boring. I always lay around there."

His son's voice sounded deeper, which prompted Isaac to look sidelong at Eli, noticing for the first time those mild pimply bumps on his nose beneath his butterfly, the downy mustache above his top lip, the somewhat darker hair sprouting from his upraised forearms, thumbs beneath his backpack straps, the flesh beneath this pasting of fur rippled with sinewy muscle. He hadn't taken enough time lately to look at Eli. He wasn't certain whether, or how, Eli's condition might interfere with the ordinary changes in boys, so was relieved to see the first glimmer of these developments. His bar mitzvah, Isaac supposed, was just around the corner. Eli's head, too, seemed to bob a bit higher up beside Isaac's torso as they lumbered along under their burdens. With hope, his son just might top off at five foot three or so. Normal, practically. He considered saying something to Eli about these positive developments, but held his tongue, not wanting to embarrass his child.

"So where to, sport?" he asked, instead.

"How about between the biggest trees. The old Valencias."

"Where you fell off the ladder, you mean?"

"Uh-huh."

They continued mostly in silence toward the ancient Valencias, concentrating on their steps, scolded by an invisible mockingbird that followed after them for a time, thwacking its way along the citrus greenery. Isaac listened for Eli's breath beneath the mockingbird chatter, could hear his thin exhalations and thinner inhalations.

"Let's slow down and take it easy."

"I'm fine," Eli insisted, refusing to slow to Isaac's new pace. "I brought my inhaler."

"Who's talking about *you*?" Isaac's joke made Eli laugh and slow down.

They finally made it to the behemoth Valencias and chose what seemed like a soft spot along the broadest row, kept that way to permit truck passage. The cowpeas, lupine, and peanuts were still green from the recent wet season. Eli poked at the ground cover for snakes with a dead Valencia stick he found while Isaac loitered above the wreckage of their overnight gear.

"All clear," Eli finally said.

"You sure now?"

"Yep. Sure."

"Better get this tent set up then." Isaac scanned down the row between the tree sentinels for the sun in the western horizon, but it had long ago dipped beneath the shaggy slash pines beyond the highway. An hour or so they'd have to set up the tent and fly, the narrow canvas cots and the naphtha stove, before the light failed. They should have started out earlier, but Isaac had gotten distracted at Eli's grove, brooding over his experiments, tree by tree, top-worked branch by top-worked branch, plucking one hopeless specimen after the other. Just months ago, Isaac had plied closed corolla buds with tweezers, emasculated the stamens, painted choice pollen to pistil with his clean camel-hair paintbrush, paper-bagged the specimens to ward off interloping insects sloppily trailing indeterminate pollen, then traded paper bag for mesh once the fruit set to let the light and air in, but keep the pests out. And what did he have to show for his meticulous labor? The Parson Brown and Hamlin crosses had broken color and were just about ready to harvest, but they hadn't broken early, as he'd hoped. No improvement, it seemed. No improvement, again. He still held out hope for the Navels, that their flavedo and albedo would thicken over the next few weeks, California-style. The experimental Valencias, too, might fare better come spring, he consoled himself, offering Florida's first summer harvest, if he could just keep their acid high enough so late in the season.

Isaac untied the heavy canvas satchel and turned it upside down. The tent and fly, the aluminum poles and stakes, the dissembled cots toppled out onto the weedy ground. Father and son gazed down for a protracted moment at the chaos of aluminum and canvas parts as if they were jigsaw puzzle pieces, which in a sense they were. It had been a while since they set up the tent. They finally looked at each other and laughed. Eli's higher peals somehow harmonized with Isaac's deeper laugh. It was a nice moment, which made Isaac wistful, somehow, for more such moments.

"Okay, let's dig in and figure this out, *boychik,*" Isaac said, grasping a corner of the tent. "Grab that other corner. We'll spread it out first, then put in the stakes."

"Yeah, *that's* how we do it," Eli recalled. "Did you go camping with *Zaide* when you were my age?" he asked, crawling across the canvas expanse to stretch out the fourth corner. Isaac liked that his son did this necessary thing without having to be prodded.

"Do you remember your Grandpa Harry?" Isaac asked, retrieving the rubber mallet and stakes. Perhaps that Yiddish word Isaac had uttered—*boychik*—summoned Eli's grandfather to his son's thoughts.

"No, not really," Eli admitted. Isaac felt these words like an intestinal hurt. He pounded the first metal stake with the rubber mallet hard, burying it beneath the soft soil. Eli was four years old when Isaac's father suffered his stroke—old enough, Isaac had thought, that he'd remember his grandfather, which suddenly seemed important. Isaac didn't want to be the sole guardian of his father's memory.

"So did you camp with him?" Eli pressed.

"No, Eli. We didn't camp."

"Not even at Valley Forge?"

"So Valley Forge you remember?"

"Uh-huh."

Isaac and Melody had taken Eli to visit the state park when they lived in Philadelphia. Isaac had meant it mostly as an educational outing and tried to explain to Eli at the park how harsh the winter had been when General Washington camped there with his troops. The morning of their visit was so lovely, however—acre after acre of rolling green hills accented by towering deciduous specimens, the placid Schuylkill winking at them in the distance below, the mild sun painting every vista with breathtaking light—that the lesson was completely lost upon Eli. "Sure would be nice to camp out here," Eli had uttered.

"We didn't camp at Valley Forge, Eli," Isaac said now. "I'm not even sure you're allowed to camp there."

Even if camping were permitted, Isaac thought but didn't say, it never would have occurred to his father to drive his family the fifteen miles to visit Valley Forge, much less sleep outdoors there, unsheltered. It was the Depression, after all. Only vagabonds and roustabouts slept in makeshift Hooverville camps along the trash-lined city stretch of the Schuylkill, cooking muddy fish over black fires.

"Then what did you do with *Zaide*, Dad? When *you* were a kid?"

"What did we *do*?"

"For fun, I mean."

Isaac contemplated the phrase. For fun. Fun would have been as foreign a word to Harry Golden as camp. They didn't do much of anything together for fun. His father slaved, instead, so that they wouldn't have to camp beside the trash-lined Schuylkill. Isaac, for his part, pored over his school books like a demon to redeem his father's slaving. That's what they did. What else was required? Still, there were plenty of good times in their small tenement, especially with his mother, who doted after her only child.

"We read together," Isaac said. "We read, mostly. And listened to the radio. *The Chase and Sanborn Hour.* They played music, and there were some comedy bits too. Your *zaide* also taught me to play gin rummy." The recollection summoned his father's cheap cigar smoke to his olfactory memory.

Through the corner of his eye, Isaac could see his son nodding as Isaac tried in vain to pound the last stake into the ground. But it was no use. There must have been a rock in the way.

"Son of a gun!" Isaac cried, rising to his feet and gripping his lower back. "It's always the last gosh-darned stake that screws us up. I'm just no good at this, Eli. Sorry."

Isaac—great lover of plants, and trees, and woods—liked the idea of camping, but foundered when it came to the application. When he thought of camping, he thought of that Hemingway story, or maybe it was from one of the novels, featuring plentiful trout nestled on fern beds beside some gurgling stream, a sturdy and spartan fireside meal, peaceful slumber beneath whispering winds, strong coffee morning-time percolating above the restored flames. When he actually tried to camp with Eli, however, he invariably struggled over the tent, or the mosquitoes dogged them, or it rained, or it was too hot, or the crickets and frogs belted out deafening cries, or his back ached so badly in the morning from the cot that he could barely rise to his feet, or he forgot to bring matches. None of this ever seemed to bother Eli, though.

"It's okay, Daddy. It's just one stake. We'll figure it out." Isaac breathed, gazed down at his son, happy to follow his boy's lead. "Okay," Eli said, "how about we tie a rope from the tent bag around the circle-thingy, then stake the end of the rope to a softer spot in the ground?"

"Sounds good to me."

They finished setting up their small camp just as purple twilight gave way to dusk, just as the whining mosquitoes turned on their infrareds, sending Isaac scurrying for the Watkins in Eli's pack of supplies.

"The skeeters'll mostly go away once it's all dark," Eli assured him, as if he feared his father might call it quits.

Isaac lit the naphtha stove and opened the can of B&M beans. Eli arranged the can of beans and four Hebrew National hot dogs on the metal slats. Isaac had considered fishing with Eli for their dinner, but decided against the plan. Too much gear they'd have to lug out, and there was no guarantee that they'd even catch anything. Besides, cooking this can of beans directly on the stove-top was adventure enough for Eli, who stirred the now boiling caramel broth with the small spoon from his fold-out utensil set. Isaac reached over and put the heat down on the right burner below the can. The hot dogs they'd cook till they were well charred. They both liked them that way.

"So we can go look for a wildcat after dinner, right?" Eli asked as he munched down on his first dog. They had forgotten the mustard, but that was okay.

"Sure," Isaac said. He had half-hoped that Eli would forget about finding a bobcat. Isaac didn't much like the idea of tromping around the grove in the middle of the night with the raccoons and opossums, their tree vandal still on the loose (whom he wouldn't mention for fear of scaring Eli), only a flashlight and the noise of their approach to ward off the snakes. Plus he couldn't imagine they'd be lucky enough to spot a wildcat before it spotted them and made itself scarce. But he wouldn't disappoint Eli.

A bird, or rather a group of birds, bleated overhead in the blackening sky—nasal, Doppler bleatings as they darted back and forth. Isaac looked up and saw the night's first stars, blotted momentarily by the speedy silhouettes of the birds. "What are they?" Eli asked.

"Nighthawks," Isaac answered. "Good birds. Eating up those skeeters." Eli nodded, shoveled up a spoonful of beans with his fold-out spoon. "Now don't eat too many of those beans, Elijah-le. We've gotta sleep in the same tent." Eli chortled, scooped up more beans in jest. Isaac did the same on his own plate, arming his intestines. "Two can play at that game," he threatened between mouthfuls, the nighthawks still bleating overhead. A stray bean, he noticed, skidded halfway down Eli's chin and rested on the shallow rise before his cleft. Eli's jawline had grown more prominent, maybe.

They scouted the grove with their flashlights for nearly two hours after dinner. Isaac's beam was powerful. He mostly used the flashlight to make occasional rounds along the ripe rows come harvest time, guarding against thieves from the river. One good thing about citrus is that it didn't ripen further once plucked from the tree, so you pretty much knew exactly which trees you had to worry about being poached. It was the bad thing about citrus too, these fairly short and crucial harvesting periods.

Father and son now followed the broad access road all the way east to the irrigation ditch, then cut up and walked all the way to the intersecting irrigation ditch at Walt's line. Eli waved his flash-light beam around as if he were conducting a discordant symphony. Isaac advised him to keep the beam down until he heard something.

No point spooking every creature about. It was quieter out on the grove than Isaac had expected. Just some crickets sizzling in the trees. He supposed that the frogs were done with their chattering for a while now that summer was over. A great horned owl hooted low and human in the distance, near the river. Isaac was used to hearing their eerie voices call out from the slash pines above the palmettos west of the highway, but was surprised to hear one loitering about the weathered palms and mangroves to the east. They didn't hunt fish, did they?

"Let's go find it," Eli suggested.

"Are you nuts? We'll never spot it way off in that bramble."

"Okay," Eli said. He seemed relieved by the discouragement, as if he only suggested going after the owl out of some vague boyhood obligation to seek adventure. "Sure are lots of stars out anyway," Eli observed.

Isaac pointed out Orion's belt and Cassiopeia, wishing that he knew the names of additional constellations. The nighthawks, silent, seemed to have given up the insect chase now that it was fully dark. He looked around for the Big Dipper, but supposed it was only visible during the summer months. "Maybe you can study up on the stars, Eli, and teach me. Never saw so many stars up in Philly, that's for sure."

Eli said okay, then yawned, a long lusty whine that he probably would have suppressed had he anticipated the consequences.

"Well, that's about it, I guess, Eli. Sorry we didn't find your wildcat. Better get back and turn in." Eli sighed, but didn't otherwise protest, tired as he was.

"Can we light a fire before going to bed?" Eli asked back at their camp.

"Awfully late to start a fire now, don't you think?"

Eli shrugged.

"Hot too," Isaac pressed. What truly worried him was the woodsmoke and Eli's embattled lungs. But he didn't want to say this, so broached the late and hot night, instead.

"Can we start one anyway?"

"Sure," Isaac relented. "Half hour or so. Then we'll turn in." How often did his son get to enjoy a campfire? Eli, before their dinner, had already gathered up dead and dried citrus twigs and small branches from beneath the canopy, most of them broken off by careless field-workers during harvest.

Isaac stood over Eli and watched as he piled up the kindling twigs in a little nest, then braced larger branches in a precarious pyramid above. Now where did he learn to do that? Isaac wondered, but didn't ask. Television, likely. One of his comic books, maybe. It was good to see his son take charge in this way. Eli asked if he could strike the match and Isaac said okay.

Father and son sat Indian style on the upwind side of the fire and stared at the dancing flames for quite a while. Eli poked at the glowing bits on the fire floor with the same stick he used to check for snakes earlier. Sparks danced above the flames, then disappeared, when Eli poked the bottom. The fire was small but grew hot all the same. Isaac glanced down to see the sweat beading on Eli's forehead. It was tough to judge his son's coloring in the ochre glow, but he was likely red with the heat, his butterfly angry and swollen.

"Fire sure is nice," Eli finally said, piercing the quiet. Then he coughed mildly into his fist, knowing full well that his father wouldn't like this cough.

"Sure is. Better turn in, though. It's getting late. And the fire's hot."

❦

The tent. Atop their canvas cots. Beneath their light cotton sheets. Too hot still for sleeping bags. Isaac had zippered open the front flap, but there was little breeze to ventilate the inside. What breeze there was came from over the river to the east. Isaac should have set up the tent to face eastward, toward the breeze. Too late now. This was just the sort of thing he botched when he camped. Something small and vital. Flat on his back (the only possible position on the shrunken cot), he laced his fingers atop his chest, shook his head, and brooded. He wouldn't sleep a wink tonight. Not a wink.

"Daddy?" he heard Eli ask. The tenor of Eli's *Daddy?* made Isaac brace himself.

"Yes, son."

"What did you and Mr. Boehringer do to those bad men at the river? You didn't shoot them dead, did you?"

It had been weeks since the incident, but he supposed the close quarters of the tent, the uncommon darkness, bolstered Eli.

"No, Eli, I didn't shoot them at all. Heaven forbid."

"Did Mr. Boehringer shoot them dead?"

"No. Mr. Boehringer didn't shoot them. That's why I went with him, Eli. To make sure he wouldn't shoot them. They won't be coming back, though. Promise."

"Good."

"Go to sleep now, Elijah-le. Sorry we couldn't find you a wildcat."

"That's okay."

Isaac listened to the thin, metronomic breath of his slumbering son for what seemed like hours. The inhalations and exhalations sounded so tenuous, as if each breath he heard might be his son's last—which was probably why he listened so intently for that next breath. He fell asleep. Isaac didn't know that he had drifted off to sleep, even though he must have been asleep, because the incessant mockingbird chatter that rattled now inside his skull seemed to have transported him to a more wakeful state of consciousness. He lifted his wrist above his head to glance at his Timex, but the glow-strips at the numbers were invisible.

"Hear that, Dad?" Eli asked, bursting the humid atmosphere inside the tent and startling Isaac. The chattering bird had woken up Eli too, apparently.

"Sure do, sport."

"Queer, isn't it? Does it think it's morning already?"

Isaac was already on his feet, having groped for, and finding, his flashlight. They'd never get any shut-eye if this mockingbird didn't stop its yammering.

"I don't know, Eli. Sometimes they sing at night, I guess. But it sounds more like scolding. Snake maybe. Stay here. I'll be right back."

"Aww—"

"Stay here!"

The brighter night surprised Isaac as he stepped out of the tent, throwing on his boots, tucking, rather than tying, the laces behind the crisp leather tongue. A three-quarter moon had risen above the ocean and tree line to the east. He could see the outlines now of the ancient Valencias and even make out the dark green globes within the foliage. He wouldn't need to flick on his flashlight to make his way toward this oddly chattering mockingbird. Couldn't be too far off. A few rows south at the farthest. Bit west, maybe. He'd scare off whatever raccoon or opossum or snake had this mockingbird so riled.

He walked across the cowpeas, which hadn't gone crunchy yet with their seeds. He soon heard rhythmic human grunts beneath the still-screeching mockingbird. It hadn't occurred to him, groggy as he was, that a human presence might have been the thing riling the mockingbird. He raised his flashlight and flicked on the beam toward the grunts, half-averting his eyes, but saw something he didn't expect to see at all, a fat child. A boy, who froze in the white beam between blows, his machete blade glinting at his thigh now. The child raised his chubby free hand to shade his eyes from the light, but didn't think to run, caught red-handed as he was. Isaac gritted his teeth at the fresh green wounds striping the bark of the towering Valencia.

"Son of a gosh-darned gun!" Isaac cried the lustiest non-curse that came to him, recognizing the child now. "Sheriff was right! Son of a gosh-darned—"

"Peter!?" Eli's voice startled Isaac from behind. His son had followed him, after all. "Peter!?" Eli asked again, advancing to Isaac's side, as if repeating the chant and drawing nearer might alter the vision of his chubby classmate before him.

"Go back to the tent, Eli!" Isaac commanded, but his son just took a single step backward. Isaac was too preoccupied with their discovery to press further. Peter dropped his machete and began to cry where he stood, both hands at his side, looking so tear-soaked and pathetic that a wave of pity churned through Isaac's insides. Yellow mucus that the boy didn't bother to wipe away pooled in the cleft between his nose and mouth. Isaac lowered the flashlight beam to the cowpeas for a moment before steeling himself, raising the beam again on their vandal.

"Well, Peter King. No way around it, I'm afraid. Looks like we're going to have to have a talk with your poor father."

Twenty-five

IT WAS NO SIMPLE MATTER ANYMORE, timing the harvest. Clay remembered when they used to just sample a fair passel of oranges off the tree. You scouted your rows for the color break and then sampled fruit off the slower-maturing north side, few a day. If eating one made you want to eat more, it was harvest time dollars to donuts. You called your fellow growers together and double-checked one another's fruit and judgment. If the acid stung your mouth something terrible, you waited a few more days then sampled some more. Didn't even have to bother with the commission and their highfalutin chemistry-set tests to determine the TSS content in degrees Brix. Horse sense is all it took. Growers still had the say-so. Since the war, though, since the California and Texas markets started challenging Florida's share, the commission had established all sorts of rules—ever-changing rules based on their secret consumer taste tests held in some secret dugout, all likelihood—to keep the Florida citrus standard beyond reach.

So here Clay was, this second week of October, sitting at the big corner booth, not their usual bar, with the other river men, huddled over their passels of Hamlins and Parson Browns, subjecting the lot to a more rigorous goin' over, commission grades on the line. Number 2 Grade wouldn't do at all. Grade 3 and the river might as well rise and swallow them up whole. Clay surveyed the crusty orbs before them, tottering nervous on the table as the river men set to their pastries and coffees and colas and cigarettes and whatnot. Tottering fruit hardly looked like oranges now, dirt-caked and mostly green right off the tree and all. Their packing house, Nevin's, would take care of the cleaning and, for the dwindling share headed for their fresh-fruit stands rather than the concentrate processing plants, the ethylene to speed up the break, the Johnson's Wax coat and polish to keep the bugs out and the dear nectar from seeping. Least Walt could do, though, was wipe the crusty bird shit off that one of his. The Negro boy with his too-short T-shirt advertising the pale bulb of his navel stood outside the plate glass, as he'd stood each Wednesday and Friday afternoon these past two weeks, dispatched by his elders, gazing toward their conference inside, making no bones about the fact that he was watching them, waiting on the first sign of their verdict so he might report back to his daddy, or his uncle, or someone. *Fieldwork next morning!* Or not. Clay, in truth, was relieved to see the boy this season. Meant the Negroes, despite Levi's meddling, would be there daybreak at the Save-a-Lot when they were ready for first harvest.

"Well river men, let's proceed," Clay said. "Won't you be so kind, Doyle Newell, to sample a Parson Brown from my fair grove?" Clay opened his calloused palm, partly toward Doyle beside him and partly toward his dusty orbs closer by on the faux-marble tabletop.

They were a casual lot, mostly, the river growers. But they still stood on ceremony time to time, certain occasions. Like sampling the season's first fruit, determining the first cooperative harvest. They adhered to something of a script, the same essential script their fathers (and Walt's and Clay's grandfathers) recited before they were even a cooperative, proper. When it was enough, simply, to be fellow growers along the river, Christian neighbors.

"It would be my right honor, Clay Griffin, to sample your Parson Brown. Might I select the fruit now?"

"You may."

Doyle reached for a pebbly green specimen before Clay, rotated the orange before his eyes, squinting against the Camel smoke he puffed, as if the Parson Brown were a crusty planet and he were its fiery God.

"Color's broke, best of my ability to determine and on my river fruit honor. Won't you agree, Edwin Hill?" Doyle handed the orange across to Win, who didn't seem ready to receive it, who seemed put out as he clanked his RC bottle on the table and accepted the offering. Young Win followed the custom, but begrudgingly.

"Yeah-yeah. It's broke."

"Now Win," Clay said, lighting up a Winston.

"Don't pay him no nevermind," Doyle said to Clay.

"Let's just get on with it," Walt added, tapping off the worm of his own cigarette. He'd ordered a pastry topped with confectioner's sugar. Some of the powder, Clay noticed, still adhered to his shaggy red mustache. Hell if Clay'd tell him he looked a fool.

"Best of my ability to determine and on my river fruit honor," Win groaned, "I agree, color's broke."

"Please use my knife to proceed," said Clay. Holding the dull side of the blade, he extended the pearl haft of his father's best budding knife beside him to Doyle, who sliced the pebbly green specimen in half on the Formica, letting the halves rock on their pebbly peels, exposing sunshine middles that shimmered against the fluorescents above. Droplets from burst septal bundles beaded across the plateaus. Clay thought he heard Ike gasp small across the table, and why not? Sure was something, these high-color October insides of such an unlikely green berry. That Reverend Brown sure did stumble across something glorious up in Webster these many years past. Shame it couldn't have been his own granddaddy. Shame the commission bureaucrats and their eggheads at the university ran things now. Ike was plain fooling himself thinking otherwise.

"That's a fine high color, best of my ability to determine and on my river fruit honor," Doyle said. "Won't you agree, Ike Golden?"

"High color, indeed," Isaac agreed, "best of my ability to determine and on my river fruit honor." Ike'd showered this morning, Clay noticed. His near-blonde hair was dark still with wet around the edges. The shower seemed hardly to take, though. Beads of sweat that he hadn't wiped away sprouted like toadstools on Ike's forehead, above his lip, and right on his normal non-Jew nose, where Clay didn't think grown men sweated. Ike had a fair bit riding on this harvest. Couldn't practically spare this passel before him, scale-stricken acres and all. Plus the squandered acres. Those experimental acres. Eli's acres, he called them. Ike'd grub out those acres spring, Clay hoped, if things didn't pan out again. He only hoped his river partner hadn't waited too long to prove up the land.

Doyle sliced both halves, making quarters, nicked under the albedos at the pointy edges to make them peel easy and handed over the wedges with his nicotine-stained fingers to Walt, Win, and Isaac, leaving himself the last quarter.

"Shall we taste, gentlemen of the river?"

"We shall," Isaac said, just now wiping his wet lip with his oversized paw.

"We shall," Walt said, and Win grumbled. Clay liked that Walt and Ike seemed to be getting on better since their business at the river with the roustabouts, since Ike figured out once and for all that it wasn't Walt dicing up his trees but Hugh King's overfed son. (Clay supposed a fat boy like that needed to hate someone worse than himself.) It came as something of a relief to Clay that it was just a kid. Not that he much suspected Walt, himself. But still.

They tasted. Parson Browns and then the Hamlins. The fruit was all sweet enough. The Hamlins were less seedy than the Parson Browns, which was why they were starting to take over early season, bird dogs offering a bit more per box for the Hamlins. But the color wasn't quite as high as the Parson Browns, seemed to Clay. Up to Clay he'd plant equal Parson Brown rows still for the early season. But it wasn't up to Clay. Long as it came down to what the bird dogs would pay, housewives and their preferences would hold sway. Which meant sweet as all get-out, acid be damned, far as Clay could determine. Color be damned, too, for who'd see the inside of an orange anymore with fresh fruit going the way of that Edsel motor car, concentrate taking over.

"It's time, gentlemen of the river," Clay said, soberly. "It's time. For the spot harvest, anyway."

Walt slapped the faux-marble tabletop with both his palms, making the cheap metal cutlery dance and issue a brief tinny song. "I'll call the commission fuckers so they can send someone," Walt announced, less soberly. "Let's get this fruit to Nevin's for Chris' sake."

"Yippee," cried Win, shaking his RC Cola bottle, stoppered with his thumb, then making it foam champagne-style over his plate before containing it in his mouth.

"Now don't you make a mess for Janisse," Doyle said, lifting his Camel to his mouth, clutching a deep dose of smoke. An overgrown cord of hair flouted Doyle's earlier efforts with a comb and pomade to dangle straight down between his eyes clear past his hawk nose and gash of a mouth.

"Oh, all right," Win said, wiping up the soda all about the dirt-caked oranges with a sheaf of paper napkins.

"Janiiiisse," teased Walt.

"Might wipe that powder sugar off your pie-hole before jawin' at me," Doyle answered, not angry but not quite smiling. He must have felt his stray cord of hair, finally, because he gathered it in the crook of two fingers and threw it back up on his sunburnt pate.

"Oh, don't pay Walt no nevermind," Clay advised Doyle. "We all like Janisse."

Truth was, Clay thought, poor Janisse looked like she fell out of the ugly tree and hit every branch on the way down, but that didn't matter none. Doyle looked like he fell off the same tree. And people should be with people.

People should be with people. His stomach sank out from under him as if he were on a carnival ride soon as the phrase rose to his mind. *People should be with people.* Erma's phrase from long ago. Releasing him, all intents and purposes, as if she had any say so. When he told her about Pearl.

And here they were these many years gone, Pearl coming home some weeks ago, lifting her fingers to her cheek, shaking her head slow with worry, talking about some sharp-looking Negro at Ike's stand looking a mite too familiar with Melody, which Clay took to mean that Melody was looking a mite too familiar with the handsome Negro, too. Clay knew full-well it must have been Levi, come back to stir up all manner of devilment, apparently.

Well, what did Pearl want him to do about it? Clay had asked, while Pearl just kept shaking her head slow, staring down at the corner of the kitchen floor. How do you tell a fellow grower that his pretty wife might be carrying on with a Negro? *Damnit Ike!* he had cursed silently to spare Pearl, the pent-up words making his forehead burn. *Damnit Ike!* spending all his time on his fool grove experiments when he ought to be minding his home fires. He'd say something to Ike if he could figure out the words. But he just wasn't sure what he might say, exactly, what words on the subject wouldn't cause all hell to break loose. For Ike. For Melody. For Levi. One thing for certain: a pretty wife sure was a curse. Maybe it was Melody he ought to speak to, it occurred to him. Before it was too late. For Ike. For Melody. For Levi. He'd have to think on that one.

"Yeah, Doyle, listen to Clay and don't pay me no nevermind," Walt said, jolting Clay from his reverie. Clay lifted his Winston to his mouth, savored the tasty smoke, exhaled. Walt rose, smiled, having already wiped the powdered sugar off his beard, or deeper into his facial foliage, having already performed a mental calculation of his likely harvest over the next several days. “Guess I’ll have a word with Jackson out there ’fore I call the commission fuckers,” Walt said, lifted his nose toward the plate glass, raising a palm to the Negro boy outside with the too-short shirt advertising his navel bulb.

Twenty-six

SHE'D ALREADY CANVASSED most of town. But not these blighted weed-choked blocks west, close to where they were talking about planting the interstate. What would they do with all these old live oaks and slash pines, these fewer magnolias and maples and sweetgum, she wondered, dropping some of their clothes now that it was fall? Probably bulldoze the poor creatures. Maybe they'd bulldoze these very homes to pour the asphalt. Melody wasn't very familiar with these blocks:the dull, chipped paint on the bungalows, the oaks dense as shrubs with their foliage, left to grow as they pleased, leaning on sunken, moldy rooftops. She'd done well these past few weeks—returned to MB twice for another stack of blue tickets, which emboldened her.

She forced herself to slow her brisk pace to keep the perspiration from rising through her foundation. She crossed the street, the asphalt scarred with weed-choked fault lines here and there, thought for a moment before approaching the first front door. The homes on this block all seemed to have unshaded cement stoops instead of proper porches. She considered skipping this benighted block, concentrating her efforts on homes with more promising frontage. Yet this didn't seem fair. The spaghetti dinner truly was a bargain. Bottomless plates. Plus an iceberg lettuce salad and sheet cake dessert. And the fallout shelters concerned the entire town, even these residents. It seemed downright churlish to exclude anyone.

She knocked on the wooden door, its cream paint stained with rust (from a hose?), surveying the eave for a slanted mezuzah (stupidly, she realized). A Negro man answered the door. That's the first thing Melody noticed, which made her hiccup a short intake of breath. She hadn't realized she'd slipped into a neighborhood where Negroes lived, that they had staked out—or been designated, rather—a separate warren so far west of Hopkins and the FEC tracks.

The next instant, she recognized the Negro man as the particular Negro man he was.

"Oh my," she said, her hand on her heart. "Hello."

"Hello," he said, his lips curving into a careful smile. Pleated suit pants, he was wearing, ironed crisp, a leather belt cinched tight, but only a white cotton undershirt above, the neckline sloping into a V to expose his near-hairless chest.

Melody lowered her eyes to the stack of blue tickets in her hand. The tickets trembled. Then she raised her eyes again.

"I didn't realize this is where you were staying." Melody might have said *living* rather than *staying*, but there seemed something temporary about the accommodations, the bare painted walls behind him, perhaps, the broad uncluttered table. He couldn't have spent much time in this room, she gathered.

"Where I'm staying for now, anyway. I move about every so often. Can't be too careful. Ever since Principal Manning and his wife."

"The man firebombed in his bed Christmas night you mean? Up in Mims?"

"Yes. Him."

"You truly think you're in danger, Levi?"

As soon as the words escaped her lips, she noticed something dance within his dark eyes.

"Where do you think you live, Melody? What kind of place do you think this is?" he asked, more amused than angry, it seemed. Then: "Where's Sarah, anyway?"

She looked about her feet as if for coins that she'd scattered. It took Levi's reference to the baby for her to gather the strange logistics of her current circumstance. That she was alone, all by herself, without even Sarah in tow. That she was out of the house, away from the stand and off the grove, in this disheveled part of town she'd never traversed before, where no one would think to look for her. That she'd knocked on Levi's door of all doors. That he was home, as if he were waiting for her to knock, waiting, maybe, all these days and weeks and months.

"Sarah's in good hands," Melody heard herself say. A distant automobile rumbled along its road somewhere farther west. "I'm on my own."

Levi nodded slowly, as if he were measuring the weight of her words against the lean muscles of his neck.

You're not the kind of person who does something like this, Melody thought, waiting for Levi to say something. But he only stood there, impassive, waiting for something. So Melody finally said, "I'm not the kind of person who does something like this."

"Of course you're not," Levi said, frowning at the suggestion. "Neither am I. All these months, have I ever—"

"No," she interjected. "No."

And since he frowned and said *Of course you're not*, since he hadn't pressed her to be other than who she was these many months, and since she was on her own now, without any people here in this Florida backwater, and on her own *now, here*, by this strange dint of circumstance she'd never have had the temerity to orchestrate, or even glimpse, she found herself scanning the weed-choked front yards up and down the blighted block, taking in the rickety, unoccupied chairs on the cement stoops. She found herself taking courage in the piercing voice of a nearby cardinal. *Alive! Alive! Alive! Alive!* it insisted from its perch somewhere. *Alive! Alive! Alive! Alive!*

She heard herself say: "But here I am."

To which Levi replied: "Here you are," swinging his shoulder open as if it were on a hinge to offer Melody passage.

Twenty-seven

Isaac might have known by Percy's shoes at the Save-a-Lot, first morning of the true harvest. Over the past couple weeks, they'd already spot harvested five boxes each with their foremen and received their US Grade 1 mark at Nevin's from the commission rep. True harvest now. For most of their early-bearing Hamlins and Parson Browns, anyway. Grapefruit in a few weeks, most likely, plus the later Hamlins and Parson Browns at the northeast parcel of the grove. Midsweets, Pineapples, and the fewer navels would be ready in December, Valencias come spring. But Percy's shoes this morning. New leather and thick rubber soles. Shoes hardly fit for climbing with those too-rigid soles. Good for walking, maybe, but too stiff for climbing. Field-workers, and Isaac, preferred to feel the ladder and the branches some beneath their curled toes. He might have known by those shoes, which he noticed at the Save-a-Lot, but didn't think about until later. Until after.

Isaac was relieved, instead, when Percy hopped up onto his flatbed at first light without even needing encouragement. For Percy was the one with whom he had spoken out on the grove about the field box rates, about Isaac being only one grower in the co-op, about their struggles all around. It hadn't been a good conversation, which was to say that Percy hadn't put his mind at ease about the upcoming harvest, about the morale of his fellow field-workers, the high-rollers or the rookies. So it was a good thing that Percy hopped right on the wood-paneled bed of the truck, that he ushered nine other fellows on board too, that they all looked fit and able to Isaac, and to Ted, who nodded his approval toward Isaac in lieu of uttering actual words. Frederick, Isaac noticed, had hopped onto Walt's truck. Nothing unusual about that. The high-rollers usually spread themselves out amongst the co-op groves in fairness to their less skilled fellows, who didn't like being crowded out by the high rollers. In fairness to the growers, too, all of whom needed the fruit off the trees in a timely fashion.

They didn't discuss this year's rates right there on the pebbly macadam. Because they never discussed the rates. Not in so many words, anyway. The pickers picked the fruit and the foremen kept tally, offered them their wages at the end of the day. Cash. Pickers got what they got. That was pretty much the protocol. Isaac had considered broaching to Percy the field box rates, perhaps inch up toward the limit he and the other river growers had agreed upon. It might offer the team a bit more incentive to learn of the upped rates in advance of the actual work—might compel their more careful twisting of fruit from stem to avoid plugging, might put some spring to their step on the jerry-rigged ladders, some actual *joie de vivre*—but it would have been a queer thing to do given the established routine. It would have seemed weak, Isaac feared. So he didn't say anything. Just hopped in the passenger seat of the cab after someone in his sleepy crew dropped the wooden gate with its square metal posts down into their female slots at the end of the truck bed. Isaac shut the cab door, which gnashed angrily like unmatched teeth, a metallic insult to the drowsy birds hidden somewhere within the still-dark magnolia foliage lining Hopkins. Clay's foreman pulled out ahead of Ted as if it were a race, cutting him off, making Ted tap the whining brakes harder than he would have liked, especially so early, especially with their human cargo. Isaac heard the shuffling and skidding of weight on the bed as the men struggled to regain their balance. Clay jutted his hand out the window, bid goodbye and good luck to Ike. *Here goes. First harvest.*

Six miles to Isaac's grove. Sun wasn't full up over the river mangroves and sloppy palms by the time Ted cut down Hammock Road, the big tires crunching and skidding over the loose seashell and rock and dirt, but it was mostly light. Light enough to start picking. Cool morning air out the window tickled the bleached fur on Isaac's forearm on the ledge, whispered promises of a temperate day. Ted nudged the Ford over the berm and onto the broad access trail, weeds thwacking the truck's underbelly, and made his way four rows inside, middle of the Parson Brown patch they'd harvest today with any luck, most southwestern exposed quadrant of the grove, earliest maturing cultivars. The truck bucked against the uneven terrain, making the human cargo bump about some, not much, on the bed, cry out in mock complaint, making Ted smile and show the metal in his teeth as he stared into his rearview mirror. The dusty brakes squealed when Ted finally brought the truck to a halt. Isaac heard the wooden gate being lifted out of its slots, but was surprised not to hear the thunk of boots from the men plopping themselves down onto the cowpea ground cover. Time to start filling up those satchels. Isaac and Ted opened their creaky doors and walked toward the back of the truck, Isaac looking up at the men looking down toward the grove owner, arms folded over the wooden gate, decidedly not making their way off the bed. They didn't seem combative so much as they seemed—Isaac searched for the proper word to describe them—noncommittal. This wasn't good at all, Isaac knew. Not good at all.

Percy was the only man with his feet on ground, waiting there to discuss matters with the foreman and the grove owner, crumpled baseball cap in his hands. A mockingbird chattered at Isaac as he made his way toward Percy, who scratched at his stubbly cheek as he waited there as if his flat chocolate mole itched. A nervous tic. Good, Isaac thought, staring down at Percy's feet again, the leather toes mottled darker from the dew-licked cowpeas. Now he thought about those darn shoes. Those stiff walking shoes.

"Aaa, shut up!" Isaac shouted toward the still-chattering mockingbird, its silhouette visible now over Percy's shoulder against the burnt dawn on top of the dew-frosted Parson Brown foliage. It was something to say, anyway, something to break the ice, and something other than what he'd have to say now to Percy, who chuckled a bit at Ike's playacting. Here was Ike, acting the irascible grove owner, no patience this morning for nonsense, avian or otherwise.

"Well," Isaac finally said, opening his meaty palms. "What's the hold up, Percy?"

"Figured, suh, we should discuss terms 'fore gettin' started."

Isaac looked at Ted, looming behind Percy, to gauge his expression, to see if Ted had known all this going in. But Ted's face was stone. His foreman finally exhaled a stream of pent-up air through pursed lips, lifted off his torn cap to scratch his patchy pate. It was tough to determine what that meant, exactly. Was Ted exasperated with Percy, or just anxious, generally?

"Terms? You mean field box rates?"

Percy nodded. Isaac looked up at the men on the truck, gazing down at the conference.

"So you're the spokesperson, Percy. Well, good for you."

Percy smiled, awkwardly.

"Well, what did you have in mind?" Isaac put his hands on his hips. "Let's talk turkey, Perc'."

"Fifty cents a box, boss." Percy winced as he stated these terms. He realized the outlandishness of the demand. "For *oranges*," Percy clarified. "Forty okay for the Marshes inna few weeks."

"Well that's very generous of you," Isaac replied. Ted laughed, but Percy just stood there, that same stricken look on his face, unsure how to read Isaac's remark. "I was being sarcastic," Isaac clarified.

Percy nodded, but didn't say anything, just kept nodding, slower and slower like a mechanical clock winding down. A worker up on the bed cleared his throat, maybe to puncture the awkward silence. The mockingbird started chattering again. Isaac could feel the day growing hotter on his neck, the sun slowly gaining its purchase, or maybe he was just hot over Percy's nervy negotiating. Who did he think he was, stating such bold terms?

And who was Isaac, Isaac wondered the next instant, wondering who this Negro field-worker thought he was? How quickly Isaac had become just another white grower, as Melody had warned, worried over his profit margin, less worried over his darker laborers in their tattered field clothes, with their own families, with their own burdens. Greater burdens, Isaac knew. Some man. Some Jew. Some sorry excuse for a human being, Isaac Golden. But then there was the fruit. These mature Parson Browns. They needed to come off the tree. No way around that. If not by this week, by next week. Week after the latest.

"I won't dicker with you, Percy," Isaac heard himself utter. "There's a top price the co-op's willing to pay. A better price than last season. Much better, you'll be happy to know. But the price is the price. No way around it. Price is thirty cents a box. There. Thirty cents. Twenty for the Marshes."

Percy stood there, weighing the offer, nodding his head slow again. A frog chirped somewhere, not yet giving up the night. Chirped again.

Percy was a good negotiator, it occurred to Isaac. Better, maybe, than even Percy realized. The frog sounded once more. For Percy seemed to know, instinctively, something that Isaac didn't know, or that he was only coming to know, anyway. That the greatest weapon in a negotiator's arsenal weren't clever words, or sarcastic words, or logical words, or any words at all. But silence. Simple silence. Which, for whatever reason, Isaac couldn't abide.

"There's nothing else I can do," he insisted, his face growing hotter now and red, he suspected. There was more of his mercurial father in him, perhaps, than he'd been willing to acknowledge.

Percy just stood there and gazed down at his shoes, brushed one of his toes across the cowpeas, as if looking for a gem hidden beneath the cover. Isaac bit his bottom lip to keep further words inside.

"Thirty's true enough a fair bit better than last year," Ted finally intervened. "Sure you can't see your way clear, Percival?"

"Afraid not," Percy said right away, speaking more freely to his fellow Negro, speaking through him to Isaac, anyway. "This's hard work, Ted, and dangerous too. You know that. Gotta factor that in. Norris done broke his leg last year falling off his ladder on Mr. Griffin's grove. We all had to pitch in to keep his boys from starving. Pay *should* be better than peppers and straw-berrs, taking risk into account. No other workplace protections to speak of."

Workplace protections? Isaac thought, but didn't say. Percy'd been coached on his talking points. That much was clear. By Levi, Isaac was now certain. Ted's boy. Ted's own son! Some pickle. The frog chirped again, followed by the mockingbird's chatter, as if the two creatures were speaking. Both Negroes looked over toward Isaac, awaited his response.

Isaac threw up his hands, let them fall back at his sides. "It's like I said, gentlemen. It's out of my hands. Thirty's the best I can do."

"Fifty," Percy uttered. "Fifty best *we* can do."

Silence. Isaac felt the weight of Ted's stare. Forty seemed a solid compromise, one way of seeing it—Ted's way, probably. But Isaac couldn't go to forty. That's not what the co-op had agreed upon.

"Listen," Isaac regrouped, "if I started at twenty-five, Percy, would you have been fine with thirty at the end of the day? I was only trying to save us some time. I know your men up there"—Isaac lifted his eyes to the field-workers still leaning over their arms—"want to make some money today."

It was a rotten thing to do, maybe, seeking to stir up dissent. But no dice.

"Wouldn't have made no difference, Mr. Golden. Fifty low as *we* can go, like I said."

"And that goes for all the workers hereabouts? Every grove? As we speak?"

Percy's eyes drifted up some toward his forehead, Isaac noticed, as if he were contemplating what he could reveal.

"You can tell me *that* much," Isaac prodded.

"Yes, then," Percy said, nodding. "All the groves."

"So here we are then."

"Here we are."

There was a protocol to this sort of thing. Not a protocol that Isaac had ever been forced to follow these past few years, but a protocol all the same, one that the river growers had apprised Ike of, worrying over this possible scenario, the strange besuited Negro in town that no one else had recognized, far as Isaac knew. It was a protocol, evidently, that Ted knew about too, for they had faced a mess like this before some fifteen years ago, just after the war when field-workers were scarce, which offered them sudden leverage for these negotiations, when river fruit and ridge fruit alike rotted on the trees, growing fuzzy green jackets, after the growers and laborers reached a stalemate in their negotiations.

"Have a nice walk back to town, Percy," Ted uttered, making his way back to the cab. They'd drive the crew back to town, but they wouldn't drive Percy. Not the ringleader. Those were the terms. The protocol, which kept things peaceable, anyway. Percy would have to make his way back along the highway, which was why he was wearing those thick-soled shoes. Isaac walked toward his side of the cab, hoping all the while that Percy would call him back, would reconsider. But no.

"You knew about this, Ted?" Isaac asked his foreman back in the truck after he clanged the door shut. He strained to keep his voice low so the workers wouldn't hear, a vein bulging in his neck from the exertion.

"No sir," Ted denied the charge. He propped his cap on the cracked vinyl dash, scratched his patchy pate. "Seen it coming, just like you, seems, but didn't know nothing 'bout it."

"Not from Levi? Not from your boy, you mean for me to believe?" The vein rose higher in Isaac's neck. "Everyone's going to know it's him, Ted. You realize that, right? No one's going to believe it's Percy, or Fred, or whoever else is speaking for the group in their new walking shoes, jabbering on about workplace protections all of a sudden. Levi hasn't said word one to you?"

"He doesn't say anything to me on grove matters," Ted answered, raising his grip some on the wheel. "Sure enough. We don't talk over grove matters, me being foreman and all. That's your business, I tell Levi. I got my business, you got yours. I can't get mixed up, I tell him."

Isaac gazed out the window, seeking counsel from the outdoors, his grove trees appearing to rock with the truck. He decided to believe Ted. His foreman really didn't factor for much, anyway, when it came to the negotiating. So what did it matter if Levi spoke with him? It was bigger than Ted. Bigger than Isaac too.

So he decided to believe his foreman, as it was preferable to not believing him.

Twenty-eight

JANISSE'S. That's where the growers had decided to meet up if there was trouble. Back at Janisse's. So that's where Isaac loped once Ted screeched to a halt at the Save-a-Lot and the men filed out of the truck, walking hangdog down Hopkins to their weary bungalows, apartments, and duplexes, too shamefaced to look up at Isaac, or even at Ted. Isaac had to give them credit. They were working men and felt out of sorts about not working, about this strange commute back to town before putting in a day's labor, their energies unspent. Clearly, they had been conscripted into the effort—Levi's effort—but they didn't seem to feel too good about how things shook out. It meant money out of their pockets, after all. At least for today. Who knew about tomorrow? That's why Isaac needed to go to Janisse's. He told Ted to head back to the grove without him, referencing vague errands he had to perform in town. He'd find his way back home. He wouldn't confide in Ted about his co-op meeting at Janisse's. There was only so much he could say to Ted, anymore.

No evidence of the other grove trucks having been back at the Save-a-Lot. No other laborers loitering about or slinking back down Hopkins, far as Isaac could tell. Not a whiff even of rich truck exhaust. So Isaac walked the few blocks to Janisse's nervously, doubting the wisdom of his earlier resolve on the grove, doubting his memory of the co-op terms. They had agreed on thirty cents a box at the absolute maximum, yes? The full sun now over the nearby river pasted his dusty neck with its heat. October and it would still be god-awful hot by noon. False promises, those cooler currents about in the predawn.

The closer he got to Janisse's, the more Isaac doubted himself. So he was relieved to see red-faced Walt and Edwin already at the big corner booth when he jangled open the glass door, entered the mentholated indoors, still AIR-CONDITIONED FOR YOUR COMFORT, read the sign. A dense plume of smoke already shrouded their conference.

". . . slap 'em all with vagrancy back before Sheriff Wright was elected!" he heard Walt cry before reaching the table. "Send 'em to the turpentine camps, they don't want to pick oranges. Else throw 'em in sweat boxes till they change their minds."

"Mmm-hmm," Win muttered.

"All right, let's just relax, Walter," Isaac said. "Don't have a conniption." Win chuckled at the strange northern word, conniption, as Isaac knew he would. Walt glanced at Isaac as he sat, but otherwise ignored him.

"What we do is go to Deland! Eustis! Apopka! Orlando! All the way to Leesburg and Groveland need be!" Walt inhaled hard, making the embers of his Lucky glow bright beyond his bulbous nose. "Scrape up niggers there!" he exclaimed through his smoke like an angry devil. "Goddamned porch monkeys there be happy for an honest day's wage! Then see how fast our boys here come running back!"

"And cut out that nigger business too, would you please?" Isaac cried. "Let's just cut that out now. Humor me." Since their river business together with the *nogoodniks,* Isaac could take this tone with his neighbor.

"Yeah, cool it," Win advised. "No point getting hot under the collar, Walt. Drink your iced coffee. We'll wait till Clay and Doyle get here. Wait till they're here to talk turkey. We'll figure somethin' out, sure enough." Win lifted up his RC Cola with the same hand that held his cigarette. Kents, with their healthier filters. He set down the bottle and held his half-spent Kent above the plastic ashtray, not so much tapping off the spent tobacco as teasing off the ash, rubbing the filter end with his thumb, waiting to see how long the gray worm would hold on. Uncharacteristically contemplative for Win. He seemed suddenly stouter to Isaac, fleshy about his razor-burned face and neck. A gradual swelling, no doubt, which Isaac simply hadn't taken the time to notice, but which he now attributed (perhaps unfairly) to too-easy living, or maybe Connie was finally making Win his pound cake at home.

"You fixin' to eat, sugar?" Janisse and her heft suddenly loomed over Isaac, blotted out the fluorescence behind her. She waved at the dense smoke with her hand, mostly a rhetorical gesture.

"Just coffee," Isaac said. He'd already eaten bran flakes this morning in the dark while Melody started in with her pies, acting vaguely put out by his unusual presence, or maybe only preoccupied over her baking, the requisite ingredient ratios and whatnot. They didn't have a whole lot to say to each other, lately, seemed to Isaac.

"Cigarette?" Win asked, lifting up his soft Kent carton.

"You know Ike don't smoke," Walt declared.

"I'm not sure it makes much sense to start driving all about looking for workers," Isaac said. "You're talking a lot of time wasted on just getting to and fro, not to mention the fuel, the wear-and-tear on the old trucks. And who's to say they're not just as"—Isaac searched his mental inventory for the word—"organized in those other towns?"

"Here you go sugar," Janisse said, sending a stream of watery Maxwell House over Isaac's right shoulder from a perilous height into the heavy ceramic mug before him.

"I thought we were waiting for Doyle and Clay to talk turkey," Win said, still troubling the shaft of his Kent above the ash tray.

"Better not have made no dirty deal, two of them," Walt said, then coughed against his own smoke, a gravelly productive cough that reddened his already red face. Water rose in Walt's eyes. Isaac and Win watched as Walt gathered himself, coughed one last time to punctuate his spasm, swallowed down the phlegm. The ginger stubble made a wave above the flesh at the indeterminate beard border around his Adam's apple.

"Goddamn communists," Walt uttered, calmer now. "The lot of them. Bunch of goddamn communists. Should ship 'em all off to Cuba."

The bell at the door clanged. "Here's Doyle and Clay," Win said.

"Look who the cat gone drug in," said Walt.

"Fancy meeting you boys here," Doyle declared, raising two nicotine fingers to tame his few embattled strands, dark and wet from some curious blend of pomade and sweat.

"Take a seat and let's talk turkey," Win said. They sat.

"Well, Clay?" Walt threw up his hands. "Got any bright ideas? So much for your thirty and holdin' firm." Clay raised his wooly white eyebrows and groaned, but didn't say anything. He seemed to be waiting for his weight to settle itself on the chair, for his innards to find the proper alignment. So Isaac spoke.

"We can still make do at forty. Might be our best bet. See us through the season, anyway."

"Forty?" Walt cried, his eyes wide. "Just like that? After one mornin' of trouble you go right up to forty? I thought Jew-folk were supposed to be good at negotiating finances." He said Jew-folk with a glint in his eye, his yellow teeth peeking out from beneath his mustache and beard like corn niblets, which made it okay, somehow—okay to rib Isaac about Jew-folk and their prowess when it came to negotiating finances. Isaac's fellows laughed at Walt's remark, mostly at the way his mouth tugged hard at the vowels in *finances*, which made it even harder for Isaac to protest.

"He got you there," Doyle said. "Can't just go right to forty, Ike. For the love of Pete."

"Why don't we just throw in paid vacation while we're at it," Win proposed.

"Cruise to Tahiti," Walt said.

"So it was the same song and dance with y'all too then," Clay finally spoke, more soberly. Janisse poured coffee for Doyle and Clay without asking, then departed, leaving the men to their business. "Demanded fifty?" Clay continued. "Not a penny less? One designated speaker for all of them? Rest of the boys just quiet as church mice on the truck?"

The river growers nodded their heads as Clay rattled off his list of salient happenings.

"Used some funny words and phrases too," Win added. "Workplace . . . workplace"—he squinted against his Kent smoke to recall the next word that eluded him.

"Protections," Doyle chimed in, lighting up his Camel within the secret cavern of his hands, a cavern he didn't need to form indoors, but one they were all just used to making from lighting up so often out on their windy coastal groves. "Workplace protections," he said, waving the flame out from his cardboard match. "Other queer phrases too. Like cost of living . . . and high-risk occupation."

"That colored in the suit got to 'em!" Walt cried. "Pickers don't know shit from shinola. Hell if they know workplace protections from . . ."—Walt paused here to locate a piquant comparison, struggled to do so—". . . from . . . from . . ."

"From cattle inspections," Win chimed in.

"From piano lessons," Doyle added, grinning.

"Anyway," Walt said, flicking the ashes off his cigarette. "It's that colored in the suit, the one running things. Bet the grove on it."

"You don't know that," Isaac said. "You don't know who's running things. Not really." He felt Clay's eyes heavy on him. Why was he defending this besuited Negro? Clay was probably thinking. Who was he to him?

"Goddamn rabble rouser," Walt bemoaned, ignoring Isaac.

"Agitator," Doyle said.

"Troublemaker," Win said.

"Does he think we won't do nuttin'?" Walt wondered. "That we'll just sit back and take it? Is he that simple?"

"Else got brass balls," Win said.

"Does he think we'll allow some outside agitator in a suit come in and stir the pot, snatch away our livelihood? A colored no less? He think we don't know people? People'd be more than happy to crack his neck for him? Cause he'll get his neck broke, what's gonna happen. His neck broke. Just knew where he lived."

"Just knew where he lived," Win echoed Walt.

"Now let's just calm down," Clay said. "First thing's first. We try again tomorrow. At the Save-a-Lot. Same terms. Thirty, final offer. Let the boys sleep without pay tonight alongside their hectoring wives. Wives are wives, I suppose. White or colored. Womenfolk won't cotton to them layin' around shiftless all day. Now they don't work tomorrow, we go to Orlando. Then Deland. Sanford. Apopka if we gotta."

"That's what *I* started off saying 'fore you got here," Walt declared. "Get out-of-town coloreds. Then see how fast our boys come running back."

"What if none of 'em out-of-town Negroes work for thirty?" Win asked. "Or busy enough workin' their own local groves?"

"Well," Clay said, seeking wisdom from his Winston smoke, exhaling long and slow out the side of his mouth. "Just have to cross that bridge, I suppose."

Twenty-nine

You're not the kind of person who does something like this, Melody thought to herself once again as she rapped lightly on the paint-chipped door, her flesh rising. Yet evidently, despite what she thought, she *was* this kind of person. The kind of person who did all manner of unlikely things. A Jewish woman who set up housekeeping in the *goyische* Florida sticks. A Jewish woman who baked with lard. A Jewish woman who took a Negro lover. Maybe that's why she let things get so out of hand in the first place, though. Because what kind of meager thing was life, anyway, if it were only about doing what others expected of you, what you had come to expect of yourself?

Still, the first indiscretion with Levi ought to have been the last. Then that word would make some sense, at least, to describe her behavior. Indiscretion. That's all it might have been, which was bad enough. But here's the thing about sexual intercourse with a strange man that Melody hadn't bargained on, not having enjoyed sexual intercourse with any man other than her husband, who had only been strange years ago, a lifetime ago, it seemed now, even though it hadn't been so many years, truly. That the first time, exciting as it was (how had she forgotten?) was mostly awkward and only whetted the appetite for more practiced encounters. That loving a strange new man only grew more pleasing the second and third and fourth times. That new bodies working against each other took time to learn the proper rhythms, and these new bodies craved this time, these new rhythms. That loving a strange man once and only once didn't settle matters at all. Not at all! So somehow, yes, Melody Golden became just this kind of person, the kind who sought out such shameful encounters, the kind of person who asked Erma (of all people!) if she could mind the stand alone, the kind who scheduled Pearl or MB to watch over Sarah while she ostensibly sold spaghetti dinner tickets in Deland or Cocoa or Sanford.

So here was Melody, locating the perfect pleasing rhythm beneath her lover. *Yes. Yes. Yes.* She relished his well-muscled but compact frame, the way he fit so easily between her hips, the way he rode her so lightly from above, the way his dark limbs looked as they rode against her less-dark flesh above clean damp sheets in the not-quite dark of the shade-drawn room, the morning daylight seeping inside like something molten. She loved the way the wet rose slowly on his curved back now as he worked for their pleasure, the rising talcum smell of his close-cropped curls, the quickening pace as he labored now with greater purpose, as she encouraged his efforts, pulling him inside with her heels at the back of his knees, again, again, again. And mostly she loved this small spot of time devoted entirely to her own pleasure.

But just like that and it was over. She felt the muscle cords clench across his wet back, deepening the ravine along the buttons of his spine, his fine but too-brief spasm inside. He was mostly quiet as a church mouse during their exercise, as if he were used to surreptitious encounters, which maybe he was. Yet upon the final crisis he released all that pent-up air to issue something close to an utterance. She grasped the knob of his shoulder, lifted a knee and nudged him off onto his back, glanced down to make sure of something.

"We're all right," Levi assured her, breathless, as he'd taken to assuring her. They'd already fallen into certain patterns, it occurred to her, physical and verbal, like practiced lovers. "It didn't go nowhere," he said.

Melody didn't understand why Levi forgot his grammar after intercourse. She didn't like it.

This was the worst part, the very instant it was over, these terrible seconds, when all that she had shut out of her mind came scrambling back inside her skull, exerting great pressure, making her lift her fingertips to her forehead. Isaac. Eli. Sarah.

These terrible seconds!

"Why do you do that?" Levi said, reaching splayed fingers now to brush Melody's moist back.

"Do what?" She rose from the bed, beyond his reach, wrapped in a diaphanous sheet, fragrant with their efforts.

"Shove me off right away. Get up so quick-like, just after we're through. That's what the man's supposed to do. Not the woman."

"I have to get to Deland if I'm going to sell any tickets," she explained, turned back to face him.

"No. It's more than that." Levi plucked a cigarette from the carton on the scarred wooden night stand, opened the flimsy-sounding drawer for a match. Found it.

"The stand, too. After. I need to tend the stand. My pies."

She was about to say she needed to help Erma, but bit her tongue.

"More than just the stand, too. The pies." He struck the match, as if to punctuate his point with the sizzle. Melody smelled the sharp carbon overtaking their humid odors. She didn't like the match smell. Her father had lit match after match in the cramped bathroom of their Philadelphia walk-up to mask the smell of his bowel movements.

"Okay," she said. "Yes. Fine. It's more." She dashed toward the small bathroom and the mildewed shower.

She felt better once she was showered and dressed, standing before him now as if nothing had happened. She only wished that he'd put on some clothes, too, rather than just lie there smoking a cigarette as if he didn't have a care in the world. Did he not realize how crazy all this was!? How dangerous, especially for him!? At least he'd covered himself with the patchwork quilt that Erma had probably stitched for him years ago before sending him off to the Normal School in Suwannee County.

"You sure look pretty, Melody."

"I'm a mess." She struggled to locate the piercing in her left ear for the simple pearl earring. Her hand was trembling. Found it, finally. "I didn't even bring any makeup in my purse."

"Skin like yours who needs makeup? Who needs jewelry? Must have some Creole in you, olive skin like that."

"At least the weather's turned," she deflected the compliment. "It won't be too hot."

"Should be a mighty fine day on God's green earth," Levi said, lifting the cigarette to his purple lips, making the embers glow.

Their postcoital conversations could best be summed up by what they didn't talk about. They didn't talk about Isaac. Or Ted. Or Erma. Or Eli. Or Sarah. Or the stand. Or the grove. Or the ongoing field-worker strike. What would they say? Her husband and Levi's father had managed to collect rag-tag crews in Cocoa and Orlando to keep the fall harvest from going completely bust, but all the growers were in a bad way. Some of the Parson Browns and Hamlins had already softened on the branches, suffered insect incursions, clouds of despoiling gnats. They both knew this. Levi was the one mostly responsible for the standoff, which made Melody's coupling with him all the more shameful. They both knew this. What would saying anything about it do?

It's not that their relationship was purely physical. A current of genuine sympathy flowed between them. Shared struggle. It was tough to be a Jew, Melody had thought. The millions upon millions in Europe, the slaughter gaining brutal clarity only now on television and in the papers upon Eichmann's trial in Jerusalem, the barbarian. Still waiting on the verdict. Even in America it wasn't easy to be a Jew. The quotas shut her father out of the Ivy League. He'd wanted to become a doctor, settled on accountant instead. Denied promotion after promotion at Philadelphia's genteel Nation's Bank and Trust. Papa's squandered talent!

But what about now? Isaac had attended Penn and then Jefferson Medical School, both of which discriminated against Jews less grossly than Cornell, and Harvard, and Yale. All their friends, practically, had moved to the main line right beside the Christian gentry, while the Negroes still suffered. The Freedom Rides on the news these months, seething bands of white men and women (women too!) spitting in the faces of brave Negroes and their white sympathizers, bludgeoning them with fists and wooden clubs, setting their bus ablaze. Levi's troubles in New York after the war. Less dramatic, perhaps, but just as real. *Niggers to the left. Whites to the right.* And if Melody and Levi were caught now, say. She'd face a $1,000 fine for engaging in sexual intercourse with a Negro. Florida law, Levi informed her. But he'd likely be beaten senseless. Or lynched. Negroes were the true Jews, maybe. In America, anyway, it seemed to Melody. Maybe that's why Ted and Erma had given Levi his name. Maybe that's why she was curiously drawn toward him. Or maybe it was just nicer to think that this was so, rather than think otherwise of herself, that she was merely a whore, answering the call of her most animal impulses. Her stomach roiled, making her reach for it above the mock-belt of her dress. Maybe she was exactly the kind of person the town gentiles probably took her for, even Pearl and MB, making their worried o's with their mouths that scalding day out at the stand. A sex-crazed Jewess, if not quite melon-breasted. The kind of person Luke surely wanted her to be. But worse, a lover of Negroes. What was that horrid phrase that the most loathsome southerners used? A nigger lover.

"You okay? When can I see you again?" Levi asked, lifting himself higher on the mattress, leaning his back against the tattered wallpaper. There was no bed frame, proper. The patchwork quilt fell just below the bulb of his navel.

"I don't know. I'll call."

"Sure you will."

She wasn't certain how he meant this. She held his gaze to see what it might reveal, waited for his nascent smile below his dusting of mustache to bloom into something else, smoothed the wrinkles from her dress with two downward strokes from below her modest bust line. But he only lifted the cigarette to his lips, gazed at her now through squinted eyes, maybe so he didn't have to say or do something else. If he were implying that she wouldn't call again, he didn't seem particularly hurt. Levi didn't need her. There were other women. That much was clear from their first tryst a few weeks ago. She felt the heat rise to her face as she summoned the memory of that first touch. Her hand rose reflexively to tuck a strand of her raven hair behind a tiny ear. Levi was a man who took lovers. Melody was only one of Levi's lovers. She suspected that there was someone else even now in Jacksonville or Orlando, one of the cities where he spent so much time. She was careful not to ask. It didn't bother her, strangely enough. Rather, it was something of a relief to occupy such a narrow and well-defined role in his life. Levi enjoyed her. But he didn't need her. Yes, this was one of the things that attracted her to Levi. Or not so much to Levi, exactly, but to these clandestine encounters themselves. That she was simply a lover, a lover who was desired as such without being needed.

They wouldn't kiss goodbye. She had only kissed him once on the lips, in fact. That first time. It felt wrong, more clumsily intimate than the more strenuous coupling that followed. That's something else Melody hadn't bargained on, that intercourse with Levi would feel less sinful, somehow, than kissing him had felt. She left the room and reached the front door, turned the dented metal knob and cracked the door open, letting a sliver of stronger light inside. She peeked her head out to look up and down the battered block. Not a soul about, thankfully. Only a mockingbird laughing from an untended thatch of beauty berry across the street, dripping with dense clusters of bitter purple fruit. "Goodbye," she called out, not expecting a reply and not receiving one. She heard the bedsprings working on the other side of the wall, instead, Levi rising now finally to tend to his own affairs.

Melody opened the door wide and stepped out into the brightness, not realizing how lucky she was that the towheaded, cowlicked stock boy out on deliveries would only cut through this blighted block a half hour later or so, upon Levi's less careful departure.

Thirty

CLAY KNEW what Melody Golden was supposed to be doing this morning. Canvassing. Because of that baby girl of hers, Sarah, squealing in their family room. That's why he worried what else she might be up to now instead of canvassing, because how often did she have someone to mind the baby? The sound, anyway, nearly brought him to his knees, made him stop thinking about Ike's pretty wife. Baby sounds under his own roof. Who would have thought? Pearl's sister in Daytona had never left their children for Pearl and him to mind, as if she felt it would have been cruel, when it actually would have helped some. Helped Pearl, and helped Clay too, maybe.

"You're awful good with the child," he said to his wife.

"It's no bother looking after a toddler."

He watched his wife sit right down on the braided throw rug to play with the tyke, Pearl wearing her dress and all, showing a good bit more spryness than one would expect of a woman her age. Seemed ten years younger with the girl, truth of it. Sarah walked clumsily about with a big plastic donut in her hand, so big it seemed a miracle she could keep it in her tiny grasp. Smaller donut thingamajigs were strewn all about. Pearl tried in vain to get the tyke to lower the donut over the plastic part on the ground.

"No, it's something special, Pearl. Seeing you with the child." He felt his eyes mist over, mostly because he was so darn old, he assured himself. Pearl looked up at him for a moment, fixed her eyes back on Sarah tottering about.

"Now don't you get started, Clay Griffin. Goodness gracious. We're past all that by now, aren't we?"

Clay nodded. "Sure," he said.

"I'm just trying to get her to stack. Stacking's important, they say."

He nodded again. "So Melody's off selling tickets somewhere?"

"Mmm-hmm. Deland, I think. All day, pretty much."

"Sure y'all ain't working her too hard?"

Didn't Pearl have enough horse sense to worry about Ike's pretty wife left to her own devices, her panties in a twist over that sharp-looking Negro?

Pearl tossed a plastic ring on the small post, making a real show of it. "Here," she said to Sarah at a high register. "Like this, Sarah. Like this." And at a lower register, for Clay's ears: "I think it's a great relief to her, honestly Clay. Gets her out of the house and that stand. That poor Eli. Change of scenery. Gets to see some new places and new people. Isaac just doesn't dote on her as he ought to, ask me. Lets her work too hard at the stand. Works too hard himself with his experiments and whatnot."

She had put the sharp-looking Negro out of her mind, it seemed to Clay, forgot all about what she had seen at Goldens Are Here, months ago now. Because it was just easier that way.

"Have you talked to Isaac about his trees?" Pearl continued. "About how lucky he is to have a wife pretty as Melody?"

Or maybe, Clay reconsidered, Pearl hadn't forgotten about the sharp-looking Negro, after all. She was smarter than she let on, his wife, smart enough to know that there were some things better left unsaid. There was no telling what manner of things his wife might know about Melody Golden, about himself too, it occurred to him. He felt a sad mood coming on again, fought it off as Pearl had asked a question, expected a response.

"Talked to him a little. About his trees, anyway. But what a man does on his own—"

"Beautiful girl like that. Down here without any people to speak of. No surprise she took to the canvassing. It's fixing to be some spaghetti dinner this year, Clay."

"So, Deland, eh?"

Clay had tried talking with Ted months ago at Sonny's Good Food, but it just didn't take. That was before Pearl told him about the sharp-looking Negro looking too familiar with Melody out at Goldens Are Here. Clay figured it was high time he pay a visit to Erma out there at the stand. Melody in Deland. Ike out on the grove with Ted, most likely, minding after those piss-poor pickers from Sanford. Clay hoped to take care of this business he should have taken care of weeks ago. Especially after what Pearl had revealed about the sharp-looking Negro and Melody. Especially the way Walt's been carrying on lately about "that Nigger rabble rouser." It wasn't all bluster, Walt's words. Or even if it was, it was a dangerous sort of bluster, the sort that spelled trouble, wrong party catch wind, if they ever tracked Levi down. Things go okay with Erma, better than they went with Ted, he might not have to speak with Melody at all. Levi up and gone there wouldn't be no need.

He drove the Buick slowly through town, so slow he could hear the engine breathe like a person, almost, driving this slow mostly because he was so old, partly because he was in no hurry to get to where he was going. His eyes lingered over the few other Queen Anne homes with their highfalutin spires (he'd humored Pearl with the purchase) built up right next to these Spanish-style stucco jobs and these rock domiciles with the fancy windows. "Greek Revival," Pearl told him once. Town fathers, Clay's granddaddy included, might have put their heads together and settled on something before throwing up every sort of house in creation. The courthouse here he liked. Fancy columns made sense on a courthouse, even if it didn't seem to get much use, which maybe wasn't a bad thing, considering. A few cars parked outside, but not a soul about on the steps. He cut down Julia and drove past the Florida Playhouse, which Pearl dragged him to least twice a year, then past the Spanish Mission Hotel and Apartments. He noticed two roustabouts sitting on the curb, sharing a liquor bottle in a brown paper bag by the looks of it. Have to get Ulee on that, Clay thought, thinking their sheriff might as well do something to earn his salary. He gazed inside the plate glass at Janisse's just long enough to spot Doyle all by his lonesome, loitering there at the bar, Janisse looming above. Well, good for Doyle—something besides his stamps and Depression glass and whatnot to play with—even if Clay couldn't figure out how something like that even worked. His own Pearl had put on some extra weight over the years. Bigger pinch of soft flesh here and there. But Janisse was something else, entirely. How'd you handle a woman like that between the sheets?

"Ah, hell," Clay said aloud, shivering at the thought of Janisse and Doyle's business together, picking up speed now on US 1 heading north. He'd been doing this a lot lately, uttering this and that oath or phrase out loud with no one around to hear. Now what was the point of that? He hoped it wasn't a sign he was losing his marbles, talking out loud to no one. If it was, he assured himself, changing his grip on the wheel, he probably wouldn't be able to think on it like this.

Just then, his mind on his questionable faculties, he glimpsed Ike's Pontiac in the road. Ike had turned right onto Clay's street some fifty yards ahead. But wait, it couldn't be Ike in the car. Ike had to be out on his grove with Ted, and Melody needed the car to get up to Deland. He sped up some to get a look inside the rear window and spied the back of Melody's raven head, as he suspected, just peeking up over the headrest. What the Sam Hill was she doing in town still? He feared that he might know. She ought to have been in Deland already, yes? He eased up on the gas, drifted farther back so Melody wouldn't spot him. There wasn't a question over whether or not he'd follow her. Of course he would.

Clay kept Melody a safe distance ahead as they carved right angles across the small grid of streets that defined town, proper. Within seconds the right-angle streets were behind them and they were surrounded by scruffier acres, heading north on the highway up toward Ike's grove. She was probably just going home now, Clay figured, unsure what he would make of it if that turned out to be the case. He gazed across the road to the west, the palmettos islands that held the rats and snakes, the slash pines spearing up into the sky, few of their trunks charred from lightning fires that didn't quite take, or got rained out. The pines seemed to stand at pretty regular intervals, not unlike their grove trees. Now how'd they work that out amongst themselves? he wondered. All that land. Perfectly good land for grove trees given the time and money. If they could just beat Simply Citrus and Joe Buck Wilson to the punch. Keep the Feds and their NASA business well clear. Keep another one of them golf courses from going up. Orange and grapefruit trees for pines was fair enough, seemed to Clay. Proving up the land. But cutting down pines and chasing the pecker-birds away for a useless carpet of grass? It didn't sit right.

New car every ten seconds or so on its way south seemed to pass Melody up ahead and then him, most of them couples smiling and showing their teeth. Kids romping across a few backseat benches. Folks on vacation, Clay figured, now that the heat broke, some of them heading clear down to Miami. More and more cars every season headed south. Some for good. Setting up housekeeping. That's why Tallahassee was so keen on building that interstate out west, well clear of town and their groves, to handle all these tourists and new Floridians. That I-95 would be the end of them if it weren't for that NASA business, Janisse thought, and Pearl thought, NASA giving folks a reason to exit and poke around. So maybe all this outer space business would turn out to be a good thing, after all. Even if the damn Feds already poached some of his island acres, laid down rules on how he could manage the rows they didn't want at the north end, what equipment he could leave overnight and what equipment he needed to tote back over the Haulover and off their top secret island now.

Melody and Clay reached the groves soon enough, whirring by on the right. He never tired of gazing into the patterned rows from the highway like this. What did Ike tell him the other day? That some famous ballet fellow, name started with a B, Bala-something or another, figured out how to arrange his dancers up there on the stage after admiring an orange grove, these perfectly spaced trees. He knew all manner of things, Ike, not much of it useful, but interesting anyway. It was good to have a fellow like Ike around. Clay hoped he was wrong about what he worried Ike's pretty wife was up to. Hardly objective about such matters, Clay. The thought bolstered his spirits some. Maybe his imagination had just gotten the better of him. Maybe Melody had an errand or two she needed to get done in town before heading up to Deland. He surveyed the fresh-painted sandwich boards side of the highway as they neared the stand. GOLDENS AHEAD, the first one. Mile later, YOU'RE ALMOST THERE. What would Ike's pretty wife do once they reached the property, and what would Clay do? He'd have to just drive past if she stopped, turn around and head back home. Couldn't talk to Erma with Melody looming. But no. She had reached her drive and the stand and just kept going north on the highway, up toward Deland, Clay chose to believe. He hoped Ike and his family would hold themselves, and their acres, together. He hoped they'd stay on.

Clay could tend to business now with Erma, Ike's pretty wife safely up the highway. Half an eye still fixed on the spec of the Pontiac off in the distance, Clay slowed to a crawl to keep from skidding as he pulled his car over the crunchy oyster-shell parking strip. It rocked on its soft suspension like a vessel at sea. Only one other car in the lot. Good. Erma wouldn't be too busy. He swung open the car door and exhaled as he set both feet down on the oyster shells. Now when did he start doing that, setting both feet down on the ground at the same time to lift himself out his car? An old man thing to do, that was. Hell. GOLDENS ARE HERE, he read the yellow-and-black painted marquee above the stand. Funny name for the stand. Ike never did give him a straight answer about that stand name. Just gave one of those cat that ate the canary grins.

The customers, a young fair-haired couple wearing crisp vacationing clothes, were busy filling up their red nets with Parson Browns. Ike had filled his wood bins to the brim, hoping to sell more than his usual share from the stand, Clay figured, seeing as they couldn't get all of them off the trees to the packinghouse. Levi and his meddling. Good thing Ike didn't know it was his own foreman's child causing all their troubles. Good thing he didn't know that. Good thing he had no idea his foreman's son was acting familiar with his pretty wife, too. Ike had a fair bit of Christian kindness in him, especially for a Jew-fellow, but he wouldn't have no choice but put Ted out on his ear if he knew about Levi. Grower could only tolerate so much.

Erma'd already spotted him, Clay knew. Because she seemed busy writing something down with a pencil next to the cash register, probably so she wouldn't have to look up at Clay and decide what face to make. What on earth did she need to be writing down?

"Erma," he said, bothering the gravel in his throat.

She looked up now. "Clay," she said. Her voice sounded the same as it always had. Eerily so. He drank in her flesh with his eyes from across the scarred wooden counter. Lovely woman still. The cheeks sagged some over her jaws, true. Crow's feet beside the eyes, but not one line across her forehead. Hair gray, like what was left of his own. But her color. Paler now, seemed to Clay. Almost coffee-cream. He glanced down at his own nut-brown forearms and hands, oddly darker than they were years ago. Darker even than Erma's color. The sun had weathered away the white and the black, leaving them both somewhere in between. Old was what mostly remained of them now. Both of them old.

"It's never sat right, way I left things," he heard himself say. That's not what he came here to say. Beside the point. So why did these words spill from his mouth?

Erma's brow knitted itself together to make a few wrinkles appear between her eyes, as if she was just as surprised by his words as he was. After all these years. "It wasn't your fault, Clay." She paused here, inhaled through her nostrils as if collecting her thoughts from the fall air. She looked over Clay's shoulder at the fair-haired couple in crisp vacationing clothes to make sure they weren't listening. "Not your fault alone, anyway."

"That's why I stayed clear out on the island those ten years. On Granddaddy's first acres."

"Let me know if you good folks need some help, hear?" she called out to the couple. Their presence made her uncomfortable, Clay gathered. Or his presence, mostly.

"We're finished," the man called. Clay stepped aside as the young fellow toted his two red nets toward the register. The woman trailed behind clasping two jars of Ike's honey in her little paws.

"Morning, praise Jesus," Clay said.

"Praise Jesus," the man replied. He set the bags down on the cement slab floor, while the wife placed the glass jars of honey on the counter.

"And these postcards," the young lady uttered, plucking a random assortment from the rack, placing them like a poker hand on the scarred wooden counter. She lifted a hand and put it between her husband's shoulder blades, briefly, before withdrawing, waiting for her husband and Erma to complete the transaction. So, Clay thought, the fellow carried the heavy oranges while the wife carted the small items. He handled the money, while she patted his back and waited. It was a nice thing to see, the way a couple got on without words. Something Clay didn't take much notice of as a younger fellow. After a moment, the couple was gone, skidding onto the dusty highway, leaving oyster shell waves lapping on the parking strip, a chalky dust cloud. Ike would have to rake the sun-bleached shells soon, maybe order a new truckload at Clyde's to keep the dust down.

"I know why you lit out to the island," Erma picked up their thread now that they were alone. "That I known, Clay. You needn't have. We were only children. Careless children. Stupid grove children drunk on orange blossoms. But only children. Seems especially so looking back. I barely remember that crazy skinny gal who got herself into trouble." Here Erma showed her teeth, lifted her fine fingertips to touch a cheek, dotted now with age spots, remembering with some fondness, it seemed, the younger, crazier, skinnier Erma.

"Well Ted swooped in and saved the day, thank heavens. Stand up fellow. That's why you can laugh now, I suppose." This sounded bitter, he knew, as if he had wished her ill at the time, or wished her ill now. Which he hadn't. Which he didn't. And so he added: "A good husband Ted's been to you these years. I've taken solace in that."

"Yes. All told."

"And fruitful. Fruitful too. The Lord opened your womb like he did for Leah. That's why you named the boy Levi. Don't suppose I'm wrong about that. Levi, son of Jacob's first wife, the unloved wife."

"It occurred to me, Clay, I admit. Daddy was a preacher, after all. But most of all I liked the name. The sound of it. So did Theodore. I could have named him Reuben. Levi wasn't Leah's firstborn son. Don't make too much—"

"And Pearl barren these many years. Me without so much as a daughter. The groves without a proper heir. The Feds'll probably have them all before too long. For that NASA business. Hard not to see the Lord in it. After what happened. Me without so much as a daughter."

These words seemed to prick Erma, who lifted a slender hand to her chest as if to keep her heart inside.

"That's how you think, Clay Griffin? That's the good Lord to you?" She made a clucking noise with her tongue. Her eyes welled. "Gracious."

A slow fly buzzed thick and lazy. Erma batted at it and seemed to make contact.

"You poor man," she continued. "Poor Pearl," she said at a higher, more strident, pitch, as if Pearl had just occurred to her, lifting a hand to her mouth now, speaking through her fingers. "Poor Pearl all these years, living under that yoke. Too much for any woman to bear. And such a brave face she wears. All these years. Such a brave face, Pearl."

Clay didn't like where the conversation had meandered. They had careened off the road. What had Clay come here to discuss? A matter of more immediate, earthly urgency. He steeled himself.

"I didn't come here to talk about me. Or Pearl. It's Levi. He's in trouble. You must know, Erma. The field-workers. Their strike. I warned Ted months ago. But now Levi's gone and done it. Riled 'em up. Oranges rotting on their stems these three counties on account of Levi's pamphlets, his rabble-rousing. Everyone knows it's him, even if they don't know he's Levi after all these years. That suit of his. The field-workers didn't get filled up with notions out of thin air. They don't know any of those fancy words, workplace protections and whatnot. Negro in the suit the cause. Growers won't stand for it. Just a nigger to them, no matter his pressed suit. His yellow tie. You hear what I'm saying, Erma!? He'll have his neck broke from some wrecking crew any day now he don't hightail it out of here!"

Clay could feel spittle at the corner of this mouth, but before wiping it away waited a moment for his words to sink in with Erma. He wouldn't say anything about his suspicions regarding Levi and Melody. Not to Erma. The topic cut too close to the bone. She wouldn't believe it, he suspected. Not coming from him, anyway. In any case, he felt he had already said enough to spur Erma into action.

Her eyes remained moist. Clay wasn't sure for whom: barren Pearl or endangered Levi, or maybe for the both of them. Maybe for all of them.

"Think I don't know that, Clay Griffin? Think I haven't told him to get? My own flesh and blood? He won't leave, though. Not yet."

Clay was flummoxed by Erma's response. With Ted at Sonny's Good Food over his chicken and waffles, his macaroni and mustard greens, it was different. Men were proud. But Erma was Levi's mother, and it was different for mothers. A mother would force her fool son to flee the kind of danger Levi faced.

"Have you all lost your godforsaken minds? What do you mean he won't leave yet? What's he waiting on?"

Erma didn't answer right away, inhaled deeply through her nostrils as if seeking wisdom from the east wind. A gnatcatcher wheezed from a thatch of palmetto and slash pine across the highway.

"Well?" Clay pressed.

"*You*, I think. I think he's waiting on you, Clay Griffin."

So it wasn't over quite yet, as he hoped it would be over after he spoke some sense into Erma. There was business still to transact. With Levi. The knowledge stretched out on its haunches against Clay's insides, making them smart.

Thirty-one

THE ORANGE-STAINED SKIN stung beneath the nail of Isaac's forefinger, the nail he'd used, forgoing his budding knife, to burrow beneath the disappointing epicarp and mesocarp peel layers of at least twenty of his experimental Navels by now. Failed experiments, all.

So how to explain this strange sensation behind his ribs? His insides, his very organs, oddly oxygenated. His respirations, effortless, as if an obstruction he hadn't known existed had been cleared. Not crushed now, Isaac Golden. No, definitely not crushed. There was a curious smile on his face. He could feel it there, stretched over his mouth, his wet teeth exposed to the cool ocean air that made the citrus leaves dance. He lifted his hand to touch his lips.

Was he losing his mind?

No, Isaac assured himself. So the Navels were unimproved. Just as the Hamlin and Parson Brown crosses were unimproved. Just as the Valencias would prove unimproved in a matter of weeks, he somehow knew.

Those pesky, miscegenate citrus embryos!

He'd have to grub out these acres, finally. That or go under. What of it? he thought, tossing up the last worthless Navel head-high before his chest, then catching it again in his thick mitt. The weight of the failed orange, its skin pitted with Isaac's inquiries, felt good in his hand, smacking down against his flesh.

There was something else he was ready to do now. Something else that would help his cash flow. That involved Ted. So that's settled too, he thought. That too. Thinking this made him breathe even easier. He knew, somehow, that he'd made the right decision, that there was a fine line between determination and stubbornness, between principle and vanity. He felt better. Funny, how losing, maybe, could turn into winning. Or maybe winning and losing were silly concepts to apply to a life. Life boiled down mostly to the big woolly in between. Why had it taken Isaac so long to absorb this simple fact?

An odd desire welled up inside him. He hadn't the will to contain it. He stepped back from the experimental top-worked tree, branches still aflutter with white mesh bags over disappointing, unimproved fruit, stepped into the clear atop the cowpeas and peanuts, gazed eastward over the treetops, then wound back his arm, took a little stutter-step and flung the failed orange in a high arc just right of the harvestable Hamlin rows. He returned to the tree, plucked a separate orange from under its protective mesh and threw it the same direction, but even farther, as if he were the Phillies' Richie Ashburn throwing the Dodgers' Cal Abrams out at the plate. (Good for Philly, Isaac remembered, but bad for the Jews.) It felt uncommonly good to heave these oranges, baseball-style. As if he was thirteen again. Again, was he losing his mind? No, he assured himself. He wasn't. He threw a few more oranges, savoring the release, the return of his boyhood form, until his shoulder began to smart.

That's how Ted found him, rubbing his sore shoulder.

"Ike!" His foreman yelled. "Isaac! You done lost your mind!"

He heard his foreman, smiled, but wasn't quite ready to listen yet. His shoulder rested, he plucked another Navel, wound up as if he were a pitcher this time, and flung one last ruined orange. "Ouch," he said, rubbing his shoulder again. Now he was ready to speak with Ted. He'd summoned, him, truly—aimed far enough rightward that he knew an orange wouldn't actually strike the party—not unlike Walt had summoned Isaac with his shotgun blasts at the swallowtails some months ago.

"You're gonna hit one of the pickers, Isaac!" Ted warned falsetto. "They're hopeless enough at harvesting as it is, these skinny Sanford boys, without you raining down oranges at them."

Isaac nodded. "I knew where y'all were." He stood there on the cowpeas and gathered his breath for his next words. A cardinal filled the silence with its lusty song. *Alive! Alive! Alive!*

"I'm thinking about selling some acres, Ted. Ten acres or so."

"Oh?" Ted's face, shiny with sweat, brightened.

"Not these acres. Not Eli's grove. I'll improve these acres myself, one way or another. My responsibility. But I was thinking of those ten-year tree acres at the edge near Hammock Road."

Ted's expression turned poker-face sober as he nodded, as he lifted his white rag to his patchy pate to wipe away his sweat. But then he shed his poker face just as fast, which Isaac appreciated.

"You sure, doctor? Good acres, those, now we took care of the scale. Those fancy wasps of yours."

"Sure I'm sure. I'm not giving them to you, realize, or even selling them to *you*, specifically. This isn't forty acres and a mule . . ."

For some reason, Isaac felt the need to clarify, even if he wasn't completely certain what he was clarifying. He fumbled through the words, instead, hoping the words that came to him would be true words.

"I'm offering them up for sale, see, and I know you're interested, and it only seems right to give you first dibs, foreman all these years. But there's no special treatment here. So no need to feel grateful is what I'm saying. If it's grateful you feel, even. You catch my meaning?"

Ted's hands were on his hips now as he listened, his white rag dripping from the waistline of his Dickies. "Yes I do, Isaac Golden," he said. "I sure think I do." Ted cleared his throat, lifted his rag to wipe the fresh wet that rose to his face. An insect sizzled from somewhere in the foliage. Isaac could tell by the new furrows that formed across Ted's shiny forehead that something else had occurred to him, something he wasn't sure he wanted to say, but something that spilled out of Ted's mouth anyway.

"Sure you won't catch the devil from the co-op?" the foreman asked. "Selling me those quality co-op acres?"

"No," Isaac said. "I'm not sure."

"The Navels, Mel."

Melody watched as her husband slid one of the oranges before her across the kitchen table, between the Lucite pitcher and the mashed potato boat. He had washed his hands in the sink while Eli recited the *hamotzi*, but two thick fingertips were still stained orange, she noticed. "Here they are, Mel. Try peeling one open yourself. Go ahead."

Melody looked toward Eli, who offered no counsel, over-chewed a brisket mouthful just so he wouldn't have to say anything, it seemed, as perplexed as she was by his father's gesture. She didn't know what to make of the proposal, these crusty, uncleaned, unwaxed Navels teetering on the table. It seemed a challenge, as if Isaac maybe blamed her for the stubbornly thin peels, which she could discern just by looking at them, the shiny, too-smooth skin beneath their dusting of grove dirt. Hardly puckered at all like those California Navels, their more peelable skins thick as tree bark. No sunburst creases projected from the stem end, as Isaac had hoped to encourage. So why did Isaac's expression seem so bright, almost euphoric?

"Is that truly necessary, Isaac?"

"Oh, I guess not. Might as well know, though, Mel. None of the crosses worked again." Isaac sighed as he chewed his meat, but it wasn't a defeated sigh. Or not only a defeated sigh. There was something else to it. Was he mad? Melody feared.

"Sorry Dad," Eli said now, cutting his next slice of meat more softly than usual, it seemed to Melody, so the knife wouldn't screech against the Pfaltzgraff.

"Thanks, sport," he said, then tousled Eli's wispy dark hair, which made Melody lift a palm high on her chest.

Sarah must have sensed the change in atmospheric pressure too. Her father's palpable intensity and frustration transformed into—what? Melody wondered—because the child reached splayed fingers from her high chair toward her father's mouth beside her, managed to touch the strange mouth that had issued all these strange words in this strange voice she hadn't heard before, as if to verify the source of the strange soundings. Sarah's gleaming fingers were sticky from the applesauce Melody had pureed. The sticky touch seemed to take Isaac by surprise, who instinctively grasped Sarah's tiny wrist and turned toward her, his eyes opened wide, as if he had just now noticed this presence at the table, his daughter, which might have been the case.

"Now let's not get Daddy dirty, Sarah," said Melody. The child was done eating, she knew, because she'd already moved on from eating the applesauce in her red plastic bowl to painting her tray with the paste. Melody rose to retrieve her so that she wouldn't bother Isaac in his curious mood, but then Melody sat down again just as fast because of what Isaac did, which she didn't expect him to do, having no reason to expect it from any of his previous exchanges with his daughter.

"Ah, Sarah-le," he said, holding her splayed fingers to his lips and looking at her now, truly seeing her, Melody noticed. His eyes were moist. "That's Daddy's mouth," he said. "Mouth. And this is your mouth." Melody watched as he touched Sarah's mouth with the orange-stained fingertips of his other hand. "Can you say mouth?"

That voice, Melody marveled. She hadn't heard her husband's voice for so long. She'd heard him speak, of course, which had tricked her, because that hadn't been his voice. Not his real voice. Not *this* voice. Which she hadn't realized until now.

Where had her husband been?

Sarah wouldn't speak, only smiled at the perplexing question.

"She can say moo!" Eli declared brightly, introducing his sister to his father, which made Melody happy and sad at the same time. She glanced toward Eli, who looked back at her, raising his fine eyebrows, also rapt with his father's performance.

"Moo then," Isaac said. "Say moo, Sarah."

"What sound does a cow make?" Eli offered the proper prompt.

"*Moooo,*" Sarah uttered now, echoed by family clapping, bounced in her plastic seat, crinkled up her nose to flash new wet teeth, delighted with the uncommon attention. "*Moooo!*"

After dinner, Melody left the wreckage of soiled plates in the sink to wash later, freed the segments of fresh Duncan halves from skin and rind and seared brown sugar across the glistening plateaus in the broiler. The family decamped for the television room with their dessert so they wouldn't miss Edwards' broadcast.

"They sure put that wall up quick," Melody uttered, the Berlin Wall having been completed.

"Sure did," Isaac said.

"What's it for?" Eli asked, then slurped a sticky-sweet grapefruit dollop from a tablespoon. Melody looked toward her husband, deferred to his counsel. He set his spoon down on the tray-table. She heard her husband exhale as he contemplated his response.

"To keep the people on one side separate from the people on the other side," he finally answered.

"It's bad, right?"

Her son could tell that the wall (or Anti-Fascist Protection Rampart, as the communists were calling it, apparently) was bad. Eli could tell, maybe, by his father's terse response, or by the sober tone of Edwards' broadcast, or by the ominous guard towers along the concrete walls in the footage over Edwards' shoulder. Or maybe walls were inherently disconcerting.

"Yes," her husband admitted. "It's bad, Eli."

Later. The bedroom.

"I've decided to grub out most of Eli's grove. Not all of it, maybe. But most. Sell some acres to Ted, too. Just ten acres or so."

"Oh?"

The room was dark, husband and wife having completed their ablutions, having slipped beneath the skin of the bed sheets. He had waited for the dark, Melody thought to herself, too ashamed or upset, maybe, to broach the subject of grubbing out Eli's acres in the light. Yet he didn't seem ashamed or upset.

A frog chirped somewhere outside, in or near the garden. She liked the muted outdoor sound of manifold creatures serenading them at night—better than the vehicular hum of Philadelphia—but didn't this frog know that winter was coming on?

"It's a good thing your pies have taken off at the stand, Mel. You're the only reason we'll survive this season. You know that, right? I'm not sure you know. But you *should* know."

Her husband's voice, again.

Melody's heart swelled with sudden sympathy for her husband, who seemed so brave now in his defeat. His ruined experiments.

"There's nothing wrong with planting ordinary oranges, Isaac," she heard herself say, deflecting the compliment on her pies. "Ordinary oranges are miracle enough, I think. Don't you?"

"Yes. I do. Commissioner wants me to plant some of his experimental grapefruit also. Irradiated the seeds. Came up with fewer segments. I already budded them." Fewer segments intrigued her, but she knew enough not to broadcast her enthusiasm for one of the commissioner's initiatives.

"So you'll plant them?"

"I'm not sure. Maybe. I think maybe I've been worrying about all the wrong things, Mel. I'm trying to sort out what really matters. But it's not easy, is it?"

Her husband didn't mean to accuse her with this question—he couldn't know about Levi, could he?—yet Melody couldn't help but hear it as such. The frog chortled. Isaac shifted his weight on the bedsprings.

"We'll have a better harvest next year," she assured him. "You'll see, darling. You'll all come to terms with the field-workers in town, don't you think?"

"I do think. Hope so, anyway. Can't go on like this. Everyone knows."

"At least you don't sound like them anymore," Melody heard herself say.

"Huh?" Isaac asked, stirred the bed sheets as he turned to open a shoulder toward her voice.

"You sound like you again now."

"Oh. Well, that's good I guess." He turned back on his side, away from Melody. "I'm tired. Real tired. Goodnight, Mel."

"Okay, dear. You sleep. Goodnight."

She wouldn't see Levi again. That much was clear to her. Isaac, her Isaac, had returned. But could things ever be right between them? If she didn't confess? She kept silent as she brooded, lifted the thin lower bed sheet to her chin for succor as she waited for counsel to emerge from some mysterious quarter. The frog continued to sing its pleasing but inscrutable tune. Nuggets of ballyhooed wisdom rattled inside her brain, absolute, unambiguous phrases that contained words such as honesty and deceit, truth and lies, husband and wife. They exerted a powerful hold, these words and phrases. Words rose within her now from somewhere deep, threatened to escape, words prompted by the absolute and unambiguous wisdom she'd absorbed from *McCall's* maybe, from the programs on the television, from the very air in America. She bit her plump bottom lip with her incisors to seal the words inside for just a bit longer. Then she released her stinging lip from her top teeth, opened her dry mouth to ask her husband to forgive her, as required, but only exhaled a harmless puff of air, deciding that she would forgive herself, instead.

Thirty-two

Hershey's syrup. Gold Medal Flour. Crisco. Brillo pads. Eggs. Milk. Jiffy Pop. Baking potatoes. Onions. Sherbet. Syrup. Cream cheese. Cottage cheese. Campbell's soup. Wonder Bread. Spaghetti. Cheerios. Melody scanned the looping cursive of her shopping list as she strolled the Piggly Wiggly aisles, having already returned Thaddeus Simpson's "joyous day" greeting upon entry. Sarah was big enough now to sit up in the cart, wouldn't tolerate being left outside in the perambulator beneath the magnolias' leather foliage. Sarah rarely napped anymore, coaxing Melody toward a heightened alertness too, which explained, perhaps, how she noticed the stock boy straight away so far down the aisle, crouched on the dingy linoleum. He was sorting cereal boxes in a huff, reaching elbow-deep inside the shelf, exasperated by whoever had rifled through their modest inventory.

"Hello, Luke," she greeted him in crisp, decisive syllables.

"Ma'am." His reply was a jagged shard he flung her way without rising, without meeting her glance, quite, his eyes barely painting her shoulder. Well, it was his prerogative if he wanted to be this way. Sour. Sullen. She plucked the box of Cheerios from the shelf at shoulder-level a few feet away, grateful that the box was well clear of Luke's hemisphere, glanced down toward the stock boy to notice his indifferent shave, the inflamed dollops of earlobe flesh. He'd worn a different face ever since Melody had artlessly rebuffed his affections that day at the stand, when Levi's visit had upset her equilibrium. Months ago that seemed like years. Sarah, her plump calves and Mary Janes dangling from the cart, stared down toward the streak of pink bald atop Luke's head, his aggressive part. Melody wondered if

Sarah would mutter something from her perch, seek to secure Luke's attentions, but Sarah held her tongue—good—seemed to realize that the stock boy, for whatever reason, just wasn't interested in her anymore. Melody went along her way, resisted the urge to hurry, the whine of her cart's wheels, the buzz of a failing fluorescent bulb overhead, punctuating their awkward encounter.

Luke wasn't so towheaded anymore. He'd taken to applying some sort of pomade that darkened the strands, taken to that aggressive part to tamp down his cowlick, which Melody didn't expect she'd miss. She barely recognized the new Luke. It seemed to her that there was the face you were born with, and not much you could do about that—Jack LaLanne's face-sculpting exercises aside—and then there was the face you presented to the world. It might be that Luke's new face was only the unhappy face he reserved for her. Yet something told her otherwise, that something larger had turned in him.

"Sarah-Sarah-Sarah-Sarah," she uttered as she turned the corner, smiled toward her daughter, sought comfort in the sound of her girl's name in the weirdly vibrating air, which made Sarah flash her corn niblet teeth, two new uppers now to make six total, four on top and two below. The dairy aisle. She reached for a Borden's cottage cheese container. The plastic cylinder felt cold against her palm. She was just about to set it down in the cart when she recognized the old man heading toward her, crouched over his empty cart. Recognized him as someone she knew, anyway, but couldn't immediately place given the strange environs. *Clay*, it suddenly occurred to her as he came closer, cracked his jagged mouth open to advertise his mottled teeth, wearing an expression just south of a smile. Clay, of course. Yet what was he doing here? He looked older. The field-workers' strike had taken a toll, she presumed. The tenuous harvest. More, he just didn't like not getting on with his neighbors, white or Negro. Poor Clay.

"Melody," he greeted her, parked beside, straightened himself to stand taller. The unforgiving glare of the fluorescents wasn't doing him any favors. Some sort of crust lipsticked both corners of his mouth. Fissures she hadn't noticed before tore across his cheeks at strange trajectories. Smelled like those Winstons he smoked all day, too. Melody tried not to shrink from the stale odor of him, because she liked Clay, who'd been kind to them from the start. She suspected, but didn't know, that he'd been their champion about town these past few years, assured his Christian neighbors that the Goldens were all right people, God-fearing in their own way. Like the Krupnicks.

"Hello Clay. Don't think I've ever seen *you* in the grocery store. What's the occasion?"

Bright notes. She'd try to pick Clay up some. No point moping about. The past few days, in truth, had been good days for Melody, field-workers' strike aside. Ever since Isaac had ambled in from the grove, sounding again like her Isaac. The experimental Navels having failed once again, he'd decided to sell some acres to Ted and prove up Eli's grove with tried and true rootstocks and scions. For the time being, anyway. Miracle enough in tried-and-true oranges. He had showered Sarah with affection that night and continued to ply her with pets and words. Just yesterday evening, as she prepared spaghetti and meatballs for supper, she heard Sarah's squeals and dashed to the den, where she spied her husband flat on his back on the pine floor, propping their giggling red-faced daughter up into the air with the oversize plank of his calloused foot, Eli cheering the pair on from the sofa.

"Sometimes Pearl sends me with a list," Clay was saying now. It was tough for Melody to gauge the spirit of the remark. It might have been a mildly humorous explanation, but not the way he said it, quite. He couldn't, or wouldn't, rise to her desired altitude. Unusual for Clay. Yes, something was on his mind. The trouble with the harvest, likely.

"Enjoying our cooler weather?" she asked.

Clay nodded, but didn't say anything.

"Isaac says you might all come to terms with the field-workers soon," she persisted, hoping to plant a seed that might take root. "That would be good. For them and for you, right?"

"Maybe. Hope so." He pursed his pallid lips to weigh the possibility inside his mouth, it seemed, extended a calloused pinkie toward Sarah, who gripped it, smiled. Melody reached a bare hand toward her daughter to wipe away the sheet of clear saliva that oozed below her smile, the neckline of Sarah's pink shopping dress stained already in a dark half-moon from the wet. Perhaps she was teething again. Melody, having forgotten to bring a nappy, dried her saliva-soaked hand on the hip of her pleated dress. "We offered the terms your fine husband first proposed, whole thing might be settled already."

It might have been a compliment paid to Isaac. Yet something about the way Clay said *your fine husband*, something sharp, accusatory—directed at Isaac? at her?—something about the way he kept his eyes trained down on Sarah as she gripped his finger so he wouldn't have to look straight at her face. It was Melody's turn to speak, but she didn't know what to say, how she might steer their conversation onto smoother terrain. She had already mentioned their pleasant weather now that the rainy season was behind them. She was about to clear her throat and wish Clay a good afternoon, cap their conversation as gracefully as she could manage, ask him to give her regards to Pearl, but then a lady in a gray dress rattled up the aisle with her cart, commanding their attention. Melody recognized the woman, roughly Clay and Pearl's age. Willa Piedmont, whom Melody didn't know very well, as Willa didn't bother with Junior League anymore, as Melody didn't attend church, of course. She took the measure of Willa's approach, her severe salt-and-pepper bob, the stern slopes and curves of her spectacle frames, the support hosiery wrapped around Willa's thick ankles below the knees of her gray dress.

"Willa," Clay said, Willa within earshot now. There was a houndstooth pattern to the gray dress, Melody noticed, a prettier dress than Melody had discerned from afar.

"Clay," Willa replied, studying the various tubs of margarine above the frames of her spectacles. Clay tried playing a thumb-wrestling game with Sarah, which seemed to amuse Sarah even if she didn't know what to do with her tiny paws. Melody wiped the fresh spittle from Sarah's chin, listened to her daughter's steady breaths, listened to her own breaths. They would wait for Willa to leave before resuming their conversation. Somehow, these were the terms that she and Clay had struck by their immovable presence, terms of sober confidentiality that unsettled Melody, the weight it leant to the words they might share next. Willa, too, seemed to know that Clay and Melody were waiting for her to retrieve her dairy items and move along. Melody could tell by the way Willa chuffed out her nostrils and twisted her lips as she finally plucked her Mazola from the shelf, deposited the tub in the cart alongside her canned goods, by the way Willa cleared her throat with unnecessary vigor. She gripped the cart's broad handle—Melody noticed her platinum wedding band glinting dully beneath the fluorescents—and wheeled the cart along across the linoleum, held her nose high to advertise her undiminished self-regard. Willa felt rushed by their conspiratorial presence and refused to hide her displeasure.

"My best to Pearl," Willa uttered as she strolled past, tilting her head toward Melody, not seeming to notice Sarah at all.

"And my regards to Bo."

Melody watched after Willa as she made her way down the aisle, the old hen refusing to take a backward glance out of pride more than discretion, it seemed to Melody. Clay waited until Willa cleared the bend before speaking his next words, which added even more heft to them.

"It's a tough thing to figure, don't you think, Melody?" He lifted his gray eyes from Sarah to look at her now.

"What's that?"

"Doing right by others. Doing right by you and yourn. A tough thing to figure. Don't you think, Melody?"

She lifted a hand to her heart to keep it inside. Clay knew something. Or thought he knew something. She could feel her heart with her hand fluttering against her breastplate, could hear her heart beating below her throat, could hear, too, her inhalations and exhalations, the hum of the refrigerants inside the shelving cooling the milk and eggs, the cottage cheese and sour cream and yogurt. A housefly zigzagged before the backdrop of breads the other side of the aisle, disappeared. Why weren't there any groceries in Clay's cart? And where was that shopping list he had referenced? He didn't have any shopping to do, Melody realized. He had seen her enter the Piggly Wiggly with Sarah in tow. Without Isaac. He'd entered the store to speak these words to her. *Your fine husband. Doing right by you and yourn.* He wasn't talking about the field-workers. Pearl, as Melody had feared months ago, had said something to him about the strange well-dressed Negro at the stand looking too familiar with Melody. Of course. Or, worse, far worse, Clay had seen her leaving that strange house west side of town.

"We're not talking about the field-workers anymore, are we Clay?"

Clay lifted his woolly eyebrows, surprised by her boldness, she knew.

"No. No we're not."

"I suppose it *is* difficult then," she heard herself say, cautious, like one in danger, Clay cutting her off now, fearful of her next words, maybe, saying, "I sure enough made my own share of mistakes. Mistakes that caused real hurt. Hurt all around. Hate to see the young folk go through the same foolishness."

It was her turn to be surprised. These words about his own share of mistakes. What mistakes? She considered afresh the crust lipsticked inside both corners of Clay's mouth, the fissures that tore across his cheeks at strange trajectories, the acrid tobacco stench that seemed to rise from his pores. A few minutes ago, she thought she knew at a glance what troubled Clay. But she didn't. The field-workers' strike, the clumsily harvested fruit receiving lower grades by the bird dogs at Nevin's, the fewer oranges and grapefruit moldering on the scaffolding of his tree branches might not be the only thing—or even the main thing—that accounted for Clay's distress. There might be something else, entirely. The mistakes he had just mentioned. The mistakes that caused real hurt. Sexual in nature? Likely. His eyes did tend to wander, despite his age, despite his finer qualities. What did she really know about Clay Griffin? Nothing. Nothing of his past, anyway. But Clay wouldn't hurt her, she realized. Whatever he knew or suspected or imagined about her, Clay wouldn't do her harm. He'd have talked with Isaac if that was his intent. He only wished to help her, help Isaac, in his own fashion. Her heart settled back down into the grotto of her chest. She lowered her hand to Sarah's plump calf above her Mary Janes, drew courage from its solidity. He only wished to help them, which made Melody want to help Clay.

"You sure they were clear-cut mistakes?" Melody heard herself say. "Sure it was foolishness? Foolishness alone, anyway?"

"Melody?"

"I've been wondering, Clay. If we're truly talking here." Clay nodded. "I've been wondering about the things we look back on and call mistakes. Wondering if it's only the looking back that makes them so. Wondering lately if some of those things weren't actually mistakes in the here and now. Or if mistake, maybe, is just the wrong way to look at things sometimes. Not the whole way, anyway. Wondering whether we ought to be kinder to ourselves."

"Afraid you lost me, Melody Golden." A new furrow rose between Clay's woolly brows to complement all the others. Melody drew a healthy plug of refrigerated air into her lungs through her fine nostrils. Clay didn't understand what she was talking about. She wasn't sure that she fully understood what she was saying. Except for the last bit she had uttered. She believed in that last bit, wished that Clay would take that last bit to heart, be kinder to himself. In the meantime, Melody would offer what kindness she could.

"It's all right, Clay. You don't have to worry." She reached for his forearm, depleted of its fur, spattered with liver spots. His arm felt cold. The skin, slack, weathered. "You don't have to worry about me. About Isaac. The children." She wanted to say Levi's name, felt she owed him that much, that he ought to be part of her moral arithmetic, part of Clay's moral arithmetic. Levi, the person most in peril. Physically, anyway. But she couldn't muster the reckless courage to summon his name from her throat, where it settled like a stone. "Not anymore you don't have to worry, Clay. I promise."

"That's a comfort." Clay's new furrow vanished. He gathered the chilled air into his lungs as if to make up for lost breaths, his chest rising and falling beneath his plaid shirt.

Sarah bucked in the cart, hoping to make it go. "Ma-ma-ma-ma-ma-ma-ma," she uttered.

"God bless, Melody. You and yourn."

"You too, Clay. God bless you and Pearl, too."

Clay stroked Sarah's cheek with the papery-soft outside of his pinkie to say goodbye, which seemed to tickle Sarah. He leaned over his cart once again for ballast as he ambled off, elbows braced on the handle, headed toward whatever meats or imperishables he'd likely purchase to justify his strange presence in the grocery store. Melody watched after him until he turned the corner, then glanced down at her hand, surprised to notice the Borden's cottage cheese container she had plucked from the shelf, warm now inside the seashell of her fist.

Thirty-three

WEEKS LATER. A freezing cold crept down upon the river. Which would have been enough.

Dr. Johnson of the Frost Warning Service in Lakeland had sent out his teletype bulletin four days earlier. The postmaster on Main, a block up from Janisse's, had taped it to the front window. Northwest winds pushing Arctic air over the entire peninsula. Growers up and down the state couldn't count on the Appalachians to buffer the frigid air on account of the western currents. The river growers could expect sustained temps, the teletype warned, below twenty-eight degrees. But they had time to see to their preparations. And the Negro field-workers in town, along with the growers themselves, had decided to set aside their dispute for a couple days, negotiate an emergency wage to pull what mature fruit they might, set up the rusty oil and coke heaters, re-bank the younger trees above the vulnerable bud unions, wrap the trunks inside thick layers of newspaper sealed tight with flax twine. Walt would use his overhead sprinklers instead of the heaters, because it hadn't been so cold for near fifty years along the river, and hell if he'd spend so much coin on labor when the shiftless coloreds would have been forcibly conscripted back in the day, a decent sheriff on patrol, and hell if he'd foot the high cost of crude when he'd mostly just end up heating Ike's grove downwind.

And so it might have only been the night of a fifty-year freeze along the river.

Which would have been enough.

Purple twilight yielded to a half-moon, half-dark night. The constellations, the major ones anyway, peeked through lazy clouds, doddering southeast with the Arctic wind. The cold mentholated air ushered most people indoors. And quieted most of the little birds, which huddled within the protective foliage. And closed up the cassia and mimosa leaves, which folded themselves shut like moth wings. And shut the lips of innumerable knee-high blossoms, roadside: sage and snakeroot and dayflower and beardtongue. And the taller wiregrass whispered secrets through the gusts. And the possums and the raccoons and the skunks and the silent bats, skittering across the half-lit sky, took over on shift work. And then quickly retreated to shelter.

And Ted was rambling past the whispering wiregrass clumps and slumbering roadside blossoms with their lips closed, having ushered the Deland field-workers onto the truck bed for the slow drive back. Town fellows had already finished their banking and wrapping and heater setup yesterday. Ready as they'd ever be, river groves. He'd flick on the heat for the cab if it weren't for the boys huddled up in back between the full-packed field boxes. Just wouldn't be right.

And Janisse shook the Jiffy Pop pan by its wire handle over the electric coils. She loved this new popcorn invention. But the fat inside the tin wasn't quite melted yet, so the kernels wouldn't rattle. She waited, then started skidding the pan across the heat again. The heat-freed kernels began to rattle. Sometimes the kernels burned if you didn't shake the pan enough. That was the only thing.

She felt his lips on her neck now as she tended the pan. They were wet, but not too wet. He'd moistened them just right with his tongue before sneaking up on her.

"Now Doyle. Now sugar. Just you wait, hear?"

And Isaac heard something on the party line, which didn't have anything to do with the weather.

And Eli checked on Sarah in her crib. Touched his fingertips to his lips, then reached down over the railing and pressed his fingertips against the greater warmth of her furry scalp. Kissed her like she was a Torah. Then he snuck out the back door, his jacket in hand, to his mother's garden. It was already a colder cold than he could remember ever feeling, which surprised him. His lungs tightened. He put on his too-small jacket. The rim of the hood was lined with raccoon fur. He tried breathing slow and deep. The air inside his bird nose made his boogers crunch. The burning crude from the heaters hurt his chest, but not too much. It was quieter, too, than what he thought was quiet before. Too cold for the bugs and the frogs and the crickets. He'd snuck out of the house with his too-small jacket to bury the bad note he'd found crumpled tight in the trash bin behind the stand, the note written in neat handwriting by someone, a man he could somehow tell, who *deeply regretted*—that was the phrase—that his mother couldn't see him anymore, who wished only contentment and God's grace for her, all of which sounded queer to Eli. There was something dirty about the letter, something Eli couldn't quite put his finger on, but definitely something dirty.

The earth would clean it all up, Eli hoped, poking his shovel beneath the soil, extra crusty on top already, on account of the cold. Few more hours and he wouldn't be able to stick the frozen ground with a shovel at all. He shoveled softly so his parents wouldn't hear him from inside. If they caught him, he'd just drop the shovel and fib that he was looking for his wildcat. And they'd believe him. The earth would clean it all up, he assured himself, just like the dirt cleaned the *flaishik* knives he used by accident on the butter. *Baruch atah adonai, elohaynu melech ha'olam . . .* He buried the note low, lower than the snapper carcasses all about. "There," he said, patting the pie-crust top with the back of the shovel. *Kashered.*

And Percy, squinting past his Spud menthol, brooded over his lousy hand inside Sonny's Good Food with Fred and Oliver and Terrance. He snatched the half-spent Spud from between his lips and flicked off the ashes in the tray.

"So it's settled," he stated more than asked, happy to get his mind off his lousy hand, stroking the slight rise of his chocolate mole on his cheek with the fingertips above his fuming Spud, wedged further down at the bottom of the V his fingers made.

"Yep," Fred said, eyeballing Terrance with greater purpose, waiting for him to play the trick. Terrance, Percy's partner, flicked down a four of spades. Now what the Sam Hill was he doing? Percy wondered, bringing his Spud to his lips. The last few puffs of his menthol were hot and bitter and made him cough.

"You done renege plain as day," Fred declared, as Percy knew Fred would declare. Couldn't get one that easy by old Fred, who chewed on his toothpick as if it were food so he wouldn't smoke so much.

"What book then?" Terrance asked.

"Second book, son," Fred answered past his toothpick, falsetto. "Five of clubs right there in your trick pile." Fred leaned back in his seat, lifted the front legs, rolled the broken toothpick across his top teeth with his tongue.

"Well played, pa'tnah," said Oliver through his Salem.

"Ah shucks," said Terrance.

"Hell," said Percy, stamping out his Spud in the ash tray. "Why'd you have to go and renege, T?" He was reckless, Terrance. Reckless like Ted's boy. Levi.

"Fetch anything else for you, gentlemen?" Josephine asked, nice as she was able. Sonny's pretty niece. She wore a wool coat over her apron now because Sonny already shut off the heat. Because the cold was already crawling under the door, which didn't have a proper sweep, Percy just noticed.

"More coffee, maybe," Oliver said, not looking up at her. She nodded and retreated, not quite scowling but none too happy, either. She wanted to close already, was sick and tired of them coming in and hardly eating nothing, low on scratch as they all were.

Josie returned with the coffee from the percolater. "Last round, Uncle says," she uttered. "Getting late." Percy liked that she lingered beside him, topping their mugs, lingered long enough to leave her smell in the air, better than their menthol smoke. Gardenias from her perfume, or maybe just her deodorant, which just barely overtook the grease and onions and cold, which smelled on her, too. If she was only five years older, Percy thought. If she wasn't likely set on college learning and college-learning men, Percy thought. All those books of hers up there on the bar.

"So it's settled, anyway, right Fred?" Percy sought again to confirm once Josephine pranced off. "I talk to Ike about the Valencias coming up if they don't fall off the trees after tonight. Negotiate terms. Christian kindness ought finally take hold, now we helped out with the freeze. And Levi knows full well we can't work odd jobs forever. Only so many hedges to prune, hereabouts."

"And houses to paint," Oliver said.

"And garbage to haul," Terrance declared.

"And porches and roofs to mend," said Percy.

"And houses for our womenfolk to clean," Fred noted. Mild laughter here, the kind that could be confused for coughing.

"And white folks' children for them to mind," Oliver picked up the thread once again. "Thirty cents a box sounding pretty dang good right about now."

"Pretty dang good," Fred echoed, then sipped at his coffee that had already lost most of its heat, having plucked the ruined toothpick from his mouth, discarding it in the ash pile.

"Better than a vagrancy charge and working the turpentine fields for nothin', like back in the day," Terrance said.

"What do you know from back in the day?" Oliver asked.

"Samuel said Sheriff Wright wasn't fixing on that," Percy said. "Not after we helped out these past few days."

"And colored vote counts for something now, I guess," said Terrance.

"Might not be sheriff's choice alone," Fred countered.

"Mm-hmm." Oliver inhaled the last of his Salem, making the butt glow, gathered the tricks without relish, laying the cards facedown in their row before him.

And Isaac couldn't believe what he heard on the party line.

And Peter King watched *The Andy Griffith Show* alone on the plaid sofa, because his little sisters were already asleep, because the show was on so late. But he was allowed to stay up and watch it, huddled beneath the warmth of the quilt, usually just draped over the sofa back, because it was his favorite show, and because he wasn't punished anymore for cutting up Eli's trees, carving that nasty word into one of them. He wasn't sure why he did all that, exactly. Eli just made him so angry, skinny and weak as he was, and Dean and the other boys lumping him in with that Rudolph the Red Nose just because his mom didn't let him do PE neither most times. *Gunsmoke* was his daddy's favorite show, so that's the one his daddy got to watch when he didn't want to watch *The Fight of the Week*, instead. Both his sisters' favorite show was the new one, that Walt Disney show in color. *General Electric Theater* was his mother's favorite show, so that's the one they all had to watch on Sunday instead of *Bonanza*, which they all liked better. Except for his mom, anyway.

❦

And Mary Beth was watching *87th Precinct*, because that Gena Rowlands could act. "Now *that's* a television program," she told Hyram, who nodded over his slice of chocolate pecan. "Now *that's* a proper young lady," she told Hyram. "Can teach that Mary Tyler Moore a thing or two," she told Hyram. "You listening, Hyram?"

❦

And Edwin enjoyed his strawberries and pound cake Connie fixed for him tonight. She didn't seem to want none. Just smiled at him across the table, not hardly looking at the children either side, squinting back the smoke from her menthol. She had reapplied her lipstick sometime after supper, he just noticed. So maybe she was feeling sweet on him tonight. Maybe she'd let him get over on her later, after the children were asleep. He wasn't so tired tonight from the grove, town Negroes having seen to the coke heaters and wrapping his liners yesterday, those Deland pickers today having done all right by him for a change. So he wasn't so tired. And Connie looked fine. He hoped she'd give him a taste tonight. He was a good husband to her, all told. Nothing he could do about the coming freeze now, anyway. He hoped she'd give him a taste tonight.

❦

And Walt, toting the popcorn in its crinkly paper, so light it was hard to keep in his calloused grip, ambled hangdog as he followed Glory down the aisle in the Magnolia. Colder than a witch's tit already. But there was nothing he could do about the witch's-tit cold. He'd already turned on the overhead sprinklers, which he hoped would coat the fruit with a layer of protective ice. Keep the crystals from growing inside the pulp. And he'd promised for weeks to take his high-society wife to this *Breakfast at Tiffany's* movie that finally made it down from Jacksonville. Two hours off the grove wouldn't hurt none. Only fair since she suffered through *The Guns of Navarone* while back. She had a thing for that twiggy Hepburn lady. Glory found them their seats. Bit close to the screen for Walt's taste. He craned his sunburnt neck backwards and up at the balcony to see how many of the town's coloreds, and which ones, were up there in nigger heaven beside the hot clacking projector. Advantage on a night like tonight, heat from that projector. Already colder than a witch's tit outside. Only a few couples up there tonight. Always dressed pretty fancy for the movies, the coloreds. Give 'em that.

Glory waved off the popcorn. Walt munched down on a fistful. Butter'd make his stomach sick, later. He knew he'd be sick, but it was hard not eating the salty popcorn, warm between his legs, cold as it was. Glory had all the discipline between them. He munched down on a second fistful.

"Just a lesson, show him," Walt had urged his hunting buddy Oscar over the phone after Luke at the Piggly Wiggly let slip who was living way up past Singleton, near where they were working on that interstate. "Same damn nigger causing all sorts of trouble up our way too," Oscar said. "Same damn nigger by the sounds of it. Suit and yellow tie, say? Don't never wear a hat?"

Oscar lived way out in Eustis. He knew people who got things done. Bragged about it when they hunted boar around his cabin week before Thanksgiving each year.

"Now just a lesson," he told Oscar over the phone, who said that's what he'd pass on, which was another way of saying that that's all he could guarantee, that he'd pass it on.

"Stop fidgeting, Walter," Glory pressed a sharp elbow at his ribs. "Honestly, the movie hasn't even started yet." Walt told his wife sorry. He tried to sit still.

Walt wished Oscar hadn't called him tonight. Telling him tonight was the night on account of the weather keeping most folks inside. Colder than a witch's tit, it was supposed to get, did Walt know? He was an orange man, for Christ's sake. Did Oscar think he didn't follow the radio reports, check the teletype every day at the post office wintertime? He'd barked this at Oscar more angrily than he might have, wishing that Oscar hadn't called him tonight to tell him. Walt only hoped those Eustis boys wouldn't get carried away. That rabble rouser had a lesson coming, sure enough. Like those dirty scoundrels at the river, messing with Jo Ellen. Eustis boys ought not get carried away, though. He wished the movie would start up already.

The lights finally dimmed.

A newsreel started up. That wormy Eichmann fellow inside his bulletproof glass cage up there on the stage awaited his verdict. Deep bass music, brass and maybe drums, resounded throughout the theater. Then Walt heard the deep announcer's voice start in:

The stage is set. Adolph Eichmann, the fifty-five-year-old former Gestapo colonel, comes to judgment before an Israeli tribunal of three German Jews who escaped Nazi persecution. Nearly four months have passed since the jurors retired to consider the massive trial evidence. Now in a three-hundred-page judgment, Eichmann is found guilty of crimes against the Jewish people, crimes against humanity, and war crimes. The verdict made Eichmann liable to be the first man to be executed under a civil court verdict in the state of Israel.

The speaker paused and the brass instruments started in louder again, reached for a dramatic crescendo.

Sentencing comes four days later. Eichmann to die in the gallows.

Deep bass notes of the music, more drums now, echoed off the walls. Walt thought he heard a gasp from up in the balcony. Then murmuring, murmuring that told him, somehow, that the coloreds approved of the verdict.

He still has an appeal to the Israeli Supreme Court and, if turned down there, an appeal for clemency to the Israeli president.

And Melody, the children abed, prepared a pie dough. The burning oil smell from the heaters outside seeped into the house with the cold. She only hoped it wouldn't bother Eli's lungs. She'd check on him before going to sleep, she decided as she held a measuring cup under the tap. She placed the water in the freezer, then meted out and mixed the no-sift flour, sugar, and salt in the plastic *flaishik* bowl. She mixed the dry ingredients with her fingertips. Then she retrieved her pre-sliced, ice-cold butter. She dropped butter bits into the mix, coated them with the flour to keep them from sticking to her pastry cutter, then set to it, issued sharp twisting jabs into the bowl. She retrieved the blue tin of vegetable shortening from the bottom cupboard and set it down with a thud on the Formica countertop. She glanced out the bay window into the half-dark that looked full-dark from the lighted kitchen, toward the poor vegetable garden (she'd lose all her tomatoes!) and the wild tamarind, toward the scruffy palmetto and lantana patches, toward the live oak triad and cabbage palms, none of which she could see. But the cold air seeping through the thin glass window felt good on her face, which was why she held her head high these few moments. What was that!? Something rustling in the garden? Eli was in bed already, yes? Probably just a skunk or possum or raccoon. She glanced back down at the counter and marveled at the blue tin of shortening she'd apparently covered with her dishtowel the moment she'd been startled by the rustling, having forgotten that she'd settled that matter once and for all, too, that it wasn't lard in that tin she'd covered on the countertop, that she'd dangled the green and white tin of Armour Pure Lard by its wire-bail handle above the trash bin weeks ago, that she'd released her grip and watched the lard drop deep into the fragrant refuse of banana peels and coffee grounds and that cheddar wedge pockmarked with mold, that she'd immediately cinched up and deposited the overripe garbage bag into the aluminum can outside, that she had nothing to hide, anymore. Nothing.

And Hubert King, Whispering Pines Champion, practiced putting into a paper cup in the hallway, not much interested in *The Andy Griffith Show.* Seemed to be doing all right now, his boy. Glad Ike didn't make a federal case out of Peter's stupid mischief. He'd give Ike that much credit. Didn't go and make a federal case out of Peter's stupid mischief, like Jews were known for. Making a federal case out of everything. Probably what caused them so much trouble over there in Germany. Making a federal case out of things. Hugh could hear the canned laughter coming from the family room now and again. That's the only way Walt would ever beat him, if he got sloppy and three-putted too many holes. Couldn't neglect the short game.

And Isaac called Clay right after calling Sheriff Wright. And he wasn't sure why it occurred to him to call Clay too. Only that it did occur to him. And so he called Clay. And then he noticed Melody looking at him, frozen within the borders of the pocket door frame, her olive cheek dusted with white flour.

And Luke, gathering his courage, released Jane Chapman's clammy hand on her lap and stroked her thigh, beneath, with his fingertips. And she let him. Over her wintertime dress of too-thick fabric, but still. He felt his heartbeat quicken in his chest. Because she let him. Or maybe she was just too distracted by that pixie-looking thing up there, that Audrey Hepburn, to notice. Glad Mr. and Mrs. Boehringer hadn't seen them come in. Glad they were seated well in front so he could carry on. Which hardly meant anything if Jane didn't notice his touch. But no, she noticed. Because she started dipping into the popcorn in his lap faster than before. She parted her legs just a bit now too, her eyes still fixed on the screen, so he stroked a bit lower in between, rubbed a bit higher, felt the heat of her lady-business now. He swallowed hard, felt his heart thick in his throat. He wished the stupid movie would end so they could go park by the river. While the cold crept down to draw Jane close. While Jane was still inclined. Woman's prerogative to change her mind, they said, cause that's all they seemed to do. Change their minds. Pug-nosed, Jane, but if she was game, who cared? A game gal was worth a hundred of those others.

And Levi, one eye swollen shut, squeezed between two expressionless white men in the back of a Plymouth Fury, was on his way . . . somewhere. The island, it seemed. Only reason to head east was for the causeway and the scruffy underpopulated island. Else they would have headed west for the scruffy underpopulated interior. It was bad they weren't wearing their hoods, Levi knew enough to know. Bad they didn't see the need to blindfold him, neither. Bad there were two Mason jars full of moonshine on the floor they didn't seem to be drinking from. For their souvenirs. Their pieces of him. His fingers. His toes. His ears. His penis.

His swollen eye throbbed with his heart. He focused on the pain, and the cold, so he wouldn't focus on the Mason jars. But there were other thoughts he was thinking. Like were these the very same men that got Principal Manning and Mrs. Manning just about ten years ago? They looked so ordinary. Just plain old white folk in their middle years, seemed. He hadn't dared stare full on them, but had gathered a scattered inventory of features. Graying hair at a temple. Ill-shaved cleft at a chin. Oversized paunch against a plaid shirt. Blood-scab on a cheek from a shaving cut. Tobacco-stained teeth. He could feel the car beneath him motoring well under the speed limit. No rush. He kept his head down, tried focusing on his throbbing eye and the cold to keep his thoughts from racing. He'd bide his time. Focus on his throbbing eye. No use raising holy hell in the car now, get himself knocked out again with the pistol butt the fat one, driving now, had flashed on the sidewalk before some other one sucker punched him. He wasn't sure which one hit him. He'd heard some names—Norbert, Shane, Ulmer—but wasn't sure who they belonged to. Was it only a fist that Norbert or Shane or Ulmer clubbed him with, or a separate pistol butt, billy club, or pipe? Not a pipe, he figured. Pipe he'd be dead. Pipe would have broke the skin, very least. He dropped his shoulders and kept his eyes down on the thin black carpet floor. He'd bide his time while his eye throbbed. Wait till they shoved him out of the car, then make a break. They tied his wrists with frayed wrappings of flax twine in front, not behind. Tight and scratchy, the flax twine, his circulation nearly cut, but in front. A pale piece of chewing gum was encrusted down on the carpet. The fabric around it was frizzy and bothered, as if someone had tried to pull the gum off but gave up. A child, maybe. A son. The driver's son up there, probably. A kid in the backseat careless with his Wrigley's. Few days ago, by the look of the gum. They were on the causeway now over the river, he could tell without looking. He could tell by the way the car rose on the road, the way the motor reached down for a lower gear. They were above the river now. He tried thinking about his eye, but he kept thinking about the gum, and the kid. Would this kid be in the car tomorrow, after his father's business was through tonight? Would the driver take his boy to school or for an egg cream or malted or something, tomorrow? Would the kid smell their human odors thick in the car now? Tobacco and sweat and somebody's citrus cologne. They wouldn't crack the windows. Maybe because of the cold. Or maybe because he'd holler, even though there was no one outside in the strange cold. Would the boy ask his father about those rich human smells? And what would his pop say? Norbert, or Shane, or Ulmer. Thinking these thoughts wasn't doing Levi any good. He concentrated on his eye, again, throbbing thick with his heart.

And what did Isaac think he was doing, heading out to the island, speeding south down the highway toward town and the causeway, which would take him across, then up past Clay's small plot and Dummitt's ancient groves that Joe Buck bought up, most all of which the government had recently confiscated for their space program? What did Isaac think he'd do without even a shotgun? Ted wasn't back from Deland, because the truck wasn't parked back beside the greenhouse yet. So what was Isaac supposed to do, hearing what he heard on the party line? Watch *The Andy Griffith Show* in the family room over his dessert? Check the newspaper wrappings on the young trees and liners and the oil heaters between the rows? Just hope that Ted's son would be okay? But, again, what did Isaac really think he'd do to stop them if he beat Sheriff Wright and Clay up there, provided he even spotted them alongside the road? Honk his horn? Give them a stern talking-to? They'd string him up too, given the chance. Nigger-loving Jew—if they knew he was a Jew—which was worse to them than a white nigger-lover, worse than a mere Jew, maybe worse even than a Negro, who couldn't help but be a Negro, whereas a Jew had the choice not to be a Nigger-loving Jew.

He'd get there first, Clay figured. He'd get there first, because Ike had to drive all the way down to town from the grove to reach the causeway, and Ulee's small Tasca could hardly keep pace with his Buick, if the sheriff's battery wasn't stone-cold dead from this godforsaken freeze. And Ulee Wright wouldn't rush, Clay worried. He'd do the lawful thing, Clay knew, but he'd take his time about it. Sort of like the whole town. Whole town in a nutshell. Do the right thing, but on their own sweet time. He glanced over at the shaft of his Browning to make sure it was there. It looked out of place leaning against the Buick's fancy upholstery. He lifted his mottled hands to feel the extra shells in his breast pocket above his heart. Every bump the Browning tip rattled against the glass of the passenger's seat window.

And Erma covered the pot of mustard greens and took the fish rolls out of the oven so they wouldn't dry out. Underdone now. She'd finish them when she heard the car. Her girlfriends thought fish rolls were too fancy, but there wasn't anything truly fancy about them. Just a simple filling. You rolled something up in a spiral and everyone thought you were being fancy. She wouldn't think of eating before Theodore came home. She sighed as she sat at the table beside the hutch, reached for her stationery. She'd write a quick letter to her daughter Winnie out at Plant City. Ask after her grandchildren. While away the time.

And Jo, her parents at some dumb grown folks' movie, pressed her foot down on the Singer's chocolate foot pedal for the final stitchwork at the wrist sleeve. She should have finished with Eli's sweater by now, but the simple fish design at the center held her up when she was doing the knitting. She kept having to pull out whole sections and start over again. Her mother had to help finally. And Eli could really use the sweater, too, cold winter they were having. She could smell the oil smoke outside, which crept in under the doors with the cold, even though her daddy was just using the sprinklers. Probably smoke drifting down from Mr. Newell's grove, which would help them some too, her daddy hoped. Jo hoped the smoke wasn't bothering Eli's weak lungs. She wished she'd given him his sweater already. Least she could do to thank him for throwing that fistful of marl in the eyes of those no-good roustabouts at the river. Seemed like forever ago, cold as it was now, hot as it still was then.

Even Dean, who was stronger, might have just run away. But not Eli. A true-blue friend, Eli was. She only hoped he wouldn't think she was sweet on him when she gave him the sweater. She'd be careful not to wrap it in anything too fancy. Because she wasn't sweet on him, small and young and strange-looking as he was, poor Eli. And "not long for this world," her mother said a while back after he was in the hospital, frowning and making sorry chirps inside her cheeks. "Not long for this world," which Jo had to think about some to pick up the meaning. "Sicker than Mrs. Golden lets on, I'm afraid," her mother said, making sorry chirps again inside her cheeks. Jo wished she could make herself be sweet on poor Eli instead of being sweet on Dean, who wasn't really very nice at all. But you were either sweet on someone or you weren't. It couldn't be helped, seemed to her. So she'd just try being Eli's true-blue friend, which maybe was enough.

And Levi couldn't help but notice Dummitt's old empty house of heart pine and shipwreck wood towering still over the silhouettes of Dummitt's very own grove trees, the old ones anyway, withered and scraggly, and which Joe Buck ought to have grubbed out by now. Very trees both Levi's grandfathers had probably worked over during harvest. His other grandfather too who didn't know he was his grandfather. The two-story mansion looked like a medieval castle with its two lofty spires either side, only made of wood instead of stone. No worse for the wear in the near-dark beneath the half-moon, even though the rats and raccoons and possums and who knew what other creatures had the run of the place now, even though just one lightning strike on top of that tinderbox would roast it to the ground, far away as it was from the fire station and from any people at all, especially now that the government was busy kicking everybody off the island.

"Quit eyeballin' me, boy!" he heard just after feeling the fresh blow at his temple, which almost knocked him senseless, but not quite. Or maybe he had been out cold and was just now coming to. Because it was the crunch of cinders beneath the tires that made Levi notice that he was awake. He struggled to lift his heavy lids, pulled his eyebrows up with the muscles in his forehead. They'd shove him out of the car, he knew. Make him walk a fair distance to the grove trees to keep clear of the mess. And then he'd run for the cover of the old trees to give himself a fighting chance, find a deep slough beyond where he could disappear if he didn't freeze himself to death, run all the way to the lagoon first, to hide, cross the river later.

And Clay shut off his headlights soon as he caught the flicker of low red lights ahead. Banking around foliage up past Dummitt's, Clay surmised. That's why the running lights seemed to blink. Else they were hitting the brakes. He drove slow in the near darkness, opened the windows despite the cold air, smelled the sulfur thick from the murky pools inside the island, heard the tires scrunch against cinders so swerved left back onto the road. His eyes slowly adjusted to the near-dark outside. The rear lights up ahead got brighter but then disappeared altogether. Brakes, he thought. They hit the brakes, then turned off the road, up past Dummitt's by the looks of it. He'd have to come up hard on them, he decided. Once he was close enough he'd pump the gas, flick on his high-beams and come up hard. Only way to go about it, being outnumbered. Being what they were set on. Being that it was no use trying to reason with low-down cowardly murdering types from backwards-ass Eustis. Come up hard and loud with the Browning and get them to scatter. He reached Dummitt's mansion, an old beast that ought to be put out of its misery, it seemed to him. There was talk of moving it to town, turning it into a museum. Clay didn't know how to feel about that.

And Isaac was glad it was winter and near freezing outside because at least he wouldn't have to worry about alligators in the road or out on Dummitt's grove in case he had to go trekking after the Eustis wrecking crew. Only thing he could do was yell loud as he could after them, hope they'd scatter like bugs, which they just might do, cowards that they were. He didn't speed too fast, because you never knew where the water would rise up on this narrow dirt strip of marshy, sulfur-smelling land between the river and the lagoon. And he'd never driven the lightless road at night. Shouldn't he have reached Dummitt's house by now?

And Walt and Glory shared pleasantries with Luke and the Chapman girl, Janie, on the pilled blood-red carpet of the Magnolia lobby after the picture show. Because how do you not stop for a moment, anyway, and say hello to Christian neighbors? Which is what Glory would say to him later if they didn't stop on the pilled blood-red carpet to say hello. Glory asked after Janie's parents, after her little brother, Dean, while Walt jangled his car keys in his pocket and tried not to look full on Luke. "Well, let's leave these young folks to themselves," Walt said, bothered by Luke's shit-eating grin. Stupid wet-behind-the-ears Luke, who had to go and start trouble, and had to wear this shit-eating grin on his face now, his biggest worry being whether he'd get a hand down that Janie's humid panties somewhere in about five minutes. Walt'd say yes, by the look on Janie's doughy face. Dressed proper enough, but a young gal shouldn't show her teeth so easy. He had a couple years yet before he'd have to worry about Jo.

And Shane Parmalee, looming above the dying old man, blood bubbling out the poor fellow's mouth, cried out, "Damn you, Norbert! You done shot him straight through!" And Ulmer McIntyre, across from Shane over the man whose mouth wasn't bubbling blood no more now that he was dead, cried, "Now why'd you have to go and do that, Norbert!? Why'd you have to go and do that!?"

And Shane crouched down over the silent fellow, whose striped shirt above the blood lagoon at his belly was still buttoned and neat and hardly wrinkled at all, and whose pale eyes above his red mouth wore an expression of placid astonishment. Shane had to look away from the poor fellow's curious expression and say, "Shucks Norbert, he's an old man. You done shot dead an old white man."

And Norbert Cross, hanging back in the near-dark, cried, "Now what d'yall think I should have done, fellow comes up hard like that, blinds us with his headlights and shoots off his shotgun who knows where!? What's a fellow like that expect us to do!?"

And Ulmer said, wearily, "Can tell by the sound he was just shooting at the sky. Could tell by the sound."

And Shane nodded, which neither Ulmer nor Norbert could see. And then he looked east toward the grove trees he didn't know were Captain Dummitt's very own withered trees, mixed in with some younger, healthier ones, and said, "I suppose that nigger's swum halfway across the lagoon by now." But none of them were too worried about what the nigger might say, because who'd believe anything a nigger had to say if it ever came to it. Then they heard a car engine, getting louder through the cold, which did worry them.

And what was Dummitt thinking, Isaac wondered, building a house so big and high out in the sticks between the river and the lagoon?

Isaac couldn't help but slow the Pontiac and gaze at the moonlit mansion, which seemed even bigger somehow than he remembered it looking the few times he'd seen it during the day. Something of a challenge issued there, for sure, a house like that. Out here in the sticks. A challenge to Dummitt's God, maybe, who never imagined that one of his creatures would have the temerity to bud oranges on this mosquito-infested wasteland of an island. And build a wooden castle out here so big and sturdy it would stand a hundred years. Isaac pumped the gas harder once the house was behind him. Or maybe it wasn't about God at all, he thought, but about all those white settlers across the broad stretch of river, who turned their noses up at a supposed Christian gentleman setting up housekeeping openly with a Negro woman, siring children with her and laying claim to the muddy offspring without even a hint of shame. Which maybe meant that things were better for Negroes along the river here a hundred years ago, before anything approaching an actual white town had established itself, when one of the first white settlers could take up with a Negro woman without the specter of actual laws, which came with actual white towns, to stop him. And so Dummitt only had to worry, if he worried at all, about the sneers of his few white and Negro brethren, while Isaac was motoring through the island now to keep Ted's boy alive, who had done . . . what? Convinced his fellow Negroes that the sweat of their brow was worth something more than what they'd been led to believe in any number of ways, big and small.

He tightened his grip on the cold wheel, shook his head. He wouldn't find Ted's poor son. He wouldn't find him. But then he heard the rifle shots—*BOOM . . . BOOM . . . BOOM*—still up ahead a ways, the shot echoes made it seem. He rolled down the window and smelled the cold as he drove toward the fading noise. He couldn't see a thing outside the gaze of his headlights, but after a mile or so he smelled gunsmoke mingling with the cold. Then the gunsmoke smell went away, so he stopped, shifted the transmission between reverse and drive what seemed like fifty times to turn himself about without pitching the car off the narrow road into the marshy earth. When his headlights shone to the southeast, they gazed on a car through the bothered dirt-fog air, the driver's-side door open wide, and it took a second or two for Isaac to put it together that it was Clay's Buick off the road that his lights were looking on, and then another second to think that it wasn't a good thing to see Clay's Buick all by itself past the bothered dirt-fog air, the driver's side door open wide. Not a good thing at all. He flicked on his high-beams to broaden his field of view, grove trees rising in the background now, more solid earth about here than he thought, orange eyes winking from the foliage. And underneath. Was that a body splayed out across the weeds, edge of the canopy? He sprang from the car, having reflexively grasped the looping handles of the medical bag he had brought along just in case, rushed across the weed-choked earth through the cold air that didn't smell of gunsmoke anymore. Lifeless, the human form. Too much blood blossomed darkly across insignificant shirt fabric, mouth agape as if to swallow the risen half-moon above the grove trees. A knee weirdly akimbo. Clay, he could no longer deny, as he knelt over the old man's head, as he searched Clay's pale eyes above the blood-spattered stubble beard, which along with that open mouth advertised a look not of terror so much as placid astonishment, as he heard the weak siren from Sheriff Wright's Tasca gaining slow strength against the frosted northern air.

And Eli was almost at the porch steps when he glimpsed the creature out the corner of his eye, just standing there on the loose chattahoochee pebbles ten yards off or so. Which made Eli halt in his tracks and turn his head toward the animal. Just a bit too big to be a common cat. Furrier ears too. But smaller and lankier than Eli expected. And right here on his driveway. The oil heaters on the grove smoked it out, Eli would think later. But not now. Now he only held his breath, and his pose, and tried not to spook the creature before him. The wildcat saw him for sure. It kept its eyes on the human invader, waiting to see if it would be seen. Or did it already know that it had been spotted? He saw the wildcat's eyes now. Really saw them. They glowed strangely in the starlight as they gazed full on his own eyes now. The eyes glowed as if they had special powers, which maybe they did. Eli felt the wildcat's gaze somehow in the pit of his stomach, which made him open his lips and exhale, his breath smoke in the Arctic wind misting his lashes with ice. Don't go, Eli thought. Don't go. Don't go. The creature blinked first. Eli could see the glowing eyes flicker beneath the lids. Then it opened its mouth and stretched its tongue around its lips, a yawn that Eli struggled to interpret. Tiredness? Boredom? Nervousness? And then the wildcat made a funny hop sideways, as if the freezing ground was hot, and sprinted without a sound past the tamarind and oaks back toward the grove, disappearing on the narrow path between the scruffy patches of palmetto and lantana and wax myrtle and privet, where the towhees and scrub jays and cardinals and mockingbirds perched. He and the wildcat walked the same trail, Eli marveled. All this time. They walked the very same trail.

And Levi, some hours later, scared the bejesus out of Isaac and Sheriff Wright and his Negro Deputy, Samuel, when he came bounding barefoot into the Sheriff's Office crying, "Help! Someone! They shot him! Help!"

"Get a hold of yourself son!" Wright shouted, lifting his palms in the hallway, the hallway smelling of the brackish river that Levi brought in with him. "We already know—"

"You're bleeding," Isaac uttered, loud like the sheriff, but calmer. Levi lifted his fingers toward the top of his shorn pate to feel the blood mixed in with his sweat and the river, inspected the wet of his fingers, the pale red-stained undersides trembling before his eyes. He was shorter and smaller than Isaac had imagined. His trousers and button-down shirt were soaked through with wet, an eye swollen shut. His teeth rattled now that he wasn't speaking. "Do you have a towel or a blanket, Sheriff?" Isaac asked in that same adamantine calm. "Both, preferably?"

Samuel answered in the affirmative for Wright, withdrew somewhere down the hall to retrieve the towel or the blanket, or both. Isaac advanced toward Levi to make sure his eye was still in its socket past the swelling (it was), to inspect the laceration on his scalp (bleeding, but slow). He pressed his palm against the wound to stanch the trickle, which made Wright hiccup with surprise, made Levi shrink some, his teeth still chattering.

"Stay still. It's not too deep," Isaac assured Levi. "You're Levi Lomax, right?"

Levi nodded beneath Isaac's palm, his eyes wide, the sclera webbed with red.

"Let's get him to the hospital," Wright suggested. "He's half-froze."

"I don't want to go the hospital. I'm okay. You gotta get out to the island, Sheriff."

"Now don't tell me what I gotta—"

"He's dead, Levi," Isaac said. "Clay Griffin. He's gone. Did you know it was him?"

"Yes," Levi answered, staring with a crimson eye past Isaac's arm, straight through the hallway wall, it seemed. "I seen him. Saved me." His voice was different now, weary for the first time.

Samuel returned, handed a blanket to Isaac, who unfolded it and held it up before Levi like a curtain. "Take off your wet clothes, Levi. Go ahead." Wright and Samuel averted their gaze as Levi unbuttoned the few buttons that still held his shirt closed, as he stripped off his trousers to his cotton briefs, soaked through to reveal his dark business beneath, as Isaac wrapped the gray wool blanket around him now. "Sit now. Here."

"Why you soaked through?" Samuel asked.

"He swam the river," Isaac answered for Levi. "Couldn't cross the bridge where they might be waiting for him, the ones who shot Clay. Swam the river instead."

Levi nodded.

"The whole river?" asked Samuel, incredulous. "I'll be."

"I can stitch you up," Isaac offered. "My bag's in the car outside. Will you let me take care of you, Levi? Will you let me do that for you?"

"Yes," Levi uttered. His teeth weren't chattering anymore. The wool blanket was coarse, but warm. "I'd appreciate the kindness, Dr. Golden."

And Melody was waiting for Isaac just inside the front door when he returned home well after midnight, saying that he'd have to go back to the sheriff's first thing in the morning, then taking a deep breath before saying that poor Clay Griffin had been shot dead, making her lift her hand to her mouth. And Melody was thankful that her hand was already covering her mouth for Clay so she didn't have to cover it again upon hearing her husband's next words about Levi, saying now that she needn't worry about her friend, Levi, that he'd made his way to the sheriff's and was all right, or mostly all right, anyway. Isaac had stitched him up, himself. "Your friend," he had said. "You don't have to worry about your friend, Levi. I stitched him up myself."

And first light, the citizenry up and down the river stepped outdoors, wrapped in layers of their useless Florida clothes, and marveled at the daytime cold, their dragon breath visible in the air. Except for Pearl, who was at the hospital with her dead husband the doctors and nurses tried their best to make look not-dead under the crisp sheets by scrubbing his blood-spattered face and neck with Borax. And except for Mary Beth and Glory, who offered poor Pearl what comfort they could in the overlit hospital room that smelled like bleach. They told Pearl how brave Clay was, seeing to the Lord's work, and they didn't say how strange it seemed that Clay would put his neck out like that for a Negro rabble-rouser who near ruined Clay's very own harvest. And except for Isaac, who was at the sheriff's office telling Ulee Wright and his Negro deputy once again what little he saw out on the island before their Tasca pulled up behind him, what he heard earlier on the party line. But most of the citizenry along the river gazed out from their porches at the tree rows. And the cold-burned leaves on all the river trees looked weirdly dark and greasy. And all they could do that second day, besides refill the crude oil in the heaters, was wait for the Arctic air to blow through when the wind finally shifted to the east. And on the third day, a fair portion of the leaves dropped, along with half the fruit farthest from the heaters. And the wild tamarind had shed all its clothes already, but no one much noticed the tamarind. And on the fourth day, they buried Clay in the morning. And in the afternoon, they finally worked up the nerve to slice open some of the unripe fruit still hanging on the trees to see glucoside crystals inside some of the sacs. And some of the sacs had evaporated to a chaffy mass already. And on the fifth day, it was clear that some of the fruit, closest to the warm oil currents, would be okay. And Walt's fruit actually fared better, on the whole, inside their igloos. But by the sixth day, he'd lost half his best scaffolding branches under the weight of the ice. The branches shattered and screamed sporadically most of the week, like fire in a canebrake. So Walt's grove suffered the worst long-term losses, even though he'd never admit it the rest of his days, even though the river men were too gentlemanly to point it out, or even to speak openly about the dangers of irrigation as freeze protection.

And on the seventh day, it was Isaac who noticed that the irradiated grapefruit scions from Commissioner Shepherd that he'd budded on sour orange stock had withered completely, four long rows of shrunken, skeletal sentries between other varietals that had fared better. And it was Eli who noticed something that looked strange in his experimental grove, which took him a moment to put his finger on. There wasn't any fruit or leaf litter beneath the top-worked Valencias, even though they hadn't been anywhere near the heaters. Most of the grove trees the farthest distance from the heaters had dropped their leaves and fruit by now. But the branches of these top-worked Valencias still clung tightly to their clothes. Eli pulled at one of the smooth-skinned berries, then twisted like Mr. Ted showed him, and was astonished by the force it took to free the orange from its stem. And so he grabbed his father away from the harvestable rows his father was most concerned with and dragged him to the experimental grove to see the Valencias. And he knew that it was something good, because the first thing his father did was lift his meaty hand to cover his open mouth. And the second thing he did was say, "Well I'll be, Elijah-le," and then the third thing he did was utter something in Hebrew four times that Eli never heard his father say before, something that sounded like *Baruch Hashem Baruch Hashem Baruch Hashem Baruch Hashem.*

EPILOGUE

July 2011

GOOD THING THE LAST LAUNCH was next week and not today. Moderate traffic. The interstate would take her door-to-door, practically, which seemed a strange thing, the difference between places. Concrete buildings, blighted housing, and oversized billboards crowded I-95 well north of West Palm. The billboards advertised Caribbean resorts and strip clubs and air-conditioning repairmen and newly sprouted residential developments and elective medical procedures (breast augmentation, liposuction, no-cut vasectomies). As the highway narrowed past PGA Boulevard, the signs mostly gave way to swatches of slash pine carpeted with palmetto. Fewer oversized billboards now and again advertised mostly pro-life pregnancy hotlines and various new Disney World offerings and inexpensive mountainside real estate in Georgia. The traffic was lighter up here even though the highway had narrowed. A good thing the last launch wasn't until next week.

The pines and palmetto seeped through the vents and into her lungs, settled heavily. They looked brave and lonely, these pines, wary of what might come their way. But brave. It might have been a leisurely drive north were it not for the pestering numbness in her left foot that flared up time to time when she sat for extended periods (lingering nerve damage from a traffic accident on the Palmetto Expressway eight years ago), and the blazing speed she was forced to maintain to keep from being run clear off the road every once in a while by behemoth semis and smaller vehicles alike. Where were these speed demons off to today? What appointments were there to keep? She was too young to be scowled at by this balding fifty-something-year-old on his cell phone as he passed her on the right in his shiny coupe (he swooped up too fast for her to change lanes). Some European model, it seemed. She'd never been a car person.

Slash pine and palmetto gave way at intervals to fragrant citrus groves and more fragrant landfills, vultures swirling above in complicated vortices, and reedy marshland accented by pretty purplish reeds, land too wet for fragrant citrus groves or more fragrant landfills or stucco housing. In one of the marshy sections, she noticed two enormous gray cranes with the red patches on their foreheads sifting through the pretty purplish reeds. Now those cranes didn't seem to be about when she was growing up. Not with all the pesticides in Florida, even after her father's whole co-op went organic. So maybe some things got better, after all, despite the blazing speeds of too many behemoth semis and smaller cars, the landfills and stucco developments. She liked to think so.

She felt a strange mood coming on, which she blamed on the pines and palmetto in her lungs.

She liked to make the trip alone on these birthdays, mostly because of these strange moods. Sometimes, though, she brought David and the boys. Evan and Jake had liked visiting their grandmother and the Space Center now and again. They had liked the squeaky white sand of nearby Cocoa Beach and the rickety pier with its labyrinthine passageway in the middle past the tacky shops and the overpriced restaurant. But before they visited their grandmother or the nearby beach and pier or the Space Center to look at the rockets and ride the shuttle simulator, before they visited the cemetery, the boys stood on eggshells around her, wondering how they should behave on their uncle's birthday. The boys were both in college now, one at the University of Miami and the other at faraway Penn like his grandfather. And David taught on Wednesdays this semester. And she liked to make the trip alone, in any case. Even though sometimes she brought David and the boys.

She pulled off the interstate early at State Road 407, what they now called the Challenger Memorial Parkway, the national tragedy meriting signage withheld from their countless local tragedies. Well, it was a terrible thing, that first shuttle disaster. Her father talked about the explosion over the phone as if he'd known the astronauts, personally, which he didn't, although he met one of them at the stand one weekend. "Nice young woman," he had said. It wasn't the teacher he had met, but the other female astronaut on the doomed mission. Sarah had finished law school in Gainesville by then and was already living in Miami, working at the EEOC for too little money, which baffled most of her Law Review friends.

Town looked pretty much the same as she'd left it when she went off to college, which might have been a comfort, but which she found distressing. She'd been relieved years ago to lay her eyes on Gainesville, its different buildings and residential blocks and scruffy hills that meant absolutely nothing to her. Not like here, where everything meant something and too little looked different. Only the town's borders seemed less defined, the shop fronts and parking lots bleeding out the edges like the fixings on an overstuffed sandwich. The NASA business never did turn the place into an Orlando, or even a Jacksonville, if that's what the town elders were after. It pretty much just helped the town carry on as usual, when otherwise it would have died a slow but sure death like so many other vanished and vanishing Florida hamlets on account of the interstate and the sucking force of the bigger cities, where all its arteries led. The river couldn't hold her, anyway.

It would have held Eli, she figured. But not her.

She glanced leftward up the few town streets she motored past. Hardly anyone outside, but that was mostly because it was summer and scorching hot, and the last launch was still a week off. The space business brought just enough workers and tourists and their money to keep Janisse's and the Magnolia Theater and the Florida Playhouse and O'Flanagan's Furniture & Electric and Nelson's Feed Store open, even if Janisse's wasn't called Janisse's anymore, now that Janisse and Doyle were long dead. The two of them sold the restaurant to a Greek family, the Christakises, sometime in the late eighties. Jo Ellen's husband, Hunter, inherited his Uncle Doyle's grove. There were other changes. Pritchard and Sons Hardware closed after the Home Depot came along. Mr. Pritchard's boys were forced to take up real estate. The Supercuts out at the strip mall near the interstate forced The OK Barber Shop to shutter up. But NASA kept the town from dying. These fifty years, anyway.

She was north of downtown and the causeway within seconds and pleased to see again the islands of slash pines and palmetto on the left, grove trees and automotive garages and a few homes off to the right. They didn't keep the grove trees as tidy as they had during her father's day, it seemed, as if the fewer growers on larger swatches of land didn't have time anymore to spend on shaping individual trees. Had she already reached Mims? Weary houses stood along the dusty street branches, but this town was hardly considered a town anymore. She spied a few black and brown children down one of the street branches riding their low bikes eastward in the heat between the groves, fishing rods thrust forward from their handlebars like medieval lances. It was good to see that there were still young boys here, and that young boys here still liked to fish the river. She passed Louis's B-B-Q Shack, which opened and thrived during the Apollo years. She was pleased, and somewhat surprised, to see a few cars out front, even though it was still early for lunch.

She hardly looked at the house or trees at all as she drove past the property, though she couldn't help but notice the sign. They kept the name. At least so far. Goldens Are Here. Respect, maybe, as respect was due. The cold-resistant Elijah orange never proved commercially viable. She had forgotten why. Too little juice in its fleshy purses? But her parents' grove, on account of Eli's illness, her father's mineral oil and beneficial wasps and tilled-under groundcover for fertilizer, was well-positioned to take advantage of the nascent organic fruit and juice craze, which conveniently coincided with the waning appeal of frozen concentrate. Suddenly, they could charge a new premium for their whole fruit and fresh chilled juice, just by advertising what they were already doing. Mail order came to account for a hefty percentage of their profits. The co-op, even Mr. Boehringer, was only too pleased to follow her father's lead, as it was the only way they'd stay afloat against the rising tide of Simply Citrus, which transitioned from frozen concentrate to fresh chilled easily enough.

But her parents couldn't run the grove forever. Safely past their trees, she reminded herself to breathe. She promised Jo Ellen she'd stop by to visit first thing. The Boehringer house was at the northernmost end of her business. Their house seemed to leap out of the grove upon her approach. Here it was, crowding the highway now, forcing her to press her brakes more firmly than she liked. Jo Ellen and Hunter had added a wing for three extra bedrooms before they even started in on children, before Hunter's Uncle Doyle died in the middle of budding a row of marsh grapefruit to sour orange stock (her father unable to revive him with chest compressions), as if to broadcast their bold procreative intentions, and maybe their entrepreneurial ambitions for their expanded holdings, the Boehringer grove and Doyle Newell's conveniently adjacent. Her mother had worried that Jo Ellen and Hunter were tempting fate with the expansion. Who knew what would happen with the organic orange market? Who knew if Jo Ellen could even conceive? But things had worked out well for them.

She felt the smile on her face as she inched the Volvo slowly up the short drive of decorative pavers. It was only a grass and weed drive back in the day, two tire trails of packed dirt the only walkway to the Boehringer home, as if they didn't want to offer too much encouragement to visitors. Now there was a clearing just behind the house with picnic tables and a (deflated) bounce-house. Jo was waiting for her on the porch, her hands clasped together as if to keep each one from flying away. She wore a broad straw hat outdoors to protect her plump, pale skin from the sun. Her cheeks, even so, seemed always flushed, clinically so. Probably rosacea. Something tamer than Eli's butterfly across his bird nose.

"Oh Sarah," Jo uttered as she reached for her, wrapped her fleshy arms around her higher neck. Sarah made sure to reciprocate, ducked under the wide brim of Jo's hat, patted the soft flesh on Jo's back that swelled above and below her brassiere strap.

"Now Jo Ellen," she said, as if to pacify her old friend. Jo smelled like peppermint oil, or eucalyptus oil, or both, maybe. Natural insect repellant for the mosquitoes and no-see-ums, Sarah surmised. A tractor rumbled from somewhere out on the grove. She wondered if it was Hunter out there in the heat.

"It's so good to see you," Sarah said as they parted. Jo's eyes were full, she noticed. Jo clasped both of Sarah's hands low to keep her eyes on her, which made Sarah lower her gaze for whatever reason. These visits always seemed to hit Jo hard, harder than Sarah would have liked. Sarah had learned to treat her own emotions less tenderly. David sometimes complained that she was cold. There were some rough years there when the boys were young, but they soldiered through it and came out okay. "Marriage is hard," her mother counseled her once, wearing a pensive expression. "Every couple goes through rough patches. That doesn't mean it's not worth it," she had added. "Most of the time, anyway." And so Sarah stuck it out. She and David were mostly happy now, she thought, which was enough to ask of a long marriage. She was pretty sure David would agree. She didn't think that she was cold, exactly.

"I see you and I see . . ." Jo stranded her words between them in the thick air. She released Sarah's hands, batted at something in front of her face, the words maybe. Or maybe a bug.

"I know, Jo. It's okay."

"Let's get out of this godforsaken heat. Hotter every year."

"Seems like."

The screen door rattled shut behind them before Jo closed shut the heavy wooden door, sealing them inside the climate control. The house had been repainted inside and refurnished several times over since the old days. And there were new frames and photographs on the walls advertising mostly the youngest generation of Newells. Sarah had lost count of the grandchildren. Yet the house still smelled the same as Sarah remembered it smelling the handful of times she tromped across the irrigation ditch and all the way to the Boehringer house with Eli. Like stale smoke and kitty litter and flowers. Jo and Hunter never could kick the habit, if they ever tried. This was what a house of cigarette smokers and cat owners smelled like, she supposed. Like kitty litter and stale smoke and flowers from the air freshener.

Jo had already set out a pitcher of sun tea in the family room where they sat, as they always sat. Diaphanous Meyer lemon discs floated at the top above the ice layer, mostly melted, which made Sarah look down at her silver watch. She had told Jo to expect her a bit earlier and was about to apologize before one of the cats, the tabby, jumped on her lap seeking affection, which prompted Sarah to say, "Oh my," and Jo to say, "Tiger-boy," without much heat.

"It's okay," Sarah said, trying her best to seem unperturbed. She patted the cat a few times, then stopped, hoping Tiger-boy would lose interest and jump down. She took a long sip of her tea, dodging Tiger-boy's flicking tail, exhaled deeply. Jo heard something in the breath that Sarah didn't mean, because she said, "It's too bad you always come in the summer, when it's so hot."

"It's all right. It's worse in Miami if you can believe that. Good tea," she added, taking another sip. Tiger-boy's tail brushed her cheek. "Okay, get down now," she said, scooting the tabby off her lap and onto the pine floor. Enough already. She brushed the orange fur off her slacks with both palms.

"Yes, leave poor Sarah alone," Jo chided as she lifted the cat up onto her lap, instead. "They just love their affection," she said, scratching the creature behind its ears, making Tiger-boy pinch his eyes shut with intense pleasure.

"You all should really come up next week," Jo suggested. "For the launch."

"Should we?"

Sarah didn't like the way this sounded. Prickly. Standoffish. She didn't mean it this way. She didn't know how she meant it. "Do you think it'll be fun?" she added to declaw her first words. She sipped at her tea again, then set it down on the coaster, an Apollo astronaut she didn't recognize (Alan Bean maybe?) smiling up from beneath the glass bottom now.

"Oh, yes. We're expecting thousands of people. From every state. Foreign countries too." *We're expecting.* Jo's comment made Sarah sad. Not so much because she felt excluded from Jo's "we," but because it brought home how much Sarah and the rest of town would miss the shuttle program, especially as nothing too exciting seemed to be replacing it any time soon.

"Then it'll all be over," Jo said, somberly now, matching Sarah's mood, as if the thought just occurred to her. "NASA folks already gone, mostly. Or seems that way."

"They're giving you all your town back, Jo. Look at it that way."

"Folks on the news already calling us the Ghost Coast instead of the Space Coast."

Sarah wasn't sure whether she should laugh or not so she troubled the rim of her glass with her thumb, instead. Jo and Hunter had profited from the space business, rented out three bedrooms for launchings, grubbed out half an acre of spent grove trees and planted picnic tables for launch fairs. They also offered grove tours and sold a fair bit of fresh fruit and other merchandise. They had purchased that enormous royal-blue inflatable bounce house—Sarah always thought it seemed incongruous and tacky on the grove—to keep the youngest children entertained. Sarah wasn't sure how much of their income depended upon the NASA tourists. They sure boosted profits at Goldens Are Here, though. Her mother's Meyer lemon and key lime pies were so popular with the NASA tourists, both at the stand and at Louis's BBQ Shack, that she began shipping them to states across the country, along with their citrus boxes, to more than a few regular customers.

"Is it going to hurt you and Hunter much? I hope not."

"Oh, we'll lose some money," Jo deflected Sarah's concern with a swipe of her hand between them. "Company, mostly, is what I'll miss. Meeting folks from every state and all. Lots of Japanese too. And they really do snap an awful lot of pictures. But let's not talk about all that. It's not important one way or the other. Let's not bother ourselves with silly things, Sarah."

"Okay."

"It must be difficult for you. This year. Your dear mother." Jo's eyes welled again. "Hope you hold on to that house, anyway. Don't listen to that Kyle Pritchard, or his brother. Charlatans, the both of them. This market, it would be madness to sell."

Sarah nodded, noncommittal. She didn't know yet what she wanted to do with the house in town.

Sarah had retrieved her mother to live with them in Coral Gables not quite a year ago, when it became clear that Melody Golden couldn't live alone in the beautiful Queen Anne home on the river in town, where she and Sarah's father retired after selling the grove. She had fallen a second time in four weeks on the cold travertine stone floor of the kitchen and that second time she could barely reach up on the counter for the cordless to call 911. She and David hitched a U-Haul trailer to the Volvo and retrieved her on a launch day, stupidly. The traffic and revelry about town annoyed Sarah.

Sarah had braced herself for her mother's long convalescence and decline in Evan's downstairs room. Life would be different. She'd have to work fewer hours. No more short but extravagant European vacations for a while. David would have to give up making love on late Sunday mornings after breakfast, a routine he coaxed her into after the boys left home. Too much light streaming in through the window treatments for Sarah's taste, anyway. She was grateful that David hadn't issued any protest when she advertised her intentions about her mother, for he must have known, too, that life would be different. He was good in that way. Solicitous. So it surprised her when her mother passed away in her sleep in Evan's bed just two months after taking over his dresser drawers. It surprised Sarah, and curiously deflated her, that life wouldn't be so different, after all. That she could toil undeterred at the EEOC and take her short, extravagant vacations and resume lovemaking with her husband on Sunday afternoons in their too-bright bedroom.

"Yes," she told Jo now. "It's tough this time. Different anyway. It feels different. Without her."

"Well of course."

They sat for a time without saying anything, listened to the silence. The soft cloth texture of the sofa arm felt good beneath Sarah's hand. The tractor's engine outside stopped, which reminded Sarah that she had been hearing it still, indoors. Sarah didn't mind the silence. She knew that Jo Ellen, scratching Tiger-boy's ears, didn't mind it, either. This was friendship, she thought. When you didn't have to fill the air between you every second with words. When you could just sit together.

"Will you be coming back up here to keep them company?" Jo finally asked.

"Of course. Once a year to visit the cemetery at least. On Eli's birthday, anyway," Sarah replied before understanding Jo's meaning. Jo's watchful expression soon told her that she'd misunderstood the question, that Jo was waiting for her words to be understood. "Oh," Sarah said as Jo's meaning finally seeped. "I guess I haven't thought about that yet. I don't know."

Jo nodded toward the ground. "It's all right," she said. "Plenty of Jewish folk now besides the Krupnicks in your section of the cemetery. And I won't be too far off in the Christian section. I'll keep them company too."

Jo wasn't one to dwell over morbid matters. Not usually. Something was different, which worried Sarah. Was Jo ill?

"So have you been to your grove house?" Jo changed the topic.

"Umm, no. Not yet. I was going to stop in, maybe, on the way back. The stand looked open."

"Your parents kept the place up better."

She inferred a racial insult here, the barely perceptible variety she frequently heard during her interviews at various places of employ she investigated for the EEOC—fast food chains, grocery mega-stores, state universities—that as a child she heard slip from Jo's mouth about the field-workers now and again. But it was nicer to believe that Jo only meant now to express allegiances, even love, toward Sarah's parents.

"Your mother's beautiful garden," Jo continued, shaking her head, chewing the fleshy inside of her cheek. "Now just grass and weeds."

"It looked all right driving past," Sarah said. "Grove trees crowding the house a bit, but I suppose they can't afford to leave too much property alone."

Jo nodded. "I just think of what your brother would have done with that place."

"I know. It's okay, Jo." Sarah leaned forward and reached for Jo's hand in her lap, the one not petting Tiger-boy, placed hers on top and patted it.

"He was a true-blue friend to me. True blue. Not easy growing up a not-so-pretty redheaded girl around here. True-blue friend, Eli." Jo slid the cat off her lap and onto the floor, its feet sounding mildly against the pine. Tiger-boy looked back up at his owner to see if there had been some mistake, then trotted off, indignant. Now Jo was crying, as if Eli had only just passed away. "I would have done anything for him," she continued. "But what could I do? I wasn't a match."

Until the bitter end, Sarah's parents had searched for bone marrow donors to treat Eli's leukemia. The town hosted a number of bone marrow drives, but the local genetic pool wasn't favorable. They couldn't find a match. That Sarah wasn't a match had filled her with shame. But she never thought that Jo carried this burden.

"Eli knew you did everything you could. That we all did. All that time you spent with us at the hospital. Your mother too."

Jo's father had dropped dead rather young from a coronary before Eli's illness. He never was the same, quite, after the freeze. After the near lynching of Ted Lomax's eldest son. After Clay's Griffin's murder. That's what people said. That something broke in him. After Walt died, Ted had managed the Boehringer property for five years before his kidneys failed. Just long enough for Jo to get her feet wet. Her older siblings weren't much interested in the grove.

"He just adored you, Sarah. Especially when you were real young. Too young to remember, maybe. The way he doted after you."

"I remember. I do, Jo." A fuzzy image of Eli chasing after her between the grove trees rose to her consciousness. *'Lish,* he called after her as she squealed. *'Lish, I'm gonna get ya!* It was the earliest memory Sarah could summon. Sarah cleared her throat to keep the water out of her eyes. 'Lish. Short for Delicious.

But what brought on such feeling in Jo? Was it one of her children, or grandchildren? Or Hunter, maybe?

"What is it, Jo? Tell me. Something's the matter. This isn't like you."

"Oh, it's nothing." Jo dabbed at her wet nose with a tissue she seemed to brandish from thin air. "Just wait here," she said, lifting her modest heft from her love seat. "Just wait here. I'll be back."

Jo returned from the kitchen in an instant, before Sarah could even wonder what she'd gone to retrieve. A stack of yellowed papers dripped from her hands. Sarah somehow knew instantly what they were. Her brother's drawings. Some of them, anyway. Using fine-tipped colored pencils, he drew any number of outdoor scenes—snook and seatrout darting for silver prey beneath the river's skin, swallow-tailed kites frozen in flight in curious angles high above grove trees, varied warblers flitting about in the lacy foliage of the wild tamarind that she only remembered as a single trunk, haloed by ferny sprigs of new growth at the ground. Drawing the outside helped him while away the time during his frequent hospital visits, the outside he must have missed inside the ammoniac hospital room. He drew on his sketch pad in the steeply inclined bed, a broad white writing board braced against a pillow on his upraised knees. Jo handed her the stack and Sarah milled through them, slowly. Her eyes settled on one she hadn't seen before, a wildcat at night, a half-moon in the backdrop looming above grove trees. Something about the drawing suggested extreme cold, but it took Sarah a moment to put her finger on it. The puffed-up fur on the wildcat, she gathered, the spindly grove tree branches, half-stripped of their foliage. The wildcat seemed to stare right through her as she looked. It was tough to take her eyes off it.

"That was from the night of the freeze," Jo said, leaning over and looking at the upside-down drawing. "When Eli saw his first wildcat."

Sarah nodded, shuffled the drawing to the bottom of the stack, finally. After a few unremarkable drawings, she came to a series of even rougher pencil sketches, or shadings rather, if that's what they were. She asked Jo about them.

"Those are his rubbings," Jo replied. "Mrs. Whitesell taught us how to do that. You wouldn't remember her."

Sarah nodded.

"Have to admit, I sort of forgot all about these drawings until I went to clean out my old dresser to give to Amelia's twins. Just found them last week. Took my breath away. I'm not sure why Eli gave them all to me."

Jo was wrong. Eli had given Sarah several pencil drawings over the years. He left a stack for her inside the top drawer of his dresser, too, scrawled her name in black marker across the blue cardboard paper wrapping. Some of the drawings featured the indefatigable wild tamarind that her father couldn't quite bring himself to grub out after the historic freeze, pruning it back to that near stump that sprouted ferny shoots. They weren't all nature drawings. Some of them featured the stand, Goldens Are Here, from various vantage points. He wasn't particularly skilled at drawing people, Sarah gathered.

"He knew you'd stay," Sarah heard herself say. "That's why he gave them all to you. He loved you too, Jo."

And then Sarah felt the hot tears drip down her cheeks, which felt strange, so strange that it didn't occur to her to wipe the tears away. One pregnant drop splashed down on the edge of a rubbing. She pushed the stack away from her leaky eyes, beside a behemoth NASA book of glossy photographs. "Goodness," she said, wiping at her tears now.

"It's okay Sarah. A good cry now and again's just what the doctor ordered. Go on ahead. Hunter and the boys won't be coming in for a while and I'll just shoo them off if they do." She held a tissue out for Sarah, who said thank you and dabbed at her eyes as if to stanch the flow of blood.

Sarah wasn't quite sure what got into her. But it wasn't these drawings, quite, or even the memory of her older brother. Not alone, anyway. She felt around for the source and brushed up against it, finally. It was her little fib to Jo, the fib about Eli giving Jo all his drawings. Her own words somehow moved Sarah, this reflexive gesture of kindness, which she realized was self-indulgent and silly. It was time she got going.

Jo followed Sarah out to the porch, asked if she was certain she had to leave so soon, before saying hello to Hunter. She could call him in on his cell. Sarah told her not to trouble him and Jo didn't protest. She asked Jo to give Hunter her regards and Jo said that she would. The sunlight from the porch looked different, less harsh, even though they hadn't been inside too long. Sarah looked up. A cloud sheet covered the shameless sun. Sarah paused there on the painted slats and looked out through the filtered light at the grove trees beyond the clearing. A pair of mockingbirds fluttered up from one of the Hamlins and seemed to lock their feet, either in battle or courtship.

"Hundred years from now, Jo, do you think there'll still be oranges and grapefruit here?"

"Sure I do. Two hundred years from now."

Sarah nodded.

"I don't know who'll be growing them," Jo added, "but the trees'll still be here. This is river fruit. Like your dear father knew. This ain't the ridge. Folks all the way up to New York and Canada will always want fresh river fruit. Can't match river soil or weather in Brazil or Texas or California, or anywhere. That's the thing. That's why the groves will still be here, even if we do have to put up with the latest scourge, plus a freeze now and again."

"It's good, isn't it? That the trees will still be here, anyway. Two hundred years."

Jo sighed, wrapped her arm around the wood post at the top of the porch steps.

"It is a comfort."

Sarah slowed the Volvo as she neared the stand to her left, tempting herself to stop. The brakes complained from the grove dust. Nearly every year she drove past the property, taking its measure, watching new grove trees slowly converge upon the house, displacing the scruffy shrubs, gauging the growth of the wild tamarind that the Lomaxes let be for some reason, a shaggy specimen now somewhere between tree and shrub. But she'd stopped in only once since her father died of renal cell carcinoma, just late enough in life that it didn't quite seem a full-blown tragedy. And she stopped then only because her boys, puffed up over the Goldens Are Here sign on the stand, pleaded with her to stop.

She brought the Volvo to a full halt in the middle of the barren highway, which was a strange thing to do, but somehow she couldn't turn the wheel left and motor onto the oyster shell parking strip. Why not pull in and roam the property now? The Lomaxes wouldn't mind. She'd make her way around back along the chattahoochee driveway to see what was left of her mother's vegetable garden, then head around the shaggy wild tamarind, past the remnant patches of palmetto and lantana and the live oaks that remained toward Eli's grove, where her brother and Jo pointed out swallow-tailed kites and ospreys and kingfishers and bobwhites for her, and taught her to play hide-and-go-seek, and where she camped out with her father and Eli, before her brother got sick that final time.

She looked across at the young dark face behind the scarred wooden counter, one of Ted and Erma's grandsons or great-grandsons, likely, who looked across at her too. It was a strange thing to do, grinding to a halt in the middle of the road, even if there wasn't anyone coming from either direction. She held his gaze long enough to see the whites of his eyes flash at his sudden understanding as he recognized her, long enough for her to smile at his greeting. He lifted a pale palm, waved her over, but Sarah had already pressed the accelerator, heading south toward her proper business.

Author's Note

On Christmas night in 1951, the Civil Rights worker Harry T. Moore and his wife, Harriet Moore, were murdered by a bomb planted beneath their Mims, Florida, home. Eleven years later, the citrus groves in the prized Indian River Citrus District surrounding Mims suffered tremendous losses in the Big Freeze of 1962. Before the specific idea for a novel set along the small towns, scruffy pine flatwoods, and orange groves of east-central Florida took shape, I found myself intrigued by these two local stories—one social and one environmental—that played out against the backdrop of the Cold War and NASA's Project Mercury. Today, we celebrate this region of Florida primarily as our Space Coast, yet a novel that imagined characters here living lives less public than our first astronauts (but no less dramatic) seemed like one worth exploring. *Goldens Are Here* is not about the Moores' lynching or the Big Freeze, specifically, but these events prompted me to imagine certain characters and their stories to explore the intersections between our relationship with the land and our relationship with one another.

I consulted several sources as I wrote this novel. I encourage those readers interested in learning more about the life of Harry T. Moore and his still unsolved murder to read *Before His Time: The Untold Story of Harry T. Moore, America's First Civil Rights Martyr*, by Ben Green (The Free Press, 1999). Other works that were especially useful to me regarding the racial dynamics of the Jim Crow era include *The Warmth of Other Suns,* by Isabel Wilkerson (Random House, 2010), *Fire in a Canebrake: The Last Mass Lynching in America,* by

Laura Wexler (Scribner, 2003), and the various works of Stetson Kennedy. Readers interested in the citrus industry and citrus fruits, generally, might wish to consult the following texts: *Oranges,* by John McPhee (Farrar, Straus and Giroux, 1967); *Citrus Growing in Florida,* by Larry K. Jackson and Frederick S. Davies (The University Press of Florida, 1999); *Citrus,* by Pierre Laszlo (The University of Chicago Press, 2007); *Citrus Fruits,* by H. Harold Hume (The Macmillan Company, 1957); *Biology of Citrus,* by P. Spiegel-Roy and E. E. Goldschmidt (Cambridge University Press, 1996); *Hesperides; A History of the Culture and Use of Citrus Fruits,* by Samuel Tolkowsky (J. Bale, Sons, & Curnow, Limited, 1938); and, finally, the book that should be on every botanist's and writer's nightstand, *The Fruits and Fruit Trees of America; or The Culture, Propagation, and Management, in the Garden and Orchard, of Fruit Trees Generally; with Descriptions of All the Finest Varieties of Fruit, Native and Foreign, Cultivated in This Country,* by A. J. Downing (Wiley and Putnam, 1845).

Acknowledgments

I WOULD LIKE to express my gratitude to the following people, who have supported this book, and me, in various ways:

Laura Strachan

Dede Cummings

Jenna Gersie

My colleagues and students at Florida Atlantic University

Chris Bernard

Erika Dreifus

Mike Branch

Dave Keplinger

Simmons Buntin

Emily Nemens

William Meiners

Nancy, Stephen, and Richard Furman

Dana and Howard Friedfeld

Wendy, Henry, Sophia, and Eva

CPSIA information can be obtained
at www.ICGtesting.com
Printed in the USA
LVOW03s2025290318
571705LV00003B/3/P